DOCTOR WHO

DRIFT
SIMON A. FORWARD

Published by BBC Worldwide Ltd,
Woodlands, 80 Wood Lane
London W12 0TT

First published 2002
Copyright © Simon A. Forward 2002
The moral right of the author has been asserted

Original series broadcast on the BBC
Format © BBC 1963

Doctor Who and TARDIS are trademarks of the BBC

ISBN 0 563 53936 8
Imaging by Black Sheep, copyright © BBC 2002

Typeset in Garamond by Keystroke, Jacaranda Lodge,
Wolverhampton
Printed and bound in Great Britain by Mackays of Chatham
Cover printed by Belmont Press Ltd, Northampton

Drift
Home is where the heart is.
This is for all those who have ever lost heart.

Chapter One

Cold perched in the trees. Talons of ice dug into white birches and the air had turned to crisp powder.

In white space, nothing moved.

Then, figures came into being like sketches on a blank page, pencilled in lightly, as though expecting to be erased at any moment. They fanned wide, drawing a grey half-circle around the brown snow-capped house, closing around it like a snare. The soldiers were clad in white, darker than the white of the landscape. The house peered out as though from a burrow in the hill, like a timid rabbit, sensing the danger.

Captain Morgan Shaw hoped those inside the house were too busy fending off the cold to be on the lookout for trouble. He clapped his gloved hands smartly together and breathed into them. The shoulder-slung SMG batted lightly at his hip.

Slowly, his gaze swept from the house to the scarred bark of the woods beyond; he motioned his platoon of ghosts to a stop. Beautiful, he thought, breathing it in deep. He remembered playing soldiers with Kenzie, weaving through those same trees, charging the high ground with stick-guns and snow-ball grenades. The memory was as solid as the crunch of snow underfoot.

The weather hadn't been quite as unfriendly and there'd been sunshine to make those birches gleam. They ran so fast, him and his brother, puffing like steam locos and leaving their breath hanging in the air behind them. No wind: the air had been frozen. Time too, that morning when Kenzie chucked a snow-bomb packed with shrapnel and smashed one of those self-same windows that were staring back at Morgan right now.

Morgan, scared as a rat, had made it home first that day. His old man had heard all about it by then and he'd waited on Kenzie, silent as the mountain, before whipping them both hard enough to crack the ice in their lungs. Winter never tasted quite as sweet after that.

Not until today anyhow, Morgan told himself.

Somewhere out in the whiteness his snipers were covering the scene, waiting for a blink from those windows. Over on his left, Bob Marotta's ammo belt was jingling like a dull string of sleigh bells. Too quiet to reach the house, but loud enough to break the spell.

'Do these people even celebrate Thanksgiving?' the big guy had asked at the briefing. Morgan had told him, 'Not this year. White Shadow is coming to gatecrash.'

Morgan was seriously back in today, twenty-plus years on, ready to play for real. This was home turf, an easy match. They'd made the forty-yard line without so much as a tackle from the opposing team.

The old doc who used to own this house was dead,. A real fearsome guy; Morgan used to reckon he was half-dead anyhow, and wished him dead more than a few times on top of that. After the wishes came true, the house had gone to ruin and this bunch had practically stolen the place. They hadn't done a lot with it either, far as he could see.

A small figure trotted out of the mist to his left, a pat on Marotta's shoulder as she passed and fell into step beside her captain. The bulk of her parka and her pack just about doubled her size. There was a black light in her eyes and the general darkness of her seemed a defiance of nature. Wearing her bead-banded cowboy hat and feathers with an ancient sort of pride, she'd have you believe she was just the opposite.

'What do we have in there, Kristal?'

6

She gripped her M16 like she was ready to drive it into someone's gut. Those eyes didn't leave the house. 'Many spirits. Or one, big enough to swallow the world.'

The cold snaked around Morgan's throat. He made sure the zipper was up as far as it would go. 'Yeah, can we have that in the white man's tongue?'

Kristal snarled, a real redskin savage. Then she spat a pearl of saliva. 'Have your fun now, Captain. I don't think this is going to be the breeze you're expecting.'

She stalked ahead of him, the same way a pony can best a horse through deep snow. She'd win any argument through sheer stamina. That face of hers, flat like an owl's with a Roman beak, might have been carved out of red rock. Morgan laughed quietly and signalled to Marotta. The Gunny grinned as he came hiking over, all set to blow the house down with a little huff and puff.

'Not if we do it my way,' Morgan murmured to the air.

Well, if it came to a messy gunfight he just hoped all these screwballs were from out of town. He'd hate to have to shoot anyone he knew.

By way of an answer the vampire sky flocked to the trees, to perch alongside the cold, waiting for a splash of red to quench its thirst for colour.

That chill sea of rolling white seemed a kinder world right now to Amber Mailloux than the lightly toasted living room from which she stood and gazed out, hoping to hypnotise herself with the wilderness. Some days it was so beautiful out there, she could float out over the deck and lose herself in the knitted trees. But not today. Today it was like that painting she'd gone over with a spray-can of white. Besides, there was nothing to focus on and her cheeks were burning from her shouting match.

Her face crumpled and she cried in tiny gasps.

'Listen,' said the voice that had made her stamp and scream,

'I'm not going to pretend with you. I never have. You can't kid a kid.'

He stopped and maybe he guessed how dumb that sounded. She kept staring out the window. If he saw her smirk, he'd only tell her how he'd wipe it off her face – but he'd never do that. Not Makenzie.

Daddy always kept that sort of promise. But he wasn't going to make it here for Thanksgiving. And nobody really cared about that except Amber.

They made like they cared, they were *sorry*, but nobody wanted him here. Only Amber – and she couldn't help that. Why should she?

Makenzie took one of his heavy steps closer; he always moved so clumsy. She wasn't afraid of him but it was a shock, when he spun her round by the shoulders to face him. 'Your Daddy hurt your Mom and I will *never* like him for that, you get that?' Amber made a face like she'd tasted poison and all she saw was Makenzie's badge.

'Don't you have to go to work?'

'Don't you smart-mouth me!' Oh yeah, Makenzie could shout. After Daddy, Mom never let any of them hit her. But Makenzie, he never went further than lifting his hand to strike, and then he'd only shout a *lot* louder. For a change his voice softened. 'I could tell you I'm not happy he's not coming, but part of me would be lying. *Part* of me, because part of me really feels for you, Amber – for what you're going through. Now, maybe we could sit down and talk about that – '

Amber glanced at his eyes and that was a mistake.

Despite the tone, his face had stayed angry and that made her want to laugh. She drank a deep breath, thought about what she might say, then the laugh broke out as tears.

Why couldn't he just hit her and get it over with? He said he wanted to talk but he was looking at her like that time she'd sprayed over that Andrew Wyeth print. A cheap present he'd given Mom: Amber had wanted to wipe out the world for that little girl sitting lonely in her cornfield.

'Get away from me!' She screamed it like she'd wanted to scream at Daddy. And, knowing she was the only one going to make it happen, she pushed past Makenzie and grabbed her coat from the hall.

She slammed the door behind her and stormed out into the kinder world, where the air swooped down to enfold her in its chill wings.

Martha Mailloux heard the ground crunching like a carpet of potato-chips and glanced up in time to catch the flap of a sleeve in her hair, and watched her daughter wrestling to get into her coat as she marched on past and on to the road. Not that there was a road.

Under the heaped snows, the road from Mak's cabin had only ever been a dirt-track. They'd taken the best part of a summer afternoon – yeah, a different world – hauling Martha's trailer up the goddamn mountain; Mak bitching at his truck every turn, like she was some horse refusing a fence.

So long as he wasn't bitching at Martha's trailer. Sure she'd moved in with Mak; it seemed the right thing to do, with her new job and all. But she hadn't really moved out of that crate-on-wheels – and Mak knew it. Maybe that was why he'd stranded the thing up here, like Noah's Ark.

Martha brooded over the piled drifts, reminding her of every birthday cake she'd done her best to frost for Amber. Yeah, springtime, maybe this flood will just melt and carry us some place where people don't beat on you with their looks.

She wiped her hair back with her sleeve, where the brush with Amber had set it loose. Glancing back at the cabin, where Mak had stepped out on deck to appeal to her with a look, she offered him a smile. Today their fight had to have been about Curt; that lame son-of-a-*bitch*, setting his little girl up for a fall.

She dug the shovel hard in the ground, clearing the snow

from around her trailer. Something to do in place of a workout.

'What do you want me to do about it, Mak? It's between you and her.'

Martha noticed the sore silence and felt kind of sorry. She wasn't up for a fight, not with Mak. No, she was going to save her stuff for Curt – the one who deserved it all – over the phone if he never turned up. 'Can't be nothing serious, hon,' she reassured Mak, this time with a smile loaded with the best times. 'She wasn't too upset to wrap herself up warm now, was she?'

'Guess not,' said Makenzie, drawing up the zipper on his police-issue parka. Looked like he'd decided work was more pressing than policing family. Hell of a lot easier too, she imagined, in a town like Melvin Village.

Martha rested on the shovel, listening for Mak's bootsteps beating a path to his truck. Amber was nowhere. Martha's only child would have disappeared long before she'd rounded the first bend, consumed in a cold white furnace.

One feast-fire story told of a hero who decided to mount a bold expedition to find a path around the barrier that guarded the Tesh fortress. He led his war party on a long and dangerous trek into unknown lands, keeping the barrier always to their right. Their journey carried them further and further from home until the jungle thinned around them and there was only open ground and grass. Yet still the barrier stood to the right of their path. The warriors often went hungry; for they were not used to hunting in these wide open lands and the herds of beasts would see them and scatter before them. On they walked and many wanted to turn back. They missed the jungle and their homes, but their leader urged them on, and told them they would eat the grass if they must. But with each day the grass started to thin and the barrier still stood to the right of their path. But none would disobey their leader for he was a great hero and they believed in him.

Their journey ended in a land colder than night. There was no colour and the few trees were like skeletons. The rain was solid, so cold it burned, and it fell on the land in great mounds and stole the warmth from the fire and made the warriors shiver. No animals lived in that white wasteland and when they dug for roots they found only hard earth and rock. They shared out the remnants of their food and began their long journey home. Their leader, the great hero, would not eat as he journeyed back with his warriors, and before he died he gave them his ration and asked them their forgiveness.

The end of the tale had often escaped Leela. She'd generally found herself wandering into that strange land, trying to see it in her mind. But no clear picture would ever come.

Now, it was as if the Doctor had delivered her to that same land, where a hero of the Sevateem had died. And yet he had told her that these lands were home to a noble people.

Leela shivered and pulled her furs closer around her. This cold smothered every scent. She blinked against the strange flakes colonising her eyelashes. She did not want to meet the tribe who could live in this place. 'Doctor, I wish to go back to the TARDIS.'

'So do I, so do I. But I've no idea where she is. I don't understand it, I can normally find my way home in any storm. Better than a racing pigeon.'

Lost. They were lost.

The feeling was by no means a new one. Still, usually the Doctor had an air of being perfectly at home with being lost. Here, in this land at the end of the world, he worried her by looking as miserable and confused as she felt. It did not help that he also looked very silly.

The Doctor had braved this hostile land in his usual garb, but had wrapped his coat around him much tighter, with the collar high to fence out the fierce cold; and he had looped the long scarf up over his hat, tying the brim down around his ears. The rest of it wound thickly around his neck like a constrictor vine. It was, she decided, the costume of a madman.

He had halted now, some distance ahead of her, with the stance of one who has lost a mate.

'I'm afraid we've arrived at the wrong time.'

'There is a warmer season? Better for hunting?'

'Yes – no, the wrong *time*.' He cast a hand back and waved her up. Wearily, Leela trudged forward, the *snow* swallowing her boots almost to the knee. It was a bit like wading through mud. She saw the Doctor nod disconsolately at a fallen structure, some sort of framework of metal dripping with shards like spearheads of water. 'A couple of centuries later than I'd intended. I was hoping to drop you off in a continent untouched by electricity pylons – amongst other things…'

Leela frowned, then gasped. 'Are these structures the work of invaders? Perhaps this tribe you spoke of toppled it in battle.'

The Doctor managed a grunt as he scanned the slopes. 'I doubt if these mountains have seen so much as a footprint from that tribe in a hundred years. A continent swept clean for the new tenants. A way of life systematically dismantled and scattered on the winds like ashes.'

The Doctor held up a hand and let a few of the flakes spatter harmlessly in his palm. 'You'll get your chance to spend some time with the Native American people, I promise. Sooner, possibly later. I'm sure you'll find it worth the wait.' He wiped his palm clean with a casual pat on his coat, then thrust both hands deep in his pockets. 'Of course, I really can't say how long a wait we might have. Could be an eternity if I can't find the TARDIS. Which would be all right for me, I suppose, but it wouldn't do much for your complexion.'

'Doctor, you are babbling.'

'Am I?' He turned suddenly very grumpy. 'Well, babbling clears the mind. It's a well known scientific – anyway, why aren't you doing your bit, instead of criticising, hmm? Your homing instincts ought to be nearly as good as mine. Think, Leela. Think.'

Leela wanted to tell him she was thinking. Instead, she sighed and searched the ghostly expanse above, behind and below.

The snowfall at the moment was a gentle swirl, nowhere near as harsh as the driving – *blizzard*, the Doctor had called it – but was dense enough to mask all but the grey bones of the trees below. And the wind still had teeth. She was sure they had worked their way downward, around this slope, projecting from the mountainside like a fist, clad in its glove of white. Their tracks stretched behind them like crudely carved script, but disappeared too soon for their every step to be retraced. They were badly exposed here, easy prey.

Leela tensed, like a deer in a hunter's sights.

The ridgeline above was invisible, but was marked approximately by the grey shapes that came pouring over the crest into view. 'Doctor.'

'I see them,' the Doctor informed her, teeth clenched. 'Never rains but it – ' He straightened. 'Do you know, I think they're only coyotes.'

Leela opened her mouth to ask the obvious question. But the Doctor shushed her and placed an arm over her shoulder. 'They're a species of wild dog native to this land, but they won't bother us. Not if we stay perfectly still, try not to attract their attention unnecessarily.' Slowly, he encouraged her into a crouch beside him. He kept his finger across his lips.

'Unless they're hungry,' he added in a whisper.

Leela whispered back, but could not quite hide her annoyance: 'And how will we know if they are hungry, Doctor?'

'Oh, I expect they'll try to eat us.'

'Doctor, we should find some better place to hide from these creatures.'

13

The Doctor never once shifted his gaze from the pack, which was beginning now to resolve itself into individual animals, dark and streamlined. They hurtled their way down the slope, battling against the deep snow, jostling like a teeming shoal of Horda. There was a predatory beauty to their motion, as well as a collective recklessness.

Leela was poised for a sprint.

'We'd never make it,' the Doctor told her only what her instincts had tried to deny.

She watched the staring eyes and the bounding grey forms, the rippling muscles beneath the frosted fur and the contours of ribs as they closed the distance. Many, the majority, looked dangerously lean. She had no choice but to sit still and hope that the pack would run past.

'They do look especially hungry, don't they?' observed the Doctor gloomily.

The lighter popped and Curt Redeker snatched it straight up, sucked at the flame through his cigarette. It was the only heat left in the goddamn car. His feet were blocks of ice on the pedals and he was getting the shakes just trying to stay on the road. He drummed his hands along to Creedence's 'Lodi'. More about stopping the shakes than keeping warm.

Jesus, I-93 was the road to hell, but this – he'd never known Martha was going to take the kid to live with the Eskimos. Bitch was frigid, she'd be right at home, but making him drive through this shit to see his kid for Thanksgiving. Amber.

Sour tears and another case of the shakes: Daddy's late, Precious, days late. Daddy's sorry, honey, can't tell you. But see, your Daddy got himself dressed up and there's presents out in the trunk. Want to step outside with your Daddy, go see?

The suit was aggravating, a bad fit. Curt swallowed dry and the drunken butterflies in his gut were coming down hard, begging for another shot. The bottle clinked around below, rolling somewhere under the seat. Cursing, he stretched down.

He almost had it, but the bottle slipped loose. Suddenly, the car was sliding like a cow on ice-skates. Curt grabbed the wheel tight, breaking out in a sweat. CCR were playing second fiddle to the sound of his own breathing. Well, hey, least he was still doing that.

Getting a grip, he scoured the slope, through the frosted windshield, a web of scratches, and all that white dirt being tossed over the hood. It was a downhill stretch, winding between trees in a fogged film. That whiter knife, that had to be a lake. And all those lines and shapes of grey, that had to be a town. A hand-painted sign, nailed to a tree, crept out of the pale murk on his right:

HASTE YE BACK, it said. A quaint local feature.

'Wish I could,' muttered Curt, deciding he really needed to pull over for a time-out. But he let the miles blur for a time. He yawned and rubbed his eyes practically into the bridge of his nose. When he looked up he blinked. And Curt was staring death in the face.

The Doctor and Leela stood slowly.

Far below, the coyotes blurred together once more and, like grey waters, ran into the trees where they disappeared, dissolved in white.

Their departure left a momentary vacuum.

'Those animals looked starved,' the Doctor noted, with a weighty glance at Leela. 'Winter. Food scarce – but even so.' He peered into the stillness below, then looked up, trying to penetrate the emptiness above the ridgeline. 'Something must have scared them very badly to make them run past a perfectly good square meal like us.'

Leela wiped her face: a great deal of the snow had stuck to her cheeks and brow while they had waited for the pack to pass them. 'I am not disappointed they did so.'

'Neither am I. But I am wondering what could have given a pack of hungry coyotes a scare like that. Aren't you?'

Leela let her shoulders fall. 'If there is danger that way,' she directed a nod up the slope, 'then we should follow those creatures.'

'Well, that's one opinion, of course,' conceded the Doctor a touch huffily. He stooped to bring his enormous eyes level with hers. 'Do you know what I think?'

'Yes.'

'I think we should take a leaf out of Jack and Jill's book.' He beamed cheerily and pointed up to where the incline met the sky. And in the next instant he was wading off in that same direction. 'Come on. Up the hill.'

Leela huffed and braced herself for a strenuous climb. 'Yes, Doctor.'

'And try not to go breaking anyone's crown.'

The Doctor's call was as faint as it was mystifying.

The snows had taken to the air like a swarm of hoary insects. Visibility was falling rapidly to zero. Just as Kristal had prophesied: not the breeze the Captain was expecting. Still, she'd like to spare him the I-told-you-so. This time. It couldn't be too lucky when it was her ass hanging in the wind.

Almost literally. Shaw had assigned her, vindictively she suspected, to the roof with Marotta. A big old colonial farmhouse, red wood, it was an easy gig to climb up, the way it huddled into the mountain. Not so easy staying aloft. Especially with the anaemic killer bees having a go with their icicle stings.

Kristal yanked her hat down far as it would go. She shuttered her eyes to fence out the swirl of flakes. White Shadow was a ghost-platoon, spread around the house in a broad arc, grey as the trees. And like the trees they waited, collecting snow.

Kristal's face had weathered some storms in its time, but none like this.

16

Winter was when the land slept, storing its energies for the renewal of spring. This day was all death without the promise of rebirth. Her hand rested on the roof and her gloved fingers confirmed it: there was more than cold beneath her fingertips.

'Whoa, Kristal. You're not about to get all spiritual on me are you?' warned Marotta, a rugged sort of Santa with a face built in Brooklyn, as he swung himself around the other side of the chimney. His boots scraped the snows loose and sent a pack of it sliding from the roof. Jerk never treated her like a real officer. None of them would ever understand.

This wasn't a two-man job. As soon as Marotta had unpacked the smoker, she dropped on her butt and coasted down on a minor avalanche of her own. She was sure even he could cope with dropping a grenade down a chimney.

Kristal hit a drift where the yard was buried. She stumbled forward but her feet were planted deep enough to steady her. She followed right through with a crouch, spun around to take in the windows. They were framed in snow, like on the Christmas cards. By contrast the panes were dark, forbidding.

A shotgun blast blew a shower of glass out among the snowflakes.

For one eternal second, Curt imagined he'd never left on this nightmare drive. He was back working the oilfields in Oklahoma, out amongst the hammer and grind of the pumps. Then his eyes fought their way open and the throbbing stepped inside his skull. Creedence had perished in the crash.

His lips resisted parting and he licked away the stickiness there, tasting blood. The wheel was pressing hard into his forehead. Lifting his head, the ache only got worse.

Every part of him was sore and some of the blood around his face was still wet. Plus the car was leaning, butt in the air, nose in the ditch. Great. Sorry, baby. Daddy's gonna be a bit late but he'll get there. Curt stopped his laugh dead, afraid he was losing it.

Straining his eyes through heavy fog, all he could see was snow. Snow and trees. And another car blocking a lonely, hostile road. Jesus-H! What was the driver thinking of? Damn near killed him.

Realisation dawned more painfully than consciousness: the other car looked like one of those Indian burial mounds, showing only a glimpse of wheel-arch and radiator; if there was any driver in that car he'd surely breathed his last by now. Past the lead vehicle, Curt made out the contours of others, a line of traffic, buried in the snowfall. He thought of a whole line of mourners scattering dust over a row of coffins.

Suddenly Curt was scared. Maybe those other drivers had done the same. Maybe they'd stayed put, been buried alive. Forget the pain and get the hell out!

He lashed out with an arm. He was trapped in here. But no, he hit the catch and the door dropped open. 'Daddy loves you, honey.' His voice a whimper. Then a warning: 'Lord, you let me see my girl.'

A shiver from outside took a hold of him and dumped him into the snow. The air whistled around him, blew flakes in his face and bit at his skin. Up on his knees, he hugged himself tight and muttered prayer after prayer to stave off the jitters. He'd prayed hard every time his Daddy came at him with that belt, the buckle he took such care to polish; Curt never prayed scared, he focused on that shiny buckle and prayed plain angry. He thought of his bourbon, *almost* the colour of that buckle, rolling around under the dash. He turned to fetch it.

And a shadow crossed the corner of his eye.

'Oh Christ, good Christ, Jesus Lord.' He was just putting words to the shivers. He hauled himself to the side of his Buick, and turned his head, aching muscles slowing the move as much as honest fear. It was freezing and the sweat was pouring off him.

A coyote drooled at him. Head down, it looked starved and mangy.

There were others – shapes was all – trailing out from the trees like wisps of grey smoke, low to the ground. And now his arm was hooking back into the car, but what he wanted was in the glove box. A mile out of reach.

The coyote, depraved eyes fixed on Curt, hadn't moved.

Curt's fingers closed on the bottle; then slipped. He swore. Then he had it again and hurled it at the coyote's face. The devil-animal snarled and jumped back, baring its fangs. The bottle shattered on the road, in one of the Buick's skid-marks. Maybe the alcohol stung its eyes, maybe the noise had it rattled. Either way, it backed off some more. Not far enough.

Curt didn't dare budge. If he lunged, so would the animal. *Think.*

The snarling of that one coyote filled his head as it padded back, smelling the sweat. Curt focused on its eyes: those twin sharp points of brightness.

Then his prayers were answered. In a bad way.

Up along the road, something stirred in the pack. The grey shapes milled about, agitated, like the smoke had been fanned. The leader caught the scent, and suddenly it was as if Curt wasn't there. The animal's ears pricked up, it sniffed the air and glanced about. Spooked.

Suddenly, it was on the run, across the road and into the trees on the downward slope. Off towards the lake. The rest of its pack followed, pouring into the woods, never looking back. Leaving Curt very alone.

Curt lunged inside the car, stretching for the glove box. He snapped it open and dug inside for the pistol. An old .38 automatic. His numbed fingers fumbled as he racked the slide.

Curt scrambled to stand with a new determination. All that sweat had turned chill under his clothes and he had to get moving. Those damn coyotes had scattered, run for their lives. Curt's precious bourbon hadn't done that. No, sir. 'Daddy's safe, baby. Daddy's okay.'

Woozy like he'd downed twenty bourbons, Curt staggered and had to take a breather leaning against the car. His eyes scoured the woodlands ahead, up the slope and down, where the coyotes had disappeared. He couldn't see a thing. Too much white.

The hairs on his neck stood like that coyote's ears. There was a whisper of motion, like the softest footfall on snow. Behind him.

He spun, backed himself into the nearest tree.

Somebody there? What in *hell* spooked those curs? What kind of Godforsaken hole have you brought my baby to, Martha, you bitch? I swear, I'll… He clutched the gun tighter for comfort, aimed it at nothing. 'Daddy's not gonna die, not now, honey.'

He flinched as the cold stung his face. Like an icicle splinter. It stung so bad, he had to touch his cheek for a moment to test for blood.

Nothing. Only a cold fire.

He ignored it and carried on scanning all around him, his back pressed to the tree. The cold closed in and the snows spattered on his jacket. He aimed the gun this way and that, searching along its sights. Nothing. Nothing he could see.

'Who's there? Goddamn you, who's there?'

'Could these soldiers have scared the wild dogs, Doctor?'

For a while there was no answer, but Leela was used to the Doctor's ponderous silences. 'They could have, but I doubt it. No, I rather think these are just men with less sense than the coyotes.'

Leela felt warmer, pressed close to the ground, her breathing almost painful after their uphill march. The Doctor was very like the hero in the elders' tale sometimes, charging on and ignoring the protests of his loyal warriors. 'Like us,' she reminded him.

They were huddled down at the edge of some silver-white

trees. The branches were all bare, but the visibility was very poor and Leela felt their cover must be adequate at this distance. A bank of snow had gathered at the foot of the trees and tumbled down into a shallow basin, across which they could see a lonely red building, half buried in the side of another rise with more trees beyond. Soldiers moved swiftly in on the house from numerous angles.

They were difficult to pick out, in their white armour. Leela suddenly felt unhappy with the furs she had exhumed from the TARDIS wardrobes. She wanted armour like the soldiers wore, so she could move unseen in this colourless land.

'The soldiers are well-armed. If there is an enemy here then they are right to stand and fight.'

The Doctor shrugged, gave a tilt of the head. 'Well, we can debate that with the coyotes when we catch up with them. Come on.'

He patted her arm and started to move off. Leela lifted herself stealthily, but hissed after him, 'Where are we going?'

'To introduce ourselves. Now stay down and stay quiet and follow me.'

And with that the Doctor was leading her on a weaving course between the gaunt trees, closing in on the house. The crack of gunfire threatened the fragile air and Leela wondered how the Doctor could be so sure none of the shots were aimed at them.

His current thirst for danger was beginning to worry her.

All hell could have broken loose, but Captain Morgan Shaw wasn't going to stand for that. He sent Hmieleski chasing after Kristal to see if she was hurt; had his snipers pour covering shots into the front windows and ordered Marotta to stay put until the all clear. Then he moved the rest of them up in the formations he'd decided on before this became a shoot-out.

By the time he'd made the porch, the gunfire and the screams were an echo. Nothing more, nothing less. Morgan nodded to young Landers who moved in to bust the door open with the butt of his M4. The guy, with his black goatee and weathered eyes, gave him a look like he knew what to expect.

Morgan knew too: a bloodbath. Had to be. Some religious cult sees itself as a modern-day Masada. Tries to make him out to be the bad guy. If only.

As boys, Morgan and Makenzie had never got to see the interior of the house. But this was the way it must have looked in a young boy's nightmares. The old doc was the local spook and he had to live in a place like this, light from the iced-over windows creeping across the floors in shafts, afraid to rouse the ghosts sleeping under the boards. The *spirits*.

They swept that house in standard two-by-two. All Morgan could hear, upstairs and down, was the breaking of doors and the shouts of 'Clear!', all to the rhythm of his own beating heart. Swinging his SMG around another chipped and peeling doorframe, it got to be so he wasn't sure any more what they were searching for. A tunnel? A secret passage?

Landers burst in on the dining room, sent a chair scraping across the tiles. Morgan swept in after him, SMG arcing left to right. 'Mary Mother,' hissed Landers.

There had been a firefight in here. They'd all heard it, straight after Kristal had nearly caught one; the shots and the screams of victims. Gunsmoke lingered in the air, mingling with their steamy breaths. A few weapons – pistols, shotguns, an automatic rifle – lay on the floor, along with a scattering of spent cartridges. The papered walls were pitted and splintered all to hell. There were even spots of blood on the table.

But by now Morgan knew they wouldn't find anything. Nobody; no bodies. The house wasn't that kind of empty. The shadows, the darkness in here, were frozen solid.

This place was empty like a recently vacated grave.

Chapter Two

Colder than a cemetery out there. Melvin Village had never looked so dead.

Painted wood, white the colour of preference, the buildings should have vanished altogether on a day like today. But from where Makenzie Shaw was parked, out front of the store, only the outskirts of the village were properly invisible. Ordinarily you could see it all: more trees than houses, the church in the middle of it all, that white spire a head or two shorter than the trees, and the lake behind. Pretty as a picture, all right.

Every day Makenzie woke up and drove down from his cabin to make his rounds, and he never really noticed any of it. Except sometimes, when he wasn't carrying a heavy load on his mind. Which, now he came to think of it, was never, these days.

Winter. Jesus. When had it been this bad? He couldn't remember. Probably never.

Never this dead. And that was the real funny part: ordinarily the town lived the whole year round. Summer or winter, everybody flocking to the lake like geese, to fish, swim, sail – sunbathe even – or to head for the hills and climb, trek, ski, get lost. But the truth was, with all those folks passing through week after week, Makenzie's town was never left to just *be*. She was doing all her living for everybody else. Between seasons there was even the motorcycle festival around Winnipesaukee; brought a horde of bikers through – like a Biblical plague, Hal Byers said every year.

Today there was nobody.

So now here she was, Melvin Village, alone at last. And not

only was Hal praying every night for visitors, customers for his store, but the one time the town could live for herself and just *be*, well, the place was past death. Like God had cut off her blood supply.

Makenzie caught a movement out of his quarterlight.

He reached over to open the passenger door as Laurie came round. She sidled into the truck, bursting his bubble of warmth and silence and bringing a few breaths of snow with her. She deposited a couple of Styrofoam cups above the dash and heaved the door to, before she was ready to offer a smile.

'Look like you wish you'd stayed home today, Chief,' she said.

Makenzie grabbed the nearest cup, and let his face soak up the steam for a moment. 'Tell you what, I'm going to be kind today, not even let you know how wrong you got that.'

'Trouble up on Walton Mountain?'

Makenzie had to laugh halfway through blowing on his coffee. Laurie's favourite joke, now there was a woman and a kid in the Chief's life. He stole a glance at his deputy: skin the colour of winter, long hair the colour of fall. Laurie Aldrich. Now there sat a mistake he would gladly have made if Martha hadn't happened. Fact was that he'd been on the point of making it when he'd been called out to the trailer park, a bunch of wasters from Wawbeek creating trouble outside of Martha's trailer; baiting the Southerners.

Helping her out, protecting her and her kid, that night it had been about doing his job. Two nights later something had prompted him to swing by and check on how she was doing. Then the same thing prompted him to ask her out. Looking after the pair of them, Martha and Amber, now it was about his life. Him and Melvin Village, living for other people, and when we're alone – well, Makenzie got by. Makenzie Shaw had been getting by since he was ten years old. Since he was Amber's age.

Laurie was attractive and she was there every day. And she was two-thirds his age. So now he woke up to Martha's head on the pillow, all that brown hair mussed up, and he could see himself with her ten, twenty years down the road. The picture was that clear. In his head, at least, it all worked out fine.

'Hey, you know, Chief, you ever want to talk about it. Over a beer, you know?'

He'd sat quiet too long, he realised.

'Nah, ain't a domestic situation been invented I can't handle,' he beamed, then raised a Styrofoam toast. Laurie was good, and the thought of red hair on his pillow was inevitable. Where would they have ended up by now? Sitting in the same truck every morning? Picking up coffees from Hal's store? Don't even go there, Makenzie. Just a different colour to your morning. Not a big enough change to want that bad.

'Appreciate the asking anyhow.' Makenzie held a bead of caffeine on his tongue. 'So – what'd Hal have to say?'

Laurie settled back in her chair. She knew when the personal door was closed. 'He was kind of worried, Chief. This couple came in early, stocked up on supplies for the road. The guy reckoned the weather had eased off, enough to try the journey home anyway. Said a few of the townsfolk were going to try to make a break for it along with them.'

Yeah, thought Makenzie. Not the real townsfolk. Just the ones who'd bought themselves a nice holiday home or two around here.

'What time?'

'Round seven. Hal told them he didn't like the way the storm was eyeing up the town. But the guy said his lady had been going stir crazy over in the hotel. So it was today or never.'

Makenzie shook his head, returned his cup to the dash. 'Never make promises you can't keep. Okay, well I guess we'd best check it out – for all our peaces of mind. They tell Hal which way their little convoy was going?'

'North. The ploughs were all along Route 109 two days ago. Guess they reckoned on a lot of traffic before Thanksgiving, huh?'

'I admire optimism,' remarked Makenzie as he grabbed the wheel and reached for the ignition. He gunned the engine and wheeled his truck gently out into the street.

'But I'd have to side with Hal on this one. I don't like the way that storm's looking at us. Not one bit. Best check it out, bring them back in. Maybe you should have had Hal fill up a Thermos or two.'

He swung the vehicle round wide to steer them north. As he started out of town the winter, for the present, was parting to let them through.

'Maybe they had a lucky break, Chief. Maybe they made it okay.'

'Maybe.' But Makenzie's tone wasn't convincing either of them.

Ten minutes into her walk and Amber's face still burned. It hadn't helped that she'd been near enough to the road to watch Makenzie when he rolled by on his way to work. That big important truck, with the rig of lights on the roof, always idle, and the Police badge emblazoned on the doors, as idle as the lights far as Amber knew.

Makenzie, driving down to take care of his precious town, like he was its daddy or something. Like he owned the place.

He hated her Daddy because he wasn't anything important like him. And sure, because he hurt Mom. But – hey, screw him. She was out on her own now, just her and the snow. She could do what she liked.

Pretty soon she was marching between the trees, away from the track – which you couldn't see anyway – and after a while the sting in her cheeks was only the wind. And as she walked, enjoying the effort it took to plant and re-plant her boots in the drifts, she imagined all sorts of craggy faces carved in the silver-white bark around her. She wished she had her knife so she could carve them some angrier faces, and the idea made her laugh.

She trotted for a while to keep warm and to get her to her secret place just a little quicker. She kicked the snows and spun about, and she sang out loud, a note of triumph she couldn't have explained if she'd wanted to.

Her own voice stopped her, like she'd screamed in the middle of someone else's party. Too loud. She searched around fast for the people who must have heard her. The ones she felt sure must be watching. Except she knew – she *knew* – there was nobody up here. How could there be? She was alone on the mountain. Makenzie's mountain.

Mount Shaw. Makenzie had joked about how it was his mountain that day they'd moved in – when taking the *family* for a summer evening walk seemed like a good idea. But they'd stopped close by another cabin, maybe fifty yards short, Makenzie said, of the view he'd promised them. Because Amber had complained she was tired, complained until Mom took her side. Today that cabin was only a shadow on the air, but the look in Makenzie's eyes as they'd trekked back down his mountain was carved in bark.

Well the mountain was hers right now. She was alone here. She ruled the mountain. She could do what she liked and it didn't matter who was watching.

She bent to scoop up a lovely helping of the ground. She pounded it together, thinking it was like a ball of frozen mashed potato.

Then she hurled it, full force, at the face in the nearest tree.

But she didn't watch what it did to the face. She was more interested in the way her creation broke apart in soft lumps, flying in every direction and falling noiselessly back to being just part of the ground once more.

Done standing still, Amber spun and carried on up the hill with a fresh spring in her step. There wasn't any movement in the forest; none at all. So perhaps it was the stillness that kept provoking her to glance around. There was never anything there, ever, and she didn't like feeling so stupid. She wanted to get to her hideout already.

Gearing herself up, she turned her run into a charge for the last stretch of the slope.

She was about ready to let out another great hurrah – but as she conquered the rise, a layer of ground, huge and purest white, flew up to smother her. And trapped the cheer in her throat.

'Don't you people know any other welcome? Honestly, put a gun in a man's hands and he seems to forget all about tea and biscuits.'

Given that the air had to escape over such a wall of teeth, the power in the man's voice was phenomenal. Sufficient to command Kristal's attention, such that she hardly noticed as Hmieleski carefully plucked each tiny splinter of glass from her forearm. There was such gravity too in the stranger's face, and eyes that could stare down an owl.

'Oh, please, you'll have to excuse the substandard hospitality,' parried the Captain, his tone a poor glue for patience already snapped, 'but you and your girlfriend have just walked in on something of a situation here and it so happens you look to me like a couple of cultists.'

'Oh really? And what do they look like?'

All the guns levelled at the prisoner might as well have been water pistols, although he kept his hands aloft as a courtesy. Or as an example to his companion.

'Well, the specifics I think vary from cult to cult, but broadly speaking they tend to look *weird*. And if I put that description out to the local cops, my guess is you'd be the first suspects they bring in for questioning.'

'We generally are. Isn't that right, Leela?'

The girl – the woman – she was an altogether different fascination. Steadfastly silent, trusting and afraid, ward and guardian both to this outlandish hobo who'd barged in on the

Captain's precious scene. They'd received advanced warning from Falvi and Barnes out on the perimeter, but the snipers' report hadn't prepared anyone for the figures that walked in. The other squads had suspended their room-to-room search and some of the men were out in the hall, waiting on the outcome like the final score in a football game.

Well hell, Kristal was ready to lay a few bucks on the outsider.

She flinched as cold liquid bit her arm. Joanna Hmieleski flashed her a wry look of apology. She was a good officer and an even better doctor, but she'd never waste anything as rare as sympathy on scratches.

'How's she doing?' Captain Shaw asked, taking a time out.

Joanna met Kristal's look, and smiled. 'She can walk and she can fight. She can even play the piano if she wants. I'm just cleaning up the cuts now.'

Right there, thought Kristal, was the first anyone had smiled since entering this house. The atmosphere didn't exactly encourage it. And despite the good news, Captain Shaw wasn't ready to echo the expression.

'Doesn't change the fact,' he rounded on his prisoners, 'I have wounded here. Scratches or no, there's a lot of firepower littered around this place, and it could have been one hell of a lot worse. So you and your lady friend will understand if my temper gets shorter when I don't start getting answers.'

The Captain's pacing brought him in line with the woman. She didn't care for the attention. 'You said these soldiers would be friendly, Doctor.'

The *quality* of the sound was like a shock through Kristal's heart: a native innocence that fit perfectly with the apparel. It confirmed everything Kristal had already seen in the young woman's eyes.

The Captain was sharp, one of the sharpest, but there were times – just some times – when he couldn't see daylight in a cloudless sky.

'Well, friendly is a relative term, Leela. Friendlier than whoever or whatever they've been shooting at, I would hope. And where there's hope there's – what exactly have you been shooting at, Captain? Because, you know, if they were very large and very green there's a good chance I might be able to find an easier way of dealing with them.'

Captain Shaw was not a big fan of condescension. 'Okay, first of all, I'm not interested in your screwy religious experiences with Martians, how you *commune* with extraterrestrials. And second of all, if you're not cultists, I want to know who you are, what you are, what you're doing here, what you know about any of – ' He gestured around, but had no words (nobody had) for the scene that possessed this house. ' – *this*. Immediately would be nice.'

'Well, as you've probably gathered, I'm the Doctor. I'm a Scientific Adviser with the UNIT organisation, although I'm mostly part-time these days. More of a traveller, freelance, you might say.' The grin could have disarmed a legion – or provoked one into battle.

'UNIT huh? And who is she? The People That Time Forgot?'

'In a manner of speaking, yes.' An answer for everything, it seemed, and now a new mask that seemed done with playing. 'Her name is Leela. You might take a little more care not to hurt her feelings. She's very sensitive you know, and probably very tired of keeping her hands up. Do you mind if we take them down, it's really getting very boring.' His arms were already lowered and those of his young companion followed his lead.

He leaned forward as though to whisper in the Captain's ear, but that voice carried to the hall and beyond. 'Now I can see you're an intelligent fellow and I know if you had anything to do with shooting the people who lived here we'd be knee-deep in bodies, which puts each of us as much in the dark as the other. And I don't very much care for the dark, do you?'

Kristal read a signal in the corner of her eye and she glanced down to see that Hmieleski had finished dressing her arm. She stood along with the lieutenant and reached down for her parka. In that time, the Captain was busy puzzling over his find.

'UNIT.' He shook his head. 'I don't know, *Doctor*. Seems to me UNIT would most likely be investigating you instead of hiring you.'

But the Captain had already been won over. And this Doctor had started work, confidently extending his hand, while his eyes conducted a grim survey of the dining room.

'Ah well, genius is rarely understood, you know,' the Doctor shook the Captain's hand absently. Kristal could almost feel his mind appraising every detail in the room, prioritising every fragment for closer attention.

His gaze fell for a moment on his companion, who waited dutifully for her own assignment.

'You know, Captain, perhaps you could see about getting my assistant some better clothing, something more appropriate for the time of year.'

'Sir, I can help with that,' volunteered Kristal before the Captain could offer his protest. 'I'll see what they have lying around the house.'

Morgan Shaw took a moment, then nodded. The message in his gaze was clear: he had no problem being railroaded as long as things were headed the way he wanted. He spun about ready to get everything moving again. Kristal stepped over quickly to usher Leela out of harm's way.

Amber kicked and thrashed for the first few seconds, and then started to realise she was making matters worse.

Forcing herself to calm down, she thought about the games she'd played, making tents of her bed-sheets sometimes long after Mom had kissed her goodnight. She had no idea where this particular sheet had come from, but it was shiny and smooth like Mom's favourite linen. And as she probed her way out from under it, she kept a hold of it to prevent the wind from blowing it any further. It flapped madly for escape, the way she'd done a moment before.

Surfacing for air, she flipped herself over and took a good look at what she had. She started to pull it together over her lap. It was huge and the strings attached seemed to trail for miles.

She wasn't happy with the way she'd panicked, but at least she could be pleased with her find. A parachute, it had to be. Wow. How cool was that?

The trace of a frown found its way to her forehead. Of course the chute had to belong to somebody, and that made her take a long look around.

Nobody. And the lines of the chute ended in thin air.

It was hers. Way too big to cart into town, but she should be able to stow it easy enough. She could go tell some of the other kids maybe, save the show for later. Amber scrabbled to a crouch and started raking in her find.

A touch of nervous excitement kept her glancing about, that was all.

'So the bed finally coughed you up?'

'Hey, I couldn't *in all conscience* leave you to mess up this surveillance all by yourself,' Parker Theroux teased his partner mercilessly as he trudged through the snow to join her.

She rolled her eyes, lowering the binoculars. 'When have you ever known me to mess up any operation?'

She had a point and Parker had expected an answer something like that. He stuffed his hands deep in his coat pockets and completed the rest of the walk with something of a sheepish gait. 'Well, never, but if you were ever going to, I know it'd be some time I wasn't around to see it happen. It's not in your make-up to give me that kind of ammunition.' The mist was sinking heavily between the trees and the scent of pine and birch rode towards him on ethereal waves. Personally, he could take it or leave it, but the view – the view was a different matter. Because there was no view. Everything ended in white.

He'd heard artist-types talking about the vanishing point, and here it was, all around him. The forest, the mountain, the air, it all fell off some unseen edge into a void.

'Will you look at that!' He grabbed a hold of his partner's shoulders and pointed her in a random direction. He perched his chin down on her head and exhaled softly into her hair. 'Doesn't it make you feel you could walk through that and you'd be stepping off this world into another universe?'

Melody relaxed into his embrace for a second. But all too soon she was wriggling free. 'Yes, Parker, yes it does. But day-dreaming isn't going to get us anywhere.'

'No, no I guess not.' Parker was used to having his spells broken like this. He yawned and blinked several times, introducing his eyes to the new day in stages. 'Whereas standing out here freezing our butts off is going to get us results.'

'Ha ha.' Parker was happy to see his customary sarcasm could still push all the right buttons. 'As it happens, it might,' she told him, all serious now. 'I came out here to see if I could get a fix on White Shadow's position. But I think we've got something promising happening on an unexpected front.'

'Yeah? Down at the sheriff's house?' Parker reluctantly coaxed his hands out of his pockets to take Melody's binoculars. The local Police Chief was family to the White Shadow Captain, but Morgan Shaw had yet to pay his brother a visit.

'Not quite.' Now it was Melody's turn to aim him in her chosen direction. 'The kid from the sheriff's house. A while ago I saw her struggling with something we might be interested in, Parker. She was taking a lot of trouble to cart it off into those trees. No, over there.'

'Yeah?' Parker tried to sound fascinated, but as he raised the binoculars to his eyes, he could barely see the trees, let alone anything moving among them. 'Um, I never like to rain on your parade, but I've had daydreams with more substance than what I'm seeing right now.'

His partner snatched back the binoculars as he lowered them. She nudged him in the ribs for his pains. 'That'll teach you to lie in, deadwood. The fact is, she was dragging a parachute. And there can't have been many of those left lying around on this mountain, can there?'

'Not lately,' admitted Parker, intrigued in spite of himself. 'You're sure you're not – '

Melody favoured him with a patient tilt of the head.

'No, you're not mistaken,' he concluded aloud.

'So, are you up for a morning stroll in the woods, Agent Theroux?'

'In your company? What, are you kidding?' And Parker thought he'd have to dodge another blow to his ribs, but Melody was too intent on leading the way on the trail of the girl. By now he was properly awake, and there was no going back.

Makenzie wiped furiously at the passenger window and grimaced at the cold, burning his fingertips through his gloves. A good deal of the ice remained stubbornly fixed, doing its best to keep the car's interior hidden.

'There's another one up here, Chief!'

Laurie was a good twenty yards ahead of the lead vehicle and Makenzie didn't need anything more to worry about. This was a bad stretch of road, the turn and the trees blocking line of sight, and the winter just made it meaner. Makenzie was a cautious driver though and he'd pulled them up in good time as soon as they'd seen the half-buried car. Then Laurie's keen eyes had noticed it was just the tail vehicle in a frozen convoy.

'This one's off the road! Looks like he swerved, coming the other direction!'

'Take it slow, Laurie! Be right with you!' He'd told her to run on, get a count of the vehicles and check further along the road. Now he was less happy with his thinking.

He shook his head. His chest hurt from all the shouting, but Laurie sounded a mile away. Damn snow ate up sound as well as all the colour.

Well, no use putting it off any longer: Makenzie swiped the worst of the ice clean and stooped low to peer into the car.

He'd kicked the snow from the plates, so he was expecting to find a couple of frozen tourists in there. The couple Byers had been concerned about. His gut was knotting at the prospect.

But all he could see in there was darkness. And the frost crusting the opposite windows.

Makenzie took a step back and his gaze hunted around. He'd popped his holster as soon as he'd stepped from his truck; they'd had a world of trouble with coy-dogs this past week, packs of them even scavenging in the town. But everyone *knew*, Makenzie had made sure of that. Surely to Christ these folks would have the sense to stay in their vehicles and wait for help. Get busy dialling on their cellular phones.

Makenzie worked his steady way along the small convoy, but as he scraped the ice at each window he thought he should be searching the wooded slopes instead. Down to the lake, or up towards Mount Shaw. Made no difference either way, none of these folks would have made it very far in this weather.

They'd gone though. All of them.

As Makenzie stalked past the lead truck he was almost hoping to find a body in the wreck Laurie had found. He didn't feel like hurrying his approach though. She was waiting on him by the upended tail.

'Oklahoma plates,' she said. And that was like a bolt through Makenzie's chest.

Dear Jesus, no. He had to inspect them for himself, to be certain. His eyes were permanently narrowed anyway, against the swirl of flakes hitting his face, but he knew his frown had just got a whole lot tighter. Along with the knot in his gut, which was never going away.

'Where the wind blows,' he tried a joke, for his own sake.

'What about the others, Chief?' Laurie was reading all kinds of stuff in Makenzie's face.

'Nothing.' Makenzie gestured up and down the road and the hillside. 'Seems none of them were for sitting still but if they'd followed the road we'd have seen them.'

Wherever they'd thought they were, they had to know Melvin Village was closest. Laurie bit her lip and was probably running through the same thoughts as Makenzie.

'I'll go take a look up the slope, Chief. The trees are pretty dense up there, might have kept the worst of the snow off their tracks.'

Makenzie didn't like it, but he wanted to have a good dig round inside this up-ended Buick. Now there was a more personal worry to add to his growing list. Laurie took his nod for a green light and Makenzie watched her go for a second or so before walking around the wreck to the driver's door. It was hanging open.

The inside was a mess: cigarette packs, take-out cartons, a flotilla of plastic cups down by the passenger seat. The glove box was hanging open like the door. And when he swung around to pop the trunk, he found the worst of omens waiting for him: an untidy pile of boxes, all shiny gift-wrap and ribbons. Makenzie gritted his teeth and delved in there to grab one of the boxes. He knew what he'd find on the label but he needed to read it anyway.

'Happy Thanksgiving. To Amber With Love, Daddy.'

The impulse to throw the box back in the car was strong, but Makenzie weathered it, holding the package clumsily for a while and thinking about collecting them all. He wouldn't need help carrying them to his truck, but he'd sure as hell need Laurie to talk to on this one.

'Laurie!' he called. 'You haven't got anything yet, I think we should be heading back!'

Makenzie looked up. Laurie's silence was all wrong. Badly wrong.

'Laurie!' Only a cold echo came back at him, sounding angry now. 'Laurie!'

But his deputy was lost in an ocean of white.

Chapter Three

White Shadow operated as a platoon-sized unit, trimmed and pruned to fit its role. Three squads plus a headquarters squad of key specialist personnel. McKim's squad, Delta, was stationed with the vehicles. That still left plenty of orders to be issued and Captain Shaw was out doing his rounds of the officers and sergeants, making sure nobody was left standing idle. Lieutenant Joanna Hmieleski was a key specialist, an Alpha female, as she liked to put it, and already had her orders: keep an eye on the Doctor, and comb these floors and walls for clues, evidence or a note from a TV magician explaining how this stunt was pulled off.

She'd ruled out any chance of the latter, but appreciated the dose of humour. Based on the reports that each room revealed a similar *Mary Celeste* ambience, she'd elected to concentrate her efforts in the one place for now and ordered everyone out of the dining room. So it was down to her and this Doctor guy, and so far her new colleague had remained mute and humourless, pouring heavy thoughts into every corner.

Actually, Joanna found herself taking frequent pauses to watch him at work. Even when she was focused, on a bloodstain or the litter of dead cartridges, his was a constant presence, impossible to ignore. Why? Because, she realised, he reminded her so much of her father.

They looked nothing alike, of course. Her father had been tall, like this Doctor, but always overweight, and with a smear of dark hair clinging to his head like a thinning oil slick. A community doctor with his own practice, he was a man who might have equated with the tribal elders of Kristal's ancestors. So loved and respected, and not least by Joanna. To her, he'd shone like an oracle, an oracle who had ultimately guided her into medicine.

But long before she'd wound up on that road, she'd seen all the unwelcome change that comes hand in hand with growing up.

Joanna had gone through the requisite teen-rebellion phase nice and early, as though to clear it out of the way; and thinned her father's hair some more in the process. It was as she started to emerge that her father began to weaken, growing old fast, losing his mystique. In fact, he had many healthy years ahead of him, and Joanna was only coming to terms with a common discovery: her father was an ordinary man. Fallible and flawed. And in his case, bearing all his private sadnesses behind the gentlest manner and a pair of smiling eyes.

Working alongside this Doctor guy, Joanna Hmieleski was a girl again. He inspired a similar awe in her. This strangest of strangers was, she reasoned, like a father seen through the eyes of a child. 'So, Doctor,' she ventured courageously, 'care to offer an educated guess?'

'I never guess.'

His face was fixed on an area of the wall, punched and scarred with bullet-holes, a single glance tracing a trajectory between the impacts and the scattered cartridges at Joanna's feet.

His brusque manner felt like a rebuke, and Joanna told herself she was being foolish as she stood to have another go. 'I just thought, since we're supposed to be working together –' She rolled a spent cartridge in her palm. 'I guess I was only trying to break the ice.'

The Doctor turned, all goldfish eyes and mystical smile. 'Medicine is your field, hmm?'

'Sure,' she answered automatically, 'but I fill a forensics role as well. Pydych is our engineer and – ' The Doctor shushed her with a mime, then went on as if she hadn't spoken.

'Do you know what interests me most, Lieutenant Hmieleski?' The way his voice made such a rich sound of her name was oddly flattering. 'We have no patients. Not even a candidate for a post mortem. These cultists were firing an awful lot of ammunition at somebody or something. But your Captain assures me not a single shot was aimed at him or his soldiers.'

'Not intentionally, no. It never got to that. Kristal is convinced she was hit by accident. One desperate guy blowing an emergency exit through a back window. She saw him run off into the snows, like a wild thing, she said. That was when the rest of the shooting started inside the house and that's when we made our move. And *that* is pretty much all she wrote.'

'Yes, well, *she* could have been a little more prolific, for all our sakes.'

Hmieleski followed the Doctor's gaze down to the cartridge in her palm. 'This little fella's a 7.62 Long, definitely not one of ours. The only shots our people fired were the covering volleys from our two snipers but – for obvious reasons – we can't confirm whether they hit anyone.' She shook her head as she scanned over the wall. 'By the time any of our people got inside the house, the shooting was all done. I don't get it. It's as if the walls might have been closing in on them and they were shooting back.'

'Well, if I were a guessing man,' argued the Doctor, 'I'd say it was more like they were shooting at ghosts, then became ghosts themselves – wouldn't you?'

Joanna suppressed a sudden shiver. There was no heat in here.

'Which only goes to prove the futility of guesswork,' concluded the Doctor, stepping past her into the middle of the room, where he could conduct a grand sweep of the scene from under that ridiculous hat.

'Of course,' he added casually, 'from a more rational point of view, we could be looking at disintegration weaponry, transmat technology; that sort of thing. Residual energy traces shouldn't be too difficult to detect – as long as they're tested for fairly soon.'

His impossibly wide gaze was meant as a prompt, Joanna could tell. 'I'll get Pydych on it. The detection gear will be back with the vehicles, but I'm sure Irving won't mind the – '

All set to fetch the engineer, she was suddenly arrested by a very paternal hand in the crook of her arm. She spun – straight into those eyes.

'Lieutenant Hmieleski, if we really are going to be working together, I think we're going to have to pool our knowledge, don't you? I mean, we might eventually persuade this house to part with its story, but some of us still wouldn't have the full picture, would we? For instance, the part about what Captain Shaw is doing here with his delightful team of soldiers? He didn't come all this way to arrest a few misguided cultists, now did he?'

For a moment, Joanna felt obliged to give him a précis of their mission. Then her training kicked in. 'I'm sorry, Doctor, but you're going to have to talk to Captain Shaw about that.'

A crumpled paper bag appeared in the guy's hand, right under her nose, like a magic trick. 'Care for a jelly baby?'

In spite of her years of adulthood and training, Joanna found herself peering inside. 'As bribes go, this is not very impressive.'

The Doctor shrugged. 'Well no,' he owned at length, moderately abashed. But the grin returned a second later. 'But you have to admit it's effective, hmm?'

Joanna inhaled and couldn't believe the turn her thoughts had taken. She dipped a hand into the bag. 'You do realise, you breathe a word of this to Captain Shaw, he'll eat us both alive.'

The Doctor plucked a juicy-looking sweet from the bag for

himself. 'I can't speak for him, but I generally prefer to bite the heads off first.'

Irrepressible. Just like her father.

Martha swore and chucked the papers from her lap onto the coffee table. She dragged her fingers back through her hair, the pen still in one hand.

It was useless: how was she expected to concentrate? School was out, but there were still test papers to mark, lesson plans to prepare. At this rate, she'd have to pray the snows would keep the school out long after the holidays.

She tossed the pen onto the papers as she stood. Mak's sofa was too damn comfortable for this kind of work anyhow. Arching her back deep, she took a lethargic walk over to the window. Well, the snow looked set to stick around forever, so that was okay.

But it sure looked harsh out there. Harsh as hell.

Maybe she could have been more helpful this morning. But no, she knew well enough, you step into the middle of a fight, everyone thinks you're on the other side. It was impossible to gauge the centre line. Anyway she'd have to stick up for Amber. The kid was ten hard years old. Mak had to tread slow and careful, something you'd think he was born to – when it came to anything but Amber. His main failing, he just didn't have the know-how to understand Amber and make her feel understood. But if it was his failing, then it was Martha's too.

School was out, so family needn't wait. Martha figured she should try. If Mak wasn't driving off packs of hungry coy-dogs, as he called them, he was probably mulling over a second cup of coffee with Laurie Aldrich. She could take a drive down and meet him for lunch, take the time to talk him through Amber properly.

Truth was, she was no expert either, and Martha had to shut down on a few tears then, the thought of those days she

42

couldn't handle her own kid. Along with all the days she could never make up to her.

So harsh out there. Martha sent out a silent prayer for Amber, out in the midst of it. And she threw in another for Mak for good measure.

The phone rang.

Martha wiped away the mood like she'd been asleep, then dragged herself to the hall. One hand went back through her hair again as she picked up the phone.

'Yeah?'

'Martha.'

Martha actually flinched. All the harshness of winter had crept inside her gut.

It was Curt.

'Listen, shut the hell up for a second and listen, will you?'

'Whatever it is you got to say, I'm not interested. Do you hear me? You're done calling the shots and you're done telling me anything. For someone who loves the sound of his own voice, have you ever stopped to listen to yourself? Not once! So why in hell I ever expected you to listen to me – or your own daughter, for Christ's sake – '

Curt Redeker was ready to beat the crap out of the phone with the receiver, just to shut her up. But he sensed the clerk watching from the counter. Why'd he even call her? Why'd he go to so much trouble to find a phone? What in hell for? Well, he knew the answer to that, and so did Martha. Amber.

'I'm not taking this from you, bitch. I've just walked a god-damn marathon through the snow to find a phone, let you know I got here.' Christ, he'd even stopped to wash his face in the snow, clean off the blood and kill the pain with the cold. 'I found a call box, it was dead, so I ask the guy at the store if I can use the phone. He looks at me like I'm – '

'Let me know you got here? You were supposed to be here Saturday morning. I told you, two days, the weekend before

43

the holidays – and that was for her, *not you*. She's been wondering where you've been the whole weekend and guess what – I didn't have anything to tell her. Same old story and we've all heard it enough, so I tell you what, you can come see her this afternoon, drop off whatever presents you're trying to impress her with this time and then you're gone. Back to whatever hole you're living in, out of our lives, you got that, you bastard? Are you hearing me, *Curt?* Am I getting through to you this time?'

Loud and clear. She couldn't do this, no way. She couldn't keep him from seeing his little girl – and for as long as he damn well pleased. What was she going to do, snatch her own daughter away, tell her Daddy's going now? She would.

He was seeing the world through a haze, much worse than the storm he'd just fought through. For a while back there, following the lake shore, stumbling blind, he'd really wondered if he was going to fall and never get up. And now this bitch was making his head spin.

He shot a look over towards the counter. The clerk was making like he was busy, like his counter needed cleaning when he probably hadn't had a customer all day. Jerk.

Damn! The bitch had said something about presents. He could see them now, back in the car, probably buried under half a ton of snow. Damn it to hell! And he could still hear her voice ranting and moaning from the receiver.

'What? What'd you say?'

'I said be at the house at four, not before, not after. Makenzie won't want you hanging around, and neither do I. You're here for Amber and that's it. And if I smell a drop of bourbon I swear I'll cut your visit real short. Be here for four.'

She hung up. Stole the last word, just like always.

Let her have it. He was going to see his little girl. But hell, he'd have to get himself cleaned up, and maybe pick up something for her in the store here.

Curt dropped the receiver back in place and patted down

his suit. Somehow he felt more uncomfortable than ever in this thing. Maybe that was why he felt the clerk's suspicious eyes on him all the time. Screw him, who the hell was he? Some hick storekeeper. The worst part was, the suit was empty of cash.

All he could feel was the bulge of the gun, stuffed into his belt and digging into his waist. The clerk might have been looking at him like he was some kind of scumbag, but Curt Redeker had never held up a store in his life. And he wasn't about to start now.

All the same, he had to get something for his little girl. No way was he showing up empty-handed. Itching inside his suit, he browsed the shelves furthest from the counter.

'Keep it loose and layered.'

Leela resigned herself to the shorter woman's attentions as she helped her on with the coat – a parka, Kristal had said. Packed off into the care of this stranger, she was feeling more lost than she had done out on the slopes. Her instincts, however, told her to trust this woman and if she could not trust them then she was worse than lost, she decided.

Kristal stepped back and Leela waited slightly anxiously on her pronouncement. She found herself wanting this woman's approval.

She had yet to make up her own mind about her new outfit, briskly assembled from the supplies stowed in various cupboards in this one upstairs room. The clothing had looked bulky, although less so than her furs, but not substantial enough to ward off the cold.

Now, Leela was beginning to appreciate the value of the materials. Her hands slid over the outer garments, testing every pocket and fastener. These were more than just coverings. At least she found she could move her arms fairly freely and the weight felt good on her limbs, nothing that would slow her down.

'These cultists were survivalists,' Kristal told her, 'so their gear is pretty much Army issue.'

'Why am I not white, like you?'

Kristal laughed – softly. 'I take it you mean your outfit. I'll have somebody bring up some overwhites from the trucks when they rotate the teams. If it means that much to you.'

'I do not wish to stand out like a sore thumb,' Leela declared, proud to have remembered one of the Doctor's phrases. She wondered then whether she had got it right, when she saw Kristal shake her head, a curious gleam in her eye.

'Welcome to White Shadow, Leela.'

'Thank you.' Leela didn't know what else to say. She recognised a sense of ceremony in Kristal's attendance and the sense made her hesitant in case she broke any tribal laws. 'What is White Shadow? Is that what you call this land?'

The smile of an elder stole across Kristal's face. 'No, Leela. White Shadow is us. It's the name of our group of soldiers. Our warrior tribe.'

'It is a good name. I am Leela of the tribe of Sevateem.'

Leela detected a stir of emotion in Kristal and believed she must have said the right thing. The small woman spoke back to her with a measured respect, as one warrior to another: 'And I am Kristal Owl Eye Wildcat of the Pasamaquoddy of the Abnaki.'

Excitedly, Leela pounced on a fragment the Doctor had thrown her earlier. 'Are these your lands? The Doctor said a noble people lived here.'

'He was probably talking about the Penacooks,' Kristal explained quietly. 'They were of the same nation, the Algonquin. These lands belong to a larger nation now, Leela. Not necessarily a greater one, whatever my captain tells you.'

The woman's gaze roamed far and wide as she stood perfectly still. Leela recalled the way Neeva had succumbed to his visions and thought of how the Doctor always dismissed such hocus pocus. There were always scientific reasons, he said.

Kristal convulsed suddenly, beginning a slow fall to her knees.

Leela started forward to brace her and came face to face with Kristal's trance. Whatever magic or science was in this woman, it had poisoned her eyes.

Martha drew herself up, boots planted squarely in the snow. 'Who the *hell* are you people?'

She'd set out right after Curt's call – after she'd tried Mak a few times on his radio. All she got was static, like the snow had taken over the airwaves along with everything else. Cheated of any chance to warn Mak, her new priority was to prepare Amber: your Daddy's here to see you, honey. Make like the bad news was good. Now here she was, all set to trespass on the ground her little girl believed she'd kept so secret and sacred, and she finds two creeps poking around. Lucky for them, the walk from the house had left her slightly breathless and her deadly mood lacked the force of volume to back it up.

They were wearing heavy winter coats, smart and expensive, and they looked at her from behind designer sunglasses. The woman was petite, even in the coat, soft pale complexion and luxurious dark hair, like in the shampoo commercials, cut in a real cute bob. The man was much taller, rising from an inspection of Amber's rock-cleft hideout. His hair was smoothed back, showing off a handsome face that dimpled with a smile as broad as his shoulders. Right now, Martha didn't much care for how they looked, but they plainly did.

'Well, howdy, ma'am,' he stepped up to proffer a hand. Martha wasn't sure if the Southern accent was intended to mock her own. She got a lot of that from the kids at the school, but she'd coached herself to ignore it.

'How do you do, ma'am,' the woman stepped up beside her partner and removed her glasses to show a pair of pretty eyes. 'We're just looking into something your daughter appears to have found. You are Martha Mailloux, mother of Amber?'

Right, like her facts needed checking. Martha wanted to tell her there was clearly nothing wrong with her facts and if she wanted any more she should take it up with Makenzie Shaw, whom they no doubt knew was Police Chief around here. Martha Mailloux handled her own fights though, and if these people didn't know that already, they were about to find out.

'I said,' she said, 'who the *hell* are you?'

'It's not here, Captain.'

'Thanks, Derm, I can see that for myself.'

Morgan Shaw wasn't proud to be broadcasting his irritation. He was less proud to be taking it out on his 2IC.

Still, when Lieutenant Dermot Beard had been christened, Morgan reckoned his folks must have intended him to acquire the nickname of Derm. The toughest hide, wrapped round an exceptional, conscientious intellect; going a thousand thoughts per second and revealing itself to the outside world only in a carefully measured gaze and soft-spoken observations. He could take any flak Morgan cared to throw, and he'd turned down a fistful of transfers so he could carry on doing just that. Well, serve the guy right.

Morgan appraised what little they did have.

The room in which he and most of Derm's squad were gathered showed the only signs, as far as Morgan could tell, of attempted renovation to the building by the current – scratch that, *most recent* – tenants. It wasn't what you'd call grade A craftsmanship: they'd simply ripped out most of the floor from the bedroom above, presumably for the effect of a high ceiling, but left the beams in place to collect dust and sprinkle it on the shoulders of the heavy-footed. It was a work in progress, the bones of a chapel to their alien gods.

The pseudo-religious trappings were few and far between: dead candles everywhere, many of them toppled, and DIY holy relics, like that mutated star-sculpture made out of copper wire, either hanging on the wall or mounted on tall stands draped with dark cloth. Heavy drapes blocked out the windows and there were more of the same leftovers from the unholy battle that had erupted throughout this crazy house.

The major difference was in the sheets, spars and lumps of metal; scorched, buckled and broken, and laid out with lunatic reverence over the floor. Metal victims of some unnatural disaster.

'Do we even have half an aircraft yet?'

'Possibly, Captain, with the sections we recovered already.'

Morgan shook his head, displeased. 'Well, I'll have Ben bring up the trucks for loading. Other than that, maybe we should let the crazies do our work for us.'

'Sir?'

'Kristal and Marotta reported two rust-heaps out the back. A cult like this, stuck in the New Hampshire backwoods, they'll have more wheels than that to their name. My guess, there are a few more search parties out there, running down every last piece of our property. And sooner or later, they're going to be bringing it home.'

Hopeful, sure, but Morgan Shaw needed something to smile about.

'White Shadow? Is that your winter name? Do you have a different one for warmer climes?'

'No, Doctor, I think it's meant to convey that we're stealthy and we're the good guys.'

Joanna Hmieleski was, in some respects, enjoying her betrayal, offering up state secrets to this self-pronounced Scientific Adviser. Mainly, she guessed, because they hadn't got very far into it, and she took care to murmur her responses under cover of the renewed activity taking over the house: soldiers everywhere. They'd moved on from the dining room when Pydych had come through with the detection gear: so far nothing. Thankfully he'd kept it short and quiet, let them off lightly with just the one wisecrack about a lovers' tryst.

'Anyway, our mission here is ostensibly a Search and Rescue.'

'Ostensibly, as in, *it's something else entirely*?'

'No. As in, *it is now*. There's a pilot we're hoping is very much alive. And – the aircraft was, well, special: a Raven EF111B – with some modifications.' Joanna glanced below as she took the stairs two at a time after the Doctor. She didn't want to fall behind him and have to raise her voice. 'We found some sections on the mountain, but the Captain had Kristal divine the whereabouts of the other fragments and she traced some of them here. A backwoods cult with an interest in United States Air Force debris.'

The Doctor fixed her with a stare from the landing. 'Do you know, the trouble with answers like those, they leave me with too many questions to know which one to ask next.'

Hmieleski drew a cool breath. 'Doctor, I'm risking a lot to tell you any of this. Trust me, I want to help you,' she kept her voice low but sharp, 'but there's a lot of stuff they don't even tell me. I told you, we're not UNIT. We're not about fighting aliens. White Shadow is about – recovery and research into the useful application of extraterrestrial artefacts.'

'Oh, wonderfully recited,' the Doctor's stinging praise was unexpected. 'Military applications, of course. What artefacts? What *modifications*, Lieutenant? What was that expensive aircraft doing flying through a blizzard?'

'Extreme conditions were key to the exercise.' Joanna hated the hole she was in here, but she couldn't bring herself to deceive the Doctor. Ridiculous, she didn't even know the guy, but she couldn't figure him as an enemy of the state. An excuse she would save for her court martial. She followed him along the upstairs hall, and paused while he examined the splintered rail. 'A conventional Raven is a two-seater electronic warfare jet. As the test platform for Operation Afterburn, our aircraft was fitted with a device, situated in the cockpit, adjacent to the pilot's seat.'

'Afterburn, hmm? The modern military loves to play with

names almost as much as it loves to play with big bangs. *What device?*

Joanna wanted to tell him to back off, she didn't need any more prodding. But she tightened her lip a moment, then opened her mouth to continue.

'The Stormcore,' said Kristal. The scout was standing weakly in a doorway and the girl, Leela, was supporting her.

'Where is the Captain? There's something he'll want to know.'

'He couldn't possibly be more interested than I am,' declared the Doctor.

Guilt warmed Joanna's insides. No way Kristal could have missed what was going on here. But you could never tell with Kristal, whether she was inclined to be frank and truthful or utterly secretive. Let her play it her way. Kristal had just blown the top-secret name anyway.

She reached for her hand radio. 'I'll call him in. Then we can all hear it.'

'Tell him it's very close,' said Kristal. 'And it's on the move.'

Chapter Four

Snow was turning this trek home into a year's worth of walking. Mitch Lagoy's bones were one big ache barely holding him together. He would have suggested they move up onto the ridge over west, where the drifts weren't so deep, but he knew Jacks would only throw one of her tantrums: too high, too visible; where are the trees up there, where's our cover? The fact she'd be right only made him ache some more.

She'd had them put a spurt on since they'd heard the shots. Running as best they could in this frozen soup. Mitch wouldn't dream of complaining, no sir, not with this lady drill sergeant taking the lead. Emilie Jacks could bitch in your face worse than any storm.

She always said he could scare off bears with his build, but from where he trailed it looked like she was having the easier time of this, and she was carrying a heavier load. Any lesser find she'd have had him following after her like a pack animal, but not this prize. No, this one was hers and she was going to be seen bringing it on home, a grand offering to impress Crayford. Well, he certainly couldn't have been impressed with her body. Wasn't hardly female, to Mitch's way of thinking.

Muscle and cement, and a face of hard edges.

Nobody had much minded when Crayford had moved the group north. The government were on their tail and they'd had to go somewhere. New Hampshire or Arkansas, it made little difference when they were this close to crossing over. As it turned out, the move to Mount Shaw had brought them manna from heaven. And they'd all raced out to join the hunt when Crayford had told them to go find the pieces of their destiny.

Mitch wished he saw the truth the way Crayford saw it, wished he had that kind of mind. But Crayford promised him it wasn't intelligence that qualified when it came to crossing over. Even some of the government people were intelligent in their own way, he pointed out, but they didn't have the eyes or the soul to see the other realm.

Yeah, it was the way Crayford spoke the truth as much as the way he saw it.

But what in Christ did he ever see in Emilie Jacks?

Lady was a freak. Sticking her ugly face of stone into the whole operation, taking charge and making like she was the only one ever had military training. Yeah, kiss my ass and watch it turn into a prince. If she was so smart and highly trained, how come she'd had them set out with a dribble of gas in the tank? And how come she hadn't kitted them up with snowshoes for this gig? Okay, they never had any of that gear at the house – all guns, no skis – but how hard could it be to get some?

Mitch ploughed up some more snow with his huge legs in an effort to close the distance with Jacks. He didn't like her being so way out in front with the major haul. He wanted his share of the credit when they rolled in.

Hell, if there was anyone left up there to slap them on the back.

They were pretty close now. He could tell from the lie of that western slope. Question was, who'd fired all those shots. Our guys? They knew the Army were crawling all over this hill, but Mitch didn't think they'd be nuts enough to get into a shooting match with the military. Least ways, not while GI Jane was out here with him.

'Slow it up, Lagoy!'

Mitch glanced ahead, saw her easing off the pace. Little hills of broken snow gathered around her shins. The prize

53

described a grotesque shape inside her pack. Something much more than just another chunk of aircraft.

Great, so now we get to slow it up. When I'm half dead. Mitch forced himself the last few yards before bending over to catch his breath.

'Someone's coming,' she said.

'Huh?' Mitch ducked down as he scanned the hillside.

'They've seen us already.' Jacks slid the AK into her hands.

Mitch rubbed the hard bristles on his jaw and worked the Mossberg from his shoulder. He pumped the first shell into position and prayed it wouldn't be needed. He wasn't afraid, exactly. He just knew these things got awful messy. They did in banks anyway, and it couldn't be any different in the great outdoors.

He narrowed his eyes at the figure sprinting and tumbling down the slope. The snow wasn't falling too bad for the moment but this runner sure as hell was. Colliding with trees even.

'He's panicked,' Jacks noted contemptuously.

Yeah, fire one of these at your tail, see how fast you run, thought Mitch. But he was feeling a shade happier that the figure didn't look dangerous. He held the shotgun nice and easy.

He screwed up his eyes a notch. 'Hey, is that – ?'

'It's Crayford,' said Jacks, and for once she sounded shaken.

No, not Crayford. Not running like that. Not the great man himself.

Leela was accustomed to confusion. Usually it was a feeling inside, a devoted companion on her travels with the Doctor. From the moment she left the chill confines of the house, it was a living force, manifested all around her.

'Coming through, miss!' Leela dodged aside as another pair of soldiers emerged from the house carrying a curled leaf of metal. In her eagerness to keep out of the way, she realised, she had strayed too close to the main doorway.

For the present the heavens had stopped shedding their cold ashes, and the chaos was confined to the ground. She saw the Doctor over by the vehicles, unmoving, except for the steady bounce of his yo-yo. He stayed leaning against one of the trucks, even as the dark-haired woman, Hmieleski, hurried up to speak to him.

Leela wandered over, avoiding the lines of men tramping back and forth, and training a wary eye on the vehicles they were loading: four large white crates on ungainly metal tracks, heavy carts tethered behind; two fat squashed trucks with large wheels; and a pack of squat but powerful beasts on tracks and skids. Many of those strange dwarf-vehicles were being unloaded when she had come out with the others to meet Captain Shaw.

He had been busy ever since, issuing rapid orders in every direction. Leela had started to feel lost and unwanted. And now she could see the Doctor was in a bad mood, sulking, so she felt less sure about asking all her half-formed questions.

'Doctor,' Hmieleski was saying, 'the Captain wants me to stay here, tear up the floorboards and anything else we didn't cover. He's taking you down to the town, help set up a lab. But I'm sure if you put up a fight you could convince him you're needed here, we can continue our conversation.'

'You know,' said the Doctor at length, following the yo-yo in its rise and fall, 'I'm grateful for the invitation, but I think I'll take the ride. I'd really like to find out what attracted the cult to the pieces of a broken aeroplane. Your good Captain politely declined my help in the search for your Stormcore, but I can always find other fish to fry.'

The Doctor was one toothy grin, and Leela caught a glimmer in the woman's eyes, something passing between them that reminded her of when she had first found herself under the Doctor's wing. 'Well I wish you luck. Just – well – '

'Ah, trust me, Lieutenant,' he made a shushing gesture, 'I never reveal my sources.'

'I'll see you down at the lab. Apparently there's some hotel the Captain knows, he's going to make the management's day by commandeering it as our headquarters.'

'Really? I hope it's a good one. I tend to work very poorly in anything less than three-star accommodation.'

Hmieleski gave the Doctor a farewell pat on the arm, so Leela prepared to jump in with her first question. But the Doctor snatched up his yo-yo and stood to face Captain Shaw and a small posse of Kristal, and two other soldiers. One was young, like Captain Shaw, but had the stride of a warrior trying to look like a leader, while the other, his skin a blend of earth and charcoal, had command written in his deep serious eyes.

Captain Shaw took charge immediately. 'All right, here's the news. Joanna, Ben's stopping here with you.' The boyish-faced officer traded nods with Hmieleski. Then Morgan gestured at the dark man. 'Doctor, this is Lieutenant Dermot Beard, he'll be riding back with us and my HQ squad.'

'You mean, you're not leaving me Pydych?' the woman Joanna asked.

'You might try hiding your disappointment,' answered Morgan, and everyone but Leela seemed to be laughing. 'Doc, Pydych is a good guy, technical wizard, he'll be a ton of help piecing together my aircraft, trust me. Okay, any questions from the civilian quarter?'

Leela wasn't sure whether she counted as the civilian quarter, but she knew she had questions. Because it was first in the queue, she said, 'What is happening?'

Everyone laughed again. But Leela was grateful to see the Doctor first to her defence. 'Captain, we really shouldn't be unfair on my assistant. The People That Time Forgot, you said – and even I managed to forget about her.' He moved to stand beside her. 'But she really is an excellent scout, capable of finding any needle in a snowstorm.'

'Well, that's Kristal's department. She's leading the search.'

'I am with Kristal,' Leela piped up, surprised to find the Doctor encouraging her with a pat.

She felt him leaning close. 'Leela,' he whispered weightily, 'if you get the chance out there, any chance at all, keep your eyes peeled for the TARDIS, there's a good girl.'

'I will do my best Doctor,' she promised.

Morgan Shaw reviewed the decisions just made around him. 'Great. That's a load off. Now can we please get moving? And Kristal – '

'Sir.'

'You'd better be damn certain. I don't want you coming back with a gaggle of wild geese.'

Kristal faced him with an iron calm. 'Have a little faith, Captain.'

A silence settled along the row of vehicles, only to be broken by a cacophony of engine noise as they were fired into life.

'Leela. You're with me.'

And as Leela followed Kristal, she felt her separation from the Doctor keenly.

Amber pressed herself against the tree and waited for the truck to roll by. She was grateful for the chance to rest, although way too excited to really benefit from it. The idea that she might have been spotted only added to the buzz.

She was amazed: you stomp off in a huff one morning and suddenly you're into the greatest adventure you ever had.

Hunkering down, she couldn't resist a peep around the tree. Her own breath was impossibly loud and fast in her ears, but she watched Makenzie's police truck dissolve in the haze like a fizzy tablet in a glass of water. Amber chuckled.

Then she fell back against the tree and let out a massive sigh.

She raised her eyes to the branches overhead, trying to untangle them in her imagination. With its leaves of frost, the tree looked brittle and old. Spooky. She wondered if she could put one of Mom's house plants in the ice box, see if it would look the same.

Damn. She glanced around the tree again, along the ghost road. If she hadn't had a go at him this morning, maybe she could have gotten herself a lift. Maybe he would have been excited to hear about the parachute.

Lifting herself up with a groan, she shovelled at some of the snow with her boot. Oh well, if she was going to walk the miles to town she'd be better starting sooner than later. She set off, sticking to the road's edge, where the snow was good and thick.

Every so often she glanced around at the trees and up and down the road, and wondered at how the emptiness always stayed the same distance away.

Why in hell did it have to be him?

The let-up in the storm was doing nothing for the atmosphere inside the truck, and in any case it was going to be a very temporary reprieve. Of that, Makenzie was convinced. The drive back to Melvin Village was the longest and loneliest of his life.

The world was locked in under a glacial roof of cloud. No way out.

Laurie was gone. Gone. Better if somebody had come up to him and told him she'd been found murdered. Tourists did dumb things, like wandering off into the worst weather known to man. Laurie Aldrich did not, would not, ever. Makenzie had searched and searched again, until he'd covered every inch of that wood, a lot further than Laurie could have walked in the time she'd had. He'd searched until his lungs were solid pain. In all that whiteness, his vision had turned black, and in all that whiteness he had found precisely nothing.

No sign of a scuffle, no tracks to show she'd been taken anywhere. No anything.

When he'd eventually dragged himself back down to the road, he'd stepped on broken glass. After that, it hadn't taken him long to turn up bottle fragments held flimsily together by the sodden label. Wild Turkey. Not his father's brand, but Makenzie knew it well enough and the alcohol smell was all over the inside of that Buick.

Disgusted, Makenzie had tossed the clue into the ditch. Rescuing the gifts for Amber, he'd headed for his truck and sat a while before making the drive back to town.

From that discovery on, there was no Laurie, no tourists, no part-time townsfolk lost in the hills. No, the part he kept getting hung up on was Curt Redeker.

For this guy, the man who beat up on Martha and terrorised his own daughter, the man who lets his kid down when he's supposed to come see her, the man who drinks himself off an icy road into a ditch – for this man, Makenzie Shaw must do more than his damnedest. When Makenzie wanted to be scouring the whole of New Hampshire for Laurie, he had to go find a hundred-proof son of a bitch like Curt Redeker. Nothing less would do.

Why?

Amber was why. Because when he'd had Martha and Amber move in with him, the spectre of Curt Redeker had moved in right after.

How did that Casablanca quote go? The problems of three people didn't amount to a hill of beans in this world. Yeah, unless you're one of the three, and then those problems are your world and there's nothing outside of that.

Makenzie shook himself alive. He didn't want to end up in a ditch like Redeker. He had to start thinking as well as driving. Real thinking, not just this circuit of doom.

The way he figured, tracks or no, Laurie had to have been abducted. Taken somewhere by somebody. Same with the folks in that sad little convoy. Even the most ravenous coy-dogs would have left a few bones, not to mention stained the snows red. That wasn't it. No, Laurie had to be alive somewhere, taken hostage. Redeker too maybe.

As he drove, Makenzie's gaze climbed the lowest slopes of Mount Shaw. Those cultists had taken over the old doc's house up there, turned it into some sort of commune. They were screwed up enough, he was mad he hadn't thought of them before.

They had themselves their own armoury too. He couldn't tackle them alone. Hm. He remembered the running gun battles he'd had with Morgan up there.

That checked him. Thoughts of Morgan weren't going to improve his mood.

'Listen, if this is something Curt's into, he's nothing to do with me, not since a long time back. He thinks he is, but that's his problem, none of mine.'

Martha was jumpy, edgy; she hardly felt the spike of caffeine as she drained her cup. The woman agent had suggested they retire here, to their cabin; the same place Amber had kicked up such a fuss that one time last summer. The man had brewed up some coffee, help her calm down, he'd said. Some chance.

Crazy, finding herself back here, inside. Not nearly as big as Mak's place, and impersonal, like any holiday shack. Personal touches wouldn't have registered with Martha anyway.

It had to be about Curt. He didn't have the spine to get involved in anything serious, but he was sure stupid enough. And now she thought of it he'd sounded real jittery on the phone. But the CIA? This just wasn't a part of her life.

The guy was pacing around all casual. The woman sat opposite, prim with a patient smile. 'I understand how difficult this must be for you, Miss Mailloux.'

'Please, call me Martha. You seem to know me well enough already.' She realised she was nodding tightly, a nervous reaction.

'Martha,' the woman corrected herself genially. 'But this really has to do with your daughter, and we honestly believe her involvement is purely tangential to our investigation. We'd simply like to ask her a few questions concerning where she found the parachute and if she knows anything about what was attached to it.'

The man, Agent Theroux, had shown her the bundled chute shortly after the badge and introduction routine. He'd demonstrated how the lines had been cut and he'd produced the pocketknife they'd pulled from Amber's hideout. Another dumb gift from Curt.

'Excuse me for a minute, but that's another part I don't get,' argued Martha, aware of how hostile she sounded. 'If my Amber found anything valuable attached to the damn chute, don't you think she might have kept that instead? I mean, what you're telling me is there was something other than a person on the end of that.'

'Sadly, ma'am, we're not at liberty to say.' He hadn't given up his Southern drawl, so she'd figured by now he wasn't mocking her; although that line belonged in a movie.

The woman, Melody Quartararo, on the other hand, was hard not to like. 'Martha, you're right. Your daughter probably only found the chute quite by accident. But I hope you understand, we have to follow up every lead and we have to make absolutely certain. This is a matter of national security.'

'Well, Curt always said I was a bad mother and I'm real sorry, Agent Quartararo, but I don't know right now where my daughter could be. Maybe you'd like to help me look for her.' She set her mug down on the table and it clunked noisily. The two agents were waiting on something more from her, a best guess perhaps. 'Listen, I don't know. Maybe she headed into town to tell Mak about her find. Sometimes she wants to impress him.'

Apparently that sounded reasonable to Agent Theroux. 'Would you like to take a drive with us, Martha? I'm sure

Amber would prefer to have her mother hold her hand while we interview her. Believe me, I know how intimidating us government types can seem.'

Melody laughed, a gentle echo to her partner. She was hard not to like, sure, but trust was a whole different matter.

Lagoy watched Jacks grab their leader as he fell into her, and they shook their heads at the creature he had become. Mitch couldn't make up his mind, but Emilie was looking at Crayford like he was a lame thoroughbred.

She didn't take up her rifle though, just gripped him hard and tried prying him open with a stare. 'Crayford,' she barked, 'it's me! *Emilie!* What happened up there?'

Crayford was on his knees, staring straight back at her but something else blocked his view. Their guru had lost it. All that hair on his face, he was starting to look like some Neanderthal raw recruit.

'Emilie? Where were you? I was – we opened the gateway, Emilie, it's *wide* open! But they cheated us. They betrayed us! They didn't want us to join them – they wanted to cross over! And now they're here, they're here, they're here, they're here.' The great man laughed like a frightened kid, then trembled uncontrollably. 'And what they are – oh God, what they are!'

Mitch wanted to say something, snap him out of it. But Jacks was in command, just about.

She shook him hard to beat the tremors. 'Crayford! How can we have opened the gateway? I've got the key here!' She tugged at the left strap of her backpack. 'We found it. It's the real thing, Crayford. Genuine United States Air Force ET hi-tech – and it's ours! Everything you dreamed of, everything you saw, it's right here in this pack! You can't have opened any gateway. This is the key right here, has to be!'

'Then close it. Use it to close the gateway, Emilie.'

For the first time Crayford was actually looking at and seeing

Emilie. And that, for Mitch, was scarier than when he'd been out of it.

'We can stop them. We can stop them sending any more. The Army can't stop them. No, the Army – the Army,' he yanked at Emilie's coat, trying to bring her down to his level, 'the Army is too busy hunting *me*. They brought a Psi with them, Emilie. She touched my mind. They'll find me. They'll find all of us and they'll finish us before we can stop them.'

Jacks swallowed on a bad taste. Suddenly she shoved Crayford off and smacked him hard, a man's punch. Mitch blinked. Crayford squirmed in the snow, squirting blood from his nose.

'What did you just do?'

'If he wants to run so bad,' determined Jacks, hypnotised by the sidewinder rhythms of the fallen man, 'he can carry on. The Army must have hit us and this one cracked like an egg. We're going to pay them back. You and me, Mitch.'

Mitch Lagoy was the one with the bad taste now. Commanders' speeches were supposed to be inspirational.

'You just knocked Crayford Boyle on his ass! And now you want to take on the Army?'

Jacks didn't like that: she turned on him, and her wild glare drove him back a pace. 'That,' she wasn't satisfied until her face was right into his, 'isn't Crayford Boyle any more. I don't know what that is, but it's all finished. *We* are finished. Our dream, our mission. It's over, *Mitch.*' She never called him Mitch.

She left him then, spinning around and ripping herself free of the pack. She chucked it onto the writhing pile at her feet. 'We won't be needing this any more. Total waste. Time we were leaving, Lagoy.' When the bitch finally looked his way, she was evil on fire.

'We should tidy up before we go.'

Chapter Five

Clad in her overwhites, Leela was looking forward to being at one with the landscape. This first stage of the hunt was not about stealth though. It was about speed. For Leela, it was also about hanging on in fear for her life.

She rode with her arms anchored around Kristal's waist. The vehicle ploughed along, churning up the snows like mushy paper, the sky and trees zipping by in flashes. Her limbs were taut, and the engine sent powerful vibrations through her calf and thigh muscles. Despite the goggles, Leela felt the full blast of wind in her face whenever she peered over Kristal's shoulder, and yet she felt a frequent need to keep looking. The fierce noise and the occasional bump did nothing to ease her fears.

'How much further?' she tried to shout in Kristal's ear, but her driver did not hear her.

Ahead and behind, other members of Kristal's squad rode more of these dumpy little monsters. The Captain had allowed seven of the *snowmobiles* for the hunt, so some soldiers doubled up like herself and Kristal, while the lead troops, some distance in front, rode singly.

Kristal glanced west. The visibility was fair but Leela saw nothing.

Kristal made a swift motion with one hand though and Leela realised they were slowing, veering around to an eventual halt. Past the trees the ground fell away fairly steeply and the open terrain below looked like a giant thumbprint stamped in the mountain. A gentler hill dropped into the bowl at the north and Kristal's gaze was trained there as she hopped from her seat. Leela dismounted to stand beside her.

Her nose wrinkled and she pulled a strand of hair under her nose for a tentative sniff.

'Smell like a tail-pipe, huh?' It was the big sergeant tramping up, carrying the large gun with its jingling ribbon of bullets.

'What is a tail-pipe?'

'You're really quite a girl, you know that?'

Leela did not know what to say to that.

'Ignore him,' Kristal advised her, still watching the far hill.

'Hey, I love that smell of gas. Never get enough.'

'Marotta,' she spared him a fleeting scowl, 'when you're done sweet-talking Leela here, take Landers and two of the guys a couple of hundred yards up. Move down slope and hide yourselves in the open down there. Hide yourselves good.'

'You got it, Kris – Lieutenant.'

'With any luck, we can take our man alive. I'm sure he's the one blew his way out of the parlour window.' She closed her eyes and breathed in, long and deep. 'He's three minutes off from that north ridge. Get moving.'

Sergeant Marotta headed off at a trot, collecting his chosen team. Kristal looked back and motioned the others to move up, even as she dropped to her knees. Leela followed her example, and inched closer to the scout's side.

She searched along the crest of the hill. 'I do not understand, Kristal. Do you see this man in your mind?'

'I see him. And I feel him in the pulse of the land. Besides, he has the Stormcore.'

Leela was wary of troubling her friend further, but felt compelled: 'What is the Stormcore?'

Ben McKim was the new kid on the block. Just over a year with this outfit, and he'd figured it was one of the reasons he'd drawn guard duty on the vehicles back there.

It was dumb speculation really, because ultimately every outfit was the same: you had to work lights and scenery if you wanted to make centre stage. Now, posted at the house, left behind again, he couldn't decide whether he was being given the bum's rush or his shot at the Oscar. On the face of it there wouldn't be a lot to do here besides more waiting. Unless some cultist stragglers started rolling in – which was doubtful at best.

McKim saw his two sharpshooters stepping through the front doorway. He'd called them in from the perimeter and they'd probably jogged all the way, although they both had their breathing under good control. Falvi was being funny, wiping his feet.

Falvi and Barnes, each a head shorter than him. They took to the waiting game like they were on a diet of time and boredom. 'Glad you could make it, people. Welcome to the House of the Dead. Find yourselves a room, high as you can go, one each flank of the house. I want every approach covered far as the eye can see.'

At least, he added with a look, as far as anyone can see in what passed for weather in the Granite State.

'You got it, sir,' the young man, Falvi, acknowledged and the two of them were vanishing up those stairs like they were keen to start the next round of waiting *ASAP*.

He let them go and moved on to the lounge. He'd seen tidier craters, but his grenadier, Pelham, had shovelled enough trash off a sofa so he could lay back. Eastman kicked the guy's boot and stood to attention. McKim signalled her to rest easy.

He ran through the list, checking it off: snipers up top, three-man patrol stalking the fences, two at the downstairs windows, three – including himself – grabbing some rest and cleaning weapons. It was a system of sorts and they were wired for action, looking out for it; something the cultists hadn't been doing. It bothered him, the way these amateurs had been about as heavily armed as his squad, give or take a grenade launcher.

And where did all that firepower get them? Nobody knew. Not even Joanna, and she was probably the smartest on this crew. Except for the newcomer, maybe.

But Captain Shaw was not going to come back up the mountain to find White Shadow guns lying smoking on these floors, the men and women of Ben McKim's team only a cold memory. Not a chance in hell.

He made that promise to the walls right there and then. He made it in silence so neither Eastman nor Pelham could hear the worry on which it was founded.

'You know, usually in any investigation I try to leave no stone unturned.'

'That's a commendable work ethic, Doc. Shows dedication.'

'Yes, but it's also very time-consuming when you find your-self in a quarry as often as I do.'

The Doctor let the edged comment ride a while, waiting for it to pierce Captain Shaw's military hide. He was a shrewd young officer and it wouldn't take very long. Not long at all.

The Doctor could ignore the constant jostling. It was, he decided, like riding the London tube during rush hour, except the Snowcat wasn't as cramped or filthy. The cabin lights on, it might have been night outside: white night. The snows had started in again, spattering softly on the panes and dying slow deaths as they met the warm air heating the interior.

Captain Shaw leaned forward in his seat. 'Doc, believe me, I want to help you turn over every stone, but you've got to realise, the Stormcore isn't my baby. I'm just the sitter.'

'But you were supervising an experiment, Captain. Some ambitious project using extraterrestrial technology.'

That had the others sitting up: Lieutenant Beard and the other soldier sharing this ride. The driver up front was well beyond earshot, with the constant rumble of the engine, not to mention the shake and rattle of the chassis to contend with.

'Who told you that?'

'The tooth fairy. Does it matter? The important thing you have to ask yourself is am I a spy and since the answer is no, can you really afford not to let me in on your little secrets?'

'Captain,' Lieutenant Beard offered a warning note.

'It's okay, Derm. The Doc and I understand one another.'

The Doctor decided this wasn't much like a tube ride after all. There wasn't even a sense of a tunnel wall slipping by outside. There were the window panes, all around, and then the world stopped. The substance was here in their conversation and this young fellow's remarkable will. He decided he rather liked this Captain Shaw.

'See, I have this problem with you, Doc. I believe what you say you are, as far as it goes. Don't get me wrong, if I had the comms to run *extensive* checks, I would. Now, I want your help and you're no use to me working blindfold, but I can't afford to let anything I tell you find its way back to Geneva, you know?'

'It's a terrible pickle to be in,' sympathised the Doctor.

'I'm not about to put my career on the line here, so I figure, I tell you *only* what you need to know and if any of it gets talked about in UNIT circles, I'm going to point my finger in your direction. There's going to be no culpability for my people and as far as my bosses are concerned, you, Doc, are a dangerous masterspy. I'm going to paint you as a James Bond with a twist of lime and they're going to come after you, wherever you roam, and they're going to poke laser designators through your bathroom window.'

'Really? All that attention, just for me?' The Doctor held his grin for a moment, and then leaned forward seriously, glad the preamble was over. 'Now, what about this Stormcore?'

'For my people, the Owl is a wise and friendly spirit, possessed of powerful love medicine. But among the Sioux, Hin-Han the Owl guards the entrance to the Milky Way, the river of stars' – Kristal swept a hand overhead – 'over which the souls of the dead must pass in order that they might reach the spirit land.' She waited, and she looked pleased to see Leela so engrossed. 'When they first asked me to touch the device and divine its purpose, I felt I had climbed upon the wings of Hin-Han and he showed me the world and the Milky Way and the endless expanse of other galaxies.'

'And did he show you the spirit world, across the Milky Way?'

Kristal smiled, the river of stars running to the horizon behind her gaze, asking her to join the scout in her memories. But Leela did not know how to take up the invitation.

'My superiors wanted something a little more concrete than that. They dabbled in what they call psychic forces, but any suggestion of the spirit world was more than they could stomach. So I had to answer them in the language of science.'

Leela recalled Neeva's claims of communion with the Great One, and how the Doctor had showed her that, then too, the magic of the Tesh was involved; the magic that was not magic. She did not believe Kristal was a *charlatan* like Neeva.

'Unfortunately, it was not Hin-Han's wings I rode, but those of a ship from another world. But, yes, Leela, I saw far across the Milky Way. The Stormcore is the key to the spirit world – and a thousand other universes my ancestors never dreamed of. And the government had no idea what to do with that kind of power.'

She looked out across the landscape and Leela saw her eyes tighten.

Tracing her line of sight to the north, she picked out the lonely figure in a blundering run, a bundle clutched to his chest like a baby at a mother's breast.

'There he is. Come on.'

'See, Kristal told them the device was a navigation system, because that was the closest term, she said, that they'd be happy with. She told them it navigated not only between the stars, but all the universes between the stars. Including a direct channel through to all those psychic forces they'd been studying for so long. So naturally they were pretty excited, hence they gave their star pupil a front row seat on the project as soon as they'd figured out what they were going to do with their find.'

The Doctor pondered a while. 'Hm. Sounds to me like a variety of multidimensional navigational system. Not something you'd find on any common-or-garden spacecraft.' He fixed Captain Shaw with an inquisitive scowl. 'You know, I have to wonder if this *UFO* of yours crashed or had the slightly greater misfortune of being shot down?'

'Sir, the Captain told you,' Lieutenant Beard broke in for the first time, 'we're just the baby-sitters. Neither the NSA nor the CIA are about to tell us whether the Air Force shot down some alien spacecraft twenty or thirty years ago, and we aren't about to ask. The folks down at Fort Meade came up with the project, assigned their staff and dropped it in our lap. We're all on the same side, different departments is all. That's just the way it works.'

The Doctor saw Morgan Shaw trying on a smirk for size, to see how he liked that. He leaned back in his seat and regarded the two officers, letting the rocking and the growl of the vehicle answer on his behalf.

Emilie Jacks could never have said she loved Crayford Boyle. He'd had something miraculous and he'd shared it with her, that was all. But once shared, it had become hers too, and she couldn't get over how he'd surrendered it so easily. All for what? Fear?

She spat to one side. Time to step up the pace for the final few yards. Her muscles were burning but that kind of pain only made her feel better.

Fear was made for giving, not receiving.

One man broken and everything lay in ruins. Everything she'd signed up for, everything they'd worked for. Now she was left with Lagoy in tow. God Almighty, of all the possible survivors, Mitch Lagoy. Not exactly *The Omega Man*.

Jacks looked back over her shoulder to make sure Lagoy was sticking close.

He was panting like a goddamn polar bear. Plenty of insulation on him, but he was one hell of a risk when it came to covert ops. She felt like ordering him on ahead, draw the enemy fire, but she figured he must be smart enough to question a command like that.

When she'd first enlisted with Crayford, Lagoy was already in situ, a trusted man in the ranks. The guy was a slob though, never been near the military. A bank robber, for Christ's sake. Okay, he'd never been caught (and Crayford had run enough background checks to confirm that) but Jacks always looked at it this way: Lagoy hadn't made a million either.

The trees were starting to thin some. Jacks hit the snow on her belly and she waved Lagoy down behind her. Gun held off the snow, she started scuttling on her elbows, to a few yards shy of the treeline.

Hopefully Lagoy was doing the same, but she didn't have the time or patience to keep checking on him every two seconds. Snaking up, she peered over a mound of snow, ready to meet a soldier's boot, the muzzle of a rifle or anything.

She saw the house: a short dash down a shallow gradient. They'd followed the arc of the woods, a safe distance in, and this was about the furthest the treeline extended.

There were three soldiers. Not easy to see, but they were there. They weren't straying far from the house, following a tight circuit out by the broken fence, more to keep warm than cover the terrain. The two old trucks, cannibalised for spares not long after they'd arrived, guarded the main line of Emilie's planned approach.

'We'll take a breather for a second. There's not much ground to cross here, but I want to be sure there aren't any more patrols.' Even as she said it, she knew she was sounding pleased with herself. And she kind of expected that would get a rise out of Lagoy.

He was shuffling up on his gut, bringing his voice too close. 'Listen to yourself. This is nuts, no matter how you dress it up.'

Then the real accusation: 'You just packed Crayford off like some decoy in hunting season.'

'Don't forget,' Jacks snorted, 'I also gave him our trophy. If the Army can't manage to track him, their Psi is going to make sure that stays square in their sights.'

'You sold him out!'

Jacks grabbed at Lagoy's collar. 'You're getting loud, Lagoy,' she bared her teeth. 'Crayford sold us out, he gave it up. The sooner you get it through that concrete skull of yours the better for all of us. And all of us means you and me. We're it. Whether you or I like it or not.'

She was satisfied to see some of the flame fade from Lagoy's glare. He said, 'Listen, I get that Crayford lost his nerve. I just don't get that the Army scared him like that. What if something did come through? Something we couldn't handle? What if it's in there waiting?'

'Waiting for what?' Jacks jerked her head to indicate the patrol. 'Say Crayford was right? Say our devotions brought some invader through from the other world. D'you think they're going to let the United States Army walk around their new territory unchecked?'

She watched Lagoy watching the soldiers.

'Say there's a bunch of ETs in there, lying low until their main invasion force arrives. They're not going to be bothering anyone much longer.' She laughed, enjoying the man's dense look for a moment. 'When we get inside that building, we are going to take care of everyone and everything in one go. Wipe the slate clean.'

Jacks enjoyed the man's look of fear that little bit more.

The way ahead was wide open, but Crayford Boyle didn't trust it. A basin of white, tainted with enemies. He guessed the soldiers were somewhere out there, but he felt *her*: watcher and hunter, a shadow on his mind, waiting for him across that bleached plain. He fancied he could even see the men in their foxholes. Enemies everywhere.

The Army's pet Psi and her little troop of soldiers.

Crayford whimpered and tried to remember where Emilie had gone. Why did she desert him? Why would she? Watch me run, then. Watch me run in empty space.

He broke right, haring along the brow of the hill and he laughed when he thought about the surprise on all those Army faces. Especially the Psi's. The thing in his embrace beat against his chest like a second heart, and Crayford felt the alien energies pumping into his bloodstream. He wanted to throw it away, but he couldn't let it go. Not now.

He tripped. He clasped the pack tighter as he fought his way up, glanced back as he ran on.

'Damn it!' Kristal had her radio up in an instant. 'Marotta, he made us.'

'Yeah, I see, Lieutenant,' the set crackled in response. 'I swear he never saw us. We're packed tighter than the snow here.'

'He made me, I think.' Kristal was on her feet and trotting for the snowmobile. She signalled with her free hand and the other troops were running for their vehicles. 'Saddle up and follow us. We're never going to catch him on foot.'

Leela ran to catch up both with Kristal and what had gone wrong. 'We were well concealed here. How could he have seen us?'

Kristal grimaced, seeming abashed, as she reached her vehicle. 'Our man sees the same way I can, Leela. I should have anticipated the possibility. We knew the cult were interested in recruiting psychics. Come on. He won't get far.'

Leela moved behind her, ready to hop on. This was not her idea of hunting, but she was almost looking forward to her second ride.

The trees, if he could just reach the trees. He could lose them, lose them all. Except the Psi, but he could kill her, couldn't he?

If he couldn't take on a woman then there truly was nothing left of Crayford Boyle. Nothing left.

He sprinted, lifting his legs high and pumping them down hard. Time and distance stretched the faster he pushed himself on. Coarse breath raked the walls of his lungs.

Then he was across the finish line and starting down the slope, brushing snow from silver tree-trunks. Bare twigs clawed at his hood.

Something snagged on his sleeve.

Crayford turned. His right foot landed wrong.

As he gave in to the tumble, Crayford realised he was crying.

He was crying because his run was over. It was the only thought he had time for as he completed a clumsy roll and thumped into the base of a stout tree. A few dumplings of snow spattered on his coat and something shifted above him.

Crayford whimpered and thrust the pack out in front of him. It was useless as a shield but he prayed it was all they wanted.

Leela leaned hard to her right, sensing the vehicle's desire to topple as it cut along the slope at a frightening angle. Even as they levelled off, Leela's butterflies refused to settle. The snowmobile chewed ravenously at the snow, spitting clouds of soft crumbs in their wake.

They raced full pelt across the basin floor, powering up for the climb ahead. Kristal glanced aft to check on her team and gestured insistently with one hand. Two of the snowmobiles broke left and upped their speed to draw level.

Goggles down, her hood pulled up to keep her hat in place, it was impossible to read anything of the real Kristal under these circumstances. And yet, Leela's arms detected a sudden tension possessing the woman's every muscle. Something more than the effort of driving.

Kristal wrenched their snowmobile round in an abrupt curve, like the slice of an attacker's blade. Leela braced herself for a tumble. But no, they were upright and unharmed

– but perfectly still. Kristal's raised hand called a halt. To everything.

The other snowmobiles coasted to a stop and sputtered into silence close by.

For a moment, the loudest thing on the mountain was Leela's own heartbeat.

Then fear found substance.

Crashing over and through the trees like a mighty breaker striking a white shore. Spilling over the far ridge, where the hunted man had disappeared: a broiling mass, exploding and reforming in a relentless drive across the land. In a few seconds it had advanced enough to blot out the treetops. The brow of the hill was engulfed soon after.

The sight of it left Leela hollow. 'What is that?'

'Death's pale horse,' managed Kristal, without a breath.

The tidal-wave blizzard crashed onwards, erasing the landscape as it came.

Chapter Six

In any creepy old house, the last place you want to head is the cellar. But, following a brisk sweep upstairs and down, Joanna knew she was going to wind up down there sooner or later. She had covered all the ground the platoon had cleared, testing for loose boards, knocking at the backs of closets, and crawling around on all fours up in the roof-space. Just to be sure.

By now she was past sure and the basement was the last stop on her itinerary.

Descending the stairwell, barely one person wide, Joanna laughed soundlessly at herself. That was the trouble when you were reminded of what it was like to be a little girl: the reminiscence wasn't limited to the good stuff.

Her nerves weren't purely childish. She didn't expect to find anything in the basement, be it clue or danger, but the cultists hadn't expected whatever they'd found. Even if they really had managed to summon extraterrestrial forces into their rundown country commune, they hadn't got the brand of salvation they'd wanted.

The briefing had told her next to nothing on the cult's principles, other than their alleged promotion of psychic experimentation and the baptism of the soul in the fire of the inner mind – whatever that meant. But Joanna had read the profiles on known individuals, and these guys were all survivalists. Which implied they wanted to survive.

The electrics were out, so Joanna had armed herself with a flashlight and, despite the platoon having pronounced the basement as clear, collected her H&K from where she'd propped it up in the hall. It wasn't big enough to encumber and she felt a whole lot safer with its weight close to her side. Shadows generally went unarmed and were a deal less scary for the fact.

The door at the foot of the stairs was wide open and the darkness beyond looked empty enough. The stairs were positively geriatric though, and if anything was lying in wait for her down there it surely would have heard her coming.

Joanna allowed herself a sense of relief when she touched bottom. She advanced out to her left, sweeping her beam over the room in a steady arc.

Darkness clung to the walls like moss and lichen, drinking up the torchlight.

Details bounced back in glimpses: dusty shelves, some sloping dangerously, others warped with the damp; the greens and browns of old bottles; a large table in the centre of the room, its surface a mess, standing on bare and rotting boards. Directly opposite there was a sink, a dripping faucet and greening copper pipes running a gauntlet of cobwebs along the wall above; the bench top stacked with plastic containers, weapons parts, heaps of other tools and clutter that the platoon had seen fit to leave behind.

There was a slim chance the junk had been stored neatly before the platoon had done sifting through it all, but she strongly doubted it. For survivalists, maintenance and basic hygiene didn't look to be one of this group's fortes.

There was a doorway, the remnant of a wooden frame, leading into another room at the far end. A faint promise of daylight hung in the air in there and Joanna could see snow blowing in. The stench of mould was the only thing to jump out at her. That, and the cold.

No danger of condensation on her weapon in here. This house was like an icebox.

Literally. As she moved, there were occasional patches of ice underfoot, and her flashlight was finding clumps of crystal white in the corners of the floor and ceiling, or clinging to some of the fittings. Give it time, this place could end up looking like that house in *Doctor Zhivago*. Omar Sharif and Julie Christie, arriving in a sleigh to find a regular winter palace.

Relocated to this New Hampshire derelict, the romance of that scene would be stillborn.

Joanna circled the room, scanning the labels on the bottles and containers: developers and fixatives, inks and toners, paint strippers, lubricants and cleaning fluids, domestic and photographic chemicals, plus a few for cleaning and maintaining firearms. Plus zoom lenses and other apparatus.

If there'd been any other photographic equipment lying around, then Morgan had certainly ordered it taken along with the aircraft debris. Cameras might have film in them.

A necklace of starlight slithered across the corner of her eye. She swung around, heart set to gallop. But there was nothing.

Only the random reflections of her flash in water. Depthless puddles patched the floor, old spillages diluted with the ice brought in on the boots of White Shadow troopers.

Joanna sighed. What more did Morgan expect her to find?

Her torch alighted on the table, where a few home-printed pamphlets lay strewn to one side and, under a thin scattering of automatic weapons parts and mechanical components, a sprawling map of the Granite State had been pasted.

A few marker-pen scrawls drew Joanna closer. Flashlight held at shoulder height, she brought the White Mountain range under a spotlight. Mount Washington was marked for special attention, a small collection of red rings with scribbled annotations in black obscuring some of the surrounding terrain. The scribbles might have been hieroglyphs, but Joanna knew a file reference when she saw one.

A beam swept over the map and it wasn't hers. She jumped out of her skin.

'Hey, sorry. Didn't mean to scare you.'

Ben McKim, right at the foot of the stairs. Jesus. 'You didn't – not exactly. This house gives me the creeps, is all.'

'Yeah, well, you're not alone there.' Ben's eyes roved the expanse of ceiling, coming quickly back down to the table and the map.

'Here, come and take a look.' Joanna's finger stabbed the ring around Mount Washington. 'I think these are references to other documents, other maps. The Captain didn't mention any being found. We might be onto something here.'

'You might be,' conceded McKim. 'Unless that fugitive grabbed it all when he ran.'

Joanna licked her lip, shook her head. 'Uh-uh. They'd be somewhere close by. He went out through the parlour window.'

She started her flashlight dancing about. 'If you're not busy right now, Ben – '

'Everyone's alert, I got the patrols set for the next thirty minutes, and if you ask me, nothing's going to be heading our way.' Ben rounded the table slowly. 'You know how it is, these squads run themselves most of the time. I'm all yours.'

Joanna nodded. 'In that case, you can give me a hand. There are two rooms to go over down here.' She met him head-on. 'By the way, I've never known anyone move as quiet as you.'

'Thanks, Hmieleski.'

As Joanna turned, she smiled for herself. She hadn't meant it as a compliment.

Leela had stared this death in the face once before. It was death exploded into countless tiny fragments, but it was death nonetheless; each splinter as vicious and merciless as its monstrous parent. That time before, Leela had stood in the mouth of a metal giant constructed by men to battle with death in its cloud form. The giant was called the Sandminer, and that storm had glimmered with the promise of untold riches. The storm that bore down on them now shone in a way that threatened to blind long before it fell upon them to tear them apart.

On any world, nature crafted foes that could not be fought. And faced with enemies of nature's making, honour was never an issue. To run or to hide: those were the only choices.

And yet Kristal chose to run and fight.

Breaking away, she drove them flat out back across the level plain. The other snowmobiles followed, digging riverine furrows in the snow. The white fury poured into the basin after them: death as a cloud, too heavily laden to reach the sky.

There was no shame in this hasty retreat, only dire uncertainty. Kristal strained Leela's trust to the limit, driving one-handed while she shouted into her radio. 'Marotta, give us all the covering fire you can, then fall back after us!'

A moment's static seemed to scoff at her. *'You want me to shoot at the storm?'*

'Save your questions! Have Landers drop some shells in there for good measure! *Now!'*

Leela fancied she had many more questions than the Sergeant, but she took Kristal's command to include herself. She held on in dread silence, prepared to endure the chaos of her thoughts so long as the chaos behind them was determined to give chase.

'Typical: playing with dynamite before you've discovered fire. A few decades attempting to turn out psionic James Bonds and they think they can command the weather?'

Morgan Shaw had been trained to withstand interrogation, but the Doc's interview technique was relentless and curiously wearing. Still, the guy had summed up the essence of Operation Grill Flame pretty accurately: it had all been about psi spies back then.

This convoy was taking its own sweet time. There were two-thousand-and-one things he'd rather be thinking about instead of arguing ethics with some mad-professor-type from UNIT who'd wandered into his investigation unsolicited. Whether McKim had been the right choice for watching the house, whether he'd been right to take Kristal's sixth-sense report at face value, for a couple of instances.

Morgan cleared his tired throat and hoped each answer would be the last required.

'Not command exactly. Just give the occasional nudge. It's no more than Bernard Vonnegut's cloud-seeding experiments back in the 40s, right? Just a hell of a lot more precise and effective. We're talking about the potential to end drought in the Third World, all of that. You're not about to tell me that's immoral, are you?'

The Doc looked surprised. 'Oh, I'm not debating the morality. I'm talking about the danger – to everyone and everything on this planet.' Morgan glanced at Derm to see what he was making of this melodrama. But the Doc hadn't done with his lecture: 'Even based on what you're choosing to tell me, this Operation Afterburn of yours amounts to a great deal more than firing silver iodide into the sky. You're talking about herding clouds around like sheep and I can assure you, Captain, the weather is a very ornery beast indeed.'

'Listen, Doc,' Morgan levelled with as much patience as he could muster, 'we appreciate the environmental concern, but the boys down at Fort Meade must have thought this through before they handed it down to us.' He settled back and let the vibrations of the Snowcat's engine pummel him a while. He tried to think of it as a rough kind of massage after a morning jog. 'They gave us Kristal, and I'm telling you I've seen her work miracles with that Stormcore: she taps into the Earth's biorhythms, whatever she does, and she never has to do another raindance.'

The disapproval was evident in Derm's impassive silence. Grill Flame was old news – and the aims of the project, if not the true results, were public knowledge. Even the limited stuff he had let slip about Afterburn could have Morgan court-martialled and watching his back for NSA hitmen for the rest of a short life. But he tried to view each serving of information as an investment in the Doc's eventual productivity.

'That's all very well and good, Captain, but the gentlemen at Fort Meade appear to have overlooked one vital consideration.' Captain Shaw glanced out the window opposite, hoping to recognise some landmark that would tell him they were nearing journey's end. There was zip. The Doctor held his audience captive and he knew it: 'Whatever miracles your scout is capable of performing with the Stormcore, didn't it ever occur to you there might be someone out there who could play much more impressively?'

Humanity had few examples on offer that hadn't, at one time or another, passed through Melvin Village, or even stayed a week or two. And they all wandered into the store.

As much to suck in the old-world atmosphere as to buy anything. And Hal Byers was happy to have them browse and walk out with only a memory in their pocket, if that was all they wanted. Normally they'd pick up something, and stop for a few words besides. For Hal, that was the best part of the trade. The store was the focal point of the village for visitors and townsfolk alike; with the church a close second.

Makenzie had talked to him before about a CCTV system. Like hell, he'd said every time. The mirrors were adequate for a store this size and a camera spying down from every corner wasn't part of the charm folks came looking for.

Of course, there was that biker who'd tried stuffing his jacket with a couple of six-packs, while he'd sent his girl over to keep Hal busy. Makenzie had seen that as meaning something, like, *what'd I tell you*. Hal saw it as just another anecdote for the bar of a Saturday night. The way that girl had draped her chest further and further over the counter, giving out her best small talk. And Hal smiling and saying uh-huh a lot, while he looked over her head and watched the idiot biker fumble the cans.

Before he sent the pair packing he'd told the girl she was pretty, but maybe she should hit on guys more her age.

Makenzie, Hal figured, was just sore for having missed out on an arrest.

A scrape of boot on the boards made Hal look up from his magazine.

Since this one customer came in, begging for the phone, he'd been doing lots of nothing as an alternative to watching the guy like a hawk. Hal preferred to give folks the benefit of the doubt, but this particular guy looked so wired. And his breath smelled like Saturday night. Day like today, anyone might take a swig to warm up their insides, but Jesus.

The mirror opposite showed an empty aisle. His customer had found the blind spot.

By accident? Hal didn't think so.

Hal shook his head. Another sorry son-of-a-bitch, probably thought because everyone in a small town moved slow they thought slow. Hal didn't feel like being so lenient with this one.

He went back to leafing through the magazine, thinking about his poor boat locked in ice down at the marina. Damn, but he should have seen that freeze coming. She was going to need plenty of TLC before he could take her out again come spring.

Hal caught the movement as a shadow crossing his page.

He sighed and flipped the magazine closed. His customer had just rounded the end of the back aisle. Moving slow, *because that's what we do here*, he wandered to the end of his counter and stepped out as though to hold the door open.

The man stopped and his eyes twitched.

Hal wanted to laugh. The guy's suit had inherited some bulk all the time he'd been browsing. Amateur didn't even cover it. But this one wasn't some kid like that biker. Hell yeah, he'd give Makenzie a call on this one.

'You mind showing me what you got there, sir?'

The guy was twitching under the skin now. His only exit was through Hal and Hal was closed for business. 'I got all day,' he added helpfully. 'How about you?'

'I haven't got anything,' the man objected, like a kid caught with his hand in the candy jar. Southern boy too, which figured. 'What? I didn't want anything okay? I didn't see anything I liked in your dead-end store. What, is that a crime in this hole?'

Hal was done with the nice face. 'Shoplifting's a crime anywhere, far as I know. Open your coat and turn out your pockets, sir. I like to think I give service with a smile here, but trust me, I can get real ugly real fast.'

'You're making a big mistake.' Real anger was creeping in now. Hal liked him even less.

'Show me what you took and then I'm calling a cop. We have one here, you know. Happens to be a buddy of mine.'

'I don't care about your goddamn buddy, jackass! Now get the hell out of my way!'

Hal blinked. Trouble with anger, it was contagious. 'Hey, you're not bullying little kids in the schoolyard now. You're caught for real and it's time to pay. It's time for regrets not excuses, friend. What, you think we're really that stupid, to be taken by the likes of you?'

Hal barked out a laugh and grabbed the guy's arm.

Suddenly the man yanked away and screamed in Hal's face. There were goods falling to the floor, toys and such, and it would have been comic if he hadn't pulled a gun from somewhere in there. A compact little automatic, looked like a .38.

'This is what's real!' the guy blew up. 'And yeah, I think you're really that stupid!'

Hal said nothing. He guessed he ought to raise his hands.

Makenzie gave up trying to raise the dead. He'd been getting undiluted silence on the phone, static on the radio. No chance of backup any time soon. Plenty of the townsfolk would willingly muster for search parties, but in these conditions he'd only risk losing more people. He'd exhausted all of his options and himself in the process.

Then he'd taken a moment to ring Martha and he was getting the dial tone on the other end, but she wasn't home. Something more to fret about. The worst part though, the office was unbearably empty with no Laurie.

Makenzie was waking up to just how alone he was here. The edge of the world had come to the outskirts of Melvin Village and everyone was walking or driving right off it. Hell, he might even join them. No, no good to anyone, thinking like that. He tried massaging some life into his eyes, hoped it might find a way through to the rest of him.

So where was he? Stuck.

No chance of a solo tour around the cult place. Oh yeah, he'd thought about it plenty, but he knew it was plain stupid – especially assuming they were involved. All he was left with was looking after the folks still here. If he ever found Laurie, he'd have to explain the delay to her then. He'd be happy to see her hate him for it.

Just as long as he saw her.

Standing, he thought he might swing over to Hal's, let him know some of what was going on. He didn't want to tell him about Laurie just yet.

'Mak! Hey, Mak! Get yourself out here!'

That was Phil Downey calling at him through the door. The old boy was padded out with coats and sweaters, but they all looked like they'd been thrown on.

'What is it, Phil? You should be home by the fire.'

'Army's here, Mak. They just rolled up. Take a look.'

Makenzie stepped out beside him and looked along the street: a line of Snowcats and a couple of Hum-Vees, outriders on Ski Doos; all of them parking up outside Janny Meeks' hotel. Armed men, answering Makenzie's prayers. Janny was going to hit her own roof.

Makenzie strode past Downey. He had to get a closer look, make sure the help wasn't going to disappear on him.

Makenzie broke into something close to a trot, uttering a few prayers of thanks to a God he'd forgotten existed. Then took them all straight back the moment he recognised the man hopping down from the lead Snowcat to take charge of his town.

The engines wound down as his boots hit the snow. Man, was it good to be back home.

Kind of.

Morgan glanced along the side of the hotel. Where a grey shape dissolved hastily into white. A toppled trash can rolled noiselessly in the snow-covered driveway.

The Doctor landed beside him. 'More coyotes. You know, I can't help thinking they must be hopelessly sentimental or desperate to be courting the company of humankind so freely.'

Morgan Shaw cleared his throat. You had to wonder about this Doc. He was on another planet most of the time. 'Hey, listen, Doc, do you think you can count yourself as a member of the human race just long enough to help us out here?'

'I shouldn't think that will be a problem. It's no more than I usually do.'

Again with the solemn, mysterious tones. Where did UNIT ever dig this guy up?

Morgan returned his attention to the town, at least the length of the main street. No, this didn't really look like home at all. Maybe that was why it felt good to be back. He was standing in the town but he was still very much outside of it. The best way to be.

'When they get the lab set up,' he began absently, 'I'll want you going over every piece of that wreck with Pydych. We need results, the faster the better.'

As he finished the last word, Morgan forgot all about the

Doctor. Another grey shape was looming out of the veiled street, and the shape had Morgan's exclusive attention even before the details had properly resolved themselves.

Makenzie. No surprise, of course, but later would have done as well as sooner.

Man, was it good to be back home.

McKim called out from the map room. Joanna heaved the cellar hatch closed and hopped off the steps, satisfied that she'd shut out the wind and the snow, if not the cold. This basement room had turned up only more shelves of chemicals, canned goods, spare parts and gas cans.

Hoping Ben had struck gold, she turned from the plank steps and switched her flashlight back on. Her small endeavour had also shut out the daylight, of course.

'Ben,' she called, her voice like an intrusion as she passed into the other room, 'don't you get a feeling there might be something still in here with us?'

Ben McKim was over by the sink. Solid old porcelain, the cracks of age in its surface, he had pulled it some way free of its nesting place and was reaching into the gap behind.

Cold feet danced over the base of Joanna's neck. She glanced over her shoulder: nothing.

'Something we can't see,' she prompted, wanting the conversation.

'You mean the Invisible Man?' Ben tugged a plastic folder from the niche and gave it a once-over before passing it to her. He clapped his hands clean and stooped to retrieve his H&K. 'Come on, Joanna, there'd have to be a whole bunch of them to take out this many. And all these guns going off, none of these invisible aliens get hit? Not to mention where are the bodies? Normally, you loot a battlefield, the corpses are the thing you leave.'

'Ben, I don't understand any of this but I know we've missed something. More than paperwork.' She drew a deep breath to flush out the tightness. She teased a few of the documents from the folder, focused on those with a lengthy frown. 'Although these are definitely interesting.'

There was a clatter and bang from the next room. She and McKim looked to the doorway.

Wind, snow and daylight had all broken in again.

Paul Falvi was up and bolting out of that attic room in a little under a second, slinging his rifle in favour of the Beretta. It wasn't a hundred per cent definite he'd seen anything, but he was going to check it the hell out right now. Lieutenant McKim was not appreciative of false alarms. Probably even less appreciative of alarms that didn't get raised.

Down a flight, across the hall, he poked his head into Barnes' room. 'Hey, you got any activity out front, Barnes?'

'All quiet on the eastern,' she told him, her eye squeezed up on the sight like his had been until a moment ago.

Falvi raced to the head of the main stairwell, leaving a shout trailing: 'Maybe I got something. Movement between those two trucks.'

'*Maybe* you got something?' her call chased after him.

Pistol locked in a firm grip, Falvi descended the stairs two at a time. Urgency or no, he couldn't help a wry shake of the head. Didn't she ever let up, Barnes? One time she'd said they were like Legolas and Gimli at the battle of Helm's Deep. Falvi hadn't even read *Lord of the Rings*, but after she'd explained the comparison he'd given it a shot. Twelve pages in and he's skipping ahead to Helm's Deep, where the two warriors are in hot competition for the most bad guys notched up. Mostly, Barnes and him were just a practice target's worst nightmare and they never counted their live ones out loud.

Now she was having a dig because he wasn't a hundred per cent. He's been watching the snow smother the woods for so long he's starting to see in monochrome. And she's covering the front, while the best view out back is out of bounds because there's no floor in the goddamn room!

Falvi hit the downstairs hall at a run, making for the back of the house. If he wasn't mistaken, then it wasn't just points at stake.

Joanna stuffed the folder inside her parka and backed swiftly against the left side of the doorway. McKim moved quietly and efficiently to the opposite side.

In the next room, light from the reopened hatch was projecting a shadow onto the dark boards. An expanding silhouette, it looked to be brandishing a rifle or a shotgun.

Joanna studied McKim's eyes, trying to gauge if he could see any more than her.

Ben had his SMG aimed high and she could almost read his mind, running through every possible play. Joanna was pretty sure she'd covered them already.

In one respect, she had reason to be relaxed: the shadow was all bulk, but human. Safety was off. She hooked McKim's gaze on hers and signalled for him to cover her.

One long slow breath and she swung around the doorframe.

Steel struck her flat in the side of the face. There was a loud slam that carried on into her head, a liquid sloshing underneath it. Her world was on the move and she reasoned she was falling. By the time she hit the deck she worked it out: *someone else in here.*

Amid the ringing pain and the underwater vision she could make out the man. He was huge, magnified, at the foot of the basement steps. Frigid light was barging its way in from above, filling the dingy space and crisping the edges of the shadows. The shotgun had a silver lining as it came up and blew a great crater in the air over her head.

Splinters blew back from the doorway. *Ben!*

Joanna's fingers closed around her weapon's pistol-grip and she wondered: is this how it begins? In this house, people

– human beings – shooting at each other, only to be swallowed into some otherworld oblivion? Fresh meat for a bloodthirsty void.

Near-blinded by the ache in her face, she brought her gun up anyway.

Chapter Seven

Riding frozen rapids. Squeezing all the speed out of the snow-mobile, Kristal would have willed it to fly if she could.

Even on the expanding borders of hell, there was a certain terrifying poetry to Kristal's situation. Leela's arms locked around her waist, Kristal found her courage shored up by the added responsibility she felt for her passenger. Nature's destructive forces make children of us all, she thought; so what, then, were any of us in the face of the supernatural?

Behind them the storm played predator.

Zooming into view on her left, she saw Landers, up on one knee with the rifle slammed against his shoulder. She didn't hear the discharge as he launched a round from the M203 grenade launcher far over her head. Then she was zipping between two shallow foxholes and glimpsed Marotta in one of them, his machinegun braced to fire the moment the other snowmobiles had passed him by.

She glanced aft to spot the blast. The eruption was negligible, a cough in the cloud front, like it had swallowed nothing more than a harmless pill. The storm carried on tumbling over the rise like the fallen walls of Jericho.

Kristal hadn't expected much more. She wanted some sign though of the effects on the forces driving that wintry smoke-screen. That was over-optimistic, maybe, but she could rely on Marotta to give it his best shot before following them.

Leela shifted her grip. The foxholes slipping far behind, Kristal aimed her eyes front – and saw they were running out of level terrain. Kristal shouted back, 'Hold on!'

Chill wind gnawed at her cheeks.

She thought hard about the storm's rate of advance, next to their own. She also thought about how the Plains tribes hunted buffalo. All right, she concluded, we're through running.

One final glance back, and she could hear the guttural spit and crack of the machinegun above the other rifles. She didn't know what good it could do, and had to tear her gaze free from the icy vortex to focus on her driving. She managed a quick signal for the three snowmobiles to follow her lead. Then, praying it was a slope and not a cliff, she made sure the accelerator was at maximum ready for when the ground dropped away.

Leela's hold nearly squeezed the breath out of her.

The vehicle cut the lip of the hill and took to the air, taking half a ton of broken snow with it. The engine whined in panic and they were flung like ammo from a catapult. They hit just as hard too, the impact jarring Kristal's every nerve.

She fought to swing them round, the vehicle's butt backing into the snow until the engine suddenly cut out. Finally, Leela lost her balance and Kristal felt herself dragged off her saddle, sliding on her back some few feet down the snowy slope.

The prow of the snowmobile peered timidly up from its burrow, like a gopher checking the coast was clear. Of course, Kristal knew it wasn't.

Three more snowmobiles fired themselves over the brow of the hill in quick succession, skiing down the incline with a deal more control than Kristal had managed. Kristal didn't have time to get all competitive. She sprang to her feet.

'Leela, you okay?' Kristal said. Leela gave a dazed nod, hauling herself up. 'I wanted to stop, but not quite like that. Sorry about that.'

Satisfied her freshest recruit was okay, Kristal launched herself onto her knees and started shovelling snow with her hands. She was pleased to see Leela pitching in, no questions asked, and she shouted across at her troops as they were dismounting. 'Get busy! We need to be under the snow before that storm hits us!'

'Under the snow?' asked Leela anxiously. 'Is that not dangerous?'

'Not if you know what you're doing.' Kristal kept shovelling, sorry she was too busy to offer any more reassurance. Fortunately, Leela was giving it her all on the digging as well. 'We can bury ourselves or we can wait for that thing to do it for us.'

Looking at the gouge they'd taken out of the slope, Kristal stayed Leela's efforts and reached into her pack for two smoothly rounded grenades, and one more for luck. She packed them together deep, eggs in a nest, and looked to make sure the troops were doing likewise.

There was no gunfire to be heard over the rise – which might mean Marotta was on his way.

'How will we know when the storm has passed over?'

'Trust me, we'll know.'

Kristal yanked the pins and hauled Leela into a dive. The crater blew out like an ice volcano and she listened to the snow falling back to earth in chunks. When she looked up she was relieved to see Marotta's crew riding the last two vehicles into view. Further along the steep bank, a second explosion punched another hole.

When the snow settled they would at least have somewhere to hide. Assuming the storm had no eyes to find them.

The town built itself around her out of snowflakes and pale shadows. The wind followed her on the last stages of her trek, but Amber never got the feeling it was helping her along. The main feeling she was getting was of being watched all the way and she kept daring whoever it was to just step the hell out and show themselves. All this white was getting to be worse than the dark in her room at nights.

Passing along the main street, she hurried her pace as she

crossed the side road by the church. Ahead, figures moved behind all the white spray paint.

Some were gathering in small knots a respectful distance from the vehicles parked in front of the hotel. Others were getting busy unloading. Something exciting had come to town at last.

Amber found a whole new reserve of energy at the thought. She ran the final stretch.

She stopped abruptly, nearly skidding where caterpillar tracks had squashed the snow to slush. These guys were carrying rifles: soldiers, wow! She watched some of them and moved slowly around the back of the nearest trailer, hitched to the big ugly tracked vehicle. The tarpaulin was still in place, and Amber thought about peeling the corner back to peek inside.

'Hey, get out of there, kid,' a man's voice startled her. Sandpaper skin and coyote eyes, the guard herded her out of the gap with his rifle. Kyle, his uniform-tag said. She peered into the mouth of the large tube under the barrel, but she decided, no, the guy was scarier.

Amber ducked onto the sidewalk and scowled back at him when he wasn't looking. Then she walked sullenly along the line of trucks, smiling secretly because of the excitement stirring inside her. This was great, the best ever.

No. No, it wasn't.

Voices had been carrying on in the background all the while. One was louder than the others and now she was closer she could hear him above the noise of the soldiers and the unloading. What was more, she could see him, not far along, in a face-off with a dark-haired soldier.

'I'm doing my *job,* Kenzie,' the soldier was answering back. 'You might try doing the same. These townsfolk of yours are getting mighty restless, looks like.'

There were other soldiers standing around him and she guessed he must have been as important as he acted. He was shorter than Makenzie, but just as solid and he stood right up to him, didn't so much as notice Makenzie's size.

Amber could have told him how smart-ass gibes never dented Makenzie.

'I'm not asking you to broadcast your secrets over town, Morg, but I have a right to know!'

She edged a step or two closer. As she did so, she noticed the other man. *Not* a soldier, she couldn't tell what he was supposed to be. He was outside the group. Even he wasn't as big as Makenzie, but somehow he towered above all of them. He watched everything from under his silly hat, but didn't seem very interested in the argument.

'You're taking over this town, bro, and jamming our streets with your goddamn trucks and suddenly I see myself having to go round to every door and tell everyone how my kid brother has everything under control. "Oh yeah, I remember little Morgan – he made Special Forces, didn't he?" That's all I'll hear, and none of them will mind that you left us all behind because you thought we were all too damn small for you. Or that you won't lend me any of your men to help with the search.'

Makenzie's brother, Morgan. Of course. She could see that flame in their eyes now, too much like her heart whenever she saw her Daddy. Angry – love. Her eyes stung and her mouth curled as she remembered a torrent of stuff.

She was aware of the tall man then and the fact that he'd noticed her. Makenzie hadn't even seen her. The man smiled. She quickly glanced away.

She realised she'd missed some of the fight, and Makenzie's brother was biting back: 'You could have made yourself a different bed, bro. But you stayed in Dad's and now you step into his boots every morning, grew up to be just like your old man, a big cop in a small town. Well, I have my orders, and my people are here to help me do my job by doing theirs. And that doesn't include searching all over the mountains for a few civilians who took a wrong turning or went out trekking completely underprepared.'

'You knew some of these people!' Makenzie roared back in his brother's face, and by now their fight was the centre of the town. Makenzie's thick finger stabbed at Morgan's flak jacket and Amber wondered if he bullied his brother like he bullied everyone else.

Everyone around looked uncomfortable at all of this. Amber hated it.

'Yeah, I'm a small-town cop and I'm short on manpower. But you know what, I'm starting to think maybe I wouldn't need so much if you hadn't brought your big-city government projects out here and screwed things up for the rest of us.' Makenzie's arm flew out like a spear to indicate the troops carrying jagged artefacts into the hotel. 'Does this have anything to do with that cult up there? Your people been stirring them up – or what?'

'FYI, Kenzie, I can tell you all we have in that truck are the pieces of an Air Force jet that crashed on Mount Shaw. End of story, or it will be when we've found the rest and the small matter of the pilot. I don't know if I count myself lucky or not we haven't found him yet. But the guy was a patriot and a hero and I'd expect you to understand that.'

Through all of the speech, Amber could see Makenzie gearing up to explode. It was as if everything his brother said just burned his fuse, like the way everything she said or did made Makenzie shout in her face. Suddenly, she couldn't stand the thought of him answering back. She could feel the idea of his voice like a pressure in her head.

'I know where you can find him,' she said. 'I know where you can find the pilot.'

Amber was amazed. Her small voice had stopped everything.

A mess. A bloody mess.

It was the way these things always turned out and if he

could only get out of this alive, he'd be laying the blame on Jacks. She'd got them both back into the house, which was clever or plain lucky, but if it got them both killed then Mitch reckoned it was neither.

The moment the patrol had passed around the front of the house, they'd crawled out of the woods, Mitch with his hood down because he was sweltering despite the cold and wet. Once they'd reached the old trucks, they were up and running to the basement hatch.

Jacks was dead quiet on the doors, give her that. Just as silent going down the steps, sinking into the dark.

Mitch was supposed to wait, stuck out in the open until she'd finished her recce. He hadn't liked that bit, watching for trouble along each approach. Anyway, he got to slow his breathing some, until she'd motioned for him to come on down.

That was the other bit he hadn't liked: trusting her judgement.

Especially as she was down there holding a gas can like a crazy pyromaniac bitch. Still, he'd made five steps down and was going okay. The gig was going so smooth, he was starting to get suspicious, edgy. Sure enough, she'd signalled a warning, pointed at the doorway.

Mitch still had the wind in his ears, but he could hear voices.

Jacks mouthed instructions at him and he could see she was getting sore as hell with him as he took his time getting it. When he did get it, he thought she was more nuts than ever. Folks probably let her watch too many Chuck Norris movies as a kid. Mitch shrugged and retreated up a step so he could get a better leverage on one of the doors. Heaving thirty or forty degrees towards him, he let it drop with a bang then started back down the steps.

The Army hadn't been a long time coming after that.

First, the woman swung in to cover him and as he saw his own shadow on the floor, Jacks batted her in the side of the head with the jerry can. Then Mitch got the idea maybe he'd been used as a decoy like poor Crayford, but the thought was broken by the sight of the other officer at the doorway – and Mitch reacted too quickly, blew away half the doorframe.

From there on in, that was all he was doing: reacting, his thinking always a second slow.

Mitch threw himself into the middle of the room. The chopped whistle of suppressed SMG-fire chased him, exploding bottles and parts of the shelf behind him. He hit the floor rolling, pumped his shotgun and brought it up to fire. Another burst from the SMG was killed by a retort from Jacks' AK-47, and this sudden hammer-pain broke over his ribcage.

He jerked on the trigger, heard the blast faintly. As a cloud of ceiling plaster showered down in front of the doorway, so the real pain filtered through. His head went for a short swim and he felt the wetness pouring out of him. Mitch fired another shot, vaguely aware it was wide.

Just as well: Jacks was ducking in under the cloud of plaster and dragging the Army woman onto her feet. She must have dropped the jerry can, but he didn't remember hearing it hit the floor. He pumped another shell into place, wincing hard and trying not to think about the warm blood spilling inside his clothes.

The stench of gasoline hit him like a dose of smelling salts.

'Get off your ass, Lagoy! We're leaving!'

Jacks had the woman officer in a fierce arm-lock, jamming the AK's barrel under her prisoner's chin. She shoved the hostage over to him before he was properly on his feet. He took a firm hold of his new charge, wheezing with the effort.

Jacks fired once into the doorway, then she was rescuing a bottle from a shelf by the stairs.

Nice. This mess was about to get a whole lot messier.

Falvi was there, waiting for them.

The whole mountain must have heard that AK, and he was

already out by the rusted trucks. That left him a very short run to the basement doors and when he saw the gunsmoke sailing up out of the entrance, he planted himself off to one side and trained the pistol on the opening.

The patrol was coming around the house at a fast trot, fanning out nicely.

'Hi, bitch,' Falvi greeted the woman as she emerged, coming up into his line of sight.

Jeez, this woman was hard as a statue, near bald with dead marble eyes.

'I don't think you want to do that, kid.'

'What do you know, what I want or not?'

She gave a confident nod back towards the basement entrance. A gorilla of a guy was pushing Joanna Hmieleski out ahead of him. Falvi took careful note of the shotgun. The Lieutenant was looking right into him, eyes loaded with an appeal, and he eased himself back a pace. This was going to take tact and timing.

'Maybe I can take you *and* your boyfriend,' he challenged, getting the bald bitch thinking.

'Don't pretend,' she said.

And she shot him in the gut.

'Storm's closing in.'

Martha realised her simple observation was a perfect summation of the turn her life was taking today. Even the inside of the 4WD seemed gloomy and overcast, although that hadn't stopped the agents replacing their shades as soon as they'd started down the mountain. They sat up front, Agent Theroux at the wheel, while Martha sat in the back with the rest of the cargo: a couple of briefcases, papers, binoculars, a flash-looking camera, a slimline laptop and some other gadgetry.

The temptation to leaf through the papers was strong, but Agent Quartararo's reflection was a permanent fixture in the rear-view; and there was no telling which way her eyes were aimed behind those shades.

Outside, there wasn't a whole lot to see. Only the storm, lashing at the treetops higher up the mountain and whipping up a whirlwind of snow.

Some of it was already pelting the windshield and the wipers were going like a couple of rapiers in a duel. She wondered if the weather might get to town ahead of them.

They were taking the longer track down, to come into town from the southeast, but Agent Theroux seemed determined to make short work of the journey. He'd taken every bend expertly so far, but he was driving too fast and casual for her liking. Showing off? Maybe. It was certainly in keeping with this pair's style.

Wait till Makenzie got a load of these two. More trouble she'd brought into his life.

Curt Redeker's arm was getting tired. Each time he lowered the gun, he'd find himself lifting it straight back up to keep the clerk at bay. It wasn't that the guy was making any moves, it was just he wanted him to stay the hell away. Out of his face, out of his life, further away than the walls of the store would allow.

Perspiration stuck to Curt like a cold skin. His mind was racing everywhere and getting nowhere fast. What in hell was he into here?

He wanted to pace, but he didn't dare move. Instead he fidgeted awkwardly in the one spot. Daddy never meant to do this, honey. At least he had coaxed the clerk into trading places and he now had a place over by the door. Dumbass wasn't taking his eyes off the gun and that helped remind Curt who was in command here.

The stolen toys, scattered at the clerk's feet, looked pathetic. He didn't want that crap any more. So he didn't really know why, but he said, 'Pick it up. All of it.'

Perhaps it was just to give him a chance to look out through the pane in the front door. There were notices and such pasted all over it, but he could still get a fair look both ways along the street. Fair enough, at least, to give him the really bad news.

'What's your problem? Don't like the look of the weather?'

'There's soldiers. A goddamn Army convoy!' Curt was stunned – and furious. Holy Christ, this couldn't be happening. No. Suddenly it dawned that the clerk had smart-mouthed him. He raised the gun again. 'What in hell is going on in this town?'

Kristal and Leela lay huddled in their miniature cave, twins in winter's womb.

A moment's extra effort had brought a thin layer of snow down on top of them, then they'd worked swiftly to pack it close and build up a wall, the intention being to leave a narrow slit for air. The vicious storm was upon them long before they'd finished their crude construction.

Kristal kept them at it though, while the blizzard tore the air to shreds outside. The wind didn't howl so much as it screamed. There was no telling when its rage would be spent.

'When the people of the Sioux nation hunted buffalo,' Kristal used the time to try to explain some of her thoughts to Leela, 'they used to herd them off high cliffs.'

The girl saw the analogy immediately. The prospect clearly frightened her as much as it worried Kristal. 'Do you think that was what it was doing? Trying to herd us?'

They had to raise their voices to compete with the tempest outside. 'I don't know. I can't – see very clearly into the storm. I only know that – whoever or whatever is driving it, they must have the Stormcore. They took it off our fugitive. It's the only possibility that makes any sense. And it's the worst of possibilities, believe me.'

'But if the Stormcore controls this blizzard, then we should try to take it back.'

Kristal studied Leela closely, smiled. She looked outside. Operation Afterburn had stirred up more than a hornet's nest, and a share of the guilt was hers. Still, she had no arguments to counter Leela's simple wisdom.

'Maybe we'll do just that, soon as we get the chance.'

As she watched, she saw the blizzard retreat past their slit-window, as if the mountain had suddenly inhaled. Or the sky perhaps, filling its lungs for another blow.

Kristal had them wait. Nothing returned.

The assault had left the air all brittle and fragile.

Eventually satisfied, Kristal broke out into that air and beckoned Leela after her. Around them, some of the troops had already emerged onto the blasted embankment. For a moment, Kristal was hesitant to shatter the stillness, but she knew she should check on her squad. She saw her Gunnery Sergeant climbing out of his burrow.

'You tucked yourself in okay, I see, Marotta? Can't have had much time.'

Bob sniffed. 'It was tight, but me and Landers made it cosy. I'm a little rough around the edges, but I'll survive.'

Kristal wished she could say the same for the vehicles. Bits of snowmobiles poked up through the deep banks of snow along the base of the slope.

'Man, you're lucky to have any edges left,' Landers put in, dusting off his parka.

At least it made a few of the troops laugh.

'Ma'am, best get up here!'

Kristal looked to where stocky Stu Garvey, her second sergeant, had shown some initiative, scrambling up the hill to see where the storm went. She blinked and let go a huge sigh. She was feeling way too tired to go running up there after him. 'What do you have?'

'Smoke, ma'am! Up at the cult place, far as I can make out.' He glanced back down at her, and suddenly he seemed impossibly far away. 'Looks like that house is on fire.'

Kristal closed her eyes. Fire and ice sounded too much like a ritual trial, a rite of passage. And she didn't think she was up to passing one of those right now.

Chapter Eight

No more than a hundred yards or so into the woods and Joanna was bitterly exhausted, drained far more by what she'd seen than the physical exertion. Somehow, when her captors shoved her face down in the snow, she figured they weren't giving her a rest break.

She felt the weight as the woman jumped onto her back and started tugging both of her arms behind her. 'You're going to tie me?' Joanna couldn't believe it. Maybe they hadn't noticed her uniform patches. 'I'm a doctor. Don't you want me to treat your friend?'

The woman carried on looping rope tightly around her wrists. Joanna lay still, aware of the document folder crinkling inside her coat. They'd come back to torch that place, most likely looking to destroy evidence. So if they found the folder now they'd probably just tear it up and feed it to the wind.

'You can treat him later. Meantime, we get moving.'

Joanna was hauled to her feet, the bonds pulling at her arms. Once she was up, she was shoved on her way again. She could hear the complaining breaths of the wounded man behind her and it occurred to her she might have read the woman's motives all wrong. She was insane, forcing her partner into a march in his condition; and the aim of torching the evidence seemed too much like the product of a reasoning mind. Ambitious, but not crazy.

'Why did you come back to the house?' she asked, keeping going and facing front like a good girl.

'Shut the chat.'

That was the woman again. Giving all the orders, letting her know who was boss. Well, she and her partner could go to hell, Joanna decided.

Where she really wanted to be was back at the house, looking after Falvi. A faint wave of nausea swept over her as she relived the horror of that moment. It was vividly preserved, a photograph in her mind. Everything that happened after it was a detached blur. A three-round burst into the abdomen: it was a picture that couldn't be erased. So instead she started to analyse it, estimating the severity of the wounds and tracing their progression with every step she took away from where the sniper had fallen. McKim had Eastman, a trained combat medic, on his squad; but Falvi needed a field surgeon.

Better still, a hospital.

Joanna shut her eyes and bit her lip. Running through the procedures wasn't doing anyone any good. All she could do for the present was make the best of a bad situation. Learn something, maybe. She had the thought that, after all, her situation wasn't so terrible.

Walking on, at least one psycho pointing a gun at her back, she had been taken prisoner, but Paul Falvi was being held hostage by an altogether different captor. And the deadline for his life had already been set.

Ben McKim was practically in mourning. He had to keep reminding himself that nobody had actually died. Yet.

One second he'd been ducking back from a shotgun blast that threatened to bring half the ceiling down, the next he'd seen the intruders herding Joanna up the stairs. He'd eased into the room after them, stepping on crumbled plaster, splintered wood and broken glass, the stench of alcohol and gasoline drying the inside of his nose and mouth. The shots had stalled him in the middle of the room.

He'd gone for the steps, taking them one at a time with forced care and patience. All the while his breathing was accelerating.

Then the bottle with the flaming tail, like a brown comet, had flown past him to shatter on the floor below – and splash liquid fire all over the basement room. Other bottles exploded a moment later and the roar of a fast-growing inferno chased Ben McKim up the steps.

Outside, he'd found the big bear of a cultist dragging Joanna further off, the woman backing up and warning his squad off with the AK; and blood-red petals blooming in the snow around Paul Falvi. The look in Joanna's eyes said it all: she didn't want anybody else getting hurt on her account. And the way McKim saw it, the house could go to hell.

Falvi was yelling: 'Barnes can take them, sir! She can take them both, I swear. Let her do it!'

But Ben McKim just swallowed and did like every other trooper in his squad: they kept their guns on the retreating fugitives every yard of the way; even after they'd disappeared behind the trees and the white curtain beyond.

Then it was over and they were into the aftermath.

McKim told Falvi to take it easy, but he had to step back to let Eastman do her best – and to escape the accusation in the wounded sniper's eyes. He glanced over at Barnes, to see if it was there too, but she reserved her attention for Falvi. Running from the top of the house, she'd been last on the scene. That had to sting.

While he waited for the word on Falvi, McKim held conference with his sergeants, Mike Lester and Kurt Bederman, to get the full picture on what had happened. They moved a few yards out from the flames lapping greedily at the back of the house. McKim listened intently to each man's report, determined not to hear each new explosion from the basement. At least he'd read Joanna right: according to the sergeants she'd ordered everyone to back off. Even as the woman whipped up her Molotov, they'd done precisely nothing.

It made McKim feel even worse about having done the same.

Watching the house burn, he reached for his radio and almost wished he was still inside.

'What is this, your job includes interrogating ten-year old kids now?'

'Take a break, Kenzie. I'll buy her a soda. This is an interview, not an interrogation.'

'No. No way. She's my responsibility and you're not putting her through a ton of questions. She can't possibly know anything anyhow. She makes stuff up, it's what she does.'

The Doctor looked bored, not merely because he was bored, but because he wanted to make a show of it. He huffed moodily and wandered away from the renewed argument. Idly he produced his crumpled bag and held it out to the side, under the child's nose.

'Jelly baby?'

'No thanks.'

The Doctor blinked. There was a first time for everything. 'Oh, go on,' he urged, 'you'll only hurt their feelings, you know.'

There was a pause, as the Doctor pretended to survey the street. The unloading operation was nearly done, which promised some useful work for his attention. He heard the rustling as a small hand dipped inside the bag.

'Do you know,' he ventured, 'with all these coyotes around, I'm surprised no-one here has heard the story of The Boy Who Cried Wolf.'

'I didn't make it up.'

'Well, that's precisely my point. Neither did he.'

The Doctor flashed her a grin, pleased to see she was frowning uncertainly, as though trying to work him out. Of course, no one had ever worked him out past the seventh decimal place before, but he would be the last one to underestimate a child's intelligence. This girl, small as she was, held the wisdom of three times her years in her eyes.

'You know,' he went on, 'everyone tells stories, for one

reason or another. I've had to tell them myself from time to time. I mean, I try telling people I travel through time and space in a blue box, but they never believe me. Don't you hate that, when people never believe you?'

'I – '

The Doctor tipped his head disarmingly and thrust out his hand. 'I'm the Doctor, by the way. You can call me Doctor.'

The girl glanced past him to where the argument was going on, before eventually accepting the handshake. 'Amber,' she said. 'Amber Mailloux.'

'Do you know what I think?' suggested the Doctor. 'I think we should go and take a close look at this aircraft they brought down from the mountain. There's a man called Corporal Pydych who's supposed to be helping me. He's probably inside the hotel with all the pieces. Shall we go and see him, and you can tell me about what you saw on the way. Hm?'

The Doctor ushered her gently in through the hotel entrance. He was sure nobody would even notice their absence, at least for a few minutes.

'Excuse me, d'you mind? I'm trying to make a call here.' Morgan Shaw held the mic up and pointed at it to make sure his brother got the point. What did he think he was doing, sticking his head in at the door? This was the Command Post Vehicle, for crying out loud.

Morgan had been so grateful when his comms officer, Kev O'Neill, had come trotting out from the CPV with the message that McKim was trying to reach him. He'd broken off the discussion with Kenzie immediately and headed for the vehicle. The radio was much more powerful in there and he wanted to make sure McKim got his instructions loud and clear. More to the point, he would be free from Kenzie.

The report from McKim contained nothing to be grateful for however, and now Kenzie was barging his way onto *his* CPV when he was trying to reach Kristal.

'Good. You can call for some more men,' was Makenzie's sour recommendation.

'Kenzie, get the hell out of my vehicle, or I swear I'll – '

'Silver Surfer, this is Wildcat. Come back.'

Morgan held his stare on Makenzie a moment longer, before lifting the mic. Kristal was coming through like she was in a frying pan and he needed to concentrate. 'Kristal, I got you. What's your position?'

He listened to her summary of the manhunt and everything that had followed. If it hadn't been for the wounded man and Joanna's abduction, her report would have beaten McKim's hands down. And if it had been anyone but Kristal giving the account, he would definitely have had them repeat it at least twice. Still, the Stormcore was involved and that meant pretty much anything was possible.

'We're heading back to the cult place on foot. There's smoke – '

'Negative,' Morgan cut her off, thinking fast, 'I've just talked to McKim. I've got him bringing his squad down the mountain. He's got a man down and Joanna's been taken hostage. Two rogue cultists, out for revenge it looked like. He doesn't know.'

'Two?' asked Kristal sharply.

'Yeah, two. Ben doesn't know how they got the better of him and he's real sorry – but not as sorry as he's going to be. Kristal, what about this storm?'

He strained to hear her answer, worried he was about to lose her. 'Seems… died down…' He gave a nod to O'Neill, see if he could boost the signal.

'Yeah, yeah. But I want to know what it is we're dealing with out there.'

'I told you, Captain. Many spirits or one big enough to swallow the world.'

Great. Typical her mystic mantra comes through nice and

clear. Morgan let the silence fill the vehicle momentarily, then sat forward in his seat. 'Fine, yeah. Strangely, in all this insanity, I recall those words very clearly.' His tone shifted up a notch on the irate scale. 'Now, what the hell does it mean?'

'It cannot be explained,' Kristal told him flatly.

Despite the fact she couldn't see him, Morgan threw his arms up in despair. 'Kristal – please – if you don't know – why don't you just say you don't know!'

'Because I mean, *it cannot be explained.*'

'Listen, I am trying to be open-minded here, I really am, but – '

'Don't, Captain,' Kristal broke in unexpectedly. 'Whatever you do, don't open your mind now. That might just give the spirits a way in.'

Morgan Shaw pressed his tongue to the back of his teeth. 'You know what, have it your own way, Lieutenant Wildcat,' he said tersely. 'Right now, you can head after those cultists and bring Joanna back safely. They headed east-south-east from the house, you should be able to get ahead of them and cut them off. Don't take any chances, but Joanna's safety is your priority numero uno. Are we clear on that?'

'Crystal,' she answered, delivering the pun humourlessly.

'And when you get back here with Joanna, you're going to explain to me the difference between I don't know and it cannot be explained. Out.'

Morgan tossed the mic to O'Neill, glad to be rid of it. He sniffed and rubbed his face from head to chin. He was aware of his brother studying him.

'You know, I might be able to help you out there,' Kenzie offered.

'Mm?'

Makenzie propped himself against the door of the Command Snowcat. 'I got myself a girlfriend, Martha. That was her kid out there, Amber. They both live with me, up at Dad's old cabin. I know them pretty well, might get to know them

110

a whole lot better if this works out.' He looked straight at Morgan then, more sibling than rival for that instant. 'But I'll be damned if I'll ever be able to explain them.'

Morgan nodded, half a smile forming. Makenzie's life had moved on a lot since they'd last spoken. Two years, wasn't it?

'You know, Kenzie, you might be the only one round here knows what my scout is talking about. You want to stick around, act as an interpreter?'

Makenzie shook his head. 'Too much on my plate right now.'

Morgan stood and made for the doorway. His brother dropped down off the step to let him pass. Morgan jumped down next to him.

'Hey, what say we call a truce, huh? Nothing permanent, you know. Just long enough to get the job done.' Morgan looked up and down the street, trying not to make a big deal out of this in front of the troops.

'What say,' Makenzie said, 'you lend me some of those men coming down off the mountain. Soon as they're rested. And I'll see if I can get Amber to talk to you. I don't know, maybe she found something.'

Morgan decided he could cut his brother some slack. For the sake of the truce, if nothing else. 'Four men, twenty-four hours. That's the best I can do. My man, McKim, is going to need something to occupy himself when he gets back.' He glanced again, up and down the line of vehicles. This time he was actively searching for something. He waved over his second-in-command. 'Hey, Derm, where did the girl go? And where the hell is the Doc?'

'Ah, Pydych, there you are, good man. I trust you haven't started without us.'

All the tables in the hotel dining room had been pushed to the walls, the chairs upended on top of them. The rustic décor was totally at odds with the shattered fossil of a military airframe, laid out on a tarpaulin spread over most of a blue carpet. Sections of the wings and the tail fin, with its distinctive electronics pod, were by far the largest recovered.

The Doctor squatted to examine the mashed remains of the jet's nose. Much of the air superiority grey had been seared or scraped away.

Pydych coughed. 'I see the experiment to shrink your assistant worked out.'

'Mm?' The Doctor looked up, mildly annoyed at being disturbed. 'Ah, yes, Amber meet Corporal Pydych, Corporal Pydych, meet Amber Mailloux.' Stooping, he moved up along the skeleton of fuselage, to where the cockpit should have been. 'Amber has been telling me how she found your pilot's parachute, and how she was clever enough to stow it somewhere safe until someone could collect it.'

'Hi, kid. Call me Irving. I hate it, but my Mom likes to know the name's getting used.'

'Whatever.'

Amber moved to stand over the Doctor, managing to block some of his light, but he had already observed the black wiring protruding from the mangled avionics bay. 'I think your comic timing needs work, Corporal. What's your verdict on the electrical systems, hmm?'

Pydych skirted briskly around to face the Doctor. The engineer did his best deep-pan puzzled expression, then sighed. 'What I can tell so far, I think all the electrics that are left in there – which is not a whole lot – are like burnt spaghetti stuck to my Aunt Clara's pan. But it looks like the rest was surgically removed in mid-air. And I don't know any aerobatic engineer display team that could pull off that kind of stunt.'

'Curious.'

'What was your major, Doc? The value of understatement? Myself, I majored in cynicism, but I minored in electrical engineering and I've never seen anything like this in my long and colourful career. And I'm talking at least as long and colourful as that scarf of yours.'

'Oh I doubt that,' the Doctor dismissed the claim airily. His thoughts were elsewhere as his gaze sailed over the exhibit. 'There's really not much left of this Raven, or its experimental modifications. You wouldn't happen to know about any of those, would you?'

Pydych laughed and polished his fingernails on his collar. 'I can tell you this much: they were experimental. Rush-job avionics and wiring to patch in the Storm – ' he arrested himself and smiled at Amber ' – device. I hadn't seen a bigger lash-up since my brother tried to spy on me and my first girlfriend with a cheap Polaroid and my remote-control car.'

'They had remote-control cars when you were a kid?' Amber goaded.

'Hey, kid, I'm only thirty-six next month and I played with cars well into my twenties. Now, if you'll excuse me, I think your learned colleague is trying to attract my attention.'

The Doctor was indeed waiting on Pydych with an expectant stare. 'Yes,' he said with tested patience, 'I didn't really want to break up your new friendship, Corporal, but I have a question I think you can help me with. The Captain happened to mention the Stormcore – '

'Uh, yeah, Doc, can we just stick with calling it the device? I'm not entirely comfortable using official designations in front of the kid.'

'Corporal, in the first place I thought codenames were intended to disguise the nature of top secret equipment; and in the second, I'm getting a nasty feeling you'll be able to forget your state and its secrets if we don't find some answers very soon.'

While Pydych tried to make up his mind, the Doctor watched Amber detach herself from the scene and drift off towards the tail of the wreckage. It struck him that she was a good deal more distant than the length of the aircraft.

'Yes, okay, yes. The Stormcore was where the electronic warfare officer normally sits. At first I was guessing it was –

disintegrated – like most of the electrics.' Pydych shrugged. 'But if the creepy kid found the chute then it made it to the ground. The pilot and the Stormcore were rigged into the same ejector system.'

'Really?' The Doctor frowned. 'Well, that's very bad news indeed.'

Pydych blinked. 'Bad news?'

'The wires looked like they were cut,' Amber said from down the room. 'On the chute.'

'Since others have apparently recovered it,' the Doctor pursued his point, 'I can only assume your pilot ended up guarding the Stormcore with his life. Which is a tremendous pity.' He rose slowly. 'Because he might have been able to tell us what attacked this aircraft.'

The humour drained from the lines in Pydych's face. 'Wait – attacked?'

'So far, we can be fairly certain most of these breaks are impact fractures. The metal is buckled and warped and what's left of the wiring is burnt, as you say.' The Doctor let a gloomy cloud descend over his face, and his finger traced a ragged course in the air, marking a wide area around the missing cockpit. 'But doesn't it strike you as odd, that neither White Shadow nor the cult could find a single fragment from this entire section? And some of these jagged edges look a little too neat for my liking: torn along the dotted line.'

Pydych's worried features were simply mirroring the Doctor's. 'The question we have to ask ourselves, Corporal Pydych,' he declared darkly, 'is who made the dotted line?'

Martha hit the door release as soon as the lumbering 4×4 had rolled to a halt. The woman agent turned in her seat. 'Hey, hey. Slow down there, Martha.'

Martha stared right back into those blank shades. '*Melody*, I appreciate your politeness and all, but if you're thinking of telling me to relax I'll save you the bother. I've been sitting quiet in the back of this car all the way down the mountain and you've told me next to nothing about what business you have with my daughter. So if you don't mind, I don't feel much like relaxing, I feel like finding my baby girl right now.'

At that, she was out of the car, slamming the door behind her. They were parked across the street from the store and despite blowing snow she could see the grey silhouettes of a bunch of vehicles up by the hotel. She couldn't see Mak's police truck, but if he was in town he'd have parked in back of the station. She thought she'd best march straight for those vehicles.

Two more car doors opened and slammed in tandem.

'Whoa, Martha,' the man called Parker caused her to turn. 'Those guys there are the United States Army. They're all here as part of our operation, you know, and they're likely to be mighty sensitive about folks busting in and asking all kinds of questions. Maybe you'd prefer my partner here to make the introductions.'

Melody rounded the front of the 4WD, her stylish boots making wet crunching sounds in the snow. 'Sure I will. Then we can go find your daughter, speak to her nice and calmly. It won't take more than five minutes, tops.' She angled her head up at her partner. 'And what are you planning on doing exactly?'

'Me?' Parker flashed a winning smile and jerked a thumb over his shoulder. 'I am going over to the store to pick up some candy. Your daughter likes candy, right, Martha?'

Martha clenched her teeth before returning the thinnest of smiles. 'Why don't you tell me, Agent Theroux? Or isn't that covered in your government files?'

'Touché, ma'am.' He tipped her a salute and turned, crossing the street with an over-easy swagger. Byers was always saying how he got all sorts coming through his store.

* * *

115

The trees materialised around and in front of them like a developing image on photographic paper, only to fade behind as they trudged on. Time, unfortunately, was the only gauge left by which Joanna could measure how far they had come, and she had lost track of that an uncertain while ago. Actually, for all the dragging minutes of their trek, she didn't think they had covered a heck of a lot of ground.

The wind was getting up, stirring the crystal flakes into a frenzy.

Jacks forged ahead like she was on some kind of route march. The big guy, Lagoy, was dragging his heels for painfully obvious reasons, and Joanna was watching her step because one slip and she might crack her head against a tree. Hands tethered behind her back, her balance was off and she'd already earned one vengeful kick from Jacks for a simple stumble.

Vengeful seemed to sum up Emilie Jacks pretty completely. There was certainly no compassion in her tone when she finally called for a rest break. 'Ten minutes,' she said, marching back to them. 'Here's your chance to take a look at Mitch.'

Joanna turned herself around to be untied, privately thankful. In spite of what he was, she'd been concerned about Mitch Lagoy. Sure, part of her had wanted him to keel over and never get up, but it was always the lesser part.

Set loose, she yanked her hood up and rubbed her cheeks furiously to get some heat back into them. Her right cheek was still sore from its meeting with the gas can. Lagoy had slumped against the nearest birch, and she knelt beside him to peel tentatively at his coat. Where the blood had stained the punctured fabric, the holes looked especially ragged. They might look neater when she got to the skin, but there wouldn't be any cause for optimism.

She worked swiftly, Lagoy breathing in thick gasps – and wanting to close his eyes.

'Hey,' she said, 'for what it's worth, it wasn't me who did this.

116

I didn't get a single shot off before your lady friend – '

'She is no way,' he butted in, 'my lady friend. She was Crayford's squeeze – or the other way round.'

Joanna remembered the name from a CIA dossier. Jacks was safely out of earshot, hovering across the clearing and trying to out-stare the whiteness. 'And there I was just thinking he was crazy for believing in aliens.'

'Come off it, Lieutenant. We know that you know. That thing we cut from the chute wasn't manufactured in Detroit.'

Joanna was peering underneath her patient to check for exit wounds. There were none and she looked up to meet the big man's gaze. She knew the Stormcore must have been in this pair's hands when Kristal had sensed it. 'What did you do with the pilot?' she demanded, her normally brisk bedside manner giving way to anger.

'Pilot?' Mitch Lagoy rolled his head side to side against the trunk of the tree. 'There wasn't any pilot, miss. Just this busted rig with this piece of alien magic inside it. Christ, we thought we'd found the Holy Grail – then Jacks just threw it away.'

Joanna felt her heart knotting up with fear. She wasn't sure she could take this man's word at face value. From what she knew of Jacks already, she knew the woman would be more than capable of dealing with an Air Force pilot standing between her and a prize as valuable as the Stormcore. But what if the pilot had vanished like the cultists at the house?

Somehow, an act of cold-blooded murder seemed like the lesser of two evils.

Chapter Nine

Curt Redeker knocked back a mouthful of bourbon and rode down the burn in his throat. It was the only thing keeping him in the present, and he was glad he'd thought of it.

The clerk had taken his time finding it, but that had suited Curt fine. He'd had the guy set it down on the counter, backed him off with the gun, then snatched it up. He'd had to twist off the cap with his teeth, but he'd barely felt the bite of metal. And the taste of it trickling down inside, man, that purged those shakes right enough.

They'd threatened to return as soon as he'd sighted the smart guy coming for the store.

He'd wanted to break down and cry at that. Today was turning into an echo of his whole life, one rotten turn after another. No lucky breaks, not for Curt Redeker. No, that'd be asking too much, wouldn't it, Lord? Once in my life, one miserable lucky break.

Screw you. And screw this new guy if he upsets the boat.

Curt jerked the pistol again, backed the clerk up another pace. They were both of them tucked out of sight along the back aisle. He kept the clerk towards him, even though he couldn't stand that ugly mask staring back at him. Ha, scared out of his wits, yeah.

The door opened and Curt flinched, even though he'd known the bell was going to ring.

Curt's sweat was turning cold and clammy against the pistol grip. Quietly, he took another swig of the Wild Turkey and kept the pistol centred on the clerk's face.

* * *

'Hi there! Anybody home?'

Parker rapped his knuckles on the counter, then flipped his hands over to turn it into a drumbeat. He whistled. Boy did he miss his music. Melody rarely let him enjoy the in-car stereo, accusing him of hogging it with his prog rock.

Sad but true, he and his partner had such diverse tastes: she had none, he had some, as he'd teased her one time. He smiled as he recalled the minor bruise he'd sustained as a result.

With a sniff, he surveyed the store.

As the town's main store its shelves were stocked with the full range of goods, from hardware to groceries, and it was one of those typical country stores you expect to find in small New England towns. Even the trace of dust in the air seemed like it counted itself as part of the establishment's charm. It wasn't the sort of place Parker would ever choose to do his shopping, and the clothing department probably amounted to a few lumberjack shirts, but he had at least anticipated some personal and friendly service.

For the moment, though, the counter stood unmanned.

I want candy, damn it! Parker thought about shouting his demand and pounding on the counter with his fist for good measure.

He sighed, craning over the counter to see if there was a door through to a storeroom at the back. It looked like there was, but it was shut. Maybe the staff were sneaking a smoke or coffee break out there and hadn't heard him. 'Hi there! Hello!' he called again.

Parker wandered along the counter to the back of the store.

He could at least see if the door was locked, have a quick poke around. It was in his nature.

As he drew level with the rear aisle, something made him look right.

'Oh, hey, I didn't realise you had a customer,' he smiled at the clerk's back and the armed drunk in the corner. 'That's okay, I don't mind waiting in line.'

119

The drunk motioned for him to raise his hands. Parker kindly obliged.

Captain Morgan Shaw brought a gust of icy wind into the hotel lobby along with his small entourage. Derm and his NCOs kept pace, while Makenzie lagged in the rear. The tramp of so many boots jangled the chandelier overhead like a fragile tambourine.

A woman scooted out from reception and headed him off. 'Morgan Shaw,' she said. 'Your man said if I had any problems I should take them up with his Captain. He didn't mention it was you.' Then, as a quick addendum, 'Hello, Makenzie.'

Makenzie must have tipped his hat like the real gentleman. Morgan settled for a courteous smirk. 'Janny. What can I say? I realise this must be a major headache, but trust me, your hotel will be fully compensated for the inconvenience.'

Janny's eyes sparkled patiently. She was a robust sort, her brown hair only now starting to silver. Morgan was sure she'd keep her good looks right up to when they put her in the ground. 'Your brother always was a smooth talker, wasn't he, Mak?' she remarked. 'Now he's out playing soldiers in other people's back yards, he hasn't changed so much.'

'Guess not, Janny.'

Morgan grit his teeth behind tight lips. What was with these people, they couldn't see the uniform? Mak too, ignoring the Captain and treating him like a kid brother. Get over it. He had enough to contend with right now and he didn't want all his ire getting sapped before he got to the Doc. 'Janny, my team gives you any trouble, you have any complaints, take it up with Makenzie. He'll pass it on. Meanwhile, I'm kind of busy, so if you'll excuse me – '

He spun for the dining room, not waiting on her answer. 'You make yourselves at home,' Janny called after him. 'Just you take care and mind my fixtures, is all.'

Lord have mercy. He felt like he'd just talked to an ex-girlfriend, and he realised the whole town was like that.

Melvin Village. Once his home, she was familiar and even retained a degree of warmth when he thought of her; but man, the distance that separated them now was a chasm. And if he could get through this mission without having to cross it, that would suit him just fine.

Now where the hell was I? Oh yeah. Morgan threw back the dining room doors.

The Doc, the girl and Pydych looked his way at once.

'Ah, Captain, I'm glad you could make it. You'll never guess what we've found out.'

Morgan Shaw took a deep breath. 'Impress me,' he ordered.

Guns or no, Martha had wanted to scream into the guards' faces. The two soldiers posted at the hotel door had helpfully told her the Police Chief was inside with the Captain, and yeah, the girl was in there too. Then they'd stared back like she was crazy when she'd demanded to be let through.

While Martha wondered which guard to scream at first, a voice of perfect calm had said, 'Agent Quartararo.' A single flash of an ID set both guards standing straight, and Melody led her through into the lobby. Simple as that. Martha was annoyed that the woman had proved so useful. She didn't want to be fooled into thinking they were on the same side.

Inside the lobby, Janny Meeks lurked behind her desk, immediately giving Martha one of her holier-than-thou looks. A voice, like a velvet-stringed cello, floated out from the hotel dining room, saying, 'Whoever attacked your aircraft, Captain, they had to be after the Stormcore.'

Martha went over and yanked the door open. She was met by Makenzie's broad back.

Past him there was a small gathering of soldiers, a dark-haired young guy – had to be the Captain – facing a tall, bizarre character with a sort of permed lion's mane. Another soldier, with glasses and a face wrinkled like a pale raisin, was standing over what might have been a junkyard sale; and at the far end of the room was Amber.

Makenzie turned his head, surprised and not ecstatic to see her. The soldiers did an about-face. There was something vaguely familiar about the young Captain.

'But if your cultist friends had brought it down with some psychic assault, I can't help thinking they should have known precisely where to look for it.' The tall weirdo didn't seem to mind her intrusion in the least. He carried on flapping his battered hat about as he spoke, and she caught his words as a kind of backing track. 'By which token we should have found it at that house, taking pride of place in their collection already, wouldn't you agree? We're missing something terribly important. *Hallo*!'

Martha realised the man was addressing her, eyes all huge and friendly – and faintly disturbing. She tried to ignore the sudden attention and looked across at her daughter. 'Amber, honey, your Mom needs to talk to you.' Then she tugged at Mak's sleeve. 'And you, Mak. Something's come up.'

'Jeez, Kenzie!' the Captain threw up a prolonged shrug. Martha recognised the face then: Makenzie's brother. Makenzie didn't keep any pictures on display but there were plenty in the old photo albums. 'Can you please take your domestics elsewhere?'

'Excuse me, *sir*,' Martha chewed, 'but this isn't any place for my little girl. You want to tell me what she's doing in here with you all in the first place?'

Makenzie laid a protective hand on her shoulder. 'It's okay, Martha. She's going to help with a few questions, is all,' he told her. 'Five minutes, Morgan promised.'

Martha had shaken off the touch before he'd finished. 'Like hell she is!'

'Martha has kindly agreed to let me conduct an interview with the child,' explained Melody in such sweet tones that

Martha wanted to slap her. Melody took a step into the room.

'All due respect, miss, but who the hell are you?' That was Makenzie's brother, putting Melody under the microscope now.

Melody smiled pleasantly and produced her ID with a practised flourish. 'Agent Melody Quartararo. My partner and I have been assigned as supervisors on this investigation.'

Morgan Shaw circled away, then came right back to study her sideways, like a bird looking for a meal to peck. 'Are you sure you don't want some other investigation down the road somewhere? Because my last orders were I was taking pole position on this one. Nobody mentioned any supervision.'

The tall hobo sauntered into the melee, clapping a hand on Morgan Shaw's shoulder. It was plainly not a welcome move. 'Ah, Captain, you must be delighted. More people to argue with. How do you do, Agent Melody? Welcome aboard. I'm the Doctor.'

He had shaken Melody's hand before she was entirely ready. Next thing, the Doctor was thrusting out a hand to Martha.

'And you must be Martha Mailloux, Amber's mother. She's told me all about you.' Martha somehow doubted that. She rated herself as better than Curt, hell yes, but she wasn't a parent worth boasting about. This Doctor character was pumping her hand though and she'd somehow lost her power to answer back. 'You know, I'm a lot happier now that we have some of the people from Fort Meade on our side,' he confided.

'She's from Langley,' Morgan Shaw corrected him pointedly.

'Really?' The Doctor was suddenly fascinated with Melody. 'What's the weather like down there this time of year?'

A few grains of the agent's confidence seemed to have slipped behind her shades. 'Captain Shaw is perfectly aware that the CIA has a vested interest in this project,' she toughed it out. 'My partner and I have been in close liaison with the people at Fort Meade from the outset.'

'Well, what's a few miles between government departments?' The Doctor beamed around at his audience. 'I've heard a lot about the CIA too and I'm sure they have a great deal of experience in dealing with extraterrestrial forces.'

'Sorry, Doctor, but this is hardly the time or – '

'The time or place?' The Doctor cut Melody's quiet protest dead. In an instant he was swooping in, full of foreboding, the way Amber's grandpa told his ghost stories at Halloween; too scary for kids, Martha had told him year after year. 'Agent Quartararo, if you know anything at all about alien menaces, you'll know that they choose the time and the place. All we can do is have the decency to show up. Now, I'm afraid I can't be sure what these particular aliens might have come looking for, other than the Stormcore, but I do know there are extra-terrestrial forces at work.' He dispelled the doom and gloom as quickly as he'd cast it. 'And I think that's rather a good start, don't you?'

Martha could only wonder why the CIA or the Army would hire such a lunatic. Melody fidgeted behind an uncertain smile. 'Um, sorry,' she said, inspecting her watch, 'Doctor, Captain. You'll have to fill me in later. My partner's been a hell of a long time at the store and I'm sure you won't want to give your report twice. I'd better go see what's keeping him.'

She held the door open for a second, then made her exit.

Her departure left the whole room temporarily stunned. The Doctor's gaze followed her out through the hall, some time after he could no longer see her.

This Doctor and the CIA Agents were plainly as weird as each other. Probably came with the job, some need to act mysterious and make out they were more complicated than they really were. Hell, her life might be a mess, but she didn't have the range of hang-ups like some.

Making like the soldiers weren't there, she pushed her way into the room to fetch Amber.

* * *

'Pydych, how's the lab coming?'

'That Meeks woman has a couple of staff clearing another room now, sir.'

'Well, go help them. Colgan, Kurzyk,' Morgan spoke to his NCOs, a fine-featured brunette and a guy with a hide of tanned leather. 'Grab some guys and make sure it's set up within the next thirty minutes, tops.' Salutes exchanged, he was moving over to intercept Martha. 'Miss Mailloux, I'm afraid I'm going to have to ask that your daughter stays a short while longer. Just to answer a few simple questions, that's all.'

Makenzie wanted to go to Martha's rescue. His brother could be a pain in the ass, most especially when he was trying to take charge of everything. Makenzie had enjoyed seeing him lose it when the CIA woman showed up.

Ideally, he should rescue Martha and take her and Amber out to the hall at least. But in the first place, he'd made a deal with Morgan for those men. And in the second place, he wanted to stay and hear more talk about aliens and psychic assaults, precisely because of how nuts it all sounded. The more fantastic the threat, the less real the danger seemed to Laurie and those other folks.

Martha had a hold of Amber's hand. She dared Morgan to stop her.

Makenzie stepped forward, but the Doctor guy interrupted him. 'Actually, Captain Shaw, that really won't be necessary. Amber told me the full story and she might even be able to show us where to find the parachute if you have a map handy.'

Martha looked surprised to hear support coming from that angle. She used it to shore up her stance against Morgan. 'Right. And even that won't be necessary, because those CIA people brought your precious chute with them. It's out in their car. Maybe you want to go talk to them, because Amber has to meet her Daddy.'

'He's here? Daddy's here? Mom?'

Martha started towing Amber across the room and she

almost reached Makenzie before the news had fully congealed. He barred Martha's exit with his arm. 'Curt's in town? Well, that means – ' Christ, he didn't know what it meant. 'He can't be.'

'What're you talking about, he can't be?' Martha planted her free hand on her hip, her features trembling with the promise of tears. 'Mak, he called me, I spoke with him on the phone. He's going to see Amber and go. Now you can be with me on this, or you can – '

'Martha, listen.' Makenzie was acutely aware of Amber following every word, but it had to be said. 'The – guy drove his car into a tree. But he wasn't there. He vanished, Martha, like those other folks. Like – ' But he couldn't say the name.

The Doctor slipped into view beside Amber. 'What other folks exactly?'

Makenzie sounded hoarse as he said, 'Out on 109.' He gave a summarised account of everything he and Laurie had found, and everything they had not. The Doctor kept a hand on Amber's shoulder, as though to cushion her from what she was hearing. The little girl looked lost, unsure of what face she should show. Makenzie focused on Martha, watching her trying to get her head round it. He finished up, adding, 'All the other cars were just parked up in the road. But he'd been drinking, Martha. He was drinking and he drove himself into a tree.'

That set Martha ablaze. 'Take the moral high ground, Mak, but I don't think my baby girl needs to hear that kind of stuff about her Daddy.'

Amber's eyes darkened as they fell. Makenzie felt like a heel. 'It's the truth,' he said.

As he led Martha and Amber outside, he noted that the Doctor had left the family group to sort out their own problems. The guy clearly wasn't as crazy as he made out.

Melody hurried her pace along the street, taking care not to slip in the snow, and wondering if she was being unnecessarily paranoid. Not over Parker: she could picture her partner trapped in a dilemma over whether to buy Reece's Peanut Butter Bars or a couple of Twinkies. No, that had just been the best feint she could think of to get herself out of there.

Her real concerns were about the Doctor.

She'd spent months down at Fort Meade running psych evaluations on graduates of the Agency's Grill Flame programme; not so long ago that she'd forgotten how to recognise a higher intelligence when she met one.

More significantly, she was sure she had read a file or several on a character going by that same alias. Parker was a wizard at remembering the most obscure facts and she needed to consult him before she was a hundred percent sure. Ninety-nine simply wouldn't do.

Besides, if her suspicions about this Doctor held water, she would need her partner's backup as well as his input in deciding what to do next.

Those thoughts carried her up the steps to the store. They were replaced by a whole new set from the instant she turned the handle on the door.

Her partner was standing with his hands up, looking along the back aisle.

Melody eased the door open and reached inside her coat.

The bell rang above the door. She swore silently.

'Who's there? Who the hell's just come in?' a man's voice demanded, spitting its words.

Melody executed a quick scan, looking up towards where the walls met the ceiling. There: over in the middle of the right wall, just above the pet foods and cleaning products. No CCTV camera here. Only a security mirror.

And in it: Parker's most immediate problem.

The figure's back was hunched and distorted in the mirror, but Melody could see the pistol, an automatic, and she could even recognise the label on the bottle. The hint of another figure curled around the edge of the mirror. The question occurred to her, was the drunk helpfully debilitated, or was he experiencing one of those moments of clarity?

It could, she decided as she drew her own gun, make all the difference.

Now that he had the Doc pretty much all to himself, Morgan was hopeful of getting a rein on his famous good mood. Chaos was okay; he could handle chaos, but only as long as it eventually learned to do what it was told.

'All right, Doc, what's the something important we're missing? Other than the flight recorder and a million other pieces of my aircraft?'

The Doc snapped out of whatever deep thoughts he'd been having and answered with a scowl. 'Do you have to keep shortening a perfectly good name? How would you like it if I started shortening all your precious codenames or addressing you as *Cap,* hmm?'

Morgan stared. This was not going to plan.

'Information, Captain Shaw,' the Doc regarded him at a curious angle. 'Perhaps you can fill in more of the blanks than you realise. For instance, tell me what happened from your point of view. Presumably your team must have been monitoring the flight from the ground.'

Morgan took a moment to realise they were back on track again. 'Absolutely. Constantly. Right up until we lost radio contact, radar contact and – everything.'

'Everything?'

'Everything.' Morgan sighed. The Doc wasn't going to settle for scraps. 'Kristal was in direct psychic – I don't know – *communion* with the Stormcore. Theory was, by manipulating the device's emissions, she manipulated the weather system. It was her directed Psi waves that kept it active. She was our co-pilot on the ground, if you like.'

'I don't like, but do go on.'

Morgan couldn't help wondering what Derm was thinking, seeing his 'Cap' put on the spot like this. What the hell, he needed to feel they were getting somewhere.

'All right. The Stormcore allowed for the transmission and reception of commands or data, what the Grill Flame techs termed psychosensation. Or what Kristal calls clairvoyance. You ask me, the name doesn't matter. What matters is, she was getting all kinds of data back from the device – visual, IR, radar, the whole spectrum – seeing through every one of its senses. Then,' he made a cutting motion with his hand, 'zip.'

'Well there you are,' concluded the Doc, as if that solved it.

'There I am what?'

The Doctor held his gaze for a heartbeat. 'If the Stormcore was kept active by Kristal's directed psychic energies, and then it suddenly cut out, I think we can safely assume her psychic link was cut. Or jammed.'

'That's one hell of an assumption.'

'Well,' considered the Doctor at length, 'it would be. But then again, I have the benefit of some additional insight.'

'Which is?' He wasn't going to stand for the Doc holding out on him now.

'Let's just say, I know how she feels.'

Curt listened intently for footsteps after the door had closed. The clerk's face in front of him was a stone mask. The man who'd introduced himself as Parker had instructed whoever it was to leave before Curt had thought of how he wanted to play it. He was furious with the guy for stealing the initiative.

'You bastard. They'll go and call the cops.'

'Well, maybe, but I think the cops in this town are busy, you know.' The man called Parker shrugged an apology. 'Anyway, I don't think that old lady saw anything too suspicious. Me with my hands up, is all. And I'm pretty sure she couldn't have seen Mr Byers here.'

Curt made a face like he was in pain, although he couldn't feel much of anything. Nothing distinct anyway. Only the threads of cold running through him and the sweat all over, making him shiver. It was getting to be the gun was the steadiest part of him.

Curt concentrated. No, there was nothing. The old lady must have gone like the guy said. Nobody could move that quietly, not on these old boards. And yet, he could swear he felt another presence in the room.

The man, Parker, spread his hands wider. 'We've got some time to talk, pity to waste it.'

'Shut the hell up! I'm trying to think.'

The clerk hadn't budged and Curt could see the tiny nervous tremors in his facial muscles. Those minute tics were starting to aggravate. He thought about putting a bullet into that stone face – then another in the face beyond it. The one with all the pretence of friendship.

'I don't know you. You're not my goddamn friend.'

'Hell, no!' shouted Parker, and the volume was like a shock of hot water. 'You're pointing a gun in my approximate direction here and it's making me nervous. I get real talkative when I'm nervous, it's a bad habit I know but what can you do to break a habit. Huh? I mean, I have a hard enough time trying to kick the smokes, you know what I'm saying?'

The rising tone was driving Curt into a panic. He felt pearls of pure ice standing out on his forehead and his breathing was feverish. He was on the verge of whimpering as he poured every grain of energy into keeping the gun on Parker. He could sense a danger here, feel it coming at him like a freight train, but all he knew for sure was he couldn't take his eyes or the gun off that man. Not for a second.

'Drop the gun and get down on your face *NOW!*'

The power of decision was gone. He was pure reflex. He wheeled around, swinging the gun onto the woman. Two shots shattered the air. The noise burst inside of him.

Then he was dropping, straight down, listening to the pinprick chimes of breaking glass. The golden smell of whisky sprayed everywhere.

He was on his back and the store was spinning.

The woman stood over him with her gun aimed down at his chest. His chest, where it hurt the most. He didn't know where his own gun had gone. He couldn't feel it in his hand any more. Then he heard it, skittering down the aisle, as the woman kicked it away.

The man, Parker, floated into view.

'You tried looking in a mirror lately, pal?' he said. 'You really don't look so good.'

Curt cried, feeling the tears pool in his eyes. Shadows gathered inside him.

'Amber? My little girl?' His voice sounded small, like a child's.

'I'm sorry,' the woman told him. She tucked her gun slowly out of sight, and she knelt beside him with one hand outstretched. Her palm came down over his eyes and suddenly it dawned that he was never going to see Amber again. He fought to build a picture of her in his mind, but somehow it kept coming out as a blur of white.

Then the storm in Curt Redeker's head fell silent.

Chapter Ten

Bad visibility was so much worse when you were riding down the mountain flat on your back. Despite all the painkillers, Paul Falvi felt the stretcher ride bouncing his gut around, as he watched his world go by through a filter of cold and pain.

There was no shine to the silver in the branches overhead, the surrounding white having lost the last of its brightness. Withered arms of trees tossed blanched confetti down on the procession and Falvi thought, blearily, that this was no wedding march.

No, man, this is my funeral. No offence to Eastman's skills, but he wasn't expecting to make it down this mountain. But every time he felt a shaft of pain, he'd grab onto it and use it to strengthen his resolve. Oh yeah, he *was* going to make it.

He was in good hands, the best. Cocooned in a sleeping bag, plus an extra blanket, borne along by a couple of angels. Well, Eastman and Barnes. Probably lost their halos a long time ago, but they both had sun in their eyes, even on a cold day. Shame was, he was getting all the wrong view of Barnes – and he had to lift his head for a proper view of that.

'I know what you're doing, Falvi,' spoke Eastman from on high.

Falvi laughed, and winced. He let his head drop back again. Man, that was hard work. 'Hey, tell Barnes these uniforms don't do squat for her figure.'

'Let me know when Donna Karan lands that Army contract.' Barnes tried a glance over her shoulder, tough work in the hood. 'How you doing back there?'

'Been better.'

Falvi rolled his head to the left. Pelham was tramping along by their side, the grenade launcher giving his M4 rifle a serious double chin. Seen through a haze of drugs, mist and pain, he was a lot less ugly. Falvi wanted to laugh again but it felt like he might retch.

Anyway, he could just make out the Lieutenant, moving down between the trees, all on his own and taking lots of looks around.

Well he might. He'd let everyone know how caution was his watchword.

'Son of a bitch. He could've let you take them, Barnes. Eyes closed, no sweat.'

The words were a battle, but he had to say them. Pelham was close enough to hear, but Sergeant Bederman, with his permanently stern gaze and a face of bevelled edges, was out on the wing, past Pelham and safely removed from the conversation. Barnes was quiet a while.

She said, 'Let it go, Falvi. It was Hmieleski's call.' The hang of her head and shoulders said the rest. 'The Kristal Ball is going after her.'

'I heard.'

Falvi straightened his neck, aimed his eyes at the sky again. Except of course it wasn't there. The white ceiling was too solid and too low to be called cloud. It smothered the treetops, hurling flakes of itself everywhere, like a moulting blanket thrown in the air. If he slipped away now, unconscious or the alternative, he supposed he'd still be seeing white.

He rolled his head again for another glimpse of the Lieutenant. McKim was the vaguest of silhouettes, walking into a lot of nothing.

'What worries me, it's what they might be dragging her into.' His thoughts travelled on ahead, following McKim into the snowfall. 'You know?'

For a moment, he thought nobody had heard him. Like

maybe he had drifted off and the real world carried on into his dream.

But then he could see the hollow response in Pelham's gaze at least. Nobody wanted to talk about it. What they'd witnessed at the house. Before the fire, before Hmieleski got nabbed.

'Maybe they're still out there,' he suggested hoarsely.

'What?' Barnes was annoyed at being spooked, he could tell.

The bad part was he wasn't playing games. Suddenly Falvi really believed it. That had to be the truth: the cult had staged everything. Blown each other away in a frenzy, and now they were ghosts stalking the landscape. Ghosts, at one with the winter. Cold and dead and white.

It made sense. Scary sense.

Falvi blinked and lay back to get a rein on his breathing. Stupid. Getting worked up over a hunch. He kept it to himself and watched the grey branches pass overhead.

The sound of the shots soared over the snowbound town like a couple of distant jets, one chasing the other's tail. Makenzie pressed on Martha's and Amber's shoulders, as if to plant them where they stood, then he was running for the store.

He'd been trapped in a fight with Martha over that deal he'd made with Morgan. Fair enough; but he'd had a bellyful of quarrels since Morgan had turned up, and he'd been searching for a quick excuse to duck out. Gunshots, though, were not a welcome pretext.

When he reached that door, Makenzie knew the drill. He took it slow, stole a good look round past the edge of the window, and he went in with his revolver up. The adrenaline was up a little higher.

The bell sounded a lonely note as he entered. Hal's store was routinely quiet. The whiff of smoke told him this wasn't routine. Makenzie knew he was too late: the shots had been fired. Hal Byers was on his feet, walking out from the end aisle and mopping his face and brow with a big handkerchief.

'Mak,' he motioned to the aisle. 'They took care of it.'

Taking him at his word, Makenzie holstered his pistol and went around to check it out.

He should have expected to find the CIA woman and her partner: she'd said she was going to look for him here. The identity of the body on the floor, rather than the death, was the shock.

Makenzie felt like his gut had been scooped out, the rest of his insides sinking to fill the pit.

The Quartararo woman stood up from examining the corpse. Her partner, built broad like Makenzie, thrust out a hand and a smile way too warm for the situation.

'Agent Parker Theroux, pleasure to meet you. We had a minor hold-up situation here, but as you can see it's all under control. It's cut-and-dried, open-and-shut, a closed case on your books, Chief.' The smile perked up a touch. 'I'm sure we're not going to run into any jurisdictional difficulties on this one.'

Makenzie shook his head and chewed on the air between his teeth. He could see the gun on the floor and Hal had pretty much told him the rest. The paperwork was the least of his headaches on this one. Yeah, he'd definitely had a bellyful of squabbling.

'No argument from me,' he assured the agent. Then he took a second look at the dead man. 'What's that all over his face?' He walked up the aisle, closer. 'Ice?'

Joanna extended her arms behind her, ready to be bound again. She felt Jacks grab her roughly and wind the cord around her wrists, and stood still through all of it.

'You're being remarkably co-operative. And it's a little early in the day for Stockholm syndrome to be setting in.' Jacks' sarcasm was truly vicious. 'I'm beginning to suspect you have a plan in that pretty head of yours.'

Joanna rolled her eyes, forgetting that her patient was in front of her. He had managed to stand, doubtless eager to prove himself to Jacks. He was wobbly already, leaning against a tree. Joanna was sure he wasn't sharp enough to have noticed a facial expression.

She didn't rate his chances. Three 9mm rounds were still lodged in his chest. The entry wounds were close together, down and in a few inches from the armpit. There were no exit wounds and God only knew where those bullets were now, rolling around in there, slicing and dicing as they travelled. All she'd been able to do was dress the wound and attempt to staunch the bleeding. First aid on a major surgical case.

Ben McKim may have shot the guy, but she was going to preside over his death.

Jacks tested the cord with a hard tug, then yanked on Joanna's arms to turn her around. 'Maybe I'd best see if you're packing anything else besides that nice H&K.'

Joanna's spirits slumped some more. Knocked out of her hand right after the gas can hit her face, her weapon was probably nothing more than a puddle of molten metal and plastic in whatever was left of the house. About as effective, she concluded, as it had proved in her highly trained hands.

But no, the loss of her sidearm wasn't any cause for depression. It was what Jacks was sure to discover when she started patting her down – like she was doing this instant.

'Is paranoia like an entry requirement for cults?'

'I just like to be careful.' Jacks was working her way from the boots up. Joanna was grateful for the layers of her winter uniform, minimising the intimacy of those touches and preventing her skin from crawling. 'No doubt your CO tells you the same.'

The patting and squeezing climbed Joanna's hips to her waist. Finally, she decided she wasn't going to stand it any longer. She backed off. 'Hey, if this is what you do for kicks, hand yourself in and wait for a nice long prison term!' She had to keep the words coming, not give the woman a chance. Behind her, Mitch Lagoy actually laughed, which would hopefully spread the venom. 'You're not going to find anything. A knife, a pistol, I don't carry any of that. I travel light.

'All you're going to find,' she reasoned a spoonful of the truth might be the best medicine for Jacks about now, 'are documents – some kind of operation you people were planning, as far as I can make out, which I don't think you're in any position to carry out any more, what with two of you on the run and one of you dying.'

There it was: she'd blown her ace. And she wasn't a gambler. She braced herself for the punch or kick or whatever was flavour of the moment with Jacks, but the woman only stood there, a scowling statue in the snow. Joanna didn't flinch.

'Don't be sure what I can or can't do,' said Jacks after a silent age. Her eyes burned black, but she spoke like she was drugged. 'Keep them. They're not going to do you any good.'

In light of what that implied, Joanna knew she'd be pushing her luck to take this any further. Still, the military had taught her that once the initiative was seized you take it as far as you can. Morgan Shaw used the football analogy: if you have the ball, run with it until somebody sacks you.

In those papers, she'd skimmed maps, schematics, plans of buildings, particularly the observatory, and even the Cog Railway that snaked up the state's highest peak. There was even a host of meteorological data, including hard copy radar maps; downloaded via the web and printed on a cheap Desk-Jet from the look of it. A sketch plan of the Observatory had been penned over in red, marked with boxes and scrawled notations, energetically drawn arrows shooting in on the plan from all angles. Joanna had seen the kind of thing a hundred times, albeit more professionally rendered. Troop deployments and tactical projections, each box representing what the cult might label an infantry squad. Terrorist squad, more like.

'What were you thinking? An assault on Mount Washington

Observatory? What was that supposed to achieve?' There wasn't any useful objective she could determine, but then she realised she was thinking like a sane person. 'Or was it one of those end of the world things, where you go climb the nearest hill and sing hymns?'

Actually, it was the weather maps that concerned her most: something in those radar pictures that didn't look right even to her untrained eye. Unnatural patterns, which she was convinced the Doctor would be able to decipher the moment he saw them. *If* he saw them.

Jacks had already stopped hearing her. She marched right up and swung her AK. The wooden butt clubbed Joanna in the chest and she dropped in the snow, the pain hardening like concrete in her lungs.

'That was Crayford's idea. Something about spreading the word.' She had the ball and she was walking away with it. 'Now we're going with my plan. So get up and get moving.'

Joanna struggled up from the ground. She watched Jacks heading into the landscape. There was a woman who could teach the winter a thing or two about being cold.

Leela was impressed with how smoothly Kristal had returned to practicalities. From the moment she had spoken with Captain Shaw, the scout had apparently put the storm out of her mind. It was a forgotten monster, a demon from a nightmare that vanished on waking.

Leela wanted to know more about how enemies might have used the storm to cover their advance or perhaps herd them over a precipice like Kristal had described. She knew more than she liked to admit of god-like beings wielding the forces of nature to their own ends. The invisible beasts that stalked the forest beyond the perimeter, for instance. No more than spears in the hands of the Evil One. Deadly powerful spears.

Puny, it seemed to her, in the face of the forces from which she and Kristal had just fled.

The snowmobiles lay scattered, flung against trees, or buried, their metal hides looking battered and scarred with frost. What damage it might have inflicted on her skin or even the hardy clothing she wore she could only wonder. And again she found herself thinking back to those inside walls of the scoops on board the Sandminer.

'A soldier – a warrior,' Kristal had told her, 'faces two opponents in cold weather combat. One, the enemy, must be defeated, while the other, nature, should be made an ally. I'm afraid our enemy has made the weather his ally and now that too is our enemy.'

Contact with the Captain had allocated them another enemy, and Kristal believed the opposition were as much at the mercy of supernatural forces as everyone else. She declared that in pursuing the kidnappers they would at least be back on a level playing field. Leela thought she understood her meaning.

'Marotta, how fit are you feeling?' Kristal had most of her squad assembled in front of her, while the two exceptions unearthed the last of the snowmobiles and checked it over.

'Fit to drop the sons of bitches who took Lieutenant Hmieleski. Ma'am.'

Ray Landers chuckled.

Along the slope, a soldier pulled on the cord that was supposed to bring Kristal's snowmobile to life. The engine gave a mechanical gargle and died.

'Leave it,' Kristal ordered.

She summoned them over to hear the rest of her briefing. Leela imagined this would be like the speeches given by a tribe's leader to prepare the warriors for battle. But Kristal made no attempt to stir her soldiers' spirits or fire their lust for blood.

She informed them, 'We're lucky. We're down the one snowmobile. It's probably a minor repair job, but we won't waste time. Everybody doubles up. Sergeant Marotta will take command of the main body of the squad.' She looked to the rugged-faced sergeant.

'They have a head start on us, but it won't be much. They've a wounded man, according to McKim. They won't be making more than a klick an hour.'

Marotta nodded, looking satisfied with the estimate.

'Their heading will take them over the mountain as far as the nearest town, where they'll probably try to get transport. Dorrs Corner is closest, or Moultonville. There's not a lot in it.'

'Maybe not a lot, Lieutenant, but enough. How is a squad going to find two – three people on a mountainside? In this?' He held up a big hand to the snow, blowing wild although without the violence of the blizzard. 'Give me a battalion, I might do it.'

'If I had a battalion, Marotta,' answered Kristal, 'would I be putting you in charge?' Leela wasn't sure if she was joking; and neither was Marotta, by all appearances. 'Take your men north east, cut in front of their escape path. Spread the squad in a line, say fifty yards apart. Leela and I will be making sure they come to you.'

'We will be herding them?' Leela jumped in. 'Like the buffalo?'

'Like the buffalo,' confirmed Kristal, and Leela was pleased she'd got it right. The Doctor would have been proud of her. 'Only Marotta is the precipice.'

'I never been called that before,' laughed Marotta, sharing it with the squad.

'If nature has been turned against us,' Kristal confided to Leela, as she led the way to their replacement snowmobile, 'we can at least borrow its tactics.'

But Leela was puzzling over how they might scare their prey ahead of them. The unnatural storm had had the distinct advantage of being utterly terrifying.

* * *

'Lester! Where are you at?' Then nothing. The same pattern repeated, like a snatch of Morse code, and it was the intervals that commanded everybody's attention.

Although there was nothing to see, Falvi kept hurting himself trying to look. His neck couldn't cope with the angles, and his ruined stomach sure couldn't. Each attempt had him collapsing back like he'd run a marathon.

McKim came marching back into view. His face was – bleak. 'All right,' he was shouting, 'everyone stay where you are! Sound off!'

'Who was with Lester?' Falvi needed to know.

'Cory,' Barnes told him quietly.

'Sturgeon!'

'Danciewicz!'

More nothing.

And that was it, Falvi realised: the only names to come out of the woods, up the trail to the rear. Bederman, Pelham, Barnes and Eastman added their names to the roll call, even though McKim could see everybody here. Falvi thought about throwing his own in, but was in danger of cracking up at the idea. At the same time, notional ghosts were haunting his head.

McKim stood there letting the snow blow around him. The moment stretched. Falvi saw the Lieutenant's grip tighten around his SMG. 'Danciewicz, Sturgeon,' he called into the storm, 'get down here!' Then he turned to the stretcher party. 'Pelham, you're with me. Bederman, take Eastman.' Buddy system. 'We have to find them.'

'Sir.' Pelham moved up with McKim.

Eastman and Barnes lowered Falvi gently to the ground.

Inside, he was hearing the timid voice of a frightened little boy. *Don't go, don't leave us,* it was begging. *Don't leave me alone.* He wasn't cocooned in the sleeping bag any more, he was trapped. It was all he could do to stop himself saying the words out loud. *Don't go!*

Stupid, crazy. Don't lose it now, Paul. Now is not the time.

McKim was looking at him. Falvi fixed on his eyes.

If he tells me to sit tight, I'll get up and flatten him, Falvi swore. But another silent oath was sworn in the Lieutenant's gaze. Falvi knew he'd do everything for his squad.

Determination drove the man's every step as he turned away, taking Pelham with him. Eastman glanced over her patient, and purged her concerns with a bitten lip. She was a mouse-haired girl, didn't have Barnes' exotic looks. She was out of her depth and she was most likely grateful to be going, to keep herself from giving anything away to Falvi. She shouldn't have bothered. They were all out of their depth here.

Bederman gave Eastman a pat and steered her off to the right. Falvi strained his neck, intent on watching until their outlines had broken completely in the swirling snow.

He was sweating.

Ghosts come out at night.

Well, if they did they were dumb. This, here and now, up on this mountain, was their natural environment. Perfect camouflage. No way you'd ever see them coming. White was hell and night would be a blessing, a release even.

Falvi tried to feel the cross at his throat. But there was hardly any weight to it and either he was as cold as the metal or his sweating had warmed it up. Was a cross any good against ghosts? He didn't know. He guessed it depended on what the ghosts wanted.

'Barnes,' he spoke to snap himself out of it. She was crouching down at his feet, the rifle off her shoulder and cradled in her lap. She said, 'Yeah?'

'You love that husband of yours?'

'I don't think I see him enough to know.'

'But he treats you right? He doesn't cheat on you or anything?'

She looked his way, an arch smile in the making. 'We have a policy: don't ask, don't tell.'

142

'You ask me, that's no kind of serious relationship.'

The smile grew by the smallest degree. 'Get some rest, Falvi.'

Falvi tensed, spoiling the mood he'd worked so hard to generate. 'Danciewicz and Sturgeon should have been through here by now.'

'Don't *create* threats,' Barnes warned, faintly edgy. 'They could have passed down twenty yards thataway,' she jerked her thumb aft, 'and we wouldn't have seen them even if we'd been looking in that direction.'

Falvi stared straight up. The wind blew screens of static across his vision.

'Lieutenant! Sir!' The voice rode up the mountain on the same wind.

Pelham?

Whoever's voice it was, a burst of automatic fire came right after it.

The Doctor passed along the street almost unnoticed, taking enormous strides as handfuls of locals watched elite troops laying siege to their village shop.

He saw little point in running. What with the Army, the Central Intelligence Agency and the local Police Chief, this town was overflowing with official bodies capable of responding to a shooting incident. Still, given that there had been no more shots following the first two, it was exceedingly unlikely there would be any lives to be saved.

No, far better to postpone his arrival till Captain Shaw finished capturing the building, or whatever it was he hoped to achieve with all those soldiers. Hm.

The Doctor glanced around, trying to pick out what he could between the buildings and trees.

His intuition hadn't betrayed him: the storm was thickening, like thick soup poured down the mountainside around the outskirts of the town. The winds were blowing harder, sweeping great plumes of snowflakes into the streets. Leela would be finding her adaptability and survival instincts tested to the limit up there. At least she was in safe hands.

White Shadow troops were on guard at the store, keeping a small group of civilians at bay while Lieutenant Beard offered them reassurances that everything was perfectly okay and there was nothing to see. The Doctor had his doubts. For now though, he was alone in finding something of interest opposite the store.

A brisk jaunt across the street took him to the lone truck, a civilian four-wheel drive affair, conspicuous only in that it had not been there when he had arrived with the Army. Unlikely that government agents would have left anything too informative lying around in an unguarded vehicle. Still, the opportunity to find more details of the CIA operation here – without the need for all that verbal duelling with Captain Shaw – was simply too good to pass up. Especially as the agents' arrival was such a surprise to the Captain.

That the vehicle was locked was a very minor deterrent, given all that the Doctor could see through the lace-curtain of frost drawn over the windows.

Making sure Lieutenant Beard and his troops were properly focused on their job, the Doctor tried not to look too furtive as he picked the lock on the rear door. Within moments he was clambering inside and pulling the door closed.

Settling back, he cast his gaze over the treasures littering the seat beside him.

He riffled through some of the documents, quietly absorbing the top few pages of each; but most appeared to be dossiers on members or suspected members of the cult. He turned over a few of the gadgets, examining each with expert indifference.

Amongst all the leading edge surveillance and communications equipment, there was a graviton distortion sensor that was definitely not standard CIA issue.

As well as a raised brow, it prompted the Doctor to wonder

unhappily about the number of spacecraft the authorities must have plundered. The Doctor considered confiscating it: the device was a possible – if imprecise – means of locating the TARDIS.

He returned it to the pile for now, and turned instead to the genuine prize of the cache, lifting it onto his lap and flipping back the screen. He wouldn't have a lot of time.

Rummaging through his pockets, he wondered if he happened to be carrying any kind of power cell he could readily adapt. He imagined CIA agents were the sort of people who might monitor battery usage on their laptop computers fairly closely. Even if they were relatively careless with their storage arrangements.

Energy was currency in some societies, and he wouldn't want to be accused of stealing.

The wind was getting pretty loud, but Paul Falvi was listening to the whispers underneath. Somehow the absence of sound was making itself heard. Whoever said silence was golden needed to be here right now. Barnes probably wouldn't object to the extra company.

They both thought they'd heard Eastman's shout, but that had been long minutes ago.

Three more bursts of automatic fire might have come from Eastman or Pelham. If McKim or Bederman had been firing, they wouldn't have heard it anyway: the Heckler & Koch MP5SD was a submachinegun with a finger to its lips.

Time ticked by to the beat of blood in Falvi's temples. The wind played Chinese whispers with the possibilities running through his mind. Whether Pelham or Eastman, the howling silence was telling him he would never know an answer.

'You see anything?' Falvi fought to keep the panic from his voice.

'I – thought I saw something. Maybe. I don't know.'

Barnes retreated, drawing alongside Falvi. He could

appreciate the closeness, but there were no thoughts of flirting in his head now. This was about security. And not any real security either, just a kid's false sense that because he was with his friend nobody could hurt him. Never mind that the friend was a kid no older or wiser than him.

For a while, he prayed to hear more voices, more shots cracking the cold air.

Beside him, Barnes held her rifle at the ready and scanned the woods. Great gusts blew in more snow to obscure even the closest trees. Even on his back Falvi could judge that they'd have ten or fifteen yards at best if anything did come at them.

Barnes raised the rifle to her eye. Lowered it straight after.

'What? What was it?'

'I – don't know. Maybe nothing.' She shook her head, nostrils flared and mouth all tight.

'Hey, Barnes, give me a pistol. Help me sit up.'

She stared down at him. 'Are you nuts?' She was about to add something more, but Falvi saw the change of mind in her eyes. Maybe it was the plea she'd seen in his that did it. Whatever, she slung the rifle and hooked her arms under him to start lifting. Falvi grit his teeth, but he let the pain out with plenty of volume all the same. In short time, he was propped against a tree, panting hard, and Barnes handed him her automatic.

She eased the rifle back off her shoulder and dropped down beside him and waited for him to flick the safety off before reaching over to clasp his left hand. She swallowed, then looked away. But she hadn't let go.

Now his arms were out of the sleeping bag, Falvi felt the cold all over. He searched around, waiting for the ghosts to attack from out of the white woods.

'You know,' he confessed, 'I only ever read that one bit of *Lord of the Rings*.'

Barnes pressed his hand tighter.

Falvi flinched and shuddered. Barnes' fingernails digging into

146

his palm were like icicles. Then he remembered: she was wearing gloves.

He turned his head, his breathing galloping away from him, and he saw that she'd gone. She simply wasn't there. He looked down at his hand.

There wasn't time for anything else.

Chapter Eleven

There was a rap of knuckles at the window.

The Doctor snapped the laptop shut. There was much more to be learned, but he would have to make do with other sources.

Lieutenant Beard stood back as the Doctor exited the truck. 'Hallo there,' the Doctor doffed his hat. He swung the car door closed behind him as a pretend afterthought. 'What can I do for you, Lieutenant?'

'Captain Shaw was wondering where you'd disappeared. They could use your help inside.'

'Of course they could. Lead on.'

Whatever suspicions the Lieutenant was entertaining, the Doctor let him keep them. Tracks left by vehicles were already refilling with fresh snow. As the Doctor trudged through the miniature rifts, he retraced his path through the information he had gleaned.

Mines of information were much like the conventional kind: labyrinthine tunnels and if you didn't tread carefully you could cause a collapse. Negotiating his way around the hard disk hadn't been difficult, but sifting the files for relevant information had been like panning for gold in the Yukon. It was somewhat distracting, if vaguely flattering, to discover numerous references to unrelated UNIT cases, including several of those in which he'd had no small personal involvement. Fortunately, surprisingly few of the key files were encrypted and those that were unravelled themselves swiftly enough in the face of a home-grown decryption program the Doctor had found hanging on a custom toolbar. That in itself was of passing interest, because the interface looked to have been written by an enthusiastic amateur.

A curiosity, but an indispensable tool nonetheless. The software trotted through a multitude of algorithms at once and blew down encryption walls without so much as a huff or puff.

The data confirmed what he had heard so far. Along with some behind-the-scenes secrets.

When Operation Afterburn was conceived in the early 60s, the CIA had been in possession of an extraterrestrial artefact they designated Prism. Grill Flame, their ESP/Remote Viewing programme, had confirmed the suitability of the device for a proposed application of those same researches. Unfortunately for the Agency, the application required a formidable psychic talent, and the Cold War had thawed by the time the first viable candidates had graduated.

Still, early test flights had been conducted during the 60s and 70s, while Agency and Air Force technicians worked out how to wire an entirely alien technology into their relatively primitive electronic systems. Given the limited number of personnel that could be trusted, working in the face of mundane threats like budget cuts and successive reappraisals, it was the work of decades.

One alleged clairvoyant reconnaissance of a sensitive National Security Agency facility sparked investigations and a pooling of resources under one umbrella, centred at Fort Meade. (You had to admire human perseverance in the face of a challenge, the Doctor supposed.)

Ultimately, Operation Afterburn had reached some sort of fruition. The device, freshly redesignated Stormcore, was mounted on a Raven Electronic Warfare aircraft. Monitored by the White Shadow team, the plane had flown a number of missions out of Pease Air Force Base, New Hampshire, in fair weather and foul. Until now there had been no incidents worse than a couple of routine electronics failures.

Schematics on the hard drive gave the Doctor both a better understanding of the device and an appreciation of how little the agencies understood their (borrowed) toy, however many codenames they chose to give it.

Various decrypted communiqués revealed the true nature of the project and its true aims. And they had very little to do with delivering rains to a parched Third World. An issue the Doctor would have to take up with Captain Morgan Shaw.

There were also copious notes and reports compiled during the latest series of flights, including transcripts of all White Shadow radio traffic, up to and including the cut-off that had preceded the crash. That final moment had been transcribed simply as: WHITE NOISE. The reports were an indication that Captain Shaw's team had been subject to CIA monitoring long before the two agents had announced their presence.

So perhaps there were other issues the Doctor would have to take up with them.

The assembly in front of the store was neither large nor densely packed. Too sparse and scattered to be called a crowd. Something bothered the Doctor about that, but for the present he placed it on the shelf with the rest of his concerns and allowed himself to be ushered past civilians and soldiers alike.

He pushed the door open and walked in on an already overcrowded crime scene.

'All right, go get a stretcher. And cover it when you take it out of here,' Captain Shaw was issuing instructions. 'His ex-wife and daughter are down the street.'

Two troopers headed out from the rear aisle, dispatched to fetch said stretcher. One acknowledged the Doctor and gestured towards the far corner with his rifle. The Doctor detoured down the middle aisle and around the end to the centre of activity.

Makenzie Shaw was there, nodding to his brother. 'I'd best go break the news.'

Melody Quartararo stood the other side of the body, next to a man the Doctor assumed was her partner. Behind the counter, he noticed a middle aged fellow, probably the owner of the store, sipping at a cup of coffee and looking at everything but the corpse.

The corpse –

The Doctor crouched down and fished in his pocket. 'Before you leave us, Chief Shaw – '

'Makenzie.'

'Makenzie,' echoed the Doctor gravely. 'I gather this was the man you told us about earlier? The man you thought had vanished out on the road?'

'The same. I should go tell – Martha. And Amber.'

For all his resolve, the Police Chief looked reluctant to move.

'Yes,' the Doctor shook his head sympathetically. 'Yes, I suppose you should. Thank you, Makenzie. You've been a great help.'

Producing a magnifying glass and a pencil, the Doctor delayed his examination while Makenzie withdrew. He started making slow passes with the glass over the victim's face as soon as he heard the bell ring above the door. He experimented with poking at the ice crystals with the tip of the pencil. 'Now there goes a man in an unenviable position.'

'Doc, I appreciate you joining us at last,' Captain Shaw leaned over, 'but Agent Quartararo here has already completed a pretty thorough examination.'

'Has she really?'

'That's right, Doc. My partner's got a list of medical qualifications long as – that scarf of yours. She's real thorough too. Never misses a trick.'

The Doctor looked up. 'Never?'

He studied the man who'd spoken. Behind the sunglasses, there was something to suggest he was the type who seldom blinked. 'Never is a bit like always, don't you think? They both make for impressive records if you can pull them off.'

The agent removed the sunglasses to present a pair of shining eyes as an appetiser to his proffered handshake. 'Agent Parker Theroux.' The Doctor shrugged to show his hands were full. Again, Mr Theroux wasn't fazed. 'For instance,' the agent cited, 'she noticed how it's a little on the warm side in here, all these bodies giving out heat, but those ice crystals on his cheeks have only just started melting. Like they're a little reluctant to obey the laws of physics.'

'And I suppose she noticed how they seem to grow through the skin like shoots?'

'Excuse me?' put in Captain Shaw.

'The tip of a very nasty iceberg,' murmured the Doctor.

Pocketing the spyglass, he used the pencil to gently tease back the collar of Curt Redeker's shirt. Tiny vines of ice clung to the neck, gathered into knots where the crystal structure jutted up through the flesh.

The Doctor rose in slow motion. This was the kind of discovery that demanded a temporary retreat. He regarded Morgan Shaw soberly.

'Captain, someone needs to conduct a post mortem before we can draw any definite conclusions. But I'm persuaded of one thing.' He cast a look at the two agents, then down at the body of Curt Redeker. 'Whoever shot this man may well have done him a kindness.'

Amber knew.

When Makenzie approached from the store to draw her Mom aside; when he said he had something to tell her, Amber knew. She knew something was badly wrong the way she always knew when Mom or Makenzie were mad with her. The details weren't always immediately obvious; sometimes she'd forget what bad things she'd done lately. So, like now, she didn't have a handle on what was wrong, just how bad it was going to be.

Avoided, left to one side, it was all too easy for her to slip free.

She heard them both, Martha and Makenzie, shouting her name. On the same side, for once. Whatever it was they didn't want her to know, she didn't want to fight for it. Quicker and easier to find out for herself.

She darted past a soldier and ran straight into the store.

All eyes turned on her. The soldier from outside followed her in. Mr Byers stood up to come around the counter. He gave her this awkward kind of look, and there was a flicker in his eye that he hid just a second too late. She followed it to the corner, then up to the mirror.

Miniature people were huddled over something. That was the bad thing.

She recognised most of the faces automatically: that Melody woman, Makenzie's brother, and the Doctor. Plus a man she'd never seen before. They were gathered over a dead body, blood pooling around it just like in the movies; only darker, less red. He was wearing a suit, but still looked kind of scruffy. He was –

Daddy.

There shouldn't have been anything to connect them, this thing reflected in the mirror and her Daddy. The two pictures just didn't match. And yet she recognised him. And the image in the mirror shrank, falling away to a distant point like Wile E Coyote disappearing over a cliff.

Mr Byers walked towards her like he was afraid of her.

Amber stared at him. Then he reached out to touch her on the shoulder.

'Get away from me!'

Hating the sound of her own scream, sore in her throat, Amber spun blindly and ran headlong out the door. The world had never seemed so far away, and all she wanted to do was run and run until it wasn't even a memory.

* * *

'Hell's *teeth!*' Makenzie tossed up his arm and watched Amber fade behind the screen of snow. He could hear Martha's trot slowing as she came up beside him.

'Leave her go. She could use some time to herself.' Martha was puffing, but Makenzie knew her pained expression had nothing to do with the run. She'd just lost the man she called a hundred different names and he had no idea how to feel for her right now. 'Christ,' she added, 'she probably would have run anyway, if I'd broken it to her gently.'

Makenzie couldn't believe what he was hearing. But then, Martha hadn't been out on that road. Martha hadn't lost Laurie.

'You don't understand, Martha.' He started for the store. The door opened and his brother was already emerging, along with the CIA agents and that Doctor character. Two troopers went inside carrying a stretcher. 'It's dangerous. The weather, and all.'

'No, I understand.' Martha stepped up to Makenzie, ignoring the onlookers and shooting him a look that was half-appeal, half-accusation. 'It's the plainest thing I've ever seen in those eyes of yours, Makenzie Shaw. Exasperation. You're about ready to give up on us and I can't say as I blame you. Nobody needs this kind of headache in their life.'

'Christ, Martha.' Makenzie felt everybody's eyes on him like the cold. 'I'll go find her, fetch her back.' He wanted to deny any sense of exasperation, feeling guilty in advance for the lie. The store door opening saved him, putting the rest of his words on hold.

His silence was joined by a collective hush as the stretcher-bearers carried their pathetic bundle from the store. Most everyone retreated as though afraid of the form covered by that plain plastic sheet. Not least of all, Makenzie, who watched Martha's eyes follow it as far as her numbed neck would allow.

Only the wind dared speak.

* * *

Parker propped himself against the doorjamb and stayed well clear while his partner marched into the room like she was storming the Bastille. She tore herself free of her coat and flung it into the nearest corner.

'Want to tell me what's got you riled, *honey-pie*?'

She paced around the centre table, flipped the sheet back from the covered corpse. 'You mean apart from your Southern-beau terms of endearment?' Flicking hair back from her face, she took a long hard look at her subject. 'That Doctor guy, that's what. He knows a lot more than he's letting on and he was playing games with us back there, I swear.'

Parker shrugged himself up from his leaning stance. 'Well, he would, darling.' He was piling on his Southern accent because he knew he had his dear partner rattled. 'He's Doctor John Smith aka the Doctor. Scientific Adviser to UNIT. I've got a profile of him on the computer – you want me to go get it?'

Melody sighed like an extinguished fire. Plenty of embers still smouldered. 'I knew it.'

'Those White Shadow boys did a good job on the lab, don't you think?'

Melody feigned patience badly while Parker passed an eye or two around the hastily converted hotel lounge. The soldiers had culled benches and tables from other rooms and neighbouring houses; equipment had been brought in from the vehicles and left a bare minimum clear as available work surface. A pool table had been rudely pushed to the wall, and its attendant light shone down on the grisly cadaver of the deranged perp Melody had plugged. The bar lights lent their illumination a little reticently to the scene.

'Great ambience,' concluded Parker.

'Yeah, well, why don't you fetch yourself a beer and I'll conduct the post mortem as well as worry about this Doctor poking his nose in where it's not wanted.'

'It's a prominent nose. The guy probably can't help it.'

'*Parker.*'

Parker beamed his friendliest beam and sauntered closer. 'Trust me, partner, I'm way ahead of him. The fact he's here could mean something, could mean nothing. You never know, a guy like that could prove useful. Meanwhile, we just stick with our programme and watch the situation like hawks.' He slid his arms around her and stooped to kiss her forehead. 'Now, you want me to go get that profile, learn a bit more about who we're dealing with?'

'Sure, I could probably use the computer anyway, when I get into the analysis.' Placated, she pursed her lips thoughtfully and tilted her head way back so she could meet his gaze. 'First, you can prepare me a few slides of those alleged ice crystals while I open up this corpse.'

'You're a true romantic,' he declared unenthusiastically.

He fished in his pocket for gloves and tweezers, and he was soon scraping gingerly at the barbed veins of ice still jutting up through Redeker's skin.

'Oh, come on! This project of yours has been about much more than flying aircraft through storms. Not only were you planning on generating storm fronts as cover for military flights, you're actually developing a system for directing those same storms against ground targets. Using the weather as a weapon. And you're trying to tell me you knew nothing about it?'

Morgan sucked in about as much air as he could take. Hemmed in outside the store, he'd packed those CIA interlopers off to start on the autopsy, but the Doc was refusing to join them until he'd had his say.

'No, Doc, I'm telling you I don't *care* about it. It's not my place to care. I'm given a job and I'm free to exercise my initiative as long as that job gets done. You might try it yourself some time.' He acknowledged the waiting troops and civilians, particularly conscious of his brother's sour expression pushing its way forward.

The Doctor cut in darkly: 'I don't appreciate being lied to, Captain.'

'And I don't appreciate being lectured, so I guess that makes us even. Give me a break, will you? Unless you have anything relevant to add, I suggest – '

'Oh but I have.' Somehow, the news came as no surprise. Morgan braced himself. 'Find that child, Captain. Do everything you can. And organise the search parties in groups of four or five. There may be safety in numbers.'

Morgan was getting used to staring at the Doctor like he was several nuts short of a pecan pie. 'Safety in – ?' He pitched his voice low. 'Are you saying who or whatever attacked Redeker – they could be here in town?'

He could see everyone around straining to catch the slightest word. The Doctor at least had the smarts to keep his voice low too. Somehow it still managed to ring just as ominously. 'My dear Captain, before we speculate on where they are, don't you think it would be a good idea to focus our attention on who or what *they* might be? It's very possible that man was contaminated in some way and if it's airborne in these winds, well – '

The Doc didn't have to finish his point and they both knew it.

Morgan pitched his voice lower still. 'Could we be talking biological warfare here?'

'Well, most warfare is biological,' the Doctor batted the question away like a philosopher swatting a nuisance fly. Not a gesture designed to appease. 'In the sense that living things tend to be involved on one level or another. But yes, we could be looking at some sort of viral agent, a biological weapon of some kind.'

Morgan steadied himself, his nerves walking a piano-wire tightrope. 'That's quite a leap, Doc. I mean, shouldn't you be weighing all the alternatives, like a good scientist?'

The Doctor pinned him with a steady gaze. He looked like some sort of mad butterfly collector, annoyed to find one of his more stubborn specimens still fluttering. 'Well, I don't like to be the bearer of bad tidings, but the fact is I can't think of any alternatives, and when that happens, Captain Shaw, everyone tends to be facing more trouble than they deserve.'

Sudden decision seized hold of him. 'Now, if you'll excuse *me*,' the Doctor batted Morgan politely on the shoulder, 'You have some search parties to organise, and I ought to make sure our two CIA visitors know what they're doing.'

'Great idea, Doc.' Morgan clapped his hands together and thanked a few unnamed gods as the Doctor made for the hotel. He didn't have any cause to be happy or relaxed about what he'd heard, but at least that was three people out of his hair now.

'Okay,' he said, 'now let's *please* have some order here.'

'Hallo!' the Doctor announced his entrance with a wave of his hat and plenty of volume. 'I was at a bit of a loose end and I was wondering if you could use an extra pair of hands and a scientific mind.'

The laboratory was a very makeshift affair, but that was the way the Doctor liked laboratories in general. Yes, a home from home.

Both agents looked up from their work: the young woman at the table, poised to make her first incision; and the powerfully built man slotting together some microscope slides over by the far bench. The two traded glances the Doctor couldn't quite interpret.

'You're qualified?' The woman's voice was slightly muffled by her surgical mask.

'In most things, yes,' answered the Doctor absently. He plonked his hat back on and scooted around to loom over Melody Quartararo's shoulder. She had cut away the dead man's clothing, and having presumably completed a comprehensive external examination, she had just marked out the standard Y-incision on his chest.

'Hm, you've done this sort of thing before, I see.'

'A million times,' she said, moving in with the scalpel once again.

'I do hope that's an exaggeration.'

Melody turned her head. She fumed behind the mask. 'Can we please get on?'

'Don't let me stop you. Actually, there were a few things I was hoping to discuss.'

'Talk to me.' Parker Theroux prodded his shoulder from behind.

The Doctor spun like a whirlwind and grasped a stunned Parker by the shoulders. 'Ah, there you are! I hope you won't mind if I take a look at those crystals while we talk. It'll save a lot of time. I take it you've got those slides ready, hmm?'

Parker blinked. 'They're about done.'

But the Doctor had barged past before Parker had finished speaking, making himself comfortable at the microscope and reaching urgently for the first slide.

'Well,' quipped Parker, rearranging himself after his brush with the Doctor, 'I realise it's a matter of life or death, but we could at least be civil, don't you think?'

The Doctor dipped a weighty eye towards the lens, not expecting to like what he saw.

'Oh,' said the Doctor, 'if my suspicions are founded in anything resembling the truth, Agent Theroux, life and death will be the least of our worries.'

Chapter Twelve

Darkness crept in like a conspiracy at the edges of Mitch Lagoy's world. He didn't dare steady himself against a tree: they looked so brittle and blasted they might snap under his weight. Besides, if Jacks spotted him, she might be tempted to shoot him like a sick dog.

Even the Army doc, roped like some rodeo calf, was doing better.

Course, she wasn't carrying the extra lead. The bullets nested inside, three hot stones multiplied into a thousand, igniting a trail of fire from his shoulder to his brain, warming the blood that squirted out of him and congealed inside his clothing. At the same time, an arctic chill had invaded his arms and his gut, while his legs had become dead weights that kept on moving like badly worn cylinders in an engine that didn't know how badly it was screwed. The shotgun badly wanted to drop from his anaesthetised grip into the snow.

He was sweating a paranoid fever. Despite the effort it cost, he kept glancing back the way they'd come, where the snows flew down to smother their tracks. Not like an ally; more like some malicious serial killer erasing all trace of the victim's approach to his lair.

Mitch felt hunted.

Jacks marched up front, her figure a broken transmission in the blizzard. So damn purposeful, like she actually had some idea where they were going.

The doc trudged between them, watching only Jacks in front, with occasional glances back at Mitch, which almost looked concerned. Or maybe that was just wishful thinking.

What he did wish was that he could hand her all three kilos of shotgun and be done with it. She could put a few shells into Jacks and get the hell off this mountain. They'd all be happy.

Jacks deserved it. She was –

Lagoy twisted his neck around hard. He came close to blacking out, but there had been something back there. Some motion that wasn't part of the storm.

No, paranoia.

Maybe another touch of wishful thinking; like he wanted something to pounce on them out of the whiteness and finish this. Could those Army boys be that good?

He tried for a tighter grip on the Mossberg. But as he faced front again the weapon was forty times heavier and the light drained out of his eyes. His knees hit the snow but he barely knew he'd fallen. He knelt there, fighting the dizziness.

He couldn't make out Jacks any more, and he wondered, desperately, if she could see him. Someone came at him out of the blizzard.

The woman: Hmieleski.

She stood there, hands tied and eyes burning. She'd come back on impulse and couldn't do a damn thing. Mitch wanted to laugh. Instead, he breathed hard and heavy, three times, before he planted the stock of his gun in the snow and levered himself up. The Army doc watched his head rise above hers, watched him sway a little.

'I think we're being followed,' he managed. 'Best keep moving.'

Her gaze narrowed minutely, the way Crayford's had whenever he knew Mitch had something more on his mind. Mitch swallowed and hefted the gun awkwardly. He couldn't look at the hostage, as he asked, 'Don't say anything to Jacks. She – doesn't need to know.'

He brushed past her and grabbed the woman's arm to shepherd her on.

Mitch wanted to rest some of his weight on her, but she

picked up her stride and resumed her prior position, a few paces ahead.

He was on his own again. They were all on their own.

Leela scurried up and stole the available cover on the left. The girl moved with instincts as animal as Kristal had ever seen. Her knife sneaked out like a puma's claw.

'They are close,' Kristal called through the spiralling shards of frozen air, 'but we still have over half a klick to cover.'

Leela blinked across at her. 'How far is that?'

Kristal sighed and trotted over. 'A short walk, in any other weather,' she explained, and gestured into the distance, far past where the trees dematerialised. 'If we're going to rest, we should do it now – and keep it short. Their wounded man will be slowing them, and Joanna will be buying herself some time. But they'll be pushing as hard as they can.'

'Then we should not rest until later.'

Kristal smiled, but looked away. She'd just heard an echo of her inner self. Outsiders knew not to show weakness in the face of their foster pack.

'We should take a few minutes to get our breath. Any more and we'll only start to feel tired.' Kristal welcomed Leela's nod before bending closer so the brim of her hat was brushing the girl's hood. 'If we do catch up with them, you might be better off with this.'

Her automatic was out of its holster and she was presenting it to Leela. She racked the slide and ran through a brisk demo – safety, trigger, point and fire, brace for recoil – knowing her student would catch on without any problem. 'There's only two bad people, you won't need more than the one magazine. Maybe not even that.'

Leela hesitated before taking the gun and felt its weight cautiously when she did. 'It is a good weapon,' she decided.

Kristal patted Leela on the arm. 'Stick it in your pocket for now.'

She wondered for a moment if she'd done the right thing. It felt like tainting the innocent – peddling guns to the savages. But there was no question, not really. No way could she let Leela go up against the armed and dangerous with only a knife.

Besides, she had an intuitive confidence in Leela.

Leela was the proverbial stranger in a strange land. But she was no alien to danger.

Bob Marotta worked his way along the line, fixing each man in place with a pat on the back and a few encouraging words. He didn't think any of them were convinced. They knew when their Sarge didn't like the smell of something.

Parking the snowmobiles and spreading out on foot, it had been a hard slog just getting here, and now they faced a waiting game in which no one would get any rest. Breathing was hard labour, even for Marotta, as he squatted down beside the last man along the row. It was Landers, laying prone and tugging a dead branch across in front of him.

'I'll be fifty yards out on your right, so don't go shooting that way.'

Landers settled his rifle on the improvised support. 'Ain't that a thin kind of spread, Sarge? We can't see twenty in this.'

Marotta sympathised. Time was short and they were committed to Kristal's scheme. 'Garvey's way out on our left. We'll just have to hope Kristal's picking up clear reception today. Just try hard to see twenty five, okay? That way no one's going to slip through.' He punched Landers' arm. 'And keep your itchy trigger finger off that grenade launcher. We want Lieutenant Hmieleski back in as few pieces as possible.'

'Amen to that.' Landers sighted along the barrel of the M4 – into a lot of nothing.

Marotta was up and on his way to his own position, the burden of the machine gun his consolation. 'Hey, Sarge,'

Landers called after him.

'Yeah, Landers?'

'Do we wait till we see the whites of their eyes?'

Marotta shook his head and strode out on the right flank. If that was the best Landers could do to make him laugh, he didn't want to hang around.

Joanna Hmieleski all but resented having to fight for Mitch Lagoy's life as well as her own. She didn't expect to choose her patients, but she could sure do without them taking her hostage. Captive or no, she didn't care to lose patients either. So at the end of the day, she knew she had to kick up a stink for another rest break, if only to take another look at the guy before she got to watch him drop dead.

The woman, Jacks, relented fairly easily and Hmieleski only stopped to question why while she waited for her hands to be untied.

'Toss me the shotgun,' Jacks instructed her subordinate.

Lagoy obliged weakly before sagging against a fallen trunk. The howling wind was everywhere, but Joanna could still hear the man's laboured breathing. She set to work, trying not to think about the woman with the two guns somewhere behind her.

Peeling back a flap of the guy's coat, she whispered, 'How many did you see? Following?'

Hmieleski watched blood ooze through sodden dressings. Lagoy made a sound somewhere between a laugh and a groan. 'It's – not your people. Not ours either.'

'Has to be one or the other.'

Joanna didn't feel the smile she gave. She could redress the wounds, kill some more of the pain, but this man was well on his way to the afterlife. The best she could do was hide the fact. If that really was the best thing.

'I don't know who they are. They're after us. Hunting. They'll get me first,' Lagoy wheezed, nearly smiling. 'Maybe it's just –

coyotes.' He gave a sick laugh.

Hmieleski bit her lip. He was losing his grip, finally. She stood and faced Jacks, who was a few yards off, one of the weapons shouldered. 'We have to get your friend to a hospital. ASAP. D'you understand? My outfit has surgical equipment.'

'What shall I do?' the woman scoffed, somehow harder than ever. 'Call them in?'

'There's got to be a shack, with a radio – or a vehicle – somewhere nearby.'

'You read my mind.' Jacks swung the AK in a quick gesture. 'Let's get going.'

Hmieleski stared. And held down a shiver.

She took a pace forward. 'You're not leaving him.'

'He's slowing us down. Badly.'

'Then run, goddamn you, and leave me here with him!'

Jacks stood planted, a coarse effigy of a human being. Joanna had no idea how the woman's mind worked, didn't want to know. She noticed the muzzle of the AK, tipped slightly downwards and she thought, *if I'm going to do this it had better be now.*

The thought wasn't even complete before she'd dived across the space between them and thrown herself into a brave tackle around the woman's waist. Incredibly, she brought the solid figure crashing down on her back. But Jacks pushed up and rolled them over.

Joanna spun with it instead of resisting and tumbled clear. She flew back at her opponent and cracked her across the mouth with her elbow. Jacks fell back in the snow and Joanna lunged over to pin her in place. She threw a follow-up punch and the woman couldn't quite pull her face aside in time.

Swearing and snarling at the jab, Jacks forced her arms up and fended off a third blow – and suddenly her gloved hands were closing around Joanna's throat. Two thumbs pressed hard and kept on pressing, squeezing Joanna's throat to what felt like a straw's width.

Choked and feeling her eyes bulge, Joanna was in a daze by the time Jacks hurled her backwards. She was on all fours, shaking her head clear, when Jacks kicked her in the ribs to send her sprawling. Just so she would be looking up when Jacks aimed the AK at her face.

Grateful to be on the move again, Leela knew what Kristal had meant: that if they had rested any longer, not only would they have lost the trail, but fatigue would have taken hold. Not that there was a trail, in the forest evaporating before her eyes.

She moved up behind Kristal, thinking about the weight of the gun she had been given, and marvelling at how the Native American woman could follow invisible tracks. Especially as this white cold dampened all sound and mercilessly killed every scent.

Kristal had explained that their prey's passage marked the land in other ways. Ways she could divine with senses immune to the weather. 'I know these lands,' she'd told Leela. 'They remember a passing creature some small time after its prints are erased.'

Leela stopped beside her and waited while Kristal scanned the storm.

'Are your homelands like this?'

Kristal met her questioning gaze fondly.

'Not really, no. My people's lands were mostly coastal lowlands and river inlets. We used to fish and hunt along the shores and rivers. I guess you could say we were among the more fortunate tribes, the government gave us lands within our natural territories.'

'The government gave you your own lands?'

'Well, they let us live there,' Kristal cast her eyes to the wind. 'What was left of us. So where I was born was close to my homeland, but it never felt like a homeland. In giving us the land, they had taken away our home. I suppose that's why I find it so easy to be at home anywhere. At home with the land, anyway, even if not the people.'

The concept was at least as puzzling as Kristal's shamanic powers. 'I do not understand.'

'The government set aside reservations for the Native Americans. They allowed us to live our traditional lives there, segregated from their civilised communities.'

'Like the Tesh,' Leela nodded sagely now, and angrily. 'They erected a great barrier to keep the Sevateem out and contain them within the jungle.'

Kristal showed her surprise. 'The government erected barriers too. They still exist. But our differences are the greatest barrier of all.'

'Then why do you work for the government?'

'Because as I grew up I became convinced that if you're to stand any chance of changing something, you have to be a part of it.'

Suddenly, Kristal threw out a hand to steady herself. Balanced, she clasped the hand to her head, and then drew it slowly down over her face – until a pained mask was revealed.

'What is it? What has happened?'

'I'm not sure. A loss of life I think. Someone in my squad.' Kristal bowed her head and took three slow breaths, her eyes closed.

Leela drew the gun from her pocket. Satisfied with the feel of it in her hand, she went around on Kristal's right and helped her up.

'Then we must go to their aid,' she said.

'Landers, with me.' Sergeant Garvey, pasty faced and dewy eyed, marched past and held up his radio. 'I can't get through to Marotta. Something's happened to him, I know it.'

Landers rolled over and was up on his feet in a second. 'Sir, you don't know that, sir.' When arguing with a superior, Landers always figured stick with the formalities and they won't notice. He swallowed, swinging his rifle up and ready.

'Sir, you think they took him hostage too?' Landers set off at a trot after Garvey. 'Cause I don't think they've had time to get here, is all. What with their wounded guy and all.'

Garvey's jaw was working, but the man was chewing nothing but air and saliva. He chucked back his hood and rounded on Landers with a half-formed fist. 'I don't know what to think, soldier, but I'm thinking back to that house from hell. Okay?'

'Know what I think, sir?'

'No, and I don't care to know.'

Landers sniffed. What he was thinking was that Marotta was alive and well with a busted radio. What he was also thinking was that if he wasn't, then they had themselves a badass *Predator*-type situation. If anything had taken Bob Marotta down then the last thing they ought to be doing was going out there after it.

Garvey went creeping ahead into a fog of fibreglass, SMG gripped too tight for his own health. 'Marotta! Hey, Marotta, where you at, damn you?'

The wind blew fear around with the snow. Landers shut up and raced after his Sergeant.

Mitch sat there like a corpse waiting for burial. He speculated on whether Jacks would shoot him as well or just leave him here bleeding into the snow. Funny, he'd always imagined himself being gunned down in a warm bank somewhere down South.

But the Army woman wasn't quite ready to die. 'Go on! Do it!' she was shouting her lungs dry. It prodded him to concentrate. 'You'll be free of your buddy here, you won't have a hostage. You'll be out on your own again, and I'll tell you what else: Mitch tells me they're right on our tail, so you fire that thing and that'll help narrow down their search fine!'

Jacks, the blessed Emilie, was silent. Mitch knew then she'd made up her mind not to kill either of them. He wasn't too surprised either when he saw her grabbing hold of Hmieleski and shoving her on her way. So that was how it was going to be.

'Wait. Wait up,' Mitch croaked. 'Army girl. *Lieutenant.*'

He had this blurred impression of Hmieleski then, turning to look back at him. She seemed impossibly far away, but he did his utmost to focus on her. 'You must know the truth, right? State secrets, aliens, all of it. Were we even close?'

In his mind, at least, he saw the woman open her mouth to speak – before Jacks shoved her on with the muzzle of the AK. He didn't even know if she'd heard him or not. Maybe he'd have his answer soon enough.

He watched his next moments tick by on a clock without a face.

There was that movement again. Out in the white. Not part of the storm. Not quite.

It was closer this time. But just as difficult to make out. It was coming for him.

And beyond it, he thought maybe he could see a pair of fuzzy silhouettes. People. But they were white too, so they weren't necessarily real.

Either way, they weren't going to reach him before he died.

One way or another.

Chapter Thirteen

The Doctor was peering into a microcosm. And much like the universe at large all too frequently, it was cause for the gravest concern.

'If I were you,' he warned, his eye trained exclusively over the lens, 'I would drop what you're doing and back away from that body right now.'

'Doctor, I'm in the middle – '

The Doctor leaped up from his stool and spun ferociously. '*Back away now!*'

Melody jumped back from the table, staring at the corpse as if she expected it to sit up and attack her. Parker rushed over from the doorway, in a hurry to play bodyguard.

'Whoa! Steady, Doc, you don't have to bite her head off.'

The Doctor met him face to face. 'Don't I? She might find it preferable to the alternative.'

Melody had taken advantage of the pause to recover her composure, and now she met the Doctor with carefully rationed patience. Her surgical gloves were dipped in blood, lending her something of a macabre appearance as she gesticulated with the scalpel. 'Doctor, you're clearly intelligent so I'm not about to dismiss your warnings – but you'll have to appreciate we need more to go on than a note of panic in your admittedly very commanding voice.'

The Doctor accepted the flattery sourly. 'I never panic. What you heard was urgency. The kind of urgency that's needed when lives are at stake. Even yours, Agent Quartararo.'

'Well, I'm safely backed away now,' the agent answered tautly, 'so we can all rest easy.'

'Oh, I doubt that.' The Doctor regarded the agents darkly as he approached the table. The corpse lay stretched and open, no longer a life extinguished; rather, a death given substance. 'Your gun may have put paid to this man, but it's highly probable that whatever invaded his system is still very much alive. I could be wrong, but I'm generally at least half right.'

He bit off two words for added emphasis: '*At least.*'

Charlene Lowell rolled onto her back and groaned. She'd been in bed way too long, but it was goddarn cosy and she didn't appreciate being woken by crazy banging on the cabin door. Crazy was right: the double glazing kept the sound of the storm out, but she remembered just how bad it had been last time she'd dared to look out.

Gary mumbled beside her. She reached over the covers and slapped his butt. He just grinned, his head firmly embedded in the pillow.

'That's all right, sweets, you just lay there. Lucky for you, I'm in a good mood.' She'd managed to drag him away from that damn CB for a few hours anyway: leaning over him, fresh from the shower, telling him if he wanted to get a response, he had to push the right buttons. Warm with that and subsequent memories, she sat up and rubbed the sleep from her eyes. Someone's fist was still hammering on the door.

She pulled her robe up off the floor beside the bed and quickly wrapped herself.

'If it's one of the neighbours come to borrow some milk, they sure don't like their coffee black. They can have one carton and a piece of my mind, they keep this up.'

For the briefest second, she wondered if it was Gary's wife, and she laughed at the picture in her head: Lynette on a crusade up from Concord, battling through the blizzard to track them down. She'd have to be one crazy-ass bitch.

Kind of like the woman waiting for her when she opened

the door. Except this one was packing an automatic rifle and pushing another woman into the cabin.

Loss, like a mountain of hurt, cut Amber off from the world and cast her adrift in streets, recently familiar, now altogether foreign. The snowfall was like fog in a blender and she ran on, ghosts of buildings haunting her from all sides.

Sobs racked her lungs and reddened her face even as she vaulted someone's picket fence and landed shakily in the snow. She dragged herself up and hared blindly down the side the house. Some junk tripped her and she dropped on one knee, steadying herself against the end wall. She cried her heart out and smothered her face with a glove.

A dark grey cold filled her insides. Her hand slid from her cheek as she hurled her scream at the sky. The sky that wasn't there.

Her rage cracked, dry and scarcely audible. It caved into a single, shattered sound: *'Daddy.'*

A slate cloud prowled at the edge of her vision.

Eyes like marbles: moon-bright colour locked in cold glass.

Amber's breathing was tight and rapid. She felt the blood draining from her cheeks.

The coyote pinned her with its glare. Saliva dribbled over its jaws and dropped in silver-wet strands to the snow. The animal looked mangy and shabby, a fur-clad skeleton. Evil, hungry. It sniffed and padded three or four paces toward her.

Beyond, towards the front yard, she could see more of them: patches of white and grey snuffling around the edge of the house.

It took her an infinity to stand and the coyote studied her all the way. It seemed to expect her to grow taller, none too impressed with her height. A few of its brothers and sisters shambled up behind, starting to show an interest. Amber had returned to the real world.

Low growls drove her back, her hand following the wall. She

nearly fell as she retreated around the corner, decided to turn it into a run.

She sprinted along the back of the house, her thoughts scrabbling around for some escape route. Where was Mom? Where was Mak? She could manage without them, she could.

Down there! A dog-flap in the back door.

Amber threw herself flat and didn't listen for the sounds behind her. She hauled herself through and turned to hunt for the catches. She found them and fastened the flap closed.

With a smile, she slumped down with her back to the door. Trembles took over her small frame, but relief escaped as a cloud in front of her eyes.

The floor felt cold through her gloves.

Ice.

There was a thin coat of ice over the kitchen floor.

Amber rose slowly, the ice cracking under her boots. Outside, the coyotes growled and sniffed at the back door; the whole pack of them, it sounded like.

Amber walked forward to where the kitchen door hung ajar. She pulled it slowly open and peered through into a lounge where sheets of ice fanned out over the rug. Some of it was broken glass, but the TV and windows looked undamaged.

There was a noise. Like a lapping tongue.

A coyote lifted its head to peer over the arm of the sofa. Amber's heart jumped. Her eyes dropped to where it had been licking. A colourful fish, fragile like a butterfly, lay dead, locked under the ice sheet.

The coyote snarled and curled back its lips to bare its fangs. Its starved eyes fixed on her.

'You're supposed to be intelligence agents – *think!* What actually killed Mr Redeker there? Or is Central Intelligence another contradiction in terms?'

Melody's patience, Parker could tell, was thin ice over cold waters, and he hadn't had any to begin with: this Doctor guy needed to be told who did the sarcasm round here. But Melody played the guy's game and said, 'Trauma.'

The Doctor had drawn them into his forum, patronising them like promising students to his brilliant professor. He wielded criticism and encouragement like twin prongs on a pitchfork.

'Precisely!' Parker was prepared to punch him if he stooped so far as to pat Melody on the back. He didn't and his grin faded, like day into night. 'And what, in your professional opinion, did you see in there?'

Parker couldn't believe it as Melody allowed the Doctor to direct her gaze over to the fourth – silent – attendant of their conference. Since she'd fired the shots herself, Parker guessed she'd skipped the painstaking examination of the wound tracks through the 'victim'. Even so, he'd watched her take her time over the post mortem, exacting as ever, peeling back the skin from her Y-shaped (*Y for yuck!*) incision, sawing through the exposed ribs and removing the breastplate. She'd been making the preparatory incisions prior to lifting out the tree of internal organs when the Doc had interrupted and flipped everyone's lid.

'I don't think any kind of professional opinion enters into it,' she murmured, a shade humbled by what she'd seen. Parker had leaned in casually, only to be rewarded by the sight of the central cavity infested with tangled roots of ice. 'But for what it's worth, it resembles the beginnings of a new nervous system, composed of ice. Except it can't be ice,' she added, 'because ice doesn't behave like that.'

'No, it doesn't, does it?' The Doctor, Parker was grateful to note, had shed his patronising tone. He stood expectantly, as though waiting for Melody to complete the puzzle.

'You think the trauma affected the invader as much as the host,' she deduced.

Parker followed the exchange intently, keen to stay in the loop. His face tightened as the Doctor laid a hand on Melody's shoulder. 'Not quite as much,' the Doctor qualified. 'Take a look through the microscope and I think you'll agree our invader was only stunned.'

Parker thought he'd missed something. 'Wait, what kind of *invader* are we talking about?'

'Well,' surmised the Doctor, 'I don't imagine it arrived in a flying saucer. Or a full dinner set, come to that. Some micro-organisms travel well, all the same.'

'So, what is it, some sort of germ warfare agent?' Parker made a meal of the words – one that was difficult to digest. 'An aperitif before the traditional ray-guns-blazing invasion? Well, gosh almighty, I can't wait for the after dinner mints!'

'Oh, I don't think we're expected to make it through to pudding. And I don't know about you, but I'm rather fond of pudding.' The Doctor hunched his shoulders and fell into an otherworldly frown. 'We could be witnessing the beginnings of something more conventional, I suppose.' With his lapels up he looked like an over-wise turtle, contemplating the world's troubles from just inside his shell. 'I'm not as sure as I was, and I wasn't very sure even then. But we might be in danger of forgetting Occam's Razor.'

Parker drew himself up. 'Don't sweat it. I cut myself on that all the time.'

'Parker,' Melody sighed, 'the Doctor's saying we should deal with the threat we know about before we go looking for complications.'

'Well done! I couldn't have put it better myself. Well, I could, but that would have been wasting even more time.' The Doctor marched for the door. 'Come on!'

'Wait up, Doc!' Parker hurried to bar the Doctor's departure. 'We don't mind helping out, but let's refresh our memories here. White Shadow's priority, as well as ours, is to recover the Prism, okay? After which, we can call in the CDC, the Pentagon or whoever we need to clear up this germ warfare situation.'

'We could stand here and argue about priorities, Agent Theroux,' conceded the Doctor, after a pensive delay, 'but I imagine our top priority isn't wasting time arguing about us. And if some of us don't adjust our priorities, we could all end up like Mr Redeker. Or worse.'

Worse? Parker twirled his finger rapidly around the side of his head and whistled. Melody just shook her head and rolled her eyes, before charging past after the Doc.

Whose side was she on anyway?

Makenzie Shaw was tired, trudging up to the command vehicle. He hadn't been out that long, but long enough to start seeing coy-dogs everywhere, and no sign of Amber.

Five troopers were assembled close by. Morgan appeared on the steps of the Snowcat.

'Kenzie, this is Lieutenant Beard,' Morgan called him up, introducing the tall black guy. 'He's my 2IC and I've instructed him to assist in the search.'

Makenzie stewed. He'd thanked the townsfolk for their offers of help, but felt the need to tell them to stay in one place, over at the station. He couldn't tell them why, but they trusted him. Only Phil Downey and a few of the other old die-hards had disobeyed orders and were out there right now, doing a house-to-house like they were some sort of militia. All the same, their devotion was to be admired. Whereas his own brother, of course, was too busy.

'Second in Command, huh? I rate that highly?'

'Chief, sir, we should find that little girl before nightfall,' Beard said. 'If she stuck to the town, she'd be a whole lot safer where someone could keep an eye on her.'

The Doctor chose that moment to burst forth from the hotel, the two CIA agents in tow. 'I couldn't agree more! We all need to be somewhere safe and warm! Which reminds me, Captain,' he pushed his way briskly to the front of Morgan's little audience, 'we need to gather all the townspeople under one roof. Safety in numbers, remember. And we have to do something to warn your people up on the mountain – not to mention my friend. They're all in a great deal more danger than they realise.'

Makenzie was almost grateful for the way this Doc took charge. For one, he hadn't cared to admit that the Lieutenant was right: he should have been thinking about Amber, not his feud with Morgan. Now he was anxious to kick-start this search.

Morgan wasn't happy. 'Thanks for the news, Doc, but I'm here right now trying to raise my teams on the radio. Meanwhile I don't have the manpower to go herding the good folk of Melvin Village out of their homes!'

Makenzie smirked at how easily the Doc put his brother's back out of joint. He sobered himself in the same second, command the best medicine for his flagging morale.

'Listen up. Lieutenant,' he gestured up and down the street, each end of which was all but invisible, 'I've conducted a broad sweep of the main streets, but I may have hurried a little. Maybe a couple of your men can go over the old ground, while we check out some of the other areas. And as long as we're conducting a search, we might as well knock on some doors and ask the folks to relocate. It needn't take that long.'

Makenzie could hear the pessimism in his own voice. He anticipated the townsfolk obliging willingly, but Amber was a difficult kid to track down in the best of situations.

The stairs were the other side of the room, on Amber's left. The coyote was closer to them, and the animal seemed to know as much. It studied her at its leisure, disinterested now in the pathetic scrap of fish locked in the pane of ice.

If it weren't for her tearless sobs, she might have forgotten to breathe altogether.

'Please don't hurt me, *please*,' she whispered, afraid of making any louder sound.

Amber tensed. But there was no strength left in her legs to launch herself into a run. She was terrified if she moved she'd simply fall over and lie stranded like that fish. And all the others, strewn around the carpet, dead and somehow unreal. Like the rainbow-tinted pair, their swim suspended in a frozen pool around the base of the lampstand.

Scuffles and bangs from the kitchen doorway gave her a start: a fight had broken out in the pack. Amber could hear them all snapping and growling out there.

The coyote before her padded into the middle of the room, wary, but building up its snarls in ferocious layers. That was when Amber realised she was playing a game of chicken: she had to be braver than the coyote.

'You get away from me!' she screamed right at its eyes. '*Get away!*'

It recoiled, ever so slightly, but that was all Amber needed. She grabbed for the lampstand, wrenched it free from the ice and hurled it at the beast with both hands. The coyote bolted back and Amber made a blind dash for the stairs.

Melody turned over the ignition and the low growl of the engine expressed her irritation admirably. Still, as Parker took his time settling in beside her, she felt the need to add something more. 'Just don't underestimate the Doctor. He'll pick up on every tiny slip.'

'What if he does?' Parker shrugged. 'Even the smartest cookie can be made to crumble.'

Melody coiled up inside. He could be so infuriatingly casual at times.

Still, they were meant to be assisting in the search. The Doctor question could wait.

The door was wide open and the wind was blasting in, driving the heat from every corner of the room. The cold only registered as a secondary symptom, ever-present but positively the least of Charlene Lowell's worries.

She hugged the robe around her and couldn't stop crying. She shuffled fitfully on her bare feet. Gary sat up in bed, wide awake and struck dumb by what was going on.

'Don't get up on my account,' the woman with the crew-cut pointed her gun at Gary. 'You! Get the keys to the pick-up.'

The woman's prisoner – Charlene guessed that was what she was – looked like she might be with the Army or something. But she stood perfectly still, head slightly bowed. Why didn't she help? Charlene wanted to yell at her.

'I said,' the voice broke in harsher than before, and something solid whacked Charlene across the face, 'get the keys to your truck.'

Charlene was in a spin, her legs folding. She threw out a hand to steady herself and the prisoner woman caught her. She stared into Charlene's eyes as she helped her up.

She sent a message clear as day: *do as she says*.

Charlene nodded, but she saw a motion past her helper's shoulder.

Gary – in his boxers – flew from the bed, diving for the gun in the other woman's hands. Horrified, Charlene fell back, and the hostage let her go. Gary actually had a hold of the gun, or so it seemed to Charlene – for just a second.

But the next thing she knew, all she could hear were these impossibly loud bangs that wouldn't go away, and there was smoke in the room, and there was Gary dropped at the end of the bed like a broken toy.

'Make yourself useful: find the damn keys.' The order sounded muffled, but the harshness in the voice was unmistakable. Charlene sat there, sobbing hysterically, her world in pieces she didn't even recognise any more.

Mercifully, someone kicked her in the side of the head.

The upstairs hall was like a tunnel, frosty light gliding in from the window over the stairwell. Amber backed her way along, scared to look around while she could hear the faint scratch of paws ascending the bare pine stairs.

Her heel slid on an old rug. She threw out a hand and caught hold of a doorframe.

The coyote loped into view, shining its eyes into the tunnel.

Amber gasped, but her voice had deserted her. The coyote pounced onto the landing and flew at her, fangs and eyes aimed up at her face. Amber forced a shrill scream and pushed herself sidelong through the doorway. She fell.

The coyote skidded on the rug.

Amber scrambled frantically to flip onto her back. The coyote faced her through the open doorway, head low and slavering rabidly.

Makenzie leaped the fence and pulled out his revolver. The Doctor and Lieutenant Beard weren't far behind, along with a couple of the White Shadow guys. But Makenzie wasn't concerning himself about backup.

The crowd of coy-dogs, milling and scrapping outside the Walsh house, had attracted his attention and he'd come trotting up. Earl's Chevy was parked in the drive and he had to wonder, *where the hell was Earl?* All he had for an answer was a memory of Laurie and the empty vehicles on the road. Jesus – and then the scream that had to be Amber's.

The soldiers spread wide over the white lawn, fingers on triggers, and started hollering and swearing at the dogs. Makenzie thought, the hell with it, and fired two shots into the air.

The pack scattered, some of them stealing bites out of one another as they fought to get clear. The Doctor, meanwhile, strode right up to the door and grabbed the handle.

Plainly, he wasn't much concerned about backup either.

The hotel looked deserted. Martha had the sense the whole town was out searching for her daughter. Well, hell, Martha hadn't asked any of them for their help. Amber was in a bad place right now, she needed to hide. She'd come running back soon enough and Martha would be there for her when she did.

Martha didn't get the special urgency this time out. Maybe Mak felt the need to over-compensate, now the girl's real Daddy was out of the picture.

Real Daddy. Sorry excuse, more like. *Goddamn* him.

'Help you, miss?'

That soldier with the premature wrinkles, Pydych, regarded her uncertainly from the doorway to the restaurant. He was turning over a piece of the aircraft in his hands.

'Where'd they take the body?' she demanded.

'Of the guy?' Pydych nodded hesitantly. 'Across the hall. But you really shouldn't be – '

Martha murdered his objections with a glance. He retreated back into his shell, murmuring an apology but appearing to lose his voice. Martha swallowed hard, then moved to the door. Only right and proper that Curt should be laid to rest in a hotel bar.

She let the door swing closed behind her, flinching microscopically, as her attention became the exclusive property of the dead mass on the table before her.

Its condition, exposed and sliced open, didn't even penetrate her. What sickened was how she still saw the living Curt: the self-loathing drunk who'd never known where to turn his hate next. The man who'd made marriage feel like breaking rocks on a chain gang; and the man who, when Martha finally slipped those chains, had hounded her from state to state for eight hellish years on the *pretext* that he loved his baby girl. Goddamn you, Curt Redeker. Why couldn't he have died in some remote hole, and Martha get a letter some day? Even in death, he had to break back into her life and hang around her neck forever.

Martha backed up to the door, nauseous. She turned herself around and walked slowly out through the hall like she was running on different time to the rest of the world. Every step, she had to fight back a fresh tear.

Martha paused out front of the hotel, trying to get a hold on her breathing. The cold air was waking her up, but she felt lost.

Snowflakes snagged at her cheeks like barbed confetti.

'Help, oh please, God, help! I'm up here! In the bathroom!'

The sound of the shots had been a shock to Amber and the coyote alike. Amber was quicker to recover and she kicked out hard. The bathroom door slammed closed.

Then she was on her feet, pressing herself to the door. She heard the door downstairs smashed open and she fumbled at the lock in a panic.

A heavy weight battered the door from the other side.

The inside of the house was surreal. Like the kid crying out from the bathroom must have been having a nightmare and they'd all stepped into it.

Dermot Beard had spent years schooling himself to think fast and react, and file away complex questions for later. This was one of those situations where he went into automatic pilot and he expected every soldier to react with him. 'Spence, stay put,' he ordered, before rushing to the foot of the stairs. Then he motioned his other man, Bertelli, ahead of him.

He showed a palm to the Doctor and the Police Chief. He was figuring on coyotes at worst, but after the house on the mountain there was no point in taking chances.

He expected an argument from the Doctor, but instead the guy relented and started toeing at some of the fish and broken glass. It looked like somebody's fish tank had exploded down here; no big deal as far as Dermot could tell. But Dermot was no scientist.

Bertelli rounded the top of the stairs. The young soldier's gun went up immediately.

'Bertelli, what is it?'

There was an agonised howl that didn't sound like any

coyote. And a thud-thud-thud like a heavy body was thrashing about on the floorboards up there. Bertelli was static, the barrel of his rifle wavering like he couldn't get a clear aim. The banging stopped.

'Bertelli!' Dermot started up the stairs, getting angry now.

He had Bertelli in his sights, but he still didn't quite see it: something stabbing out, solid and gleaming. Bertelli dropped his gun and clutched his face.

Dermot shrank back into the wall as Bertelli stumbled back over the top stair.

The soldier, Spence, brought his gun to his shoulder, sheltering behind the bulk of the grenade launcher. Makenzie rushed forward, hoping to God the man wasn't about to use that thing in here. The Doctor came up on Makenzie's left, but even he was stopped dead in his tracks.

The Italian, Bertelli, was being eaten as he fell.

The soldier was caked in frost and underneath it he was rotting away. It was like watching a time-lapsed movie, all super-fast: a joint of frozen meat, thrown through the air and consumed, packaging and all, by a plague of maggots. Except there weren't any maggots and the man was unravelling in a wire-mesh vortex, woven from ice.

All the while, Amber was upstairs, crying her heart out, begging to be rescued.

Charlene hauled herself up, leaving her long hair hanging untidily over her face for a few moments more. A few moments more of not seeing anything.

No, that wasn't true. If she lifted her eyes, she could see Gary vividly enough, even through the cascade of hair. The cruel holes were lost in the blood welling in his folded abdomen.

The carpet was damp under her hands and knees and she knew, while she'd been out of it, he'd been busy bleeding himself empty.

Their affair seemed stupid, childish, pathetic. Everything was pain. And Gary was free.

Then she remembered his irritating obsession with his radio.

Amber slowly uncupped her hands from her ears. The coyote out on the landing had fallen silent. Maybe it was dead.

The cries of the coyote had been so extreme, she'd endured them with her ears covered and her back wedged firmly against the door as though she might actually bar the sound from entering her sanctuary.

Tremulously now, she turned and stared at the door.

'Amber!' The voice was the velvet bass of the stranger. 'Stay where you are! Lock yourself in if you can!'

Amber wiped a sleeve across her eyes. She grabbed for the bolt and drove it home hard. 'Ow!' She snatched her hand back and sucked at where the metal had pinched her skin.

Thinking, glancing about, she went to the wash-basin. The medicine cabinet had one of those mirrored doors and in it she could see how pale and drawn she was from all her crying. Sniffing, she eased her hand from her mouth and looked down to inspect the damage.

The mark was minute, without the redness she'd expect.

But it burned all the same. It burned *cold.*

Where the unfortunate Bertelli should have landed, there had been nothing left of him to hit the floor. The Doctor wasted no time after that, dancing spryly sideways, and calling to Amber as he launched himself up the stairs three at a time.

Below and behind him, Spence and Makenzie had been manoeuvring clear of the ice storm that had erupted in Bertelli's place.

'What in the name of *God*?' Spence was practically screaming.

'Take it out!' bellowed Lieutenant Beard, on the edge of panic. 'Take it out!'

The Doctor stole a hurried look along the landing and saw what must have been the last thing Bertelli had seen: the very thing Bertelli had become. For the Doctor, it was like gazing into the microcosm he had studied under the lens. Before him, and now down in the lounge, it was magnified and translated into a livid mass of crystalline tendrils, shooting in every direction.

An electrical storm, frozen and re-frozen in a shifting nexus of white fury.

Some of the tendrils dug like spindly claws into the bathroom door.

An automatic rifle cracked fire. The Doctor glanced downstairs.

Spence was firing point blank into the maelstrom. Parts of the chaotic ice sculpture shattered like glass, but Beard was having to duck out of the way as most of the rounds shot straight through and blew the staircase to splinters. The Doctor threw up a hand to shield his face.

He caught a motion from along the landing.

The ice elemental fired forks of frozen lightning straight at him.

Chapter Fourteen

It didn't *move*.

It consumed itself. Particles of itself, burned up like white coals feeding a neural furnace, to be ferried along crystal threads and restructured as matter at the opposite end, in whichever direction it wished to travel.

A cycle as fast as thought. Inevitably, in that cycle, some energy was expended.

Energy that had to be replaced.

Even the Doctor's reflexes were pushed to save him, diving aside as the twin forks of iced lightning flashed through the air. Sparks of frost played over the wall behind him.

'Quick, man! A flare!' Huddled close to the banister, he snapped his fingers at Lieutenant Beard. 'Amber!' he shouted up the stairs. 'Do exactly as I say! Turn on the hot water – full!'

There was no answer, but as the Doctor caught the flare that Beard tossed his way, he *hoped* he heard the rush of water churning into a large bath. Difficult to tell, with the bursts of automatic fire pulverising the manic ice sculpture and the lower stairs alike.

Above, the icicle sparks were drawing an erratic spider's web through the painted wood, sending out strand after strand from where they had struck the wall, reaching for Beard, who was determinedly breaking open another flare for himself.

'Get everybody out of here!' the Doctor yelled at him, breaking the head off his flare. The two flares erupted like synchronised volcanoes. 'Now!'

Packing the man down the stairs, the Doctor was up and advancing on the micro-blizzard, the flare thrust forward to spout its flame at the heart of the beast. A hundred crystal tines snatched back, like a child's fingers from a roaring hearth.

Each thread tried to feel its way around the heat, desperate to embrace him.

Amber needed no second prompt: white lines were creeping through the crack between door and frame. She grasped the faucet in both hands and wheeled it round.

Behind her, ice was racing across the wall in knotted scratches.

Hot water splashed up from the tub and Amber narrowly avoided a scalding as she dropped the plug into place. Done, she retreated to the window and prayed for the steam to come wafting up from the tub like a fog bank. Like whenever Mom tried to run a bath.

At least, that way, she wouldn't be able to see the ice, eating up the wallpaper in tracks like fevered sketches of winter trees.

Captain Shaw vaguely recalled a Laurel and Hardy classic, where Stan was guarding a trench during WWI and was left forgotten; cut to ten years later, the hapless sentry has dug himself a deep ravine with all his pacing back and forth. Morgan looked down at his own tracks in the snow and he could see where he was headed if he didn't snap out of it soon.

It wasn't so funny when you had men and women out there in the worst storm this side of the birth of Christ – who he hadn't heard from for what seemed like the same length of time.

Every so often, Morgan would hop up into the CPV and bug O'Neill for some news.

Morgan kicked the crown off a pile of snow. Ben McKim was long overdue.

And where in hell was Kristal? Joanna?

'Sir!' Kev O'Neill poked his head out from the CPV. 'Think you'll want to take this!'

Morgan leaped aboard, giving his comms guy scant time to back away. 'Which team?'

O'Neill passed him the mic. 'CB, sir. Civilian was attacked, sir, by some screwy bitch with an AK and a hostage. She described Lieutenant Hmieleski, I swear. Sir.'

Morgan clicked to transmit. He mouthed a question at O'Neill: *Name?*

'Lowell, sir. Charlene Lowell.'

'All right, Charlene. Cavalry's here. Take a breath, then tell me your position.'

Now they could be getting somewhere.

Makenzie Shaw charged from the Walsh house in a daze, feeling like a criminal for leaving Amber inside. Trusting that Doctor guy was the toughest choice he'd ever made.

Lieutenant Beard, in any case, had shoved him outside, backing through the doorway after him, submachinegun levelled and shaking ever so slightly. Makenzie aimed his revolver at the same point. He jumped – and nearly pulled the trigger.

Spence was there in the doorway – but he was dead. Or dying.

Makenzie hoped it was the former.

The grenadier's face was fixed in a scream that never made it into the world of sound, his eyes as wide as they'd go; and what was left of him was enmeshed in barbed threads of ice. They whipped around him and through him and the man diminished with every second.

The Lieutenant gave an anguished, almost animal yell and fired into the face of his trooper. Makenzie told himself there was no life there to kill. Even as he fired his own two shots.

It was his turn to grab hold of Beard's arm and haul him into a retreat as the remains of the corpse thudded onto the steps.

The ice wires thrashed a while like beached eels and lay still. Makenzie tried to ignore them, searching the second floor windows for any sign.

'Sir!'

A White Shadow man was hopping the fence onto the snow-covered lawn.

'Kyle!' Beard bellowed at him. 'Get your ass over here and put a Willie Pete in that house!'

The grenadier nodded fiercely. 'Sir, yessir!' He was already ripping a stubby nosed grenade from his belt and popping it into the tube under the barrel of his rifle.

'Wait!' Makenzie waved him back, and frantically searched the windows again.

There! Above the porch, the legs of a bathroom stool smashed through a frosted window. Within seconds, the stool was tossed aside and the Doctor was helping Amber through and out onto the roof of the porch. He kept a firm hold of her as he clambered out and slid down the roof ploughing great clumps of snow with his heels. He hit the ground and rolled like a paratrooper, Amber locked in his arms and shielded from the fall. Then he was up and she was running with him for the fence.

'It's all yours, gentlemen! Be my guest!'

The Doc had taken the scene in like that, fully up to date in the space of a blink. The grenadier, loaded up and sighting keenly along his barrel, waited for the word from his senior officer. Beard practically exploded himself: 'Torch it! NOW!'

The grenade launcher coughed, blowing in a window before the whole interior was alive with a blinding white inferno. Willie Peter: white phosphorus.

Makenzie couldn't think of anything more appropriate. Squatting down, he gratefully took Amber from the Doctor, and pulled her into a hug, which she didn't even think to fight.

* * *

Melody swung the 4×4 smartly around and parked in front of the drive. Whatever the gunfight had been about, it was clear they'd found the girl.

Melody jumped out of the car in perfect synch with her partner, and they trotted over to join the party watching the savage flames spitting and hissing out of every window, as the snow fell over the scene like white ash.

'Ah!' the Doctor rounded on them. 'Just the people!'

'Well,' Melody shrugged affably, 'Parker here was concerned for your safety.'

'Was not,' Parker mumbled childishly.

'Well, naturally I'm flattered,' the Doctor said, barging past and making a beeline for the 4WD. 'In any case, your help couldn't have arrived at a more opportune moment. Lieutenant Beard, run ahead and give a full report to the Captain, won't you? A *full* report,' he stressed, looking over his shoulder and throwing open a passenger door. 'And do tell him I'd like to borrow one of his snowmobiles, there's a good fellow.'

The Lieutenant appeared to evaluate the order a moment, then led his grenadier away after a firm but silent assent. Melody traded looks with Parker, and hoped he was going to maintain his cool after his earlier slip.

The Doctor barely acknowledged their departure, too busy rummaging around in the back seat of the 4×4. 'Meanwhile, we have a young patient here who could use plenty of rest and I'm sure you two won't mind conducting her back to the hotel.' Apparently satisfied, he beckoned to the Police Chief. Makenzie Shaw obliged, steering the girl tenderly to the truck.

'Hey, Doc, what do you *suppose* you're doing?' Parker covered the ground in a few steps. '*If* you don't mind me asking.'

Melody sighed and wondered why Parker's hackles could never rise quietly. Obviously the few quiet words she'd had with him after the previous quarrel hadn't taught him anything. She decided to position herself close, in case Parker needed a kick to shut him up.

'I don't mind you asking, Agent Theroux, but it could be a costly delay for what amounts to an obvious answer. The fact is,' the Doctor was lecturing Parker severely, 'someone needs to warn those people up on that mountain just what they could be facing.'

Just as soon as he was done being dark and ominous, the Doctor slipped seamlessly into considerate paternal mode, bundling Amber gently into the back of the vehicle. 'There you go, young lady. Try not to sit on the nice agents' computer.'

The girl looked shell-shocked and Parker, Melody had to give him credit, lowered his voice for her sake. 'Doc, we need to discuss exactly what *it* is.'

The Doctor scowled, but his tone emerged as vaguely conciliatory. 'Of course, neither of you have seen what we're facing – not its true extent. I doubt I have. But I think we can stop searching for unseen enemies in the mist. The mist and the enemy are one and the same.' His gaze wandered out into the blizzard, and it was some moments finding its way back to them. 'Now, listen, I'm relying on you two, because you appear to be in the know.'

'What the hell is that supposed to mean?'

Melody clenched her teeth behind a civil smile. She wished Parker would just play it cool. 'It's true, Doctor,' Melody interceded hurriedly, 'we've had more than our fair share of *special* assignments over the years. Um, what sort of tests do you want us to conduct?'

'Everything you can think of,' the Doctor declared, hovering over Melody. 'I'm sure Corporal Pydych can help you out in the laboratory if you need it.' Then he motioned to the Police Chief again, encouraging him to sit with the girl in the vehicle. 'Perhaps you'd best look after Amber, there's a good chap. She's had a nasty shock.'

Melody wandered over, putting a lot of effort into her patient tone, but feeling free to speak openly with Makenzie tucked out of earshot. 'Okay, but Doctor, are you implying this *ice* is *intelligent?* Because I haven't seen it display any evidence of rational thought.'

'What makes you think intelligent beings have to behave rationally, hmm? Intelligence takes many forms. Whatever this entity is, it has motivation – it attacked that aircraft to reach the Stormcore – and it has awareness – it reacts to heat and it detects its prey. That puts it at least on a par with the coyotes.' The Doctor pondered a moment, rubbing his chin. 'Coyotes.'

Parker beat Melody to it. 'What's on your mind?'

'Fish, Agent Theroux. *Fish!*' He strode over to the fence and studied the blaze. 'This house was deserted – in the same way that the cult house was deserted. Ask Lieutenant Beard, and he'll tell you what must have happened to the members of that cult.' He wheeled about ponderously. 'I think our uninvited guest got hungry – hungry enough to rupture the tank to get at the tropical fish. It must have lain inert, waiting for the warm water to freeze. Then it infected the coyote when it came in search of a fish supper.'

'So it can't detect low levels of heat and it's inert in liquid form,' reasoned Melody quickly.

The Doctor regarded Melody like she was the star pupil, then clapped a hand on her shoulder and steered her back towards the truck. 'Precisely. You know, with thinking like that I'm sure you'll go far. Anyway, you two are going to have to bang your scientific heads together. And bear in mind, it has an aversion to alcohol.'

'Sorry, Doctor, remind me,' said Melody, 'how is it we know that?'

'Well, there's been nothing left of anyone else to examine. We can't be sure when Mr Redeker was infected, but something slowed the process in him. And Makenzie confirmed that he'd been drinking heavily. It's the only obvious factor that sets Mr Redeker apart.'

'So the thing's teetotal.' Parker applauded theatrically. 'Now *there's* something we can use!'

Melody wondered whether the rules of reasonable force applied to shutting her partner up. 'Doctor, you might have something. The spread of infection has certainly been – *insane,* in everybody but Redeker. And he'd pickled most of his organs in advance of any autopsy.

'So maybe the freezing point was sufficiently depressed by the alcohol to – I don't know – make it hard work for this – *ice* – stuff to crystallise within the body.'

'Well, I'm sufficiently depressed,' commented Parker.

'What is this?' The Doctor was rapt. 'The old good cop, stupid cop routine?' Before Parker could land one on him, he shook Melody by both shoulders.

'Do you know something, Melody? You're extremely clever! But it might equally be something in the neurological effects. Be a good girl and examine every angle.'

He glowered at Parker. 'You know, you really could learn a lot from your partner, Agent Theroux. I'd take very good care of her, if I were you.'

Melody fluttered her lids at Parker before strolling around to the driver's side of the 4×4. Her partner couldn't but agree with the Doctor's sentiment. 'Well, we see eye to eye on something anyhow, Doc.' Parker sniffed and scratched his neck sullenly. 'And by the way, I hate it when your thinking actually starts to make some sense.'

'So do I,' declared the Doctor, gloomy thoughts flocking to his brow. 'That's the nature of uncovering the truth. It's like condensation on a mirror. Wipe it away, and you're stuck with your reflection whether you like it or not.' He twirled a finger in the air, as if his lingering thoughts needed stirring into positive action. 'Good luck, you two. We need to learn everything we can if the world is going to survive another winter.'

Melody hesitated at the door of the 4×4. She was drawn to the sight of that house, the snows falling on the fires in wave after wave; and in it the sense that even the near-solar heat of that white phosphor blaze could not hope to survive such a war of attrition.

The Doctor doffed his hat as a good-luck gesture, before stalking purposefully down the street. '*Now* is the winter of our discontent!' he shouted into the wind.

Then he was gone, disintegrated in the blizzard, his voice trailing in the wind like an omen.

No sooner than they had driven up with the girl, the agents had withdrawn to the lab, promising to produce results as soon as humanly possible. *If* there were any results to be had, Morgan Shaw had qualified silently. Meanwhile, his brother had gone to the station house to organise the townsfolk and quell the rising panic, now the whole town had heard of old Walsh's disappearance. And the kid, she was safely stowed in one of the hotel rooms, looked after by her mother and Janny Meeks. Chained to the goddamn bed, if they had any sense. As far as Morgan Shaw was concerned, her little flight had cost him two good men.

Of immediate concern, though, was Derm's report, which had been disturbingly thorough and, Morgan noted cynically, demonstrated a newfound respect for the Doc.

Wherever he was.

Captain Shaw expected to have to do a lot more pacing before he finally showed up.

But no, there he was at last, striding into view like a walking headstone. Morgan headed to meet him, eager for a little clarification. The Doc, though, hopped straight onto the waiting snowmobile that Morgan had cleared for his use.

'Hey, hey, wait right there. What kept you?'

'Oh, nothing in particular. You know what the roads are like these days.'

'All right, you know what, I don't care what you've been up to. All I care about right now is when can I expect some answers?'

The Doc apparently felt the need to adjust his hat, and he ruffled his ridiculous mop of hair irritably. 'We already have our answers, Captain. What we need to do now is ask a lot more questions. I hope to have a few by the time I get back.' Morgan folded his arms and waited to hear something more. The Doc sighed. 'We've seen the face of our enemy, Captain. We know what it does. Hopefully, our two CIA friends are working on the how. But the question we really have to ask is *why*.'

Morgan could see he was going to have to settle for the pith and hope the flesh of the fruit turned up soon. He was hoping the Doc would be able to contact his teams out there. 'Okay, so what do the rest of us do in the meantime? Sit around and warm our butts by the fire?'

The Doc offered him a shrug. 'Well,' he said, 'you could. But I'd suggest your time was better spent searching every house in this town and torching every one of them where you find any trace of this creature.'

'Okay. Good.' Morgan Shaw wasn't happy, but it gave him a course of action.

'Just be sure to leave some buildings standing,' the Doctor advised. 'The people are going to need some shelter. And whatever you do, don't put them all under one roof. Spread them between several buildings, some distance apart. I doubt it will help very much, but it should make them feel a little safer. For a while.'

'Thanks,' Morgan said, but meant the exact opposite. He licked his teeth and exhaled. 'All right, Doc. But before you go, listen up. There's been some new developments up there you should know about.' He briefed the Doc carefully on the incident at the cabin and indicated the site on his map. The Doc thanked him and gunned the engine of the snowmobile. It spluttered and he had to gun it again.

'You sure you've driven one of these things before?' Morgan shouted above the noise.

'Oh,' the Doc waved a farewell, 'I'm sure I must have done. In a previous life.'

And with that, he was off, racing headlong into the hellish blizzard.

It didn't *see*.

It touched without fingers. Its tactile consciousness dipped into the streams of energy that flowed between its scattered threads. And sometimes other minds would wade through those streams, lighting up in its consciousness like solar flares on animal retina.

There was a nest of many such minds nearby, aglow like the core of a galaxy.

And out from that core came a single mind, brilliant and intense, like a comet arcing across the night sky.

Chapter Fifteen

As soon as they'd seen that cabin, Joanna Hmieleski had known another life was on the line. Now as they headed for the truck, that loss seemed manifested in the dragging depth of snow.

Jacks shoved her at the passenger door of the couple's pick-up. Joanna stood firm, and looked daggers at Jacks' reflection in the wing mirror.

'You don't have any plan, do you? All this killing is just so you can run away.'

Emilie's reflection twitched, but her eyes were stone. 'Crayford said the winds at the summit would be perfect. They could have carried the word to everyone. Well, it's all dead now. We're all stuck in this world.' Her sneer was bitter and primitive. 'Survival's all there is. Something you should think about, before you open your mouth again.'

'You know,' Joanna said, 'I should have given him an answer. He deserved one.'

Jacks spat. 'What are you talking about?'

'Your partner. Lagoy. He wanted to know the truth – about extraterrestrials. All those secrets I'm supposed to know because I work for the government.'

Jacks raised the AK like a polearm, ready to slam Joanna against the cab, but she looked trapped, caught between wondering if she could spare the time and whether she could afford not to. She asked, 'So what would you have told him?'

Joanna savoured the woman's pretend disinterest, while her throat burned from the acid medicine she was busy swallowing. 'I would have told him he was wrong,' she said.

'Extraterrestrials are nothing to be worshipped. There's very little to get religious over. Do you know what they're really like? They're like us. There's good and there's bad. But I don't think any of them have sickened me as much as you do.'

'My heart is bleeding. Open the goddamn door and get in.'

Joanna knew she'd effectively lost her audience, but she turned around, slow and deliberate, to aim her hate where it would do the most damage. 'I'm an officer in the United States military. You know, for me a gun is a tool I'd prefer not to use unless I have to. I don't get off on muzzle velocity and cyclic rate of fire. Do you hear what I'm saying?'

Jacks was a fortress. 'So you stand back and let people get killed. How big of you.'

'Fine, so you figured out what's eating me. The difference is, you don't have to tell me where I've gone wrong. I have this thing called a conscience, does that for me on a regular basis. People like you make me regret my calling.'

'So you'd prefer I shoot you now?' Jacks gave a twisted grin and presented the muzzle of the assault rifle like an offer not to be missed.

'No – no, I guess not.' Joanna turned away. She opened the door and climbed into the passenger seat, trying to find some way of seeing that grin as a crack in Jacks' armour. 'Maybe some day one of these alien threats will learn to discriminate. Weed out the trash.'

Jacks kept her gun on Joanna as she drew closer. 'Keep praying for the day,' she sneered.

Joanna saw the butt of the AK swinging around to club her skull. Just before lights out.

Leela found it demanding enough simply to walk through this haunted land. Now they were having to run. Or at least to drive their limbs with the power of a run, while the land straggled by with aching sloth.

Kristal had been running a hand gingerly over the surface of a fallen trunk, as if, through the fabric of her gloves, she could feel the last breaths of the dead wood. A few dribbles of blood stained the lustreless bark. 'Whatever was here,' Kristal determined, with a cryptic wisdom to rival the Doctor's, 'has gone now. Carried on the winds, and taking its victim with it.'

That was when the sound of the shots reached them through the wailing wind.

The sheer effort of the run seemed to indicate otherwise, but perhaps it was only a few minutes before the dark grey silhouette of the cabin emerged from the snowstorm, its gaping doorway venting all the heat, along with the scent of death.

There was a machine roar, finely chopped and tossed around with the snowflakes. A truck broke from beyond the cabin and skidded into a frantic turn, ploughing a fresh trail between the trees, its headlights edging the branches with ghostly silver.

Kristal cut across the open to the cabin door.

Leela followed her indoors, her pistol braced in both hands.

A female was crying over her dead mate, lagged in his blood from where she had embraced the body. Leela lowered the gun. There was no danger here, only distress.

'Where's the nearest cabin? *Miss!*' Kristal squatted to shake the woman roughly by the shoulders. Leela had seen this before: mourners had to be dragged back to the land of the living if they were to be of any use.

'Help,' the woman bawled feebly, teetering on some inner precipice. 'You have to help.'

Kristal stood, abandoning the woman and snatching up her radio. Her features formed one of the harshest masks Leela had ever seen.

If only Sergeant Garvey's radio had been an effigy of Kristal Owl Eye Wildcat, he could have wrung its neck. As things were, he had to settle for a mute growl at the crackling voice coming through on the speaker.

'Maybe you're not getting me, *Lieutenant*,' he strained as though shouting the full distance, 'but we've lost Marotta. We're still engaged in the search.'

'*I know.*' The radio made the woman sound even more callous. *Of course you know,* he swore in his head, *I just told you.* 'We don't have a choice, Garvey, so I'm not giving you one. Drop the search and haul ass up to this cabin. Detail two riders to try for an intercept and you and I can argue this face to face – later.'

Garvey swore again and surveyed the squad, who had been busy gathering around while he'd been on the radio. Landers looked like he knew he wasn't going to like his orders.

Damn it. Garvey was definitely going to take up voodoo after this was over.

The Doctor bent low behind the visor, teeth clenched like some ivory grille over a jet intake, and braced his frame for another impact. The snowmobile bounced, full throttle, off another ridge and its chassis rattled, while the Doctor grimly kept it on course.

From a distance, the vehicle might have resembled a skimming stone, clipping the crests of glacial waves. For the Doctor, riding that stone, the reality was a very bumpy ride and a series of rough shocks that any lesser system might have had trouble absorbing. Such was the price of driving as the crow flies, although the Doctor sincerely doubted whether any crow had ever experienced this level of turbulence.

His hat was clamped tightly over his head with the scarf once again, while the tails of his great coat flapped behind him like grey wings. In his pocket, the weight of the graviton distortion sensor loitered on the periphery of his senses. He had already taken a preliminary reading from within the town and he hoped he might soon be able to triangulate on that signal to pinpoint the TARDIS.

But before he could complete that search, he needed to find Leela. And the only way to do that was to drive straight into the heart of the curse that had befallen this mountain.

White death.

Makenzie wondered if it was his own shadow, looming large over Amber's bed, that was keeping her awake. Even so he couldn't bring himself to leave, mindful that his movements might break the fragile emotion in the scene, as a tearful mother stroked the child's hair and urged her to sleep.

Amber seemed oddly at peace, paying scant attention to Martha's caresses and continuing to stare from her pillow out through the frosted pane, like a kid mesmerised by a blank TV screen while she waited for her favourite show to come on.

Drawing a sharp breath, Martha finally stood and let go of Amber's hand with a kiss. Makenzie's gaze fell into that small upturned palm.

And he backed up from the bed. Because he dared not take a closer look.

'I guess I should be going,' he announced, cursing himself for sounding too hurried.

A spark ignited Martha's eyes, but she defused it in good time. She walked briskly from the room and beckoned him out into the hall with a swipe of her hand. Makenzie moved slowly and pulled the door so it was left ajar.

Martha kept her voice to a brittle whisper. 'Isn't it time you thought about your priorities?'

Makenzie was genuinely confounded. Maybe because his mind was still in the bedroom, standing guard over Amber and feeling just as helpless as when he had lost Laurie. His own low voice couldn't hide his impatience. 'What are we talking about here?'

Martha was holding back on a scream of rage. 'The Army. Your brother, the goddamn CIA – Curt lying dead downstairs, for Chrissakes. This town of yours is turning into a nightmare around us, and God only knows what it's done to *her*.' She hammered on her heart. 'I'm talking about *us,* Mak. Maybe you should be thinking about *us.* About getting us the hell out of here. Think fast, Mak, because it's our future hanging in the balance.'

'Martha, I don't have time for – '

'Make time!' Martha seethed and for a moment her eyes couldn't find their target. All too soon they were right back on Makenzie. 'What is it you want, Mak? You want to be a father to this town of yours, or you want to be a father to my girl?'

'I want you, Martha. I want us to be together. But there's things I have to – '

Martha shook her head, her face a portrait of disgust sketched with heavy strokes. 'That's not the right answer, Mak. Go think about it some more, and let me know when you're done. Just don't take too long, is all.'

Makenzie swore and lifted a fist to the doorframe, only to find his eyes drawn by the narrow band of hall light that strayed into Amber's room. He couldn't tell Martha. He couldn't do it.

He considered taking a second look, but there was no need. He knew what he had seen.

A tiny scratch glistening in Amber's hand. So much like a sliver of ice.

Easing the door closed, he spun and hurried down the hall. He had to find the Doc.

Night and the blizzard waged war over Melvin Village, and the fighting poured down into the streets, every available space or niche seized by white drifts or black shadows. For once, darkness was on the losing side.

Morgan gave the order, another window was smashed and another Thermite grenade lobbed into another house. Five so far. Kyle withdrew as the flames erupted inside this one and sent the shadows running. Morgan didn't care for the way Kyle was grinning.

No blaze of glory this. In fact, the opposite.

He turned away so he didn't have to watch the house go up, but the view in the other direction was, if anything, more solemn. Derm and the remains of White Shadow were fencing back the folks of Melvin Village who had gathered to watch the pyrotechnics.

One of the hardest things Morgan had faced was the way they had all gazed on him like some sort of hero when he'd arrived. They looked like they'd been saved and he hadn't the heart – no, the guts – to tell them straight: sorry, that ain't my job. Now they were growing expectant, and that, for people who lived life so slow, amounted to a rapid change of mood. A mood which was even harder to take than their unqualified admiration.

Morgan had to give them something more than bonfires.

Putting on a business face, he walked up beside Derm and raised his hands. 'Okay, folks hear me out.' They had been utterly silent, but he was buying himself useful seconds.

Long before he had joined the Army, Morgan had learned one thing: if you are going to lie, you had best make it a damn good one.

'The coyotes have brought some form of infection into town. We're sanitising the affected households, but in the meantime you folks ought to prepare for a possible evacuation.' Yeah, that would work. 'It might not come to that, but maybe some of you folks can get organised, gather all the vehicles, fuel and supplies you can, assemble them alongside our convoy.'

Already they were murmuring, happier with some action being taken.

For the moment it was make-work. But, since he didn't really know the truth, the story about the coy-dogs didn't exactly qualify as a bona fide lie.

The cold mask that Kristal had donned went by the name of necessity. Necessity, which made its wearer at once less than human and superhuman. Kristal trusted Leela to recognise it as such, leading a swift run through the woodlands behind the cabin, seeking out, like a hunter seeks the spoor of a deer, the warmth and life that signalled another lonely home.

Kristal had done her best for the bereaved woman, and Garvey's squad would not be overlong in coming to take care of her. Meanwhile Kristal's mind was running over the prey's escape route, calculating how much time they would have to make up even if –

Angular silhouettes in the blizzard answered the prayers she had offered up on the run.

Directing Leela around to the right, she charged around to the driver's side of the Cherokee, parked close to the A-frame shack. A couple of spare jerry cans were racked on the rear.

Well, they wouldn't be needing the extra fuel, she hoped, patting the vehicle's flank like a good horse and clambering in behind the wheel. Now all she had to do was hotwire the thing – pronto – as Leela climbed in and heaved her door shut.

After that it would be a matter of an insane drive to catch up with the fugitive. And after that, since nobody could risk firing on the pick-up, their options would be severely limited.

A spasm of cold and fatigue coursed down Emilie Jacks' spine, and her eyelids were shutters that couldn't make up their mind. She smacked her elbow against the door for a swift dose of pain – her preferred brand of uppers.

She had eased up on the gas right after that first skid, but even the trundling pace wasn't much help in this mess. Lurking behind the screen of snow, the trees were her only guide, shining in her headlights like streaks of silver frost on a charcoal window.

Beside her, the hostage mumbled, head rolling like a seasick passenger on rough waves.

Emilie could only afford a fraction of a glance, but it was enough to start her wondering why she was still keeping the woman with her. Hell, it wasn't for the company.

In fact, Jacks realised, she was a liability. Another direction to focus on, when she could barely concentrate on the one that counted. And just having her there, was a reminder of all her holier than thou speeches. All that righteous flame burned Emilie's gut.

Like the government were the good guys, and the Army were safe from whatever was out there. So *they*, like the Army, were out for the blood of Emilie Jacks. Jacks snorted. No reason why the hunted couldn't use a decoy as well as any hunter.

Slowing up some more, she reached over the slumbering hostage for the door-release.

Head down, Derm and some of the squad in his wake, Morgan Shaw was about to step up to the CPV and check on O'Neill, when the familiar bulk of Makenzie's police truck drew by.

Shots were singing out sporadically around the town, percussion to the wind's tuneless lament. A coy-dog cull was under way, as a direct by-product of Morgan's minor deceit. Morgan didn't mind so long as the folks kept busy and there were no accidents.

He stepped out and waited as Kenzie rolled down his window. The impatience in his brother's eyes was so evident for a moment Morgan thought he was ill.

'You're not telling me you got a call-out? Somebody's cat stuck up a tree?'

Makenzie's eyes were narrowed tight against the windblown snow and he managed only a colourless smile. 'Nothing like. Listen, I have to find the Doc.'

'You do?' Today was full of surprises.

The wind was blowing hard, streaming the flakes into vaporous plumes, like the frigid breath of some Norse god. The town's perimeter vanished behind scudding clouds of chill smoke.

'Well, I wish you luck, big bro. He made for the Wentz cabin. There was a shooting.'

'Yeah, I heard.'

Morgan leaned close in to the quarterlight. 'Kenzie, it's a hell of a drive.'

'I'll make it. Just take care of my town while I'm gone.'

Morgan shook his head and grimaced, watching the vehicle recede into that gusting maelstrom, past which there was no suggestion of existence. And he felt the distance between himself and his brother more keenly than he had in years.

Leela's trust in Kristal did not extend to the machine she was driving. She rode high, as though they were not properly anchored to the ground, and but for the fact they somehow remained upright, it felt like they were riding a boulder in a landslide, the way they bumped and crashed down the forested slope.

Kristal's grip on the wheel looked the equal of a Voc's, solid and unrelenting. Every so often she would compensate for a bad bounce with some minor nudge of the wheel.

Leela stared into the blizzard through which they appeared to be falling. Flakes died softly on the windscreen, despite the speed with which they were hurled out of the night.

Suddenly they broke from the trees and spun wildly onto a broader trail, freshly furrowed. A new tension seized Kristal, and Leela knew their prey was close.

There: up ahead and crawling around a bend, a man-made smudge on the specked canvas. It was the fugitive truck, one door flapping open like the broken wing of a lame bird.

Kristal jammed one foot down hard. Leela grasped around for a handhold.

Ray Landers was dead on his feet, but on balance he figured he'd rather be standing guard in the cold than intruding on that poor woman's grief. Pathos was Garvey's field of expertise, so maybe he'd see the woman okay. Meanwhile Landers could stay out of Garvey's way.

Ray's thoughts were still out there in the void, wondering about Marotta's last moments. Since they'd had their orders from the Kristal Witch to abandon the search and head straight here, it was somehow easier to think that way: if the big guy was dead, it felt a little less like desertion. With all they had found when they'd got here, death was getting to be a theme.

A shout went up.

Landers trotted around to the nearest sentry. Jen Godzinski, with her blanched freckled cheeks, nodded over at the western flank.

Jeez! Talk about a ghost rider. Landers shouldered his M4.

Then lowered it again, even before Jen had raised her sights. The figure on the snowmobile was a strange shape, but not scary strange.

The scarf securing the floppy hat to the head like some hobo's Easter bonnet was the ultimate giveaway. Landers slung his rifle and hurried up to welcome the Doc. 'Yo, Scientist Guy, what the hell brings you to these parts?'

The Doc brought the snowmobile pretty smartly to a halt. He grinned, but not entirely happily. 'You haven't happened to see a young lady with limited social graces go by?'

'You're talking about your girlfriend, right?' Landers marvelled at the devotion this guy showed to his lady: driving up a mountain to find her in this crud-storm. Maybe he should take notes. He gestured to where the path of the truck was being steadily erased. 'The fugitive went thataway, Doc, and I think your lady went after them with Kristal. Nobody tells me nothing though, so you'll have to take your chances.'

'Thank you, Private Landers. It's something I tend to do naturally.'

The Doc made as though to doff his hat, like a gent, but then appeared to remember the thing was lashed down like a tarp. He opened the throttle and rode on into the storm.

It was the warm proximity of another human being, in

consort with a blast of icy air, that woke Joanna up. But as hazy realisation dawned that the being was Emilie Jacks, Joanna fought for consciousness the way a drowning man fights to reach the surface.

Jacks' palm was like a rock pushing against her chest and the passenger door gaped open beside her. Groggy from a dozen hangovers, Joanna threw out her hands, one finding her opponent's face and pushing back and the other latching onto Jacks' arm. Barred from her full senses, Joanna had only desperation in her favour.

That and the way Jacks wasted energy in raw screams.

Whereas Joanna shoved with everything she had, pressing Jacks against the driver's door.

Then it was as if that single shift had overbalanced the entire vehicle. A sudden slide and a tug on her stomach told Joanna they had left the ground behind. The truck nose-dived and their wrestling match was suspended abruptly, the crash sending them into a deafening roll; they were trapped in a crippled dryer, blowing cold as it tumbled.

As she felt consciousness slipping, Joanna dug in her mental claws, riding it out until a religious stillness descended on the truck's interior. She couldn't focus, but she registered that Jacks was preoccupied, wiping a bloody river clear of her eyes.

That, she surmised, was the good news.

A blurred picture of the windshield told her it had been badly shattered. But when she looked a second time, the hair-line cracks seemed a little too white. Gleaming like diamond twine.

It was dumb, impossible. She was hallucinating.

But Joanna stared at the intricate webs of ice extending inside the cab.

Chapter Sixteen

They would be travelling light this time. Time and the weather were against them. Makenzie would be too if he knew. And Martha's need to act and never once – *please Lord, don't let me* – stop and think was against them most of all.

She'd warned Mak not to take too long to reconsider, and almost in the same moment she'd given herself no time for that at all. Out into the night, she'd moved like the storm, furious and giddy with the headache of the century.

Somebody brushed past her, too busy to register her let alone apologise. She was fired up to shout at the guy, but saw only the broad retreating shoulders of the CIA agent. Parked across the road was the agents' 4WD. He must have been fetching something.

Head bowed, Martha raced through the wind and seized hold of the door release. The door swung open, and Martha grinned like she'd found an exit from hell.

Her skull was still fit to burst, but the ache had evolved into purpose, and she threw herself into it, riding it like a wave. Nudging the car door closed, she ducked back across the road in a half-run, thankful her small stature would help her go unnoticed in this friendless place.

She marched into the store, breathless, tearing her hood down and searching about. Probably Hal was out scouring the town for coyotes with the rest of the amateur hunters. Didn't matter. She grabbed a cardboard box, then set about collecting a few essentials from the shelves with a haste that bordered on random. When she was done she took a time-out, planting the box at her feet.

Next minute, she was scrawling out a note and her credit card details for Hal. Picking up her box, she carted it out into the storm, and part of her sank like plunging mercury.

Maybe she was the dumb Southerner everybody reckoned. She'd spared herself a charge of looting only to commit Grand Theft Auto.

A twitch of satisfaction, heavily ironic, played at her mouth as she finished loading her goods into the back of the 4×4. She sniffed and drew a gloved finger across her upper lip, looking about and waiting for the guilt and fear to overpower her and tip her back into indecision.

But no. Goddamn you, Melvin Village. And goddamn you too, Makenzie Shaw. She made a dam of her teeth against the threat of tears. She was back on her own now and there was no great wounding guilt, but there was plenty to fear to make up the difference

Not of prison. Why fear prison when you were breaking out of hell?

No, what she feared most was the storm and how much she was going to hate herself for what she was going to have to do to her baby. Again.

She had more than the wind to fight as she forced herself back across the street to the hotel.

Leela had used nets before, trapping the larger grazers that rooted through the jungles of her homeland, then pouncing from the branches to wedge a blade in behind the armour that rendered spears and crossbows impotent. Down the slope before her, a net of ice had been cast over the front of the renegade truck.

But the net was in constant motion, threads forming and reforming, barbed and forked in countless directions as though seeking entry through the metal hide of the vehicle. The net's frenzied attack was all the more fearful for its silence.

Leela sprang a pace down the slope, preparing to brace the pistol as she had been instructed. Kristal stopped her with a shout and ran instead for the rear of their truck.

'Whatever we are going to do we should do it quickly!' Leela warned.

From this angle it was impossible to tell if the crystal vines had found their way in yet, but Leela could see front portions of the truck being eaten away as the tendrils multiplied and struck out at the air like frozen whiplashes. Fissures of ice coursed all over the surface of the wrecked truck, cracks in an eggshell.

She backed up the hill to help Kristal.

And saw a figure coasting up on a snowmobile. She called out to Kristal, but the scout barely glanced around, and instead untied the two metal cans from the cargo frame.

'Quick thinking, Lieutenant Wildcat!' the Doctor commended her loudly, hopping off the snowmobile the moment it had halted. He strode up, ready to take charge, and Leela all but sagged with the sense of relief. She trotted up to join them as the Doctor came swooping in like a bird of prey, to snatch up the discarded rope that had secured the cans to the rack.

'Old rope! Never underestimate its value, Leela!'

'Doctor,' Leela's relief turned to frustration, 'we haven't much time! This snow is evil!'

'Well,' he squinted down into the teeming mesh of ice fibres, branching and dividing all over the stricken truck. 'Ordinarily I wouldn't say a spot of inclement weather would be anything to grumble about, but in this case you might be right! You just might be! Now, Lieutenant Wildcat, will you pour or shall I?!'

'Doctor!' Kristal was suddenly handing Leela both cans. 'Now you're here, I'll try to commune with it!'

The Doctor's expression was an instant prohibition, of the sort Leela had seen before. 'I really wouldn't do that, if I were you! No matter how much we might want to, I don't think any of us can even begin to communicate with this creature!'

'No, I know that. But I might distract it long enough for you to cut a path to the truck!'

'All the same, I wouldn't advise it, Lieutenant! I wouldn't advise it at all!'

Leela caught something dark flashing between their respective gazes.

Whatever it was, it was apparently something with which the Doctor couldn't argue. While Leela puzzled over its significance, she was adjusting to the weight of the liquid slopping around inside the cans. And she wrinkled her nose: they gave off a strong smell of 'tailpipe'.

'The Doctor will tell you what to do!' Kristal squeezed Leela's arm encouragingly, making the pressure felt through her gloves and the coat's padding.

The simple gesture turned the hairs on Leela's neck cold. 'What are you going to do?'

'Open my mind,' said Kristal, and she knelt straight down in the snow, shutting her eyes just a shade too late to conceal the fear that possessed her.

The Doctor was advancing along the road with one eye on the crashed truck below.

Leela stared down at their enemy, with the feeling she was facing it alone.

Morgan Shaw narrowed his eyes and only just resisted closing them altogether, looking instead along the line of civilian vehicles queued up behind his small military convoy. There were nearly a dozen now – some with chains looped around their tyres, others with roof-racks piled up like Native American funeral pyres. Appropriately enough.

There wasn't going to be any evac. Not out of this place.

It had taken him years of effort, mule-headed determination and a conscious betrayal of paternal hopes to break out of this place before. No way was the town letting go that easily today. Not when she was as trapped as the rest of them.

Morgan heard Derm stamping up to present himself for orders. 'Kind of the meteorological equivalent of a noose, wouldn't you say?' he asked his 2IC.

'Sir?'

Morgan directed the man's glance, past the vehicles, between the buildings and the trees, to where the street broke apart in hoary pixels. In all the blowing whiteness, it was difficult to make out with any solid certainty, but tangible enough to close around their throats with chill fingers. Down along the road by which they had entered the town, there lay a new-formed barrier. Like a shifting dune of white, angry spumes of snow-flakes blowing over the uppermost ridge to fall at its base and pave the way for its slow – but definite – advance.

Not as dramatic, he imagined, as the swollen tidal wave of snow that Kristal had reported up on the mountain and by no means an avalanche. But in many ways, it augured more menace, like a B-movie zombie, perhaps, safe in the knowledge that no matter how slowly it progressed, no matter how fast its victims attempted to flee, it would ultimately have its prey. And above the advancing drifts, which Morgan now knew had to be actively encircling the town, the skies themselves were thickening and filling with a frozen swarm. Snowflakes teeming like glass mosquitoes in a hurricane, any number of them carrying a deadly bite.

'What do we do?' asked Derm, and Morgan knew he'd recognised it too.

How in hell did anyone hope to defend this town?

And then it struck Morgan, hard, like a slap in the face from his old man, that he couldn't hope to do anything of the kind. Not really. He'd set the townsfolk going through the motions, hadn't he? Now he had to do the same to his men.

No, *for* them.

They were soldiers and they had to be doing something when they saw the enemy charging at them over the hill. And when the enemy was the winter? Well, it wasn't a situation he'd ever encountered, but he was guessing you just dug yourselves in and prayed for spring.

Houston, we have ignition. Parker shoved through the lab doors like a plough through a snowbank. He dumped the laptop and all the other gear and documents in a heap on the nearest table.

'Pydych,' he snapped his fingers loud enough to break the name in two. 'Would you kindly step outside and fetch in some equipment from your electronic arsenal?'

Pydych hovered in a wanna-be helpful way just behind Melody at her microscope. 'Uh, sure,' he did a half-assed job of sounding alert. 'Did you have anything specific in mind, or is this just a means to get rid of me to talk about secret stuff?'

'Actually,' smiled Parker tautly, 'the latter. Find something to do for fifteen minutes. Who knows, maybe the Captain can use you in his defensive preparations.'

'Unless it's piling me up with the sandbags, I kind of doubt that.'

Parker thrust an arm out wide to point the man to the exit. Pydych departed promptly.

'You sound a little agitated, my love,' commented Melody, turning from her microscope to Redeker's corpse. 'You think you could channel all that nervous energy into setting up the computer?'

'In a minute,' grouched Parker, and he rested his hands either side of the corpse's feet. 'Remind me again why we're working away on all this research at the Doc's beck and call?'

His partner turned liquid blue eyes on him, traces of sympathy swimming in their depths. 'That should be obvious, Parker. This thing is everyone's enemy here. And even if we wanted to be entirely selfish about this – which we don't – it has the Stormcore.'

'Oh yeah.' Parker gaped into the open corpse. 'That living storm.'

'For sure.' Melody clearly didn't like being right this once. 'Lieutenant Wildcat's report made it pretty clear to me: like the entity was flexing a brand new set of muscles right after it grabbed the Stormcore.'

'Okay, but how come it failed on its first attempt? You know, when it attacked the jet.'

'Don't know. Can't say for sure, can we?' Melody pursed her lips, as if tasting an idea. 'Except that aircraft wasn't just an aircraft, was it? That entire plane was alive with psychic energy, functioning as an extension of Lieutenant Wildcat's mind. Its circuits were a crude artificial relay for the psychic equivalent of a nervous system, and we know what happens when it gets its hooks into one of those.'

Her gaze dropped slowly to indicate the ice still laced throughout the dead man's innards.

'Sure, right.' Parker was getting it now. 'So it eats up the electronics, the plane takes a nosedive and the ice-creature-virus-thing perishes in the crash, I guess.'

'Good work, detective. Trust me, the Doctor will have worked all this out already.'

Parker was just waiting for that name to come up. 'So do you think he wants the Stormcore?'

'No, why would he? He strikes me as something of an altruist.'

'And what if I told you your altruist has driven into the mountains with our graviton tracer.'

Parker was satisfied, if not altogether cheered, to see that he could still surprise his partner once in a while. She looked about as happy as he'd looked when he'd been out to the car.

Open your mind. Open the window, let the light in and see beyond your walls. The danger: the beyond can see inside you, the window shatters under its glare, laying you bare to the currents and the undertow of streams with all the power of the oceans combined.

Kristal never stood a chance.

A spirit quest was never a matter of lengthy meditation for Kristal. She could cast her mind into that other-realm with the briefest focus of her mind and heart and soul, like the deft flick of the wrist as an angler casts out his line. Except, here, her catch was pulling her in.

She could never have pinpointed the moment when she lost her hold on the earth, when she had crossed over – even if she had been granted the chance to tell anyone, which she knew she would not be. She knew that with the clarity and certainty with which she could suddenly see through the tempest; through the natural storm and into the spirit that had invaded it.

The same spirit that was driving hairline cracks through her consciousness.

She imagined rolling her mind over in the air, to look down and see all that she could of the shore she had left behind.

And there it was: the rescue scene being played out on that lonely wooded slope. The Doctor casting the rope like an expert fisherman, laying his line dangerously close alongside the crashed truck. Her *friend*, Leela, dutifully moving in to pour the gasoline. And the Doctor, igniting the flare pulled from his pocket; holding it a moment before tossing it into the petroleum stream, channelled along the right flank of the pick-up by the rope. A rail in the snow, along which the fires sprang up like a torched fence.

Kristal felt sad that she couldn't feel the heat on her face. She felt it instead like a blinding light that blanked out every sense she had left to her. And she couldn't hold on to her last thought, because it splintered into a billion fragments, scattered on the winds with the snows.

Tunnel vision. Except the tunnel looked to be collapsing under some incredible pressure. Martha wiped the condensation from the inside of the windshield and carried on driving right through. The shadow-buildings of Melvin Village were lost in their wake, engulfed in the cold inferno that blazed in the rear-view.

Buckled into the seat next to her, Amber blazed too.

It had been a battle, as always, to get her to the car. She fought harder than ever this time, as if her opposition was pitched specifically to match her mother's desperation. Martha had argued it out with her until she'd flipped at the sound of her own voice repeating itself; and then she'd shaken her child violently – unforgivably – until all she could hear were the screams digging their claws in on the way up her daughter's throat. At that sound, Martha's violence had turned to tearful pleas, while Amber's protests broke down into the same.

Bustling her into her coat and out of the hotel, Martha had ignored the looks of the few soldiers charging by as she had installed her daughter, still crying, in the truck. Since this wretched drive began, they had each fallen into their own silence.

Amber's silence was the kind that made the loudest noise of all. It filled the vehicle with a darkness that cut Martha deep, and so between blinks, she stared hard and fixed out through that tunnel of night and falling snow.

A massive body, like a beached Beluga whale but too white, rolled under the beams. Only after she swerved left did Martha realise it was a drift. A drift the size of Moby Dick.

'Merciful Lord!' Martha offered up a prayer of thanks for her quick reactions.

Too soon.

A sudden bump almost jolted the wheel out of her hands and the 4×4 bounded off the road into a rocky, stuttering downhill slalom. Martha held on to the wheel like it was Amber's life in her hands and she fought to steer, the sides of the vehicle slamming against tree-trunks and shaking loose clumps of snow to play an evil percussion on the roof and hood.

'Mom…' The appeal was so remote, so plaintive; had it

not been Amber's voice it might have gone unheard. Martha wanted to cry right there in the midst of the nightmare.

The 4WD dipped and hit something hard, then bounced level on its suspension, only to skid into a drunken spin. The engine growled frantically but nothing was happening.

Then the earth cracked underneath them.

The 4×4 lurched to the left and stayed that way. Martha sat statue-still, shaking on the inside.

'Honey,' she said, nervous of the damage her voice could do, 'we're on the lake. We need to get out of the car, real careful. We need to get out on your side, okay, honey?'

Amber nodded stiffly. The truck seemed to be lodged fairly securely, and that was helping to gradually steady their nerves. Martha focused on breathing while her daughter unfastened her belt and worked the catch on the door. She shut her eyes in sheer relief as she saw Amber step safely out and enjoyed, for just a second, the cold air blowing in against her cheeks. Now it was her turn.

She reached down for the belt release. Clicked it free.

Murmuring prayer after prayer, she slid over to the passenger seat, thinking she could almost hear the sloshing of the chill waters under the vehicle. Then she swung her right leg outside, then her left – and stood, expecting the truck to sink suddenly behind her.

It stayed put, but Martha sank. Down on her knees on the ice, she pulled Amber to her for a year's worth of hugs. 'Oh my God, I'm so sorry baby, I'm so sorry.'

Through her harrowed gasps she could hear the creaking ice and the lapping water and she knew she couldn't keep the embrace forever. Just a moment more.

Martha opened her eyes, seeing over Amber's small shoulder through a screen of tears.

She tensed. And Amber's heart beat a note of panic against her breast.

The Lord had no mercy. None.

Impossibly, the drift had unfurled and piled its snows down the banks of the lake after them. Now, it was reaching out with spiny fingers, talons of thorny ice that stretched out over the frozen lake towards them. To kill a mother and daughter in cold blood.

Chapter Seventeen

A blade of ice cut cleanly down Parker's spine. He leaped up, kicking his chair backwards, and nearly knocked the laptop clean off the table. 'Jesus! Oh my God! What the hell was – ?'

While he was in mortal contortions, his partner was muffling her giggles poorly behind one hand. She also happened to be standing right behind him.

'Ice,' she smirked. 'Honestly, just the common on-the-rocks variety from the ice bucket on the bar.' She playfully twirled the ice-tongs. 'What's it doing right now?'

Parker took a moment to be sure he'd heard right. 'What do you think? Introducing my coccyx to the concept of absolute zero! Goddamnit!' It took a good deal of squirming to work his hand inside his coat and yank his shirt loose in search of the offending cube.

Meanwhile, Melody was saying, 'It's melting, Parker. Heat is transferred from your body into the ice and it's effecting a transformation between states.'

Parker winced as a cold sting dropped into the centre of his palm. 'Ow.'

'You big baby. Think how cold he feels.' Melody sauntered over to the corpse. She was still fiddling with those tongs, tapping them against her lips. 'Now I didn't take a body temperature, since it wasn't exactly important to establish time of death; but I can pretty well assume it wasn't anywhere near zero, based on the fact that he was a little too lively and animated. Before I shot him, I mean.'

'Okay I'm with you so far – but how does that justify pulling a stunt like that?'

'Parker, let it go. The point here is that this invader looks exactly like ice – it shares an identical crystalline structure, but is selective about the properties it shares.'

'Yeah, so you're saying that stuff wouldn't melt if you dropped it down my back.' Parker could still feel the sliver of cold as he went about tucking in his shirt.

Melody afforded him a candy-coated smile. 'No, it would probably burrow into your spinal column and head straight for the cerebral cortex, reconstructing your nervous system as an intricate and fully functional ice sculpture.'

Parker decided he would let the matter of the ice-cube prank go. 'Sure, we know that much.'

'It would have to be colder than the surrounding biomass, so heat transference has to take place. Simple physics. The question is, where does that heat go?'

Parker was seized by a thought and rolled with it. 'Something in the ice stores the heat, uses it somehow. Energy, maybe, used to power movement and multiplication.'

'Well, I don't think you're far wrong. Except movement and multiplication are effectively one and the same where this beast is concerned. Adding particles to itself is the only way it can effect any level of controlled motion. Otherwise it's subject to air currents, I guess.'

'Blown on the winds.' Parker was nodding vigorously now, caught up in his partner's reasoning. They were travelling the same track now. 'So, okay, let's cut to the chase. What can we do against it?'

'I don't know. Alter its structure somehow.' She gave a shrug, undeniably more fetching on those rare occasions she was stuck for answers. 'Recrystallise it, effectively, and in so doing alter its basic nature.'

Parker offered a facial shrug in support of the idea. 'Sounds good. Let's do that.'

'Parker, we'd need some form of neural interface in order to tap into the ice, coupled with a governing processor capable of molecular level reconfiguration.'

Parker realised, suddenly, he was ahead of her. He took a pause to savour his moment, then perfected his delivery. 'You mean,' he said, 'sort of like cellular regeneration?'

'Oh my God,' said Melody. And she was suitably awed.

Joanna couldn't explain where it had come from, but now there was a heat-haze to add to her confused and murky senses.

Fire was the least of her worries, though.

Jacks stopped screaming long ago. Maybe that was when Jacks had stopped being Jacks. Or was there something of the woman's kevlar heart left in there? Beating away and crying out inside that thrashing mass of ice that looked like nothing more than an insane man's portrait of his own nervous system. Staring at what had become of Jacks, Joanna prayed to every god there was that the fuel tank would blow before she found out what that felt like.

Tendrils zapped across the air like neural pulses and started tearing the dash and the seating and the wheel down to basic lines; stripping the wrecked vehicle back to the designer's original drawings, sketched spasmodically in ice. White lines, boxing her in.

Suddenly the door behind her was wrenched open, the outside hurling in cold and heat in one breath. Strong, paternal hands grabbed under her arms and hauled her out. Icicle contours flashed out at her but recoiled just as instantly.

Joanna's face was awash with rosy heat as she was carried, fireman-style from the truck.

'Doctor, will she be all right?'

'Leela! Get down!' That voice breached even the barriers of her dazed mind.

Then she was thrown to the ground, cushioned in the soft snow, the Doctor a shield above her. The explosion killed her hearing but lit up what little she could see of her surroundings. The Doctor was shifting again before the drumroll in her ears had faded.

'Doctor! The evil snow! It is in her hair!'

Suddenly the Doctor was up on his knees, his eyes looming over her like twin dark moons. Ill omens for Joanna Hmieleski.

Makenzie Shaw was rapidly running out of detours. It was as if the goddamn drifts were manoeuvring around him, fencing off his routes out of town. Hell, maybe they were. Except he couldn't figure why even alien ice would be wasting its time on him.

He put it down to the blizzard's natural ability to frustrate and antagonise. And he thought of Amber lying back in her hotel bed, unaware of the threads of unnatural ice that had carved new lines in the palm of her hand and burrowed their way inside. Like a parasite.

Christ. The kid was ten. Had a father that was – hell, no, didn't even have a father any more. Where was the justice in the world?

Swearing at another snowbank meeting his beams head-on, Makenzie threw the truck into reverse then hit the brakes recklessly hard. Luckily he didn't pay for it – that time. Except it made him think: don't go killing yourself. Aren't you supposed to be the justice round here, anyway? You owe it to Laurie, and you owe it to that girl, Kenzie Shaw, to do what you can. Which involves staying alive and finding the Doc.

Meanwhile, every delay biting great chunks out of his nerves, he had to know how Amber was doing. He reached for the mic clipped to the radio. 'Be there, little bro. Be there.'

In the midst of this poisonous winter, Melvin Village had come alive with action, civilians working with the troops to erect barriers and construct crude moats at key points. Somewhere to the south, a pneumatic drill was busy chewing up the asphalt. Others were ferrying all the spare gas once intended for the evac to those defences, ready to fill the moats or soak the blankets that had been thrown over the barricades. Sergeant Kurzyk was distributing grenades to every soldier as they hurried past on some new errand for the defence, his grey Slavic features layered thick with satisfaction.

The only soul no happier for all this was the man who had set it all in motion: Captain Morgan Shaw. Possibly because he knew the town hadn't come so much alive as undead. Living past the point of no return.

Morgan wondered cynically what – apart from a morale boost – he hoped to achieve here.

O'Neill called from inside the Command Vehicle. Morgan gratefully hopped in and took the mic. The static was bad, but Morgan was skilled at filling in the blanks: *'It's Kenzie. Can you just have one of your guys check in on Amber? It's real important.'*

Morgan rolled his eyes: was that it? He went to the door. 'Hey, Kurzyk. Go check on the little girl will you? The manageress will tell you which room she's in.'

'Sir,' the Sarge's face paled, 'the mother drove off with her a while back.'

Morgan chewed on a curse or two. Running away must run in that family. 'Kenzie, did you get that? Your girlfriend drove out of town, took the kid with her. You want I should send someone after them? Repeat – '

'Okay.' Kenzie sounded mad. 'No, I'll turn back. Which way was she headed?'

Morgan looked expectantly at Kurzyk.

An age passed, locked in ice. Snowfall was the only movement for miles around.

Martha shoved Amber around behind her, mind racing everywhere and nowhere. The veins of ice seemed to float in indecision, waving in the wind like impossibly delicate branches on trees of ice. 'It's afraid, Mom. It's afraid to cross the water.'

Martha shook herself awake. She spun her head round to stare at her daughter.

Amber backed up, scared. Martha realised her utter disbelief had emerged as plain anger.

Lips clamped tight, she dug at the back of her teeth with her tongue. Then nodded and braved a smile. 'Is that right, honey? Well, let's see if your Mom can't scare it some more.'

Martha stood, glanced back at the shore, where the icicle tendrils had started to snake out again, forking here and there like slow lightning. A steady, predatory advance.

The Doctor's brisk examination was a race against the ice tracing erratic lines through the dark strands of Lieutenant Hmieleski's hair and extending roots down over her forehead to burrow into her face. Leela was a helpless spectator.

'Mild concussion,' the Doctor pronounced, pocketing the slender torch he had shone in the patient's eyes. 'Slowing down the rate of growth.' Apparently this wasn't cause for any great celebration, and Leela could only echo – and amplify – the Doctor's anxious expression as she waited for him to *do* something.

She had followed in his wake, arms up to shield herself from the flames, and helped him shovel mounds of snow to force a parting in the curtain of fire. The Doctor had leaped through, opening the door with one hand wrapped in a length of scarf; and she had seen past him into the cab as he had hauled the Lieutenant clear of the truck. She had seen the monster that the driver had become – before the fireball had consumed the creature, the truck and the evil net of ice that had enveloped it all. The flames burned still, down the slope, setting the trees and hill-side awash with the colour of sunset. Snowflakes fizzled and died, but the white night and Leela's fear starved the scene of any beauty.

'Neurological effects. Something to do with the transmission rate of neural pulses traversing the synapses, I expect.'

'Doctor, you speak the language of the Tesh,' Leela told him off. 'What does it mean?'

'Well, at the very least it means we have some time to slow it down even further.'

'Before you do anything, Doctor,' the Lieutenant suddenly insisted, her voice firmer and stronger than Leela would have expected, 'I think you'd better take these.' She tugged at the zipper on her coat and reached inside to pull out a sheaf of papers in a clear folder.

'I'll read them later if you don't mind,' the Doctor grinned, taking the folder and stuffing it into one of his implausibly deep pockets. 'But you get full marks for handing in your homework on time.' He tipped the woman's head slightly to aim her eyes straight into his own. 'Focus on my eyes, there's a good Lieutenant.'

'Doctor, what are you doing?'

'Leela! Shh!' The Doctor's hiss was as angry as the fires below.

Leela retreated a few steps, cowed and reverent, as the Doctor practised his dark arts. And she saw the Lieutenant's gaze empty of all light, as though he had bewitched her spirit from her body. Leela threw a hand up to cover her eyes, fearful her own spirit might succumb.

Then, unhappy with the protection that afforded, she turned away altogether and trudged back up the slope to where Kristal was –

Leela powered herself into a sprint and dropped beside Kristal, panic taking hold of her as she craned to look into those eyes so full of wisdom. But the wisdom was gone. There was nothing beyond the dark hazel and their black centres were empty of life.

'Kristal!' Leela touched her friend's face, only to snatch back her fingers at the feel of dead flesh. 'Doctor! Come quickly!'

There was more she wanted to add to her cry, but she was

226

stopped by the burn that locked around her throat like the lifeless metal hands of a Voc robot. Yet far, far colder.

Ordered around the far side of the truck by her Mom, Amber gaped around the front bumper to watch the great drift topple like a glass tree, reeling in hundreds of its branches only to extend new skeletal limbs ever closer over the lake.

Her Mom nearly slid into the listing rear of the truck and now she was steadying herself, popping the trunk and rooting around inside. Amber watched her Mom's footing at the edge of the cracked ice. Panic rose in her throat but couldn't find any sound.

Oblivious, relentless, Mom hoisted out a tyre iron and skidded hard onto one knee.

Amber flinched at the impact, but her Mom advanced a few feet from the truck and just set at the ice, driving the iron in like a spike or swinging it like a sledge hammer. She hacked and hacked, hurling raw shouts at the veins pumping white blood through the air towards them.

'STAY AWAY FROM MY BABY, YOU BASTARDS! YOU COME GET ME!'

Amber whimpered silently, her Mom's rage turfing up a graveyard of memories.

Water was spilling up around her Mom's knees. Her Mom shifted back and hacked again. Then the iron went in like a drill and something lurched.

Amber screeched a warning – too late. The truck continued its suspended roll, crashing down and sinking a great crater in the ice. The frozen lake cracked like thunder. Mom threw herself flat and tried to dig the tyre iron in, but she was spread unevenly on a treacherous island of ice and the whole thing tipped her sideways into the swelling waters.

Amber lunged forward on all fours, bawling and screaming, but even through her tears and the falling snow, she could see the icicle tracks retreating at last, like the scratches of ghostly blades in the air above a lonely skating rink.

The Doctor had made the Cherokee his makeshift ambulance. He was driving flat out through appalling conditions, willing the vehicle on and fighting every skid and swerve.

His two patients were strapped securely in the rear, Leela's window-like gaze occasionally seeming to pass silent comment on his driving from the mirror. Her hypnosis hadn't taken long, but a lace of frost had extended over her entire throat by the time she was under.

The sight put the Doctor in an ugly mood.

A mood that didn't dissipate even as the sight of the cabin resolved itself out of the snow ahead. The Doctor brought the Cherokee to a controlled halt before the house.

He jumped out and was met by Ray Landers once more, and a couple of other troopers.

'I need one of you to drive while I attend to my patients,' he demanded. 'Come on!' he snapped at Landers because he was the closest. 'Don't stand there dithering, man!'

'I got to go check with my Sarge,' Landers was infuriatingly apologetic. He glanced into the truck behind the Doctor. 'Where's Lieutenant Wildcat?'

The Doctor reined himself in from ferocious to merely gloomy. 'There was nothing anyone could do for her, I'm afraid.' He'd had to leave her there, kneeling in the snow, unable even to close her lids. Ultimately, her physical form would disintegrate, consumed as he was sure her mind had been. 'But we still have time to save my friend and your Lieutenant. Surely that's enough to motivate your Sergeant?'

Landers nodded, apparently infected with the Doctor's note of determination. 'Okay, Doc, you got yourself a driver.' He turned to the two female troopers standing close by. 'Godzinski, go tell the Sarge. Maybe we should take the shooting victim down with us. And Zabala, you're with me: you get to be navigator.'

While the woman ran for the cabin, the Doctor busied himself panning around with the graviton distortion sensor he had borrowed. He was intent on interpreting the readings as Landers explained about the woman and how, if it was okay with him, they ought to transport her down to the town with the rest of the patients.

'The more the merrier,' the Doctor said, from the opposite end of the galaxy to merry.

Amber lay flat and pulled herself towards the still churning waters. She cried every foot of the way, her convulsive sobs squeezing her young heart dry.

Close to her left she was conscious of the 4WD, which had lurched again but was now wedged at a severe angle, hanging on with its front wheels and dipping its rear bumper into the lake. The ice was straining under it and threatening to give at any moment.

Amber was busy being sorry as well as scared.

She had wished for this. Back in the truck – no, before that. When she was being dragged from the hotel, dragged out of town, dragged and tugged everywhere all her life. It made her hate: herself, her life, the things and the people around her. Sometimes it was blind hate, black and shapeless inside. Sometimes it was hate in the shape of a wish.

The worst of all wishes.

Amber gave a start and screamed hoarsely as her Mom broke up through the surface, coughing and spluttering so hard Amber could feel the pain in her own chest.

'Mommy!' she screamed. 'I never meant it! I never meant it!'

But Mommy couldn't hear her. Nobody could hear her.

Amber threw herself forward and grabbed for her Mommy's hand.

But the waters pulled harder and dragged her Mom under again.

* * *

It looked to Ray Landers like the Doc ought to be reading last rites over Joanna Hmieleski and the native girl, instead of constantly checking on their heartbeats and pulses and whatever the hell else might be going on inside their comatose forms.

It was weird as *weird* seeing them sitting up in back like a couple of zombies.

The Lowell woman wasn't much better back there: shrinking into one end of the seat, resting her forehead against the window like she hoped it might freeze there.

Gluing his eyes to the road wasn't easy when there wasn't any road.

Lucky he had Michaela Zabala along for company. Even if she was a diminutive and aggravatingly quiet Spanish chick. She didn't seem to be having any trouble training her eyes exclusively ahead. How she could focus in this was anybody's guess.

Well, Ray knew why she was more quiet than usual. Same reason as him: they'd all loved to rib Lieutenant Wildcat, their very own Pasamaquoddy witch doctoress. Now she was gone, Ray was wondering if he and Marotta had loved to rib her because they loved her.

Damn, was he going soft or what?

'*¡Atención!*' Zabala slapped his upper arm. 'You want to kill us all?'

Ray blinked. The white out front had solidified. A giant white arm thrust out across the road. Zabala's sharp eyes had given them a fair slice of breathing space. He hit the brakes and eased up on the gas, swearing to thank her later.

'Uh, Doc, the road to town is blocked. And then some.'

'Take a detour along the shore.' The Doc sounded like he didn't want to be bothered with such petty stuff. 'The edges of the lake should hold.'

Ray didn't like that word: should.

The arms of a bear hauled Amber back from the edge and

locked her in a powerful embrace.

'I'm right here. Right here. Now you stay back, you stay right there, d'you hear?'

Amber heard. She nodded and closed her eyes tight, afraid she was going to just cry and cry if she let herself see Makenzie's face right then. She heard his bulk drop onto the ice and there were loud splashes. The sound of her Mom's coughs opened Amber's eyes.

In time to see Makenzie lock his great arms around her and lift her bodily out of the water.

Makenzie: stronger than the lake, even.

Makenzie had seen the beams of the 4×4, hazy but still bright, arcing suddenly upwards like searchlights. He'd driven down through the trees and parked close to the shore, running the rest of the way, navigating through the snowstorm by the sound of Amber's screeches. Now he stomped back to the truck, the weight of Martha Mailloux a welcome burden in his arms.

Amber, bless her young heart, raced ahead and opened the door of his police truck.

'Fetch a blanket out of the trunk, there's a good girl.'

Makenzie glanced at the snowflakes flitting across the beams of his headlights. Looked to be just common flakes, along with all those plastering themselves to his truck.

He hurried to stow Martha's shivering form safely inside.

'Stop!'

The Doctor was far from the only one to have seen the snow-blurred silhouette, sweeping the puny beam of a flash-light back and forth across their path. Landers was guiding them in for a gentle stop as the figure came trotting up, the silhouette magnifying enormously like a projected shadow. The Doctor knew that something was amiss.

Up ahead, the bulky police truck, with its crest of lights,

waited on the incline under the trees, identifying the figure before he showed his face at the driver's window. Landers helpfully rolled down the window and shrugged. 'I was only doing thirty, officer.'

The Doctor could see the Police Chief wasn't in the mood. 'What is it, Makenzie?' The Doctor opened his door and hopped out, brushing his mop of hair back before jamming his hat down firmly. 'What can we help you with?'

'Doc, I need you to come take a look at Amber. Thank God you came when you did.'

'Well, you can thank Mr Landers for that.' The Doctor weighed his choices in a moment and stalked forward to the driver's door. He rapped on the vehicle's flank. 'Make sure you deliver my patients safely, Mr Landers. And when you transfer them into the hotel, move them *very very* gently. And *don't* touch the ice.'

The Doctor was satisfied with Landers' nod, and he grinned to soften the threat considerably. He ushered Makenzie Shaw back a step to allow the departure of the improvised ambulance, and then marched ahead to the police truck.

Makenzie shone the flashlight in past him, showing Martha Mailloux laid out, wrapped in a blanket and in a fevered kind of sleep. Amber sat quietly alongside her mother, apparently in shock and very clearly dead to the world.

'Your mother did a very brave thing trying to protect you. But it was you who worked out it was afraid of the water. What made you think of that, hmm?'

As rich as the voice sounded, it didn't really reach through to Amber. How could it, when her thoughts were such a personal blizzard? Swirling and dancing like the snowflakes over the lake as Makenzie drove them carefully along the shore, back into town.

Doesn't matter which way we go, Amber was thinking. Doesn't make any difference.

She looked up. The Doctor leaned over the back of his seat, holding her hand.

'That's a nasty cut,' tutted the Doctor, his sympathy not grating like some, but somehow forced nevertheless. Amber glanced down at her palm, and watched him prod at the tiny crystals with a tweezers. 'If you like, we can do something – to stop any infection.'

'It's nothing,' she said, and realised how much she meant and felt it. Her voice still sounded dead, the way it had as she had answered the man's questions, relating the story of all that had happened out on the lake. 'It's tiny, nothing. It doesn't hurt. It doesn't want to hurt any of us. That's just it – that's how I knew. I know how it feels.'

Makenzie's eyes glanced at her out of the mirror. She looked away, but that left her looking down at her Mom, sleeping fitfully beside her. She didn't know where to look and felt her face burning under the attention.

'I feel what it feels. I do. I know how it sounds, but it's the truth. I'm not lying, I'm not!'

'I believe you, Amber,' said the Doctor. And she found that steady, infinite gaze waiting for her when she looked up.

'Sure,' Makenzie weighed in, 'we believe you, Amber. We do.'

It was awkward and fumbling, unlike the Doctor's assurance. But there was something in it that cooled Amber's resentment, if only by a degree or two.

'What does it want, Amber? Can you tell me that?'

'No, I only know how it feels. It just wants – a home, can't you see that? It wants its life back. It wants – ' Something new came to her out of the blizzard in her head. She stared into the Doctor's eyes, as deep as she could go. 'It wants you.'

The Doctor stared back at her, far from flattered.

She had effectively silenced him for the rest of the journey, and she felt satisfied with herself but wounded and sorry at the same time. But that was only to be expected.

That was what it felt like when you were the centre of a storm.

The Doctor hopped out as soon as they'd parked up, and Makenzie hurried to join him outside. Across the street, stretcher parties were gathering to convey the patients from the other vehicle into the hotel. The Doc was searching the snows as though the flakes were his thoughts and he might pluck the right one out of the air at any moment.

'I don't think there's any cause for concern in Amber's case,' the Doc assured him.

'You're kidding, right?' Makenzie kept a check on his anger, for the moment.

'Quite the opposite,' the Doc turned to face him. 'Those crystals barely penetrated her skin. They were so utterly inert, in fact, I went so far as to scrape the wound clean of them. No, I think we can assume your child has remained unharmed.' He arched his brow darkly. 'Why. That's the question we should concern ourselves with.'

'Doc,' Makenzie still wasn't happy. He could see Amber's face at the window of his truck, and he was thinking of Martha lying in there beside her. He, Makenzie, was the only one looking out for that kid right now. 'You have to understand, she's not my child, and – '

'Yes, tell me about that.' The Doc was very interested, all of a sudden. 'What goes on inside that child's head, hmm? What makes her tick, would you say?'

Makenzie was stumped. Then he figured, well, the Doc wouldn't ask without good reason. It was just a shame he couldn't tell the guy much. 'What can I tell you, Doc. She's a mixed-up ten-year-old kid. Runs away a lot, but she learnt that from her Mom. She's been dragged here and there across the country, every time Martha felt the need to run – like she did tonight. Well,' he gave it some long thought, 'I guess she's seen enough to make her feel all grown up, like she wants to take control of her own life before it's time.'

'Hey there, Doc! You're wanted!'

The technical guy, Pydych, was trotting across the road. 'Our Agency buddies want you in the lab,' he yelled. 'They got some kind of major breakthrough they need to discuss.'

The Doc glanced at Makenzie. 'Hm, it's only a shame we can't say the same. But you know, I think we might be on the brink of something. Either that, or a precipice.'

At that, he hared off past Pydych to the hotel, abandoning Makenzie to the blizzard.

Parker stood poised behind the laboratory door, rehearsing the ambush in his mind. The door swung open and caught him off-guard.

'Relax,' said Melody, rolling her eyes. 'They're bringing in Lieutenant Hmieleski and the Doctor's friend right now. He'll be in here any minute.'

Parker nodded, casual and content. 'Well good, he's kept us waiting long enough.'

'Parker, are you sure there isn't some more subtle method we could try first?'

Parker shook his head and sighed. He felt like cupping Melody's face in his hands. 'Your touching naivety is one of your attractions, hon, but trust me. On this, Parker knows best.'

'Whatever.' Melody sauntered over to her microscope, and leaned against the bench.

They only had a short wait.

The Doctor entered with his usual stoop, and glanced around. Parker was already rushing up behind him and swinging the tall guy's arm up for a half-nelson. Nicely does it.

He grasped for the other arm, but suddenly it wasn't where he expected to find it. The Doctor spun and ducked under Parker to fling him over his back. Parker landed on his feet, just about but went staggering backwards to bang the base of his spine against the bench. By which time the Doctor was assuming a defensive stance and Parker was thinking, the *hell* with this.

He brought up his .357 Desert Eagle and aimed it at the Doctor's fish-bowl eyes.

'All right, that was fun, Doc. Now if you'd kindly roll up your sleeve, perhaps we can persuade you to donate some blood. We'd prefer it fresh, and personally speaking I'd rather collect it with a needle than a mop, if you *really* don't mind. So how about it?'

Chapter Eighteen

Morgan Shaw felt something like a dog playing fetch, but if anyone was throwing sticks he couldn't afford not to go pick them up. Pydych had reported a research breakthrough and he collared the engineer in the lobby. 'Pydych, with me. You can interpret the science for me.'

'Sir – ' Morgan shut him up with a wave then shoved the lab door open. It took one long breath to register the scene that confronted him.

'Can I take it,' he spat, 'you guys haven't quite hammered out your theories?' He reserved a special glare for Parker. 'And you, put that piece away, because I have a submachinegun and I am borderline psychotic right now. One of you had better have a real good explanation.'

Theroux tucked the sidearm away. 'It's kind of difficult,' he shrugged.

The woman stepped forward, too keen a volunteer for Morgan's liking. 'Actually, it's really quite simple. We've identified that the Doctor has a special blood type; one which might help recrystallise the iceform and subvert its currently hostile structure. Render it inert, perhaps.'

Morgan followed the signal glance she sent at the Doc.

The Doc, give him credit, played it smooth. Advancing on Quartararo with a grin, he pumped her hand energetically and guided her into the sort of huddle a happy coach would give his favourite team member. 'Yes, that was exceedingly clever of you. Did I mention how clever that was, hmm? Where did you study? Somewhere very prestigious, I imagine.'

The Doctor discarded her, adopting a lop-sided and rather

theatrical pose for Morgan's benefit. 'Of course, I told her it couldn't possibly work on the scale we would need, but it would almost certainly be a splendid way of cleansing and repairing the nervous systems of those already affected.' He pounced on Theroux with a hearty pat on the back. 'That was when Parker here came over all noble and insisted we use his blood instead.'

'You're telling me he has this same rare blood type?'

'Ah, well, that's just what I asked him. But he really was insistent on being noble.' The Doctor snatched up a syringe from the bench and seized hold of Theroux's wrist. The needle was plunged instantly into a vein on the guy's hand and drawing off a tube of dark red.

'Ow!' Theroux yanked his arm free before the syringe was full. He shot a shrug of appeal at Morgan. 'You're going to stand there and let him attack a government agent?'

Morgan wasn't ready to upset this piece of theatre. 'If you want to be noble, sure.'

The Doctor held the syringe up to the light and studied the dark red liquid the way a wine taster studies a fine claret. He stopped short of swigging it back. 'Hm, just as I thought.' He quietly pocketed the syringe. 'Completely the wrong type.'

'Okay,' Morgan finally folded his arms. 'It's been an entertaining routine, but spare me the encore. Whatever it is you people are hiding here, sort it out. Do whatever you have to do. Spill whoever's blood it takes. Because we've drawn our lines in the snow out there and I don't want any more of my people shedding theirs, do I make myself perfectly clear?'

The Doctor brought his leaden eyes to bear. 'Crystal.'

Morgan drew a steely breath. He turned and exited quickly before the hollow wells at the corners of his eyes chose to fill.

The young man marching out through the hotel lobby looked nothing like Makenzie's kid brother. Too tender about the eyes, too drawn and fatigued. Actually, yes, there was a resemblance to Morgan, that time after he had lost his first fight in the schoolyard.

He hadn't wanted to talk then. He certainly wouldn't now.

Makenzie barred him with a hand planted on his chest. 'Morgan. I know a way we can get these people out of here. Every one of them. Across that lake.'

Morgan regarded him for all of a second. Then shook his head. 'Uh-uh. Too dangerous.'

Makenzie practically growled. 'God, Morgan, come on! You can't save this town – and don't pretend you ever came here to do that!' Makenzie raised a fist, but didn't quite know what to hit. It hovered in the air uncertainly, then descended for a firm but controlled landing on his brother's shoulder. 'You left this town to save your own life, Morg. Can't you just stop and think about saving some others for a change?'

Morgan's gaze was starting to toughen up again. Makenzie took heart from that.

Lieutenant Hmieleski and the girl, Leela, were laid out on a couple of single beds, blank and lifeless, while Corporal Pydych busied himself setting up the tubes and saline drips according to Melody's instructions and the Doctor supervised in a detached manner from the end of Leela's bed. Parker stewed silently in the corner armchair, massaging his hand.

'Our intruder attacks the nervous system,' the Doctor had reasoned aloud, 'so as long as my blood is operating outside of its normal jurisdiction, so to speak, the antibodies should start doing their work completely unopposed.'

He made it sound so simple, and yet he was so plainly wary of potential complications. If there was ever going to be a safe time to make amends, this was it, Melody supposed.

She sidled up to the Doctor. 'Doctor, I'd like to apologise for my partner's behaviour.'

The Doctor wheeled around. 'Mm?'

Melody steered him gently out of Pydych's earshot. 'I tried to tell him there were far more civilised ways to request a simple blood donation,' she laughed under a sigh.

Fingers gripped her wrist like a handcuff. 'I would hardly call pickpocketing civilised.'

Melody swore under her breath. 'Sorry,' she said, easing her hand out of the Doctor's pocket. 'But you must understand, as government agents we can't allow things like blood samples to fall into the wrong hands. Someone less scrupulous than yourself might construe all manner of highly personal information.'

'Ah, well, I'm not as scrupulous as all that.' The Doctor let go of her hand and retrieved something from his pocket. He slapped the graviton distortion sensor into her palm. 'But I do like to return things when I've finished with them. It's more neighbourly.' He turned to face her, cheerfully curious all of a sudden. 'Do you suppose we could be neighbours? I mean, technically I'm of no fixed abode, so it's difficult to say who my neighbours are, but I'm sure I must have passed through your area at one time or another.'

'Excuse me?' Melody fluttered her lashes, retreating behind a shallow smile.

'Oh come on, I've complimented you on your intelligence. Don't insult mine.' He dipped his face level with hers. 'It's not medical information you're anxious to conceal. You're worried I know enough to construct a DNA profile from that sample, a profile I might pass on to the relevant authorities – a profile the Captain might have to investigate, hmm? Come on, you can tell me. Am I getting warm?'

Melody's smile evaporated under the heat.

Little more than a mile. And yet, for all Makenzie could see past the church, it might as well have been the exodus to the Promised Land. The view was a silk screen, falling to pieces before his eyes and beyond it, maybe, the darker streak of ink was the wooded headland where they would find the small resort town of Winnipesaukee and salvation. Meanwhile the folk of his town were filing past to assemble in the church, and he was starting to feel like the only usher at a mass funeral.

Men, women and children, collected in little bundles. Far fewer faces than there should have been. The congregation would be a severely diminished one.

The Lowell woman was being lead past by old Phil Downey – apparently he knew the woman. Locked inside with her personal trauma, she looked like she'd need leading around for the next ten years of her broken life. At least.

As Martha was carried by on a stretcher, all jittery under her blankets, Makenzie decided to follow her inside, sit with her awhile. They were all waiting on the word from his brother anyway, and Makenzie couldn't think of any better place to wait than inside the church.

The Doctor whipped out a plastic folder full of documents, then cast his coat over the armchair, (apparently) forgetting it was occupied. Flopping indecorously on the couch alongside Leela's bed, he swung his long legs to make himself perfectly comfortable.

Predictably, Parker leaped up, fit to explode. Drawing on all her reservoirs of patience, Melody coolly dismissed Pydych and wandered over to perch on the edge of the couch. She waited there with the needle, while the Doctor rolled up his shirtsleeve.

'I do hope you'll be gentle,' he said, settling back to read. 'You won't need much. About an armful, I should think.'

'So,' Melody hazarded, 'you found some time to browse our computer files.'

'Well, there was a great deal of non-standard software which started me wondering,' he answered, skimming the top sheets of the documents. 'Too many files relating to things extraterrestrial and not much else, that sort of thing. Of course I had my suspicions, both of you wearing sunglasses without bumping into things. And you're really too intelligent for intelligence agents, for another thing. Well, one of you is.'

Parker's shadow tensed, but Melody waved him off. 'Then Mr Theroux here chose to refer to the Stormcore by its original designation – Prism. Over thirty years out of date.'

'Quite, well, we have been here a long while,' conceded Melody tightly. 'Anyway, you must have seen the files we've collated on your good self, Doctor. Your UNIT file.'

'Ah, blackmail is an ugly word, but it never seems to stop people using it.'

'No, that's not what I'm getting at.' Melody waited for him to look up from the pages. 'Doctor, we've been stuck here for longer than I care to say. Our best chance of finding some means of transportation home lay in securing positions within the government.'

'The government that brought our craft down in the first place!' complained Parker.

'Ah, well at least you're a species who appreciates irony. That's something.'

'Anyway, Doctor,' Melody smiled patiently, 'we came across your file years ago, and it didn't take much to work out your race of origin. All your different guises, as it were. And there's no way you stayed on Earth voluntarily – not for that long-term stretch you did. So I'm betting you understand – what it's like to be stranded, unable to get home or even just leave, travel where you want.'

'Oh, I don't know, there was always plenty to see and do.'

But Melody saw straight through the glib front that time.

'Oh, all right,' the Doctor dropped the documents in his lap grudgingly. He searched her gaze like he was scanning a familiar star chart. 'Well, since we have so much in common, we really should be playing on the same team, wouldn't you say?'

'I'm all for that, Doctor,' Melody stood, openly relieved. 'Where do we start?'

Behind her Parker remained silent. Sulking, no doubt.

'Garvey.' Morgan clapped a hand on the older sergeant's back as soon as he'd found him. The man looked like he'd had a rough time up on the mountain, and his depleted squad had only rolled into town on the snowmobiles a short while ago. 'Take two of your men and break me a trail out over the lake.' He brought his arm down like a knife, cutting a line out past the church, where he had sent his brother to gather in the flock. 'South west heading. Make damn sure we've got a minimum eight inches of ice all the way, otherwise those people are heading out on foot.'

'Sir, I'd like to respectfully request – '

'Denied. Get moving. When you're done you can come back and guide the convoy across.'

Morgan spun on his heel and marched off, mad at the guy for wanting to be a hero. Nobody in their right minds would ask to stay behind and defend this place. Nobody.

Parker refused to pace the room – he wasn't an expectant father – but he was rapidly getting bored of watching the Doctor's blood meandering through the tubes, its course diverging to each of the beds. Melody reckoned on an hour or more to infuse the two patients and it was starting to feel like double that, when the Doctor leaped off the couch like Archimedes out of his bath.

'What have we got?' Parker darted forward.

The Doctor shushed him while he leafed through the papers a second time. 'Melody, would you be so good as to check on our patients?'

Parker bit his tongue, irked to see Melody obliging without a word. He could see from here that the frozen lattice was clearing from both patients' complexions.

'Looks like your antibodies are doing the trick nicely, Doctor.'

'Delighted to hear it.' The Doc yanked the tube out of his arm and tossed it aside along with about half the papers. He made a beeline for the dresser, and cleared its surface of everything but the lamp. Then he set out several sheets of one document under its illumination.

'Take a look at this. Most of it's some nonsense about a commando raid on a local observatory.' Presumably the sheets he had left strewn over the couch and floor. 'This is the interesting part: weather reports.'

'Sure, they get me leaping out of bed every morning.'

'When your enemy appears to be meteorological in nature, they should do.'

Melody fetched a Band-Aid for the Doctor's arm. Parker shook his head at the sight of his partner playing nursemaid, then moved to peer over the Doctor's shoulder.

The fact that he didn't care for wind and rain, and was rapidly losing what admiration he'd ever had for snow, was essentially the full extent of Parker's meteorological expertise. He'd seen radar pictures before though and the pages looked ordinary enough to him.

'See this area of low pressure,' the Doc pointed, 'driving a severe cold front in from the north-west. Here it runs into drier winds from Canada, and we get this cyclonic storm system that seems to be very taken with the state of New Hampshire.' He whizzed his finger around in a hurricane-like spiral, then tapped the next snapshots in sequence. 'But look: the key storm centres divide and multiply – into increasing numbers of microstorms.'

'Like cellular division.' Parker searched the others' eyes for confirmation.

Melody dropped into a crouch for a closer look at the last few frames. 'No,' she said. 'The concentrations of nimbostratus increase with each division. It's more like accretion.'

The Doctor stood tall and straight, like a monument to the dead.'Precisely. Each storm centre amasses greater and greater energy as it forms and the cycle continues. Increased density and mass around gravitational centres, like the formation of star systems. Except this one is very much a living system.'

'So where's it getting its building blocks?'

'Parker, we already know how it accumulates mass,' Melody rose slowly.'Biomass.'

Parker was sorry he asked.

'*There* is where it's formed its nucleus. Right above Melvin Village.'

'Let me guess, Doc – you pinpointed the Pris – the Stormcore, using *our* device.'

'It's no more than you were hoping to do.' The Doctor gave Parker pause to digest that, then he was off, headed for the door.'In any case, that's our key. Come on!'

'Wait, Doctor.' He didn't, leaving both Melody and Parker to chase him along the landing. 'What are you going to do?' Melody was asking.'Try to communicate with it?'

But the Doctor ploughed ahead, launching his answers behind him like depth charges in the wake of a destroyer.'No! Too many people have already tried that. The cult, Kristal.'

'So what is it with this thing? Some alien intelligence that rejects all communication?'

'Who said anything about rejection, Agent Theroux?' The Doctor stopped at the head of the stairs.'No, I think it wants contact. Think about it: if a child reaches out to touch a flame, they're very likely to get their fingers burned. But we can warn our children of the dangers, they can learn. But what if the fire reaches out to touch the child. What does it feel? What does it learn? Nothing. It just burns because that's what it does when it touches.'

'So that's all it wants to do?' scoffed Parker. 'Reach out and touch somebody's hand?'

'It reached out to touch Amber Mailloux. Why do you suppose she hasn't been burned? I'll tell you what I think: I think it recognised something in her as a part of itself. Something that had already been burned. It *empathised*. It found itself a friend.'

'You're saying this thing is emotionally charged?'

'Yes, and extremely needy. I don't believe it's sentient, not in the strictest sense. It's self aware and it's motivated, but only on a very fundamental, emotional level.'

'So what does this sensitive icicle works want with the Stormcore?'

'What does anyone want with a Dimension Phase Multiplexer? You wanted it to help find you a way home. It's a sort of navigational roulette wheel. It bands together interfaces between a multiplicity of dimensions into one central hub, then controls where the ball lands – and that's the dimension your interstellar craft enters. It's a pathfinder.'

'Well, surely, if it's got a navigator,' said Melody, 'what it needs now is a pilot.'

The Doctor fell silent and stared into a multiplicity of dimensions.

This is it. General George Custer, eat your heart out.

When the first shots reached Morgan's ears, he looked south. A diffuse ribbon of flame leaped up across that end of town, dissolving away in the blizzard. And yet, somewhere down there, Derm's troops still had an enemy to shoot at.

Morgan looked out over his own line of defence.

The drifts had rolled in with the patience of the tide, but now a spray was curling up from the crests of those great waves, tempting the imagination to draw shapes in the mist. Until the shapes left the imagination trailing and started to draw themselves.

White threads, barbed and entangled, wove surreal skeletons of crystal in the air. Only to dash the sculptures down from the drifts and reconstruct themselves anew in their advance on the barricade. Tumbleweeds of ice rolled along spiking the air with lashing tongues.

'Torch it!' yelled Morgan, and fired off the signal shot with his automatic.

Flares were lit, the bonfire roared up in several points at once and the raging flames raced to meet each other. The sculptures seethed and recoiled from the wall of heat. Morgan, likewise, had to take a step back, an arm coming up to shield his face.

Somebody whooped in triumph. Morgan glanced right.

Past the premature sound of victory, a fork of crystal lightning stabbed through a deserted house, writhing over the timber façade like snakes. The strands converged and sprouted a thicket of ice across the driveway, cutting off the men posted at the back of the building.

Their defences were breached before they'd even begun.

Chapter Nineteen

It was not a large church, but to Amber just then it seemed vast and hollow. The murmurs of a frightened congregation filled it to the ceiling and the colour had drained from the stained glass. She felt the eyes of every kid on her, as if they all knew who to blame.

Most of the grown-ups were comforting each other; or praying alone, like Janny Meeks, who had agreed to baby-sit while Makenzie went about his police business.

Makenzie was out front, kneeling over Mom, laid out on her stretcher. He'd promised Mom was going to be okay, and Amber wondered how he could make promises like that.

Shots cracked out, more like on the news than in the movies. Janny Meeks prayed louder, next to her in the pew. Murmurs stirred all around the church.

'Settle down, folks,' Makenzie rose to appeal to them. 'Everything's going to be fine.'

More promises. Not like the ones Daddy could never keep, but lies all the same. She stole a sidelong glance at the Meeks woman to make sure she was immersed in prayer, and she was sure then that she knew how to make everything fine.

She slipped out of the pew, making for the church door. And the storm beyond.

The ice latched onto the next building, the thorny hedgerow severing Morgan's front line.

He squeezed off a few bursts from the SMG, the suppressed fire shattering whole lengths of the glassy thicket with whispered blows. Sprays of shards forced Ray Landers to seek cover, tumbling behind a couple of trashcans, while the hedgerow started knitting itself together.

Time for that evac: Morgan called the retreat, and spun to make for the church.

Its spire, like a monument to this abortive battle, was fading in the thickening blizzard.

The Doctor continued briefing Melody and Parker all the way downstairs and across the hall. His voice boomed, but not so loud that they couldn't all hear the sporadic gunfire outside.

'This creature concentrates mass around dispersed centres, but the maps indicate that it developed a nucleus before it laid claim to the Stormcore. In theory, all we have to do is apply our solution to that nucleus and the effects should be relayed throughout the entire creature. Like pain conducted through a nervous system; except of course our attack will be travelling from the centre outwards.'

'Yes, but what is our attack? Where are we going to look for this miracle solution?' Melody was finding it frustrating, having to chase the Doctor and address his back.

'Well, solutions usually originate in the forebrain, so I'd recommend – ' Whatever his recommendation was, he apparently lost sight of it and instead fixed his gaze on empty space, halting suddenly just inside the laboratory. He snapped his fingers and flipped his hair back as if angry with himself. 'Of course! I've been positively snow-blind.'

Parker came around in front of the Doctor. 'What have we got?'

'Not much time,' he warned the agent morosely. Then he was springing into action, assembling a few simple pieces of apparatus on one of the bench-tops. 'Melody, be an angel would you and rouse our patients – they need to be ready to move in a short while. Oh and perhaps you could have Leela bring me my coat. I'm going to have to rush this test, but if the results are positive, then I'm going to need to wrap up warm. Very warm.'

Melody opened her mouth to speak, but the Doctor wasn't quite done.

'Oh, and Parker, make yourself useful and pour me a dozen Scotches from the bar. And make it a single malt, will you?' He smiled. 'Nothing under 12 years old.'

Parker formed a slow frown. 'Hey, the world's about to end, why not? Hell, I might even join you.' His sarcasm soared sharply. 'How d'you want yours? On the rocks?'

'No – no, I don't think so,' said the Doctor, having apparently given the matter some thought. 'But you might add a splash of water, take the edge off, there's a good fellow.'

Melody turned tail to run her errand. More shots were fired out in the streets, further reminders that if time had ever been on their side, it was fast deserting to the enemy.

Derm's eyes were impenetrable walls, hiding a sense of hopelessness. They'd been that way since the initial assault, when the ice rained in over the flames in high arcs of frozen lightning. Most melted in the heat; but enough touched earth inside the barricades. And two hooked into living targets.

Derm saw Kyle, wild-eyed and looking for something to kill, so he gave the nod. The men, already unravelling, burst apart like glass under a dozen hammers. And the ice raining in converged on the splinters, spinning icicle twine from fragments of the dead.

Derm ordered the squad to fall back, knowing he was buying time at a high premium.

Makenzie had always been a solemn church-goer, but amid the reverent silence of a Sunday morning the Lord might easily prove a good listener. Here, with the gunfire never frequent enough to subside into the background, and everyone besieging him with worries and questions; well, Makenzie wondered if even the Lord might have given up by now.

He raised his hands for calm one more time and surveyed the faces turned towards him.

Janny Meeks waited expectantly on what he might say. She waited alone.

Amber. God, he'd been praying so hard for the mother, he'd clean forgotten the child.

'Folks, I have to step outside,' he announced. 'Look after Martha, here.'

Makenzie Shaw turned away from the folks of Melvin Village, just this once. The brisk walk down the aisle seemed endless, and he was still far from free when he made the exit.

Joanna felt curiously revitalised, as though she'd been infused with energy rather than blood, but she was grateful for the support afforded by Leela's strong shoulders as they followed Melody down to the laboratory.

Her nerves were still a little edgy, and the background rattle and thunder of the small battle outside wasn't doing her any favours.

'Ah, Leela! And Lieutenant Hmieleski! Good to see you're doing well!'

The Doctor's greeting was a welcome dose of warmth, but sounded a little too exuberant for the occasion. Joanna gently shrugged off Leela's help, thanking her with a nod, before attempting to make sense of everything going on in the laboratory: the covered corpse; Melody helping the Doctor on with his coat; even the sight of the woman's partner – she assumed – playing bartender, she noted in her stride. But the Doctor, perched on a stool and working his way along a row of shot-glasses, was hard on her battered skull.

'Oh, I'm a long way off well,' she answered coolly. She was afraid she wasn't awake yet; this seemed so unlike him. 'It sounds bad out there, Doctor.'

'And getting worse, I've no doubt.' The Doctor returned to his mournful slouch, as though to show he plainly wasn't enjoying himself. 'Which is precisely why I'm resorting to such extremes. I'm normally more of a ginger pop man myself.'

The agent behind the bar jerked a thumb at his solitary customer. 'Don't mind him, he's trying for a drunken moment of clarity.'

Joanna pushed her way forward, stooping to turn the Doctor around on his stool and peer into his eyes. Beneath the faint alcohol-induced glaze, she wanted to find the same foundations for trust she had discovered there before. If he was lost, then so was everybody here.

'Doctor, tell me this is part of some plan.'

The Doctor revolved on his stool, and laid a paternal hand on her; a father who has some bad news to impart. 'Lieutenant Hmieleski, it's a beastly job but someone has to do it. Melody, tell them how my experiment in electrolysis is going, won't you?'

Melody patiently crossed the room to the side bench, where twin electrodes had been fed from a small power supply into a beaker full of clear liquid. The woman gingerly lifted one of the electrodes out of the liquid and held it up where everyone could see it: a diamond bud had formed around the electrode stem, so fiery white it hurt the eyes.

'Positive results, Doctor. Very positive,' concluded Melody, revealing a degree of surprise. 'I guess this means your drinking time hasn't been wasted.'

'No, indeed,' agreed the Doctor glumly.

'Doctor, what does this mean?' Poor Leela was more anxious than anyone for answers.

Melody smiled around the room. 'It means, I think, we have a way to fight back.'

The Doctor stood, swirling the remnants of another Scotch around in its glass and watching the whirlpool motions. 'Yes, all we need now is for some poor fool to venture into the nucleus of the storm and entice it down the mountain for a swim.'

A motion flashed in her eye: Melody tossed the crystal gem towards her. Joanna nearly choked on a rise of panic, and she fumbled the catch. The Doctor dipped expertly down and the jewel fell neatly into his palm.

'Butterfingers,' he said, kindly, flipping the crystal between his fingers. 'But you needn't be nervous. This is our invader in its purest form – and the good news is, it's perfectly inert. It's as if the creature can't multiply without its chosen vector, its building block here in our dimension. Something with a suitably crystalline structure, like ice.'

Joanna stared, all but hypnotised by the crystal. Leela approached slowly for a closer view.

'It was the fish tank, you see,' the Doctor gazed deep into the impossibly white facets. 'Not the temperature of the water, so much as the fact that it's rendered inactive in solution. Which is exactly where it needs to be if we're to stand any chance of fighting it.'

The Doctor planted the jewel in Joanna's hand. To her, it felt as cold and lethal as ever.

'While it's inert and defenceless, it's really a very simple matter to decompose the electrolyte, separate the alien crystals from its earthly – or rather, watery – host, so to speak. After that, it's just a matter of making sure your Captain stores it somewhere safe, where it can't recombine with water and re-freeze.'

He examined his hand and flexed the fingers experimentally. 'Hm, still reasonably good co-ordination. Perhaps a couple more for the road? Parker, if you please?'

While the man, Parker obliged, Joanna frowned. She was scared – scared of the thing in her hand, and just as scared of the funereal chords playing in the Doctor's voice.

'Doc,' Parker poured a Scotch and tipped in a splash of water, 'don't get me wrong, we all appreciate your scientific brilliance, but as far as I understand this thing is encircling the town. So unless you're expecting to fit the entire nucleus of this thing into that beaker, I don't see how electrolysis amounts to much of a master plan.'

'Hm?' The Doctor absently registered the extra drinks being lined up for him. 'Oh, trust me, Agent Theroux, this is no storm in a teacup. No, we need a much larger receptacle. Which is why I'm doubly glad you're here, Lieutenant Hmieleski.'

The Doctor patted her heartily, before returning to his perch on the barstool. 'There are a few details of this operation I'll need you to pass on to your Captain. For one thing, I'll need one of his vehicles; and you can have him prepare a supply of timed explosives. I don't very much trust my demolitions skills under the influence, you know. Which reminds me, I'll drink while we talk, if you don't mind. I have a few more of these to get through before our enemy calls time.'

Joanna regarded the diminishing row of Scotches and wondered if she was watching a man bracing himself for a suicide mission.

One premature whoop of victory and Ray Landers realised he'd be paying for the rest of his short life. The ice monster is out to get him, the Captain damn near blows his head off, he's damn near showered in lethal crystals; and now, to cap it off, the Captain's shouting at them to fall back and he catches sight of two comrades fenced in by buildings and monster ice.

He didn't stop to check his own escape route. He swung the grenade launcher and popped a shell into the house where the ice had broken through. It lit up beautifully – and the stretch of thicket went into spasms. It was still an obstacle, only now it was thrashing insanely.

Ray swore and thumped the nearest trashcan. The garbage hadn't been collected lately.

Ray pulled and primed an incendiary, flipped the lid and dropped the grenade in the trashcan. He threw himself on his back and kicked the can hard at the lashing thicket of ice.

It went flying into the tangled mass, belching superheat out of one end. Ray was up on his feet and charging forward, giving it everything for the vault of his life. The heat and the frost were on him in different places, but he hit the ground roughly, rolling onto his back.

Godzinski was there, helping him up. Zabala was there too, eyes so wide she looked little more than a kid. Neither of them looked too impressed with Ray's rescue bid.

The walls of their arena were the only enemy. And they were closing in fast.

Leela was crestfallen. The Doctor was continually forbidding her to follow him into battle, and on this occasion the blow to her pride was especially hurtful: the enemy that had driven Kristal's spirit from her body was the same one the Doctor was intending to fight alone.

'I want you to stay with Parker and Melody here,' he commanded her sharply, gesturing with an arm thrown wide. Then he cuffed her chin affectionately. 'You came out of that last encounter rather well, I think. A frosty expression and a few grey hairs.'

At that, he left her to brood, a slight sway to his stance as he turned to the agents. 'Now, is everyone clear on their role in this? I'm sure you took the opportunity to search my coat pockets, Melody, but I'm afraid the item you were after is safely tucked away here.' He patted one side of his waistcoat. His face sank – until he patted the opposite side. 'Here,' he looked relieved. Then he shoved his hands in his coat pockets and mastered the most serious of expressions. 'You'd best find Corporal Pydych and brief him on what's required.'

'Hey, just one thing you overlooked, Doc,' the man, Parker, assumed the posture of a male contesting leadership. 'I don't do menial labour. I *investigate*.'

The Doctor stood straight and gave the man a patronising slap on the arm. 'Then I suggest you investigate your versatility, there's a good fellow. Good luck, everybody! And remember, Leela. Stay close to Parker and Melody here. They need constant guarding.'

With that direst warning – and a gentle collision with the doorframe – he made his exit. Leela regarded her two charges uncertainly.

Only a couple of the guys from Morgan's HQ squad had managed to follow him up the main street, tossing a grenade or two and letting rip with burst after burst of automatic fire; covering their retreat and shoring up their shaken morale at the same time. He just hoped the others could find a way out round the back of the houses.

'Little bro!' Makenzie came running out of the churchyard to intercept him. Morgan could tell he had a problem on his mind, but he said, 'How bad is it?'

'Getting worse.' No sense in dressing it up. 'You have to get those folks moving now.'

'I can't. Not yet.' There was a hesitation, as if Makenzie had a bullet to bite. 'I have to find Amber. She upped and ran.'

Morgan bit a magazine full of bullets. He badly needed to yell, but he didn't know quite where to start.

'Captain!' Joanna Hmieleski came to his rescue. He guessed she must have emerged from the hotel. She looked a little dazed, but was holding it together – probably better than he was, give her credit. 'Captain,' she halted in front of him, puffed out a breath or two, 'the Doctor's got a plan together. We need to get some things set up for him.'

Morgan held up a hand to wall off his brother for the present. 'Give it to me.'

He listened intently while Joanna parcelled up the list of wants concisely and took him through the various components of the operation. 'And he wants a gap broken open at least a half mile wide in that ice.'

'He wants what?' Far as he knew, he hadn't been wounded,

but Morgan felt the blood draining out of him all the same. 'What the hell does he think I am? The Moses of the North? I've just been praying that ice can support a convoy. Eight inches! There's no way in hell we're going to blow that much of it open!'

While there was garbage in there to burn, Ray Landers gave the trashcan a shove with the butt of his rifle, sent it rolling into the other icicle thicket. Give that side something to think about, while he checked out the two buildings walling them in here.

There was only one window, and that was in the side of the house he'd torched. Hell, least ways it would be warm in there.

Head down, he charged into a headlong dive through the window. Layers of armour saved him from the glass and padded out the worst of the impacts as he crashed over the sink unit. Burning timbers collapsed overhead and hit the kitchen floor about the same time as he did.

'Come on in, ladies!' He kicked the timbers away and ducked clear of the window.

Flames were crawling all over the woodwork in livid streams. They'd have to get back out into the snow pretty damn soon.

White Shadow's demolitions maestro had been Ben McKim: one more option Morgan Shaw didn't have. Still, the two guys he'd brought with him could handle it, and O'Neill knew more electronics than just comms and sensors. He set them on the modest production line in the second Snowcat. Which left him to concentrate on coming up with a miracle.

Makenzie was still hanging like a spare limb, and Morgan was grateful when the Doctor burst out of the hotel, looking up and down the street and not really focusing on anything.

'Doc,' he motioned him over, 'I can give you six pounds of C4, timed detonators and a remote trigger. We're going to need the rest for the lake.'

'And then some, I should imagine,' the Doc commented sagaciously. There was something unnervingly mystical about the guy's gaze right now, more so than usual.

Morgan let it go. 'Just let me worry about that.'

'I will. And your first priority should be evacuating the town.'

Makenzie, predictably, barged in: 'I can't supervise all of that until I've found Amber. I know she picks her times, but she's gone missing again.'

The Doc fixed Makenzie with an omniscient stare. 'Oh, I doubt she's run away this time. Trust me, I'll find her. And don't worry, Makenzie. She's safer than any of us right now.'

Makenzie took his time reading the Doc. Morgan alerted him with an upward nod. 'Hey, bro, you heard the man. Best get those people moving. Okay?'

He softened the last word considerably. He'd never seen his brother looking so lost.

Orders from the Doctor were one thing, but when Parker had instructed her to wait right here – alone with the dead, in the middle of the room – Leela was inclined to be suspicious, as well as disobedient. She crept towards the door and pressed her ear to it.

She could hear the two conferring in hushed, insistent tones.

'This is the Prism we're talking about here, Melody! Even if this nutball scheme of his blows up in his face, our ticket out of here is probably going to get fritzed!'

'Sure, I take your point, but I don't see how your going after him is going to – '

'Well, honeybun, I would nominate you, but he's a guy and he's twice your size. No, you're better off sitting on Pydych and doing what you can to fix things from your end.'

'Parker, I'm just not sure – '

'Shush.'

Leela backed away from the door. She knew now what the Doctor had meant when he had told her these two needed guarding.

Dermot Beard's squad was scattered and running, but they were only following their leader's example. Derm didn't know where they all were: it was down to him and Kyle by the time they reached the third line of defence.

Picket fences dowsed in gas, and a shallow trench dug across the avenue between them. Derm squatted down in one of the yards and looked at Kyle as he hopped the trench.

Kyle shook his head as he hunkered down next to Derm. 'Sorry, sir. I'm all out.'

Derm let out what felt like his last breath. They'd exhausted their incendiaries and even the frags just getting here. He wasn't even packing any more flares.

Through the snowfall, he could make out the drifts, rolling in like crystallised fog.

'Damn, soldier,' he forced a pained smile, 'we need a light.'

Makenzie played shepherd to the refugees of Melvin Village, packing them into every available vehicle and sending them on their way with a wave or a slap on each vehicle's rear. As the cars and trucks filed past the church, it was like watching his town breaking apart and flaking off in pieces across the desolate lake.

He had them slide Martha into the rear of his Police truck.

The cold he felt right then was something new. Martha without Amber would never be the warm, shining Martha he loved; the Martha who smiled so fine with just half her mouth.

Makenzie realised he was mourning a family, as well as a town.

'Lots of luck, Doc. You're going to need it.'

Joanna wondered just how much luck was on offer. The Captain was standing there watching the Snowcat trundle down the street, the ferocious engine noise eventually lost in the winds, and she was fairly sure he had no idea that the Doctor was drunk in charge of a vehicle packed full of jerry-rigged bombs. She muttered her own personal good luck wishes to the back of the Snowcat before it vanished altogether in the storm.

'Sir,' she spoke her next thought loud, 'what about the lake?'

'I'll think of something, don't rush me.' Morgan scanned the street, and stamped. 'Okay, let's get organised. Joanna, you'd best find yourself a place with the evac.'

'Uh-uh.' Joanna stood straight and blinked back on the remains of her headache. 'I'm staying.' She made sure her eyes said how much she meant it. There was a clear understanding in Morgan's nod, and she relaxed immediately. 'Thank you, sir.'

Morgan's shake of the head was rueful, but the slam of a vehicle door distracted him from what he was about to say. Joanna looked back along the street to where Agent Theroux was bundling the girl Leela into the rear of one of the Hummers. Irving Pydych and Melody Quartararo were clambering into the front.

Theroux simply waved them goodbye then came striding up to greet the Captain.

'Captain, I'd like to commandeer one of your snowmobiles. I figured I'd ride shotgun.'

Joanna figured the man's smirk alone was enough for a trial and conviction, but Morgan wasn't in any mood to argue. She looked away as he assented all too easily.

And she frowned at the departing Hum-Vee.

The rear passenger door swung open and she swore she'd seen something tumbling clear as the vehicle pulled away.

The Doctor was getting the distinct impression he had never driven a Snowcat in a previous life. Still, he had to make allowances for the appalling conditions, of both the terrain and his reflexes.

He had to filter out the engine noise in order to focus; and yet focusing was one of the worst things he could do. He could purge his system of the alcohol at any time, but for the moment its effects were vital. He only wondered if they would prove as effective as he was hoping.

Flakes of snow hurled themselves against the windscreen in their millions. If the Doctor had been prone to more fanciful thoughts, he might have imagined they were ganging up on him.

The Doc was a wuss. Whereas Parker could take his liquor neat. He had armed himself with a bottle of Jack Daniels from the bar and once he was safely out of sight, he brought the snowmobile to a temporary halt to permit a few precious swigs. (He wasn't, after all, too proud to admit that the Doc might know what he was doing on that score.)

Better safe than sober.

He stowed the bottle back into his coat pocket and grasped the handle bars.

Before he opened the throttle, something substantial landed on the seat behind him. The same thing poked him in the side with what felt like the muzzle of a pistol.

'You can go after the Doctor,' Leela allowed him generously. 'But I am coming with you.'

Parker sniffed and debated whether to try the old reverse thrust with the elbow.

But no. The pressure from the gun held him off; along with the thought that if he really wanted to stay the Doc's hand – just long enough to recover the Prism, of course – a bargaining chip could be priceless. And bargaining chips didn't come much prettier than Leela.

'Sure,' he consented. 'I always say, a biker's nothing without a pretty chick to back him up.'

Parker gunned the throttle and steered the snowmobile for the back streets, searching for the safest route out of town.

* * *

Pydych stretched back to pull the rear door shut. Next to him, Melody looked tiny behind the wheel of the Hum-Vee, but she was handling the stocky vehicle with ease.

'I wonder why she left in such a hurry,' he said. 'I'm sure it can't be your driving.'

'She's going after my partner. Let's just concentrate on what we have to do, shall we?'

Pydych decided to shut up for a while. He tensed as they bumped down the bank and onto the lake. Up ahead, the lights of the evacuation convoy were diluted close to nothing in the swirling blizzard. The pale gloom made the line of vehicles look like a cortège.

Even Irving Pydych was all out of humorous comment at that point.

The storm was waiting to embrace her, urging her on. Amber was sure she could feel it pumping energy through her arms and legs, driving her onwards up the snow-blown hill.

The grind and growl of a large engine reached her through the wind and her hood.

She looked down to see one of the military vehicles struggling up the slope, churning up the snow with its big tracks. It wasn't veering towards her, so perhaps the driver hadn't spotted her yet. There was only one place it could be heading.

Ducking slightly, Amber trotted a short way down the slope to draw level with the vehicle. Then she raced across the open, like a hare darting from hiding.

The crawling speed of the vehicle was enough to make it hard work, but Amber flipped back the tarpaulin on the trailer and hoisted herself inside.

She was sure the storm would be pleased with her, now it wouldn't have to wait so long.

The ice creature didn't care for inanimate materials, but it would eat through them to get at what it really wanted. The

Doctor presumed his dulled wits had preserved him up till now, but this close to the core, he knew he was pushing his luck.

And luck had a habit of pushing back hard.

In his next glance away from the snow-smeared windscreen, he could see the first threads of ice weaving their spidery lace over the interior of the Snowcat.

Melody didn't dare drive too wide of the evacuation convoy for fear the ice was thinner off the marked route. Pydych confirmed that Sergeant Garvey's squad had been assigned as trailbreakers and they had done a fine job, planting poles in the ice and attaching coloured rags as markers. It implied there would be some extra help waiting for them on the far shore.

Still, it wasn't the best of news.

It meant she had less time than she'd hoped for making her decision.

If there were White Shadow people waiting up ahead, then any act of sabotage would have to be committed in front of an audience. It made life just a little more difficult.

Magnesium threads lanced across the Doctor's view like crooked laser beams: crystalline fire quite distinct from the blizzard, and a telling sign that the nucleus wasn't far.

The Doctor slowed the vehicle and reached for the handbrake.

Cold teeth bit deep into his palm. He snatched his hand away and grit his teeth. He defied any palmist to interpret the chaos of white lines embedded in his skin.

A smudge, no bigger than a child, crossed in front of the vehicle, then vanished into the maelstrom of threads. Amber!

The Doctor leaped up from his seat and grabbed the backpack full of explosives.

He lunged for the door and practically fell from the vehicle, all but sinking to his knees in the snow. He could already feel the alien crystals coursing through him, like sand through an hourglass, one deadly grain at a time.

Amber walked into a giant nest.

That was what it looked like: a vast bird's nest; icy fibres whizzing around ferociously like pencil lines in a cartoon tornado; except white, so very white. They scrawled themselves over and over, doodling in the air around her as she passed through the wall of the nest.

Spinning in the centre was an egg. A glowing egg.

A yolk of alien light housed in a framework instead of a shell, it seemed to take hold of her and tug at her, as though dragging her from her body.

Amber screamed.

The nest went insane.

Chapter Twenty

The Doctor stumbled through a cyclone of barbed threads, the colour of bleached silver. Every strand a frozen spark against his skin, stabbing and searing with each pinprick impact.

The alcohol wasn't slowing the rate of conversion as effectively as he had hoped. Instinct urged him to fight, to erect a psychic barrier against the alien invader. But the very act of concentration would feed its appetite for mental energy and speed the neural traffic into an inevitable *dead* end.

His vision blurred, and he knew it had nothing to do with the alcohol.

He whipped up a hand to fence out the light that had tugged at his eyes. Before the shield came up, he had caught sight of Amber, hurling silent screams into the light. And a familiar blue lamp poking up like a timid periscope directly under the Stormcore.

The tracked vehicle looked abandoned, its door gaping open. As to why, the spinning ice storm now as wide as the mountain offered a portentous explanation.

Leela mastered her fears and leaped from the snowmobile before Parker brought it fully to a halt. She drew a few deep breaths, preparing herself for the sprint to the Snowcat.

She realised her mistake as soon as she heard the heavy footfall behind her.

Before she could complete the turn, Parker knocked her to the ground.

There was nothing else for it, but to put their heads down, run like crazy and sweat. The heat and the smoke were the worst barriers by far. At least the collapsing timbers and the fires could be dodged if they kept their wits about them.

Ray was first out into the yard, the frosty air flooding his lungs and forcing out the smoke in hacking coughs. He managed to get a few choice swear words out along with the fumes.

Zabala darted out past him and made for the fence, Godzinski right after her. Another mighty crash erupted from within, and Ray figured it was time to get moving. He followed the girls at a fast jog; the best he could manage with starved lungs.

The fence was sprouting a lightning crest of ice.

Mary Mother! Ray conjured up an extra burst of speed from nowhere. He hopped the fence, hit the ground. He coughed hard. And skidded.

Flat on his front.

Zabala, up the street, stopped and stared. Godzinski hovered, then came running.

Ray was scrabbling up, trapped in a coughing fit. Godzinski was close and she thrust out a helping hand. Gratefully, he grasped at it and pulled.

Then looked up into the icicles stabbing through Jen Godzinski's eyes.

Hellish mockeries of human figures danced out of the crystal fog like marionettes. Skeletons of ice with shifting wire-thin bones and icicle-tendrils pulsing around inside.

Derm didn't have time to shout orders: Kyle just opened fire.

Derm lifted his own rifle. He was down to four magazines, and the frozen fogbank was already throwing more of its macabre infantry ahead of its advance.

The eastern shore wasn't the most scenic, so there were a couple of points where the power lines had approached the lake. One tower stood a short way down the road from the church, camouflaged to a degree by the surrounding trees.

Morgan nabbed Joanna, O'Neill and the others and led the run to the other Hum-Vee. He yanked the door open and turned to climb in behind the wheel.

The sight at the north end of town stopped him dead.

A solid snowdrift, rolling down the street like a slow tsunami.

Strong fingers gripped Amber's shoulder and spun her around. She'd been so busy screaming – voicelessly, like in a nightmare – she was about to let out another one, but she was met by a strange calm, deep in the centre of the Doctor's eyes.

'Amber,' he mouthed her name precisely, and she could feel the vibration of his voice through the fingers at her shoulder. 'We have to leave here. *Now.*'

She noticed his other hand: veins of ice crawled where they should have run blue.

Amber shook her head, determinedly.

It wasn't as easy as he'd anticipated. Parker had the advantage in size and strength, but Leela was one tough chick. Not to mention agile and vicious.

She wrestled him over at one point, striking out at his jugular. Parker took the blow with his forearm, saw his opportunity to throw her off as she reached for the knife at her belt. As soon as she landed, she went for the knife again. Parker dived at her and pinned her.

He groped for the gun inside his coat, but as he pulled it, she freed an arm from under his knee and smacked it flying. He watched it land too many yards away in the snow.

'Now, why did you have to go and do that?'

Sighing, he pulled back his fist to punch her out.

Ray Landers yelped. Godzinski's grip had seized up, like she was in some sort of electric shock. Her hand was a vice around his wrist and the rest of her was turning to ice.

Lines of it ate up her arm, racing one another to get to him.

Ray tugged so hard it hurt his wrist.

He rolled onto his side and swung his rifle like a club. It smashed through the limb of ice and the hand flopped into the snow, tiny crystals starting to eat through the glove.

Ray hauled himself out of there and ran for Zabala, who was sighting along her rifle at what had once been Jen Godzinski. Ray turned to follow her example.

Raising the rifle, all he saw was the ice eating its way along the weapon towards his eye.

Joanna racked her brain so hard she was almost in danger of blacking out again. She'd volunteered – insisted on volunteering – to hold back the drift. Moments after the Hum-Vee had burned off in the direction of the electrical pylon, her two troopers were announcing they were all out of grenades – of any kind.

The drift was holed and cratered in places, but it mended itself and continued its advance.

This stand of hers was more about guilt than courage, she was too aware of that. Action to compensate for inaction, the way a belated card is supposed to make up for a forgotten birthday. If anything, though, it made her all the more determined she wasn't going to fail.

'Explosives!' Joanna motioned the soldiers to follow her. 'Pack a charge on board that Snowcat and send it into the thing!'

'Lieutenant, we're short of charges – '

'Just do it!' Her throat was so raw, she didn't even sound like her any more.

The Stormcore was only doing what it was designed to do: multiplexing energy streams and drawing them into a central nexus. It was powerful enough to reel in all sound and even play tug-of-war with the neural pulses travelling the optic nerve.

There wasn't time to explain any of that to Amber: the Doctor lifted her up and carried her away from the centre. She pummelled him with furious blows, but when he could hear her cries he planted her down again and knelt to bring his gaze to bear on tearful eyes.

'Amber, listen to me. You don't share any connection with the storm. This ice creature is an alien creature; it doesn't belong here. It was pulled or fell through a gap opened up by that device you saw.'

'That's the thing that's making it do all this! Get rid of it, take it away from here! Then I can talk to it, I know I can. It'll listen to me.'

'No, Amber,' the Doctor argued, keeping his voice firm, but his gaze gentle. 'That device is a sort of steering wheel. It's using it to help control its actions. This creature won't be appeased or controlled, not by you, me or anyone. Control is what it wants for itself. It wants nothing more than to be master of its own destiny.'

'You can't know how it feels,' the girl complained bitterly.

'No, I can't,' the Doctor told her honestly. 'Not for certain. But in the absence of being able to communicate, we have to put ourselves in its place, try to see the world from its point of view. I think it's raw emotion, crystallised, and I think it recognised you as a friend because you shared so many of the same feelings. That's why it seeks out intelligent minds: it craves an intelligence to govern all those mixed emotions and make sense of the world around it. A world where it doesn't belong.'

The Doctor wasn't so very old that he couldn't see the world through the eyes of a child. 'It's a frightening world,' he said, 'when you feel very much alone.'

He thought he saw the first roots of understanding in Amber's frown.

* * *

Leela turned her face aside from the blow. But it never came.

She risked a look: Parker had lowered his fist and relaxed his hold. He shrugged. 'What am I doing? I can't hit a girl.'

Leela blazed. 'Then that is your weakness.'

Dragging herself from under the agent, she kicked out with her boot and struck him deep in the crotch. It was satisfying to see him crumple to his knees, eyes bulging painfully.

Irving Pydych had been cheered a little when they had rendezvoused with Garvey and his guys on the western shore. Now, peering up at the pylon, all that cheer had evaporated.

Sergeant Garvey had bravely driven the Hum-Vee back onto the ice, while Pydych held the free end of the tow cable. The winch having unwound the steel cable to full stretch, there was plenty of slack. More than enough, Pydych was sure, to hang himself.

'This strikes me as a tiny bit dangerous. Especially with my vertigo. I did mention my vertigo, right?' He hefted the weighty hook in his hand. 'Are you sure that's where they want this thing attached?'

Melody regarded him a little too sympathetically for his liking.

'If it makes it any easier,' she offered, 'I can make the climb with you.'

Pydych glanced up again at the tip of the pylon, all the power lines swinging in the wind. Even if he wasn't a born cynic, it was hard to believe anyone would make an offer like that.

Morgan watched the distant figure of O'Neill clinging precariously near the tip of the pylon. He wasn't shy of such hazardous work himself, but his comms man knew what he was doing around electrical things. He'd parked the Hummer out on the ice and now all he could do was wait while O'Neill hooked the cable to the power.

Hopefully without –

A massive explosion turned his attention north. A petroleum fireball ballooned up from the wrecked silhouette of one of the Snowcats.

Morgan broke into a run. Then slowed up some, as he worked out it was some distance past the hotel and the other vehicles. Then broke into a run again, as inspiration lit up inside him, at least as fierce and bright as the burning vehicle.

He badly needed to talk to his brother.

When the police band crackled to life, Makenzie was glancing in the rear-view for a glimpse of Martha, hoping to be able to tell how she was doing back there.

He recognised his brother's voice under the static, but didn't believe what he was hearing.

He snatched up the mic. 'Are you out of your mind, bro? The lead car's almost – '

'Trust me, Mak,' the voice came back, clearer this time, as if the radio wanted to convey all of the emotion in that simple appeal.

Makenzie swung his truck out of the convoy and accelerated along the line of vehicles.

Ray tossed the rifle away like it was a rattlesnake. He backed up in the same instant, turning over his hands and searching every inch of his jacket and sleeves for signs of ice. Snowflakes kept spattering on his uniform and giving him miniature heart attacks.

Zabala rattled off burst after burst at the raging tangle of ice now turning its attention towards them. She emptied her magazine into it, shattering it away to nothing.

Apparent nothing, Ray reminded himself.

He tapped Zabala's arm and urged her to follow him as he belted down the street.

Derm backed up and rammed in his last magazine. Kyle sprayed the ice creatures with carefully rationed three-round bursts. Derm raised his rifle – and shifted aim: downwards.

He opened up into the trench of gas and prayed for sparks off the asphalt.

The trench lit up – *after* one of the ice-marionettes lashed out with a whip-like limb.

The spindly arm grew frozen claws into Kyle's face. Reflexively, Derm swung his rifle and squeezed back on the trigger. The weapon clicked on empty.

Derm roared and charged at the newly forming ice creature.

Rifle held forward between both hands, he drove it into the wall of flames. The face of a man Derm once knew was still attached to the creature as it was swallowed by the fire.

It was an image to penetrate even the thickest of skins.

There wasn't any time for niceties such as precision place-ment of the explosives. The Doctor had to simply set the timers, and arrange the six charges in a rough circle under the Stormcore. He was relying on the TARDIS force field to deflect most of the blast upwards and outwards.

'Sorry, old girl,' he patted the lamp as he finished planting the last charge in the snow. 'Best cover your ears.'

Ducking back, he turned and grasped Amber's hand to lead her in a mad dash through the wind-woven threads of the blizzard.

'Will they kill it? Those bombs?'

Even in the screaming winds and the lashing ice, the Doctor could hear the worry in Amber's shout. 'No! Hopefully they'll break the creature's hold on the device and send it tumbling down the mountain! And with any luck, the storm nucleus won't want to let go of its prize!'

He could have done with being able to cross his fingers.

But he had lost all contact with his free hand, the nerves in that arm having turned to ice.

They may have left Melvin Village behind, but they were still a community. Anyone else might have found it impossible to persuade all those frightened folk to leave the convoy strewn in a broken herring-bone pattern and make the remainder of the trek on foot. And the extent of their trust might have overwhelmed anyone other than Makenzie Shaw.

There wouldn't be any milk and honey flowing in Winnipesaukee, but Makenzie would settle for the chance to get Martha to a hospital.

Watching the folks file briskly past, he managed a smile, and prayed for Amber's safety.

Parker lay flat on his back, with only his head and his hands raised in grudging deference to the pistol that Leela had produced and aimed at his chest. She didn't seem altogether at ease with the automatic, but he didn't doubt her intention or her ability at this range.

Behind her, the mountainside erupted like a nuclear volcano.

Leela turned to take one look, then she was bolting for the nearest trees. Parker didn't hesitate to scramble to his feet and follow, as the mushroom cloud collapsed into an avalanche.

White, he decided, was the colour of holy crap.

Joanna couldn't help thinking of Emilie Jacks, out to burn all her bridges the moment her cult had disintegrated. This *was* different, though, she told herself.

She rode pillion behind Captain Shaw. She held a gas can, tipped at an angle to spill its contents in a trail behind them. The snowmobiles slalomed between the abandoned vehicles on the lake, each of them trailing gasoline.

Sure, this was very different: they were saving something here.

For her though, any victory would carry an aftertaste, like the acrid fumes drying her mouth.

Melody waited at the base of the pylon and welcomed a decidedly pale Corporal Pydych with a congratulatory pat on the back. He was shaky on his legs but he would survive.

'I hope you realise it was hell up there.' He stamped around, as though to make sure the ground was real. 'This had better work.'

The cable trailed all the way back to the Hum-Vee out on the ice. Makenzie Shaw had led the refugees of Melvin Village ashore, taking them on to the town of Winnipesaukee. But they couldn't sink that vehicle until Morgan and his people got here. Whatever they were doing about cracking the lake open, they were cutting it mighty fine.

'Have a little faith in the technology,' Melody advised, sounding a little maudlin despite her brave smile. 'According to the Doctor, the Stormcore should do most of the work.'

Drawing the current into a concentrated stream, she thought. And, in the process of channelling all that raw electricity, probably burning out its own circuits.

She didn't suppose Parker would be happy for one minute. But there was a limit to what she was prepared to pay for a ticket home.

The snowmobiles were all they had left. Morgan had sent his Command Vehicle onto the ice to crack it open and sink the Hummer into the cold waters, as one essential component in the Doctor's bizarre scheme. The human cost had been so high here that the expense of the vehicle hadn't even entered into the account.

He swerved the snowmobile around and rode it up the bank of the western shore. Hopping off, he spared a look for Joanna, then watched the other snowmobiles cruising in to join them: among them, Landers and Zabala; O'Neill and Derm. His faithful second had been the last to emerge from the blizzard, cutting it close to the wire.

Morgan raised the remote detonator and thumbed the button.

It died like a giant wave on a lonely shore: spectacular and largely unseen.

The drama was played out behind a white curtain and the lighting could only do its best under difficult conditions. There wasn't even much of a soundtrack.

Most of the lakeside audience had the sense to cover their ears as the multiple blasts ripped apart the vehicles in a great firecracker chain; and they kept them covered as they watched the snake-formation of the convoy sink, shedding its skin of fire on the waters. But the pyrotechnics were only for openers.

Melody had the sharpest pair of eyes here. She grabbed a pair of binoculars off one of the soldiers in the hope she might see *something*. Anything.

She could make out the avalanche, exploding out over the lake, but she guessed her imagination was doing most of the work. Painting it as a galaxy of ice cast down from the heavens, to break apart over the burning waters. Cold stars formed in the nebula, ice particles clustering together in fear of the flames. They were the last to die, melting away in scattered islands, like polar ice caps on an overheated globe.

After that, there was nothing left to see.

Melody handed the binoculars back to the soldier and shrugged like she'd seen nothing. In her mind, she could visualise the chemical reactions continuing beneath the surface, steady currents setting to work on the dissolved particles.

Mostly it was just cold science. But there was an element of poetry even in that.

Currents. It was always the victim of currents.

Drowning in fire and water, grains of consciousness, crystals of emotion crying out to one another, dragged away by currents as powerful as destiny, to die in a burning energy field.

No, not to die. To sleep.

The Doctor stood close to Amber, letting his gaze fall slowly down the mountainside. Parker and Leela had joined them only a moment ago. A snake of fire rippled across the lake, faint but satisfactory under the veil of the blizzard.

'That should do nicely,' said the Doctor.

'What will happen to it?' He didn't need to see the child's face to know she was crying.

'Electrolysis, essentially. The purified crystals collect around an electrode. In this case, a small truck.' The Doctor pressed Amber's shoulder kindly. 'A crystal that size, I imagine it'll be taken somewhere safe, where it can be properly looked after.'

Amber raised half a smile. The Doctor answered with a full one.

'Which reminds me, I'm sure Agent Theroux here will be delighted to conduct you safely down the mountain. I expect your mother will be anxious to know you're well.'

Predictably, Parker was set to object, but the Doctor grinned and waved the blood sample like a bribe. Parker marched over and grabbed it. 'Okay, okay. But where are you going?'

The Doctor tapped his nose, then looked dismayed at the veins of ice still lacing his hand. He was having some trouble focusing, but he was fairly sure they were starting to recede. 'Leela and I are going home,' he said.

'Doctor!' Leela raced up, excited. 'You have found the T– '

He silenced her with a finger to his lips. 'Shh! Leela! One wrong word now and you could cause another avalanche.'

Parker huffed indignantly. 'Don't sweat it, Doc, I might have hijacked your ship if I'd thought about it, but I'll be damned if I'll accept a lift.'

'Ah, well, we're often better off finding our own way.'

He beamed at Amber.

'But it doesn't hurt to accept a little help now and then.'

He spun about and strode off up the slope. 'Come along, Leela, and do throw away that gun, they're terribly habit-forming, there's a good girl.'

* * *

The TARDIS peeped nervously above the snow, buried nearly to her middle. The Doctor reached over and patted her roof. 'There, there.' It wouldn't take too long to dig the doors clear, at least; especially if Leela put her back into it.

He looked around for her. She was turning the gun over in her hands.

'Leela, what did I tell you about – ' The Doctor stopped short of snatching the weapon from her. 'Kristal gave you that, didn't she?'

Leela nodded minutely. She ran her thumb over the pistol, absorbed by the texture. 'Doctor, do you think that she crossed into the spirit world, as she would have wished?'

The Doctor weighed his moment carefully. He eased the gun from Leela's hands. 'Well,' he said, 'that's the thing about belief. It's not important what I think.' He draped an arm around her. 'It's only important what you think.'

Just occasionally, there were things that science couldn't explain; and equally, there were some occasions when it shouldn't make the attempt.

'Amber probably still believes she was connected to that creature in some way. Empathy is a common phenomenon between like minds.'

'Is that why the girl was crying? She felt for the creature?'

'Yes, and who can blame her.' The Doctor pocketed the gun, thinking it might be made safe. 'Lost, adrift and alone in an alien dimension, only wanting some basic needs common to most: a home and some control over its own destiny. Someone should shed a few tears for it.'

Leela glanced up at him. 'You feel for the creature too?'

'Well,' the Doctor shrugged off the notion, 'I expect it's just the drink talking.'

Shaking himself alert, he turned back to the TARDIS. 'Come on, a spot of digging might be the very thing to help me metalobise the alcohol out of my system.'

'Metalobise?'

'Yes, *metalobise,*' the Doctor insisted defensively. 'If I tried to operate the TARDIS in my current state, I'd have no idea where we were going. Then where would we be, hmm?'

Thanksgiving

Thanksgiving morning was trying its damnedest to bless the trees and hills with a gold trim, working hard at it through a still-hazy sky. Like a priest determined to exorcise the demons of the past few days.

The storms would be back, for sure. It was that time of year. But they would be natural, and for now the world of New Hampshire simply needed to take a breather. And for once, it seemed, the weather was uncharacteristically inclined to give everybody a chance.

Captain Morgan Shaw wandered back to the chopper, squatting on the hill like some mutant mosquito adapted for winter. The Nighthawk was a taste of the outside world, the military machine; in some ways as heartening to Morgan as the sunrise.

His medical officer was hoisting her pack on board. She'd been glancing into the dawn, but not really seeing it. Morgan reflected on all the reasons why he shouldn't be seeing it either.

'Hey,' he felt the need to break the moment.

'Hey, yourself,' she worked hard on her smile. '*Sir.*'

'Don't go quitting the team, Joanna. Not after all this.'

Hmieleski looked out over the trees and ridges. 'I don't know, sir. The team is – ' She stopped herself, then looked right in his eyes. 'I made some wrong choices, sir, and they cost lives. I should have – '

'Hey,' Morgan shut her up. 'Want to know what I think? What I think is – totally irrelevant.' He gave a friendly smirk, because he had her attention now. 'They were judgement calls, Joanna, and stuff happened. But you know what's making you sick to the gut right now? I'll tell you, it's not because they were the wrong calls or the right ones. It's because they were *yours*. Sometimes you just have to be satisfied you were able to make any decision at all.'

'Sir?'

'Yeah?'

'Can I go now?'

Morgan laughed and he wished her bon voyage with his eyes. He could have used her support and expertise a few more days, with the whole cleanup operation; but he was hopeful if he let her go now, she'd still be his queen of Alpha Team. His Alpha female.

He helped her on board the helicopter. She settled into her seat and her expression was like a huge Thank God. Morgan ducked back and signalled to the pilot: take my girl home for some quality R&R.

Morgan knew he'd be here a while himself. Long enough to exchange goodbyes with his brother, he guessed – whenever he got back. Morgan wanted to make some sort of personal resolution, to keep in touch with Mak more. Make an effort.

But, like all those forefathers who'd landed on the East Coast and offered up their thanks to the Lord, and then, as Kristal had constantly reminded him, trashed their new paradise and wiped out the natives – some promises were best left unmade.

Melody tapped the keys hanging from the ignition and watched them jangle like a poor set of chimes. She wondered how much longer she was going to have to sit here.

Her partner was standing at the lake's edge, gazing out across the ice at the 4×4 as though willing it to finish sinking properly. Where the ice had cracked open, the waters had re-frozen and locked the vehicle in that ridiculous angle. Parker looked like he was paying his respects to a memorial – a memorial to their failure, perhaps.

With every plough in the county mobilised to take advantage of the first respite in days, it had been a relatively simple matter to obtain a replacement car.

Melody was all ready to get the hell out of Dodge, so to speak, but she'd driven back to the cabin so they could collect their personal belongings; or rather, the belongings that had become personal to their lives here. They were on their outward journey, when Parker had asked her to park up by the shore.

He'd been so sullen, she'd given in without a word. Now, she wanted to honk the horn.

Finally though, he walked briskly to the car and hopped in beside her, shutting out the cold air with a satisfying slam. Melody offered her partner a pitying gaze, but he didn't seem to rise to the bait. 'Hey, partner, chin up. It's not that bad.'

'Isn't it? We were so *close*.' He spat through his teeth and clenched a fist over the dash.

'There'll be other cases.'

'Yeah. And a lot more Dimension Phase Multiplexers. There must be, what, dozens out there. You know, it's not like the lottery – we can't buy a goddamn ticket every week.'

'No,' agreed Melody softly, and she gently took hold of the keys. 'But even if we have to wait another twenty or thirty years, the waking hours will go by that much easier if you're not in a permanent sulk.'

'I guess.' His huffy response and the folded arms said otherwise.

Melody left the keys in the ignition and reached over to stroke her partner's hair. 'Try to look at it this way: what were we back home? Just a couple of nobodies, really. Here, we're really something, Parker. We're special, different. We have talents and gifts, and a whole lot more time than anyone else on this planet.'

Parker sniffed and rocked his head from side to side, weighing up the advantages. He ended by tipping his head more Melody's way. 'Keep doing what you're doing. Yeah, maybe I can live with that. When you put it that way it doesn't sound so bad.'

Parker held her gaze and moved in for the kiss.

'Knock it off.'

Melody sat up and grabbed the wheel, turning over the ignition. There would be other cases, guaranteed. They'd just have to do like they had been doing: keep an eye out for the really *special* ones, manoeuvre their way into them.

Meanwhile it was time for a vacation. Somewhere warm, she fancied.

The road around Winnipesaukee unfurled into a different world, like an early Christmas card. The sun was shining and the clearer skies implied that the land could sleep snugly under its blanket of white this winter. Amber had seen only a few Thanksgiving mornings, but this was by far the most beautiful.

At least it gave her something other than Makenzie to look at as the miles rolled by.

Amber could tell he had something other than driving on his mind, like he'd been building up to saying the words from the moment they'd left Concord. Amber wished he'd just get on with it, get it over and done. Then leave her to her silence.

At last, Makenzie said, 'You know, your Mom and I were talking at the hospital.'

'I know.' Did he think she was stupid? Mom had packed her off to the vending machine with a few quarters and when she'd come back, she'd stopped outside the door, slurping at her soda, and listening to their low voices – Mom and Mak – engaged in one of their quieter arguments – the ones they called *discussions*.

Amber had entered and answered their twin smiles with all the sincerity they deserved. Since then, she'd confined her conversation to *yeahs, nahs,* and *uh-huhs*.

Makenzie braved it out. 'Well, anyhow, we made up our own minds what would be best for us. And your Mom's hoping you and I can talk about what's likely to be best for you.'

Amber blinked at Makenzie. Big Mak. She didn't quite get what he was saying, but he was all serious and earnest and he wasn't looking at her like she was a kid.

'You know, I can't ever be your Daddy,' he went on. 'The best I can ever be is your friend. Fact is, it's down to you and me whether we make that a good thing or a bad thing.'

'Uh huh.' This time she said it because it was all she *could* say. Because Amber thought she understood: her life, her choice. They were putting her first. The final decision was hers, and it was partly a comfort, partly a fragile weight that she felt scared to drop. She chanced a sidelong look at Makenzie, and he caught the glance.

'Your Mom'll be out of hospital within a week. You know, I think I talked her into getting rid of that old trailer of hers – kind of spoils the view out front, doesn't it? Put a For Sale sign down by the road. The town will be coming back to life soon. Plenty of folks sure to be driving through before Christmas. It'll be gone in no time. What's your take on that?'

Amber let her gaze ride ahead of the police truck some distance and for some reason she suddenly felt like she might cry. Courageously, she shook herself clear of that and aimed an uncertain expression up at Makenzie.

'Can I help hammer it in?' she asked. 'The sign, I mean.'

'I'll need someone to hold it steady.' Makenzie smiled. Pretty soon, Amber noticed, he had relaxed some more into his driving.

They still had a few miles between them and home.

But with Makenzie driving, Amber felt confident they would get there.

About the Author

Simon Forward was born in Penzance in 1967. From the age of three he was probably dreaming about writing for *Doctor Who*. For a while he was a computer programmer, but between reading, films, role-playing and writing, much of his life has been based in fantasy. He bears little resemblance to the person who wrote 'One Bad Apple' for *Doctor Who: More Short Trips*, although he is of course the same individual.

ALSO AVAILABLE

DOCTOR WHO: THE NOVEL OF THE FILM by Gary Russell ISBN 0 563 38000 4

THE EIGHT DOCTORS by Terrance Dicks ISBN 0 563 40563 5

VAMPIRE SCIENCE by Jonathan Blum and Kate Orman ISBN 0 563 40566 X

THE BODYSNATCHERS by Mark Morris ISBN 0 563 40568 6

GENOCIDE by Paul Leonard ISBN 0 563 40572 4

WAR OF THE DALEKS by John Peel ISBN 0 563 40573 2

ALIEN BODIES by Lawrence Miles ISBN 0 563 40577 5

KURSAAL by Peter Anghelides ISBN 0 563 40578 3

OPTION LOCK by Justin Richards ISBN 0 563 40583 X

LONGEST DAY by Michael Collier ISBN 0 563 40581 3

LEGACY OF THE DALEKS by John Peel ISBN 0 563 40574 0

DREAMSTONE MOON by Paul Leonard ISBN 0 563 40585 6

SEEING I by Jonathan Blum and Kate Orman ISBN 0 563 40586 4

PLACEBO EFFECT by Gary Russell ISBN 0 563 40587 2

VANDERDEKEN'S CHILDREN by Christopher Bulis ISBN 0 563 40590 2

THE SCARLET EMPRESS by Paul Magrs ISBN 0 563 40595 3

THE JANUS CONJUNCTION by Trevor Baxendale ISBN 0 563 40599 6

BELTEMPEST by Jim Mortimore ISBN 0 563 40593 7

THE FACE EATER by Simon Messingham ISBN 0 563 55569 6

THE TAINT by Michael Collier ISBN 0 563 55568 8

DEMONTAGE by Justin Richards ISBN 0 563 55572 6

REVOLUTION MAN by Paul Leonard ISBN 0 563 55570 X

DOMINION by Nick Walters ISBN 0 563 55574 2

UNNATURAL HISTORY by Jonathan Blum and Kate Orman ISBN 0 563 55576 9

AUTUMN MIST by David A. McIntee ISBN 0 563 55583 1

INTERFERENCE: BOOK ONE by Lawrence Miles ISBN 0 563 55580 7

INTERFERENCE: BOOK TWO by Lawrence Miles ISBN 0 563 55582 3

THE BLUE ANGEL by Paul Magrs and Jeremy Hoad ISBN 0 563 55581 5

THE TAKING OF PLANET 5 by Simon Bucher-Jones and Mark Clapham ISBN 0 563 55585 8

FRONTIER WORLDS by Peter Anghelides ISBN 0 563 55589 0

PARALLEL 59 by Natalie Dallaire and Stephen Cole ISBN 0 563 555904

THE SHADOWS OF AVALON by Paul Cornell ISBN 0 563 55588 2

THE FALL OF YQUATINE by Nick Walters ISBN 0 563 55594 7

COLDHEART by Trevor Baxendale ISBN 0 563 55595 5

THE SPACE AGE by Steve Lyons ISBN 0 563 53800 7

THE BANQUO LEGACY by Andy Lane and Justin Richards ISBN 0 563 53808 2

THE ANCESTOR CELL by Peter Anghelides and Stephen Cole ISBN 0 563 53809 0

THE BURNING by Justin Richards ISBN 0 563 53812 0

CASUALTIES OF WAR by Steve Emmerson ISBN 0 563 53805 8

THE TURING TEST by Paul Leonard ISBN 0 563 53806 6

ENDGAME by Terrance Dicks ISBN 0 563 53802 3

FATHER TIME by Lance Parkin ISBN 0 563 53810 4

ESCAPE VELOCITY by Colin Brake ISBN 0 563 53825 2

EARTHWORLD by Jacqueline Rayner ISBN 0 563 53827 9

VANISHING POINT by Stephen Cole ISBN 0 563 53829 5

EATER OF WASPS by Trevor Baxendale ISBN 0 563 53832 5

THE YEAR OF INTELLIGENT TIGERS by Kate Orman ISBN 0 563 53831 7

THE SLOW EMPIRE by Dave Stone 0 563 53835 X

DARK PROGENY by Steve Emmerson 0 563 53837 6

THE CITY OF THE DEAD by Lloyd Rose ISBN 0 563 53839 2

GRIMM REALITY by Simon Bucher-Jones and Kelly Hale ISBN 0 563 53841 4

THE ADVENTURESS OF HENRIETTA STREET by Lawrence Miles ISBN 0 563 53842 2

MAD DOGS AND ENGLISHMEN by Paul Magrs ISBN 0 563

53845 7

ANACHROPHOBIA by Jonathan Morris (Mar '02) ISBN 0 563 53847 3

TRADING FUTURES by Lance Parkin (Apr '02) ISBN 0 563 53848 1

THE DEVIL GOBLINS FROM NEPTUNE by Keith Topping and Martin Day ISBN 0 563 40564 3

THE MURDER GAME by Steve Lyons ISBN 0 563 40565 1

THE ULTIMATE TREASURE by Christopher Bulis ISBN 0 563 40571 6

BUSINESS UNUSUAL by Gary Russell ISBN 0 563 40575 9

ILLEGAL ALIEN by Mike Tucker and Robert Perry ISBN 0 563 40570 8

THE ROUNDHEADS by Mark Gatiss ISBN 0 563 40576 7

THE FACE OF THE ENEMY by David McIntee ISBN 0 563 40580 5

EYE OF HEAVEN by Jim Mortimore ISBN 0 563 40567 8

THE WITCH HUNTERS by Steve Lyons ISBN 0 563 40579 1

THE HOLLOW MEN by Keith Topping and Martin Day ISBN 0 563 40582 1

CATASTROPHEA by Terrance Dicks ISBN 0 563 40584 8

MISSION: IMPRACTICAL by David A. McIntee ISBN 0 563 40592 9

ZETA MAJOR by Simon Messingham ISBN 0 563 40597 X

DREAMS OF EMPIRE by Justin Richards ISBN 0 563 40598 8

LAST MAN RUNNING by Chris Boucher ISBN 0 563 40594 5

MATRIX by Robert Perry and Mike Tucker ISBN 0 563 40596 1

THE INFINITY DOCTORS by Lance Parkin ISBN 0 563 40591 0

SALVATION by Steve Lyons ISBN 0 563 55566 1

THE WAGES OF SIN by David A. McIntee ISBN 0 563 55567 X

DEEP BLUE by Mark Morris ISBN 0 563 55571 8

PLAYERS by Terrance Dicks ISBN 0 563 55573 4

MILLENNIUM SHOCK by Justin Richards ISBN 0 563 55586 6

STORM HARVEST by Robert Perry and Mike Tucker ISBN 0 563 55577 7

THE FINAL SANCTION by Steve Lyons ISBN 0 563 55584 X

CITY AT WORLD'S END by Christopher Bulis ISBN 0 563 55579 3

DIVIDED LOYALTIES by Gary Russell ISBN 0 563 55578 5

CORPSE MARKER by Chris Boucher ISBN 0 563 55575 0
LAST OF THE GADERENE by Mark Gatiss ISBN 0 563 55587 4
TOMB OF VALDEMAR by Simon Messingham ISBN 0 563 55591 2
VERDIGRIS by Paul Magrs ISBN 0 563 55592 0
GRAVE MATTER by Justin Richards ISBN 0 563 55598 X
HEART OF TARDIS by Dave Stone ISBN 0 563 55596 3
PRIME TIME by Mike Tucker ISBN 0 563 55597 1
IMPERIAL MOON by Christopher Bulis ISBN 0 563 53801 5
FESTIVAL OF DEATH by Jonathan Morris ISBN 0 563 53803 1
INDEPENDENCE DAY by Peter Darvill-Evans ISBN 0 563 53804 X
THE KING OF TERROR by Keith Topping ISBN 0 563 53802 3
QUANTUM ARCHANGEL by Craig Hinton ISBN 0 563 53824 4
BUNKER SOLDIERS by Martin Day ISBN 0 563 53819 8
RAGS by Mick Lewis ISBN 0 563 53826 0
THE SHADOW IN THE GLASS by Justin Richards and Stephen
Cole ISBN 0 563 53838 4
ASYLUM by Peter Darvill-Evans ISBN 0 563 53833 3
SUPERIOR BEINGS by Nick Walters ISBN 0 563 53830 9
BYZANTIUM! by Keith Topping ISBN 0 563 53836 8
BULLET TIME by David A. McIntee 0 563 53834 1
PSI-ENCE FICTION by Chris Boucher 0 563 53814 7
INSTRUMENTS OF DARKNESS by Gary Russell ISBN 0 563 53828 7
RELATIVE DEMENTIAS by Mark Michalowski ISBN 0 563 53844 9
HOPE by Mark Clapham ISBN 0 563 53846 5
PALACE OF THE RED SUN by Christopher Bulis (Mar '02) ISBN
0 563 53849 X
AMORALITY TALE by David Bishop (Apr '02) ISBN 0 563 53850 3
SHORT TRIPS ed. Stephen Cole ISBN 0 563 40560 0
MORE SHORT TRIPS ed. Stephen Cole ISBN 0 563 55565 3
SHORT TRIPS AND SIDE STEPS ed. Stephen Cole and Jacqueline
Rayner ISBN 0 563 55599 8